Love Never Dies

By Gerry Pratt

"When the world is at war, blind forces are at work behind the scenes. All other considerations become secondary to the will to win and armies of people do their utmost to hurt, if not destroy, each other." Takeo Ujo Nakano, *Within the Barbed Wire Fence*

For Barbara June

BOOK I: Costello

Chapter 1 Belfast

Eamon Costello's mother, Deidre, was the first of four daughters born to Ellen and Desmond Costello. Her three sisters died before their fifth birthdays, the last buried alongside the mother. Eamon was Deidre's first son, seeded during her fourteenth year in the alley behind Colcannon's pub on a night in November of the year 1890. Desmond Costello, Deidre's da and Eamon's grandfather in a small sense of the word, worked for the Belfast City Maintenance Department pushing a metal bucket on two wheels through the city streets sweeping up the horse manure. He would occasionally moonlight for a shilling or two and a glass of Guinness sweeping out the Colcannon pub.

Deidre left her widowed father's flat the day she turned fourteen, reappearing eight months later, her teenaged body swollen with child. There was a moment when her da failed to recognize the drenched urchin in his doorway. Upon seeing the condition she was in, he shouted in her face. "There's nothing here to feed you or that bastard in your belly, if that's what you are hoping." Deidre felt the spittle of his anger spraying her face and never budged. "I'm not opening the door to you," he shouted with slightly less resolution.

Deidre, who like her soon-to-be-born son was able to muster a tear on call, sniffled loudly, conscious of the rain dripping from her coat. "I'm sorry, Da," she muttered quietly, beginning to back away, her tears in full flow. Desmond Costello hesitated before stepping back from the open door.

"It's only for the memory of your departed Ma that I'm letting you in for the night. But mind, once the rain stops..." The rest of what he never intended to say remained unspoken in his uncertain scowl. Within a month Deidre delivered the baby and took him to the priest where he was christened Eamon, the name preserving the identity of her passing lover. Her da never forgave her for giving her bastard son the Costello name.

Shortly after delivering Eamon, Deidre resumed her career along the Belfast waterfront, making it necessary for Eamon to vacate the Costello flat once he grew old enough to become curious. He was in his teens the night Deidre turned him out to find refuge from the winds off the Irish Sea. Eamon ended up choosing a derelict delivery wagon in a junkyard a turn off Shankle Road, ignoring the fact that the wagon lay beyond the territorial line of security for Bally Murphy Catholics. Wrapping himself in a rug-like overcoat he had stolen from a seaman's bar, he bedded down and was beginning to feel the warmth in his bones when he was startled by the sound of others poking about the junkyard.

The three Prods discovered the lanky red-headed Mick pretending to be asleep on a pillow of old newspapers. When Eamon attempted to flee, the oversized coat tangled about his legs, landing him on his backside. It was such an inviting target the visitors took to warming themselves by putting their boots to his tumbling body. Dougal Mulhern would later preach to his light-fingered friend that it was the coat's rightful owner that had reached out to trip him when he fell.

Dougal Mulhern was a Catholic-born orphan adopted as a baby by a tolerant Protestant Belfast policeman and his wife who agreed to raise him a Catholic in compliance with their adoption agreement. It was Mulhern's religious training that caused him to smile whenever recalling how Costello's ecclesiastically tainted cursing had saved him from a severe beating. Eamon's invoking the name of Jesus and Mary carried clear out onto Shankle Road where Mulhern was on patrol for the Belfast Constabulary. Recognizing such blasphemy could only be coming from one of his own, Mulhern, who was enormous even as a young man, had the Prods on the run the instant he stepped up to the wagon. Eamon, unsure of the intentions of his large benefactor, hurriedly picked up his coat, preparing to hurry off without a backward glance.

"Is it an ungrateful lout you are?" Mulhern hollered after him. "Do you have nothin' to say to the man who saved you from the beatin' you probably deserved?"

"I was about to handle them myself," Eamon sniffed.

Mulhern, recognizing an immediate kinship with this gawky redhead, grinned as he looked into the hungry eyes facing him. "Aye," he added with mock solemnity, "and what a bloody business that would have been." Eamon's affirmative nod brought a chuckle from Mulhern. "I'm near through for the night. What do you say we celebrate your sparing those Prods with a hot sausage or two and maybe a jar to see it down?"

"Your shilling?" Eamon replied, cautiously. "That being the case, I don't suppose I would mind at all." They ate together that evening, the first solid food of the day to visit Eamon's belly. That night began a friendship that would lead the pair through service with the Royal Irish Constabulary and on to the Vancouver, British Columbia, Police Department. Through it all, Eamon was never far from Dougal Mulhern's watchful eye.

Together on the Vancouver force, they patrolled adjoining beats for eight years, dispensing night justice with their own brand of territorial imperialism. The mere appearance of either of them in the doorway of a Chinese gambling room, Japanese hotel lobby, restaurant, or barbershop would be acknowledged with head bobbing obsequiousness. In any barbershop, they had only to slip off their coat and the chair was quickly vacated. Should Costello or Mulhern let it be known they would be in need of a past midnight trim, the Powell Street Japanese barber was always there. All-night Chinese restaurants greeted the pair with unintelligible welcomes acknowledged with chairs appearing conveniently at kitchen tables. And in the backrooms of the Sun Rise Hotel there was always a bottle of Azumo's whiskey. That kind of homage earned Eamon two departmental reprimands and buried his chances of making a better place for himself on the force.

Chapter 2 A Failed Reconciliation

March 31, 1940. Daylight sleeping never came easily to Eamon Costello, having been awake on the morning side of midnight, most of his 48 years. It had become habit for him to remain in bed throughout the day, drifting in and out of sleep. When he finally opened his eyes in the early afternoon, his vacant gaze settled on the blue daisies on the bedroom wallpaper. He began mindlessly counting the daisies, counting fifty or more before the vague recollection of his previous night's activities slipped into his consciousness. Suddenly uneasy, he shifted his eyes from the wallpaper to the uniform tunic draped over the back of the lone bedroom chair. His eyes then swung to the department issue Sam Browne hanging from the bedroom doorknob, where his department issue .38-caliber service revolver rested quietly in place, the wooden handle visible above the black leather holster.

Drunk or sober before falling into bed, Costello removed the shells from the revolver, placing all five bullets on the bedside table at the feet of the color portrait of Jesus Christ. Jesus and His silver frame were parting gifts from his mother-in-law to Eileen Murphy on her eighteenth birthday. It was a gift her mother hoped would discourage the girl from marrying Eamon Costello, the newly committed Royal Irish Constabulary recruit. Eamon's wife placed Jesus by their bed, never failing to turn the picture to the wall during their infrequent mid-morning couplings. Costello reached out to the bullets, rolling each in his fingertips, confirming that he was awake in his own bed.

Reassured, he began gingerly untangling his long legs from the bed sheets, gradually becoming aware of what had awakened him. Michael and Seamus, his youngest sons, were wrestling on the grass beneath the bedroom window. Their grunts and curses pleased him, the sounds stirring memories of his own boyhood battles in alleys of Belfast's Bally Murphy. Eamon's younger half brother Cormack had never walked without a cane following a fight that was a far cry from two boys wrestling on the grass. Costello scratched absently at the scattering of ginger hairs over his chest and uttered a silent Hail Mary in thanks for the great distance separating his sons from Belfast's public housing stalls.

After a moment of studying his two bare feet, he lurched off the bed, uttered a muffled groan, and shuffled across the room to peer into the mirror atop the bedroom dresser. "By Jesus, old son" he swore softly at the image in the mirror. "There were many quick to call you a traitor to your own kind, though they damn well knew that you never once arrested one of your own while wearing that bloody RIC badge. And that included Michael Collins' killers and the Defense Leaguers as well." He glared into the glass half expecting a rebuttal, working his fist over the stubble of his two-day beard. The image in the glass grinned back, unable to disguise the guile in his green eyes.

"Come on now, it's Mulhern and the promotion that's got you talkin' to yourself," he muttered. "Better for the two of you if the job goes to Dempsey or even one of the Italians." He was whispering to the glass as he would to an intimate friend—though he had none other than Mulhern – while picturing the two of them over a jar in the St. Regis Hotel beer parlor mourning at the injustice of such a decision. "Just you and me Dougal, bitching, like old times, eh?"

He stepped back to the bed resuming the study of his feet until Eileen Costello burst into the room, her hand clapped over her mouth. She shot a deprecating look at her husband and released the window blind in a flapping flurry. Catching sight of her sons, she threw open the window. "Away from there. The two of you, wakin' your Da with all your carrying on." She wheeled, marching from the room, her lips buttoned tight, leaving the door open to the fresh air from the open window. Eamon heard her take-it-or-leave-it grumbling from the hallway. "There's eggs and sausage getting cold on the table."

Eamon pulled on his trousers, snapped his suspenders over his shoulders and proceeded on naked feet into the kitchen. The loud ticking of the hand-wound clock atop the warming oven broke the quiet as he pretended to be absorbed in the day-old evening newspaper. Furtively he raised his eyes over the top of the page with a glance at his wife's behind. He had reconciliation in mind, yet hesitated. At forty-one, Eileen Costello's hips had lost their once tempting contours and her breasts — the wonder of his eyes when first witnessing her undress — had collapsed so that what he once fondled as "two lovely tits" had softened to form a bulging, waist-high cushion.

Eamon released an audible sigh and reached for the radio atop the kitchen sideboard. Uncle Billy Brown's British Empire Program was playing Gracie Fields singing *On the Isle of Capri*; the song eliciting pictures of sandy beaches bathed in warm palm swaying winds. He turned up the music, set the paper on the table beside his un-eaten breakfast, and slipped up behind his wife. Leaning forward to kiss her neck he ran his hand up her thigh. Before he could utter a word, she spun around, the venom in her voice causing him to jump back.

"And what is it you think you are up to, Eamon Costello? Coming into my kitchen stinking of whisky and whores and wanting to put your hands on me like I was a tart on your beat?" She stormed out of the kitchen, leaving him alone with the radio and Gracie's cockney voice. *"I can still see the flowers blooming 'round him, when we met on the Isle of Capri..."* Eamon felt the warm blush of guilt, despite his attempting a sense of indignation that failed. He remained toying with the cold eggs until the song ended, then shuffled back to bed.

Throughout the rest of day he lay dozing in and out of a lingering headache until his wife reappeared at 9:30 p.m. "Time for you to go to work," she announced, snapping on the ceiling light. Believing he detected a softening in her voice, Eamon pushed up on one elbow, forcing a bleary-eyed smile. He dressed hurriedly, dousing his armpits and the hairs on his groin with a splash of Bay Rum cologne. He then stopped before the bedroom door mirror to buff his boots with the back of his trouser legs, uncertain of what he was about to face in the kitchen.

The smell of frying meat hit him at the kitchen door, bringing back the nausea of the queasy hangover that had kept him tossing throughout the day. At the sight of the two slabs of calf's liver waiting like melted chocolate on a puddle of melted butter, his throat filled with bile. Eileen Costello saw the revulsion on his face.

"Liver is good for the blood and the butcher has it for ten cents a pound. Eat it," she snapped, busying herself over the stove. Eamon swallowed hard, determined to keep a civil tongue, avoiding even a passing word that might ignite the hostility hanging over the kitchen.

Chapter 3 A Bitter Night

April 1, 1940, started as an unseasonabley cold night. Constable Eamon Costello slouched into the circle of light over the police call box at the intersection of Powell and Dunlevy. He cast an uneasy glance up the deserted Powell Street: the buildings silhouetted against the night sky, the roadway, and the sidewalks—nothing moved. Costello fished the bronze call box key from his tunic and turned, once more searching for signs of life along Powell. His eyes settled on a dim light over the entrance of the Sun Rise Hotel. The sight brought a slow grin to his face as he put the key into the lock, and he began softly humming the ballad. *"T'was on the Isle of Capri that I found her..."* His thoughts drifted to the warm sands of the Caribbean. He reached into the box, lifted the receiver from its cradle, and spun the crank. "Officer Two-thirteen. Costello. Dunlevy and Powell."

Leaning into the power pole he propped the receiver to his ear, his attention caught by a second light that came on further down East Powell. The Jap barber, one of the few Costello trusted to trim his curly red hair, had appeared from the back of the storefront barbershop. Costello watched the old man settle into the barber chair with a newspaper on his lap. *'Funny time for the old Jap to be catching up on the news,'* Costello thought, absently fingering the length of hair down the back of his neck, pondering whether he had time for a midnight trim. An empty streetcar rumbled through the intersection of Hastings and Main, leaving a quiet emptiness over Vancouver's East End.

Following a long pause, Costello took the receiver from his shoulder, pulled down the telephone hook with his free hand in a series of impatient jerks and spun the crank a second time. "Officer Two-thirteen..." Before he could finish, a familiar brogue barked in his ear.

"B'Jesus, Eamon. Are you tryin' to make a deaf man out'a those of us at this end of the line? You need crank that thing but once. Just give us a chance to pick up the call."

Costello immediately connected the brogue with Dougal Mulhern, the mountain of muscle who had volunteered over the years to assume the role of his surrogate conscience. "It's true then, Dougal? Have they given you the desk?"

"And does that come to you as such a big surprise, Eamon?"

"No. I've heard the talk, Dougal. You know it's been around the station, you getting the promotion and all. But I confess, I'm wondering why anyone would choose the likes of a lout like you, when they had an outstanding policeman like myself standing ready. Eh?" Both men laughed, Eamon less enthusiastically. "Donahue and Dempsey and Vigna, the Italian dick, they were all counting on a shot at the job. You'll have to deal with them for a while, Dougal. But tell me, do you have the job for good? And will they be handing you the stripes and the pay that goes with all that?"

"It's acting sergeant for now, Eamon. But who knows?" Mulhern was trying for a note of modesty. "Tell me, is that a tear I'm hearing in your voice? Are you missing me out there already, Eamon?" Mulhern asked with exaggerated concern.

"Miss you? Like a boil on my arse, I'll be missing you. But I'm happy for you, Dougal. You know that."

"That I do, Eamon. I do. And with me here at headquarters, who knows? Down the line there could be a potato in the pot for you as well if you keep your nose clean. Like we promised, eh?" Mulhern was making Costello's promise a joint commitment, aware that his friend's word by itself was questionable at best. "Hold on a minute, Eamon. I've half a dozen bloody boxes coming in all at once."

When Mulhern came back on the line his voice carried a note of acting sergeant authority that had not been there a minute earlier. Costello suspected other ears were on the line. "Constable Costello. There's a vandalism complaint at the Campbell Packing plant at the foot of Dunlevy Street. The big metal shed on the water at the foot of Dunlevy? It's mostly Orientals, packing fish all night.
"

"Got it," Costello replied impatiently.

"The complaint didn't make your sheet. They report thieves have been stealing gear from the yard. There is a Mister Hoople who wants us to keep an eye out tonight. He will be there around seven in the morning. Best you stop by and see him before you sign off. Let him know we have been on the job." Mulhern's voice dropped, defying other ears. "And Eamon. You and I will have a word or two on your two-thirty call once things settle down. Now mind yourself, lad."

The line went silent. Eamon replaced the receiver, turned the key in the call box and began to hike briskly up Dunlevy Street toward the Sun Rise Hotel, humming his dreams of the Isle of Capri.

Chapter 4 A Man Is Missing

By 2:45 a.m., Acting Sergeant Dougal Mulhern caught himself glancing up at the wall clock. Eamon Costello's second call was forty-five minutes late. Exercising his newfound authority of being in charge of the night desk, he ordered a side door to the street propped open, hoping the night air would soothe his nerves. A rookie uniformed officer was seated directly in the path of the sudden draft and, failing to hear the acting sergeant's order, got up from his bench and started toward the open door.

"If you're too damn cold, get off your arse or pick up a broom." Mulhern's bellowing command stopped the rookie in his tracks even as he recognized that Mulhern's temper was rightfully directed at Costello. Muttering a muffled curse, Mulhern quickly grinned at the young patrolman hoping to ease the man's sheepish retreat. "It's no use my getting upset over all the troubles Costello could be getting himself into," Mulhern muttered, glancing again at the station clock which was pacing on toward 3:00 a.m.

***

Mulhern's concern at leaving Costello on his own on a beat they had patrolled alongside one another for the past eight years began the morning of the previous day, when the big policeman had arrived at police headquarters at the end of his shift. He was standing up to the urinal in the locker room when Constable Ian Eadler sauntered up alongside, a know-it-all look on his face. Mulhern stepped back, buttoning his trousers, recognizing Eadler's smug look as that of a man with information he wanted to be begged to share. Mulhern, without so much as a nod in Eadler's direction, busied himself blotting a wet paper towel over a blood stain on the breast of his tunic. Eadler knew better than to ask about the blood, though he would later seek out the story from the jail sergeant.

"There was a Mutt and Jeff fight between a couple of drunks in the Good Eats Café toilet," the jail sergeant revealed. *"Mulhern went to break it up when he saw the little guy had a knife. He arrested them both on a drunk and disorderly. The little Indian,*

Chief Tommy Hawk or whatever they call him on the street, had cut the big guy. I had to have the jail medic take a look at the cut. Once he saw the blood on his uniform, Mulhern's Irish temper got the best of him and he broke the Indian runt's jaw."

Mulhern continued scrubbing at the blood on his tunic, determined to wait for Eadler to spill his secret or burst. Eadler, looking over his shoulder from the urinal, finally broke. "Chief Inspector McCathie has been looking for you, Mulhern."

Mulhern looked up suspiciously. "What's up, Eadler?"

Eadler shrugged. "All I know is that he's been asking for you for an hour or more." Eadler grinned smugly. Mulhern knew Eadler as a windbag and a gossip but a solid policeman. Only in that moment, Constable Eadler was a hair's breadth from being slammed into a puddle of his own piss.

Chief Inspector Archie McCathie's office cubicle sat atop the stairs overlooking the squad room, giving the night commander a view of the second night shift row-call. Mulhern took the steps two at a time, the sound of his boots thundering on the steps and alerting McCathie of his approach. The inspector waved him into the office before he could raise a hand to rap on the doorpost, the customary signal for those seeking permission to enter. Mulhern was quick to detect the hint of a smile on McCathie's face; at least it was as close to a smile as he had ever seen from the taciturn Scot.

"You and I have been at this business awhile, Mulhern," McCathie began quietly. Mulhern began to relax, sensing a hint of paternal pride in the Inspector's voice. He had come up the stairs worried over his handling of the Good Eats arrests.

"Yes, sir. We have at that."

"How long is it now? Six or seven years here, a half dozen in the Old Country?"

"That's about it, sir."

"No complaints, Mulhern?"

"You have been good to Costello and me, sir."

"It's been no bother dealing with you." McCathie grunted the words. "I wish I could say as much about your friend." The inspector sighed. "But we won't go into that. Costello is not the reason for my wanting to talk to you. I have been thinking about you taking a shift or two on the desk for the second night shift, now that Sergeant Collins is retiring. How do you feel about that, Mulhern?" The Chief Inspector was fully aware that a second night shift patrolman in the city's East End would not consider the desk a financial promotion. Even for Mulhern, whom he knew to be a more-or-less by-the-book policeman, the move would more than likely mean a cut in what he took home at the end of a week. The inspector's cold, hazel eyes fixed on the big man, watching to see if the promotion would mean more to Mulhern than the extra money he came across on the beat. "The desk carries two dollars a day premium, Mulhern," McCathie added, noting the sudden flush of pride that he was looking for.

"I'd be honored to be considered, sir."

"Well then, you show me that you can handle the job," the inspector said gruffly, "and we may find a permanent spot for you here at headquarters." Even before the first flush of pride began to settle, Mulhern's thoughts immediately went to Costello on his own on the street.

***

By the time the walk clock read 3:20 a.m., Mulhern was out of patience. He was answering a box call from Constable Danny Sweeney at Main and Hastings, and as Sweeney was about to sign off Mulhern interrupted in a voice warm with fraternal confidence. "Hold on a minute, Danny." He was aware that Sweeney, a policeman with shadows in his own closet, was not one to go about with a loose lip concerning another man's adventures. Mulhern glanced furtively across the room. Detective Jack Marshall and the rookie had their heads together over the racing edition of the News Herald. By the door, beyond hearing, he could see the backs of detectives Al Vigna and Inar Dempsey reviewing mug books.

"Danny." Mulhern spoke the name in a near whisper. "I don't suppose you have run across Eamon Costello out there tonight? No. No. He's not the type to be nosing around your beat. Nothing of the sort, Dan. It's a matter of his being more than two hours late with his box call. I'm worried. You understand?" he added meaningfully.

"Danny. Suppose you take a few minutes and head on over to Powell, eh? See if you can find out what's holding the man up. Anything comes up on your beat, I'll have one of the radio cars cover. And Danny," Mulhern hesitated meaningfully. "Take a look in at that Sun Rise Hotel. Eamon may have come up with the trots. Could be he's holed up there having an all-night dump, eh?" Mulhern's attempt to make light of his concern went right past Sweeney.

"He'd have a helluva time resting his ass on one of those Jap toilets. They got no seats on those toilets," Sweeney muttered and hung up.

An hour later the call came back from Sweeney on Costello's Dunlevy call box. "There's no sign of your pal, Mulhern. Whatever he's got going, it isn't east of Main Street, as best I can tell. Maybe he's slipped home for a midnight cuddle?"

Mulhern cut short Sweeney's uncertain laugh. "Damnit, this is serious, Danny."

"If it is, it's all because of the way you and that pal of yours have set thing up out here, Mulhern. All I can get out of that Powell Street bunch is their 'no speakee d'English' crap. You two trained 'em to keep their traps shut when it comes to talking about a policeman."

"Jesus Sweeny, he has to be out there somewhere." Mulhern began cursing and shot another quick glance at the clock. "Keep checking. Maybe he's stopped in an all-night chow mein joint. Maybe he's not feeling good and...maybe..." Both men realized Mulhern was grasping for straws. "Call me back in twenty minutes with whatever you have. Understand?" Sweeney's line went dead.

The minute hand on the wall clock seemed to leap past 4:20 a.m. Mulhern felt his heart thumping as if an invisible band was tightening around his chest when he signaled for Detective Marshall for relief and started up the stairs to the chief inspector's office.

The crown of Inspector McCathie's head protruding above the pages of the afternoon racing edition of The Vancouver Sun had the appearance of being carved out of pink marble. But for the sparse strands of hay-like hair stretched over the dome, the head was a Roman sculpture. Mulhern rapped on the doorframe. Neither the paper nor the head moved.

The chief inspector's dry voice sounded from behind the newspaper. "What is it, Mulhern?"

"It's Constable Costello, sir," Mulhern began uncertainly.

Chief Inspector Archie McCathie lowered the paper slowly, his brow drawn into a foreboding frown. His eyes, set deep in the recesses of his pink cheeks, narrowed as if he were looking down a gun sight at the three-hundred-pound acting sergeant filling the doorway. McCathie, a Belfast Scot and a Presbyterian, wore his Scotch-Irish breeding like a pedigree which he consciously complimented with his dour demeanor as evidence of his Irish loyalty to the Crown. Loyalty was important for an Irishman in government service in the very British Columbia. The clacking of a typewriter at the booking desk on the station's main floor and a distant telephone ringing somewhere off in the station filled the silence. Mulhern waited for the inspector to speak again. When he could stand the silence no longer, he blurted out: "The man's first call came in at 1:15, sir. That's the last we have heard from him." Mulhern shuffled his feet, apologetically awaiting the inspector's opinion. After a long pause, when it became obvious McCathie was waiting for more, he went on.

"I had him checking a burglary complaint at the Campbell Packing plant, the cannery at the foot of Dunlevy," he added, consciously raising the vandalism to a burglary, hoping that would help mitigate whatever it was Costello was going to have to explain. "There was little else on his sheet." Mulhern resolved to say no more. Finally the inspector shook his head.

"This is your first night on the desk, Mulhern." McCathie laid his paper on his desk, his voice dropping condescendingly. "Could this be a matter of your being overly concerned? You worried Costello can't make it through the night without you seeing him home?"

"No, sir. That's not it, sir." Mulhern lied, aware he was answering defensively. "I have sent Sweeney from East Hastings to take a look for the man on the possibility Costello may be tied up in a street arrest." He hesitated, unwilling to put the rest of his thoughts into words. "Sweeney reports there's no trace of him."

McCathie picked up a long yellow pencil and began doodling on the newspaper crossword puzzle without looking up. Mulhern sensed his tenure on the night desk slipping away and suddenly no longer gave a damn, setting his chin in to-hell-with-it defiance. His gut was telling him Eamon was out there somewhere in trouble.

"I know that beat," Mulhern blurted. "With your permission, sir, I'd like to take a ride over to Powell and see what's up."

McCathie dropped his pencil, folded the newspaper, and let it slip into the wastebasket. He leaned forward and tilted the desk lamp so that it was shining in Mulhern's face. The inspector was confident he could read Mulhern as clearly as he read the damn newspaper. The two of them went back to 1921, Mulhern serving the Royal Irish Constabulary under McCathie during the "Irish Troubles." When the Black and Tans came marching into Ireland, the chief inspector, who had watched Mulhern and liked him, summoned Mulhern to his new command with the Vancouver force. Costello came trailing after him like an unshakable shadow, with Mulhern looking out for his friend like a bitch over a crippled pup.

McCathie studied the big policeman. To appearances his thoughts were on Mulhern, but passing before his mind's eye was the litany of Costello's departmental reprimands. The chief inspector boasted he knew the men of the second night better than he knew his own children, and what he knew about Costello was presenting discomforting probabilities.

"You are telling me that your man has not been heard from for more than half his shift, Mulhern?" The phrase 'your man' carried deliberate meaning.

"Correct, sir."

"And what is it you think he's up to?" McCathie demanded, weighing Mulhern's ambition against his loyalty to a friend.

Mulhern knew how to play that game. "Hard to know what's in another man's mind, sir," he replied.

McCathie answered without moving the light from Mulhern's face. "Mulhern, when your man turns up, you are to bring the details to me. I'll decide how far it goes from there. Am I understood?" McCathie was about to say more, something about policemen messing with Oriental women, then shrugged the thought aside, hoping it would prove unfounded. "Go ahead, Mulhern. Go find your man. Dempsey and Vigna are downstairs trying to look busy. I'm sending them along so there will be less chance of things being clouded by brotherly love."

Mulhern threw himself into the unmarked police car, gripped the wheel in both hands and stamped down on the gas pedal, feeling in control for the first time since Costello failed to call. The corner streetlights glowed meaninglessly in the first light of day as the black Plymouth shot up the garage ramp into the gray April morning. Mulhern gave a clumsy wrench at the wheel and braked in the middle of the road, caroming alongside the detectives' car at the curb. Detective Alfonse Vigna was at the wheel; he was a tall, sallow-faced man dressed in dark, expensively tailored suits. Vigna's suits added to his questionable reputation in the East End. He rolled down the window.

"You got a license to drive that thing, Mulhern?"

Mulhern grinned sheepishly. "Al, don't you boys have something better to do than come trailing after me?"

"We do," Vigna said. "But we got this roundup call from McCathie to put a tail on you while you go hunting for that buddy of yours. So let's get on with it." Vigna pushed his snap-brimmed fedora back on his head and released the brake on the detective car.

"Al. You know I can straighten this thing out in two shakes of a lamb's tail. How's about you two catching a cup of coffee? Then we can all go home on time." Vigna, not slow to recognize that Mulhern's promotion to the desk could one day put him on track for a command commission, rolled his lower lip. He glanced at Inar Dempsey who, was known to have occasionally shared in Costello's late night shenanigans. Dempsey shrugged.

"Okay, Mulhern. But if this blows up in your face it's strictly your funeral." Vigna put the detective car into gear. "Meet us at the corner of Powell and Dunlevy at six thirty with or without Costello. And Mulhern. Sergeant Mulhern. You owe us."

"I thank you lads and I'll remember. So too will Eamon," Mulhern hollered hurriedly. He turned the Plymouth toward East Powell Street with never a moment's doubt where he was headed.

***

Earlier that the evening. Eamon Costello, dressed for the cold in his department-issue great coat and leather gloves had boarded the Number 4 streetcar on the corner of Fourth Avenue and Yew Street. The motorman admitted him through the front of the car, a courtesy reserved for police, and firemen, and B.C. Electric employees. "Good evening constable." The motorman smiled a greeting as Costello brushed past without a nod. He was so preoccupied with his plans for the night that at the start of his shift he had even failed to catch the winks trailing after him across the parade room, leaving a cloud of Bay Rum aftershave lotion lingering in his wake. It was the sweet smelling Costello that alerted the entire crew that he was up to no good.

"He came into the hall smelling sweeter than Rosie's crotch on a hot summer night," Detective Donavan Dempsey later recalled. Dempsey, a day- and night-time drinker himself, his bloodshot eyes evidence of having missed another day's sleep, had raised his nose like a dog on scent howling after Costello. "My Gawd, you smell like a two dollar tart, Costello. I'm half mad for you myself." Dempsey, lips puckered, stretched his neck toward Costello's cheek. Eamon ducked.

"Is your belly tight with envy, Dempsey?" Costello whispered, his glance scanning the ranks for the one face he was praying he would not see. Dempsey's charade had drawn the attention of the entire second night shift. Dougal Mulhern would have known in a heartbeat that Costello had plans for the night.

Escaping the midnight roll call, Costello stepped out of the building, and paused at the top of the headquarters steps to adjust his eyes to the dark. He hocked into the shrubbery in an attempt to relieve the lingering indigestion from his supper of fried liver. The effort left him sweaty and unsteady. He reached for the frost-crusted steel railing, seeking the touch of the cold metal to steady his legs. He then sniffed indignantly and started down the steps two at a stride, muttering: "You are as fit as any man half your years, Eamon Costello."

The freezing rain was forming shards of ice along the sagging power lines, the ice breaking loose and crashing to the pavement with the sound of shattering glass. "That alone is enough to give any policeman indigestion," Costello assured himself. "And that promise you made to Mulhern didn't settle your stomach either."

"You have to promise me you will stay clear of the sun Rise Hotel. There's trouble for you there, Eamon. Trouble we both know you cannot handle." Eamon was undecided.

"Oh, you have my word, Dougal," he had promised, raising his arm to imply his word was as good as an oath. *'Even if it was a promise, it was a promise made under duress and that is no promise at all,'* he thought to himself.

'Besides. Isn't this the day for April Fools?' The thought brought a mischievous smile of reassurance.

As he went marching on into the night, he was humming the tune that had been playing over and over in his head since mid-day. *" 'Neath the shade of an old walnut tree...I can still see the flowers blooming 'round her.."* His fingers moved absently over the rosary Eileen Costello kept planted in his tunic pocket.

Chapter 5 Puzzling Clues

Vigna and Dempsey parked the detective car on Dunlevy, a few feet from the corner of Powell, looking down the hill over the waterfront where the corrugated steel walls of the packing plant stretched out over the water's edge. For the fifth or sixth time Vigna looked at his watch. "Six forty-five," he muttered. "I have a shitty feeling that our acting sergeant is a no show." He rolled the window down, tossed his cigarette onto the wet pavement and put the car in gear. He had his foot on the gas pedal, cursing for having listened to Mulhern, when a last-minute glimpse into the rear view mirror revealed Mulhern's Plymouth caroming into the intersection.

"I'll be damned. He's here." Vigna slammed on the brake, the car shuddering as Mulhern bounced the Plymouth bumper to bumper against the detectives' car. Along Powell Street the Japanese barber sweeping the ice fragments from the sidewalk in front of his shop stopped to look up at the two police cars. Further down Powell a boy in a grocery smock stacking crates in front of the produce store next to the Sun Rise turned to stare up at the intersection. In that same instant Chief Inspector Archie McCathie's black Buick turned into Dunleavy from East Powell Street with McCathie in the front seat alongside a uniformed driver. Mulhern was out of the Plymouth before either of the detectives could move. With an almost imperceptible reassuring nod at Vigna he started toward McCathie's car.

"What in hell did you do with Costello?" Vigna demanded in a loud whisper. Before Mulhern could answer, McCathie rolled down his window.

"We have covered the man's beat, sir. Door to door." Mulhern said in a voice loud enough for the others to hear; a point that did not go unnoticed by the Chief Inspector. "There is no sign of Constable Costello."

"He's vanished," Vigna added by way of reinforcement.

"Not likely." McCathie answered coolly, his glance shifting to the two detectives who were silently nodding their confirmation of Mulhern's account.

Inspector Archie McCathie's sense of protective paternity for those who administer the law by night without benefit of judge nor jury was momentarily holding his temper. He stepped out of the Buick and looked up at the low-hanging clouds as if the major question on his mind was the threat of a late spring snowfall. "What we don't need now is more of this rotten weather," he said quietly.

Vigna, eager to build on Mulhern's story, stepped into the moment. "We checked every doorway, every alley and—" He stopped in mid-sentence, aware that the attention of the others had been drawn to a thickset figure humping up the road from the waterfront. "Who in hell is this?" Vigna mumbled, turning to Mulhern for an answer.

Mulhern shrugged.

"You checked the Campbell plant, Mulhern?" McCathie demanded. Before Mulhern could answer, the man was in their midst, his momentum threatening to knock Vigna from his feet. Mulhern's arm came down like a railroad crossing barrier, checking his rush. "Hold on a minute," Mulhern growled, his massive arm sending the stranger staggering back.

"Mulhern." McCathie's brittle bark lowered Mulhern's arm as the stranger, one loose eye roaming aimlessly, struggled to focus on McCathie.

"Never a cop in sight when you need one, eh? Now our place has been robbed, and I find half the bloody force standing on the corner." His words were coming angrily and loud between his gasping for air. "Someone has kicked the bloody office door off the hinges. Scattered half the office about the bloody road and you—"

Mulhern squeezed the man's arm.

"Ooww. Who do you think you are dealing with, you bloody gorilla? You're breaking my arm."

A second look from McCathie was enough to release Mulhern's grip.

The chief inspector turned to the man. "Suppose you settle down a minute and tell us who you are?"

"Morgan Hoople, that's who I am. The bloody Campbell plant manager. That's who," he added with searing sarcasm. He waved an arm toward the building stretching out from the shoreline. "The same Hoople who telephoned you yesterday asking the police to keep an eye on our plant. Then this morning I come to work and find our safe in the alley and what's left of the office scattered from here to hell and back." The man's loose eye began rotating again, seeking to focus on each of the policemen circling him, finally settling on McCathie.

"Then I look up here and I see three police cars, eh? A-ha, I say to myself. They have nabbed the buggers." Hoople again scanned the surrounding circle, shaking his head ruefully. "But no. It's pretty damn evident you haven't nabbed anybody. Right? Just passing the time of day, were you? Well, you damn well better know that Alderman Earle E. Adams is a personal friend of mine. Bridge partner friend. And you can be sure Earle is going to hear about this big bugger damned near breaking my bloody arm." He snarled, fixing his wandering eye on Mulhern, his words all but lost in his struggle for breath.

"You are not helping the situation, Mister Hoople." McCathie's chin thrust forward like a scolding school master. Hoople's appearance was awakening a different level of fear for the chief inspector. "At the moment we are dealing with a missing policeman. It is possible his disappearance may have something to do with your burglary." McCathie hesitated, judging how much of the Costello story to reveal. "Our officer was assigned to check out your plant last night, Mister Hoople." He turned to Mulhern. "You indicated there was a second night sheet on the cannery, Mulhern?"

Mulhern nodded.

"You had Costello check the place out?" Before Mulhern could stammer an answer, the inspector demanded: "Have you or the detectives been down there, Mulhern?"

"No sir," Mulhern muttered. "We have been canvassing Powell. Officer Costello was to meet with Hoople at the end of his shift. It didn't occur to me that maybe..." The sentence trailed off in an embarrassed hush.

"Mister Hoople, the best thing for us to do is for you to get in the car with these detectives and we will all go down and have a look around." McCathie signaled the detectives. "You two lead the way. You come along as well, Mulhern."

***

Tire ruts running through the grass formed a trail toward the water's edge from the foot of Dunlevy, the twin ruts passing scattered machine parts rusting in the winter grass and ending at two dismantled fishing boats resting on wooden cradles. The three police cars, their headlights a useless dull glow in the gray light of morning, pulled up short of the plant, Vigna's leading car blocked by a scattering of office papers and broken furniture. A table-top metal safe with the door sprung open lay in the grass at the side of the road. The plant office, a fragile shed connected to the road by a wooden walkway, stood ten feet to the side of the tire tracks, the shattered door hanging from the frame.

Chief Inspector McCathie went directly to the safe. "Didn't take much to open this box," he observed quietly. Producing a pen from his pocket, he began probing a lacquered cash box. "Much cash in this?" he asked, glancing up at Hoople.

"Maybe two, three hundred," the suddenly subdued plant manager replied. "We pay the fishermen in cash."

"Looks as if most of it is still here. Let's you and I have look inside the office," the inspector said. "I don't need to tell you not to touch anything."

"I have been inside already," Hoople replied.

Mulhern remained immobilized alongside the police car, the sweat growing cold over his body.

"Snap out of it, Mulhern," Vigna barked, assuming command now that the inspector was out of sight. "Make yourself useful. Start looking around in that tall grass by the beached boats."

Mulhern nodded like a man in a trance and started off through the knee-high grass. He had taken four or five steps when he let out a cry. Vigna would later recall sounded like the whelping cry of a woman in labor. Vigna looked up in time to see the big policeman drop to his knees. What he couldn't see from where he was squatting over the safe was the body of Eamon Costello at Mulhern's feet, stretched out to his full six feet four, his head twisted to one side with both arms at his sides. One visible eye stared vacantly toward the clouds, leaking a jelly-like substance over his cheek. Two thumb-size holes in the fabric of his great coat were clogged with threads of fabric. The peaked police cap lay jammed beneath his red hair, the silver maple-leaf badge twisted askew.

Mulhern's cry froze the detectives at the open safe and carried over the alley to Inspector McCathie, who heard the sound inside the office and was instantly certain that the morning had gone bad. With a quickness that surprised the detectives, he came out the shattered doorway and cut through the grass. Vigna and Dempsey were only a step behind though McCathie was the first to see the body sheltered beneath Mulhern's heaving shoulders. He eased the big man aside. Vigna, who had six years of working out of the coroner's office, leaned over the body and pressed two fingers to Costello's throat.

"Dead," he announced, confirming what the others had already determined. He looked up at Mulhern's ashen face without removing his fingers from Costello's throat. "Cold dead, Mulhern. I'd guess he's been dead a couple of hours. Christ. Get a hold on yourself, man."

The only visible signs of violence on Costello's body were the two holes in his heavy coat. The empty pistol holster attached to his Sam Browne belt indicated someone, perhaps Costello himself, had struggled to pull the revolver free.

Dempsey leaned over the body alongside Vigna. "J'heesus, Al. What do you suppose could have happened to make the man so damn blue?"

"He's been shot in the back," Vigna answered with deprecating sarcasm.

"Mother of God." Mulhern wailed, pressing his fists to his lips.

***

Chapter 6 The Last Call

Vigna and Dempsey were quick to come up with their own theories of how Costello's killing went down. "Must have been a bungled safe job," Vigna announced, the tone of his voice leaving no room for doubt.

"Probably shot right where he is," Dempsey suggested.

Vigna accepted that with a non-committal frown while working the hairline beneath his hat with the rubber end of a pencil. He was unhappy at having his theory usurped, particularly with the chief inspector looking on. But Dempsey wouldn't quit. "I'd say the man never got up from the grass. The bullet holes say as much. You can see where he managed to turn his head while lying there dying, eh? Probably had a good look at the shooter," Dempsey rattled on. "Too bad we can't read a dead man's eyes. You know, a photographic reflection of what he saw as he was shot?"

"He was shot in the back," Vigna muttered.

Dempsey never lost a beat. "The evidence is in the man's eyes if only somebody could figure out how to get at it. Someday some smart guy will figure how to do that. I once saw Charlie Chan do something like that in a murder movie. Only he was just pretending, making out like he could see the killer in the dead man's eyes. Helluva trick. The guy confessed."

Vigna's head shook in despair. "Sober up, Dempsey. Whoever did this caught the man off guard, probably while on his hands and knees crawling through the grass waiting for them to come out of the office.

"You mean he didn't see the lookout," Dempsey added, still trying to be a part of the theory. "Then we should be able to find the cartridge casings."

"The man was dragged," McCathie offered pensively.

"Dragged?" Vigna slipped the pencil behind his ear, hurriedly closing his notebook. "Yea. I can see it now. He was dragged." Vigna aimed his forefinger at the body and pulled the trigger on an imaginary pistol. "Two shots. Nobody hears a damn thing. The plant is going full blast, noisy as hell. Then the shooter drags the body deeper into the grass. That's it. " The detective rose up from his crouch with the air of a man having solved the mystery of the universe.

Chief Inspector McCathie cleared his throat, signaling he was still thinking. "First, we know whoever did this job, and the man who probably shot Costello, is an amateur," he mused quietly, tilting his head as if trying to focus on a picture, his face totally devoid of grief or shock. The policeman in the grass at Archie McCathie's feet was no longer a living, troublesome night patrolman. Costello was merely a body of a murder victim; a crime. Vigna and Dempsey remained silent.

"Whoever it was that broke down that office door and attacked the safe with a sledge or a rock was not a safe man," McCathie said, still speaking as if he were talking to himself. "A professional could have opened that office door like it was a box of chocolates. And the safe? It's a key lock. A teenage car thief could open that in less time than it takes to set your watch. Safe men more often than not have a misguided sense of pride in their work. What's more, I don't recall arresting a single safe cracker who was armed. Men in that trade take great care not to be sentenced to prison as armed criminals. A safe man would face too much time on a weapons charge. No, there's something here that none of us are seeing."

McCathie pushed the toe of his polished brogan through the grass, nudging Costello's open holster. He turned to Vigna. "Forget for a minute you are looking at a policeman. Use your eyes as if you were looking at an incomplete picture puzzle. See it unfolding. See it the way it happened. What we are seeing is what someone wants us to see." The others remained respectfully quiet.

McCathie turned away from the body, the detectives following him to where the two tire ruts cut through the grass. "There is money in that cash box," McCathie went on quietly. "The shooter doesn't seem to have been interested in the money."

"Didn't Hoople say it was empty?" Vigna asked.

"No. He didn't," the inspector replied.

Vigna, unsure of what to answer, nodded wisely.

"It doesn't make sense," the chief inspector continued. "What happened to Costello's weapon? Either of you…?" He shot a questioning glance at the two detectives. "No. I thought not. Nobody found the revolver? I have a feeling we are going to learn the slugs that killed him were from a .38 service revolver, possibly his own. But we won't know that unless we come up with the weapon." The inspector returned to the prone figure in the grass. "It is almost as if the man had been put to rest, laid out like he is. The shooter is telling us something but I'm damned if I can see what it is he's saying."

Mulhern, standing by the road watching and listening silently, unsure of what was expected of him, suddenly blurted: "Whoever shot him, Eamon had to have surprised him. He wouldn't have been shy about getting a shot off himself. Not the man I know."

"That makes no sense, no sense at all," the inspector said irritably. "Where are the signs of a struggle? The holster is still fastened to the belt. From the look of things the man's weapon was removed after he was shot."

Dempsey began probing through the nearby grass and let out a loud: "Hello." He held up a mutilated, fingerless cloth glove. With a theatrical pose, he pushed his hand into the glove wiggling his fingers through the holes where the fingers had been cut away. "How about this?"

McCathie groaned rising from his crouch over the cash box. "I'm too damn old for this business."

"That could have belonged to the safe man," Vigna offered cautiously, unsure of how the glove fit into the inspector's theory. "A safe cracker would cut out the fingers, so he could feel the tumblers fall. A glove leaves no palm prints."

McCathie turned a weary look at the detective. "The man who kicked that door down didn't have the brains to know he has fingerprints. Besides, you are forgetting the safe has a key lock. There is no combination." Vigna, whose promotion to detective was founded on his willingness to go along with whatever authority happened to be at hand, replied by mimicking the inspector's sad shake of the head as if someone else had uttered this stupid remark.

McCathie slipped his hand into the glove, his long, surgeon-like fingers popping through the finger holes. "Fishermen," he suggested. "Gill-netters cut their gloves to free their fingers for mending nets. Could have come from anybody around the fish plant." He slipped the glove into his coat pocket and began issuing orders. "Vigna, I'm leaving you in charge. See that nothing is disturbed until the coroner's people finish here. I'll have a uniform team seal off the area and help go over the ground. We have probably made a mess of what tire tracks there were. Let's see if someone can come up with Costello's missing revolver." The inspector looked over at Mulhern's tear-stained face. "Mulhern, you think you have a grip on yourself?"

The big policeman nodded silently.

"Good. Best you keep busy. You get into the packing plant. See what you can come up with from the people in there. I have told Hoople to hold his night crew over. Someone may have heard the shots last night. That would give us a fix on the time of the shooting."

"It's mostly Japs in there," Vigna complained. "Why not..."

McCathie cut him off. "Don't concern yourself with Mulhern. The man has been dealing with Orientals for eight years. Vigna, you find out how much of the company cash is accounted for. And if Mister Hoople," he paused to look over his shoulder for Hoople, who was standing well off by the office door. "If he is as cozy with Alderman Adams as he claims he is, we better know more about him as well."

"You suspect Hoople may have been into his own kitty?" The spectrum of intriguing possibilities lit up Vigna's face.

"Detective. All I am looking for are the facts so we can begin to make some sense of all this. Right now I'm concerned with who shot Costello, and damn little else." The discipline that won McCathie the gold braid on his cap was kicking in. "Mulhern, I'll take care of your relief on the desk. You may be able to help the detectives with what you know about Costello's activities," he added with a note of regret.

"Yes sir," Mulhern replied. "There's Costello's missus. Would you want me...?"

McCathie started back to his car and hesitated, turning to study Mulhern who stood sagging like a beaten man in an ill-fitting uniform. "No, Dougal," he said. "I'll make that call. It's only proper that she hears this from me." Struck by what he was about to undertake, he added thoughtfully. "The widow is going to need what help you can give her another day." Mulhern stood watching the inspector climb back into the Buick, then turned and started back into the grass, reluctant to leave Costello's body unattended. Vigna wrapped a fraternal arm across the big man's shoulder.

"You are a terrible sight, Mulhern. Remember, this is what they are paying us for. That could be you or me lying there." He lead Mulhern away from the body. "Just the sight of you is enough to scare the shit out of those monkeys in the plant. Listen to what I'm saying. This is no time for rough stuff. Japs kow-tow to a uniform. Go in there with your temper turned off. You won't learn anything kicking ass." Mulhern twisted free of the detective's arm, grunted an unconvincing reply, and started into the plant. Morgan Hoople was trailing two paces behind.

Mulhern started down the long passage between the fish gutting tables, his boots splashing through puddles of fish blood and severed fish heads scattered over the concrete floor, unable to escape the feeling he was passing through a vast morgue. The eyes of the silent night crew followed his progress, their heads turning like spectators at a slowly moving tennis match. Hoople continued to trail after him for a short distance, then stepped ahead to face the big man.

"See here, officer. There's nothing these men can tell you," he said, an unlit cigarette bobbing loosely from his lower lip. "None of 'em speaks more than two words of English."

Mulhern brushed past. "If that's the case, I have no need of you. So go on about your business, Hoople."

"Now you look here, constable." The plant manager rose up to his full five foot five inches before recognizing the menacing look in the big man's eyes. He quickly attempted an indifferent shrug and mumbled. "Well, it's obvious, there is no way we are going to be packing fish this morning. The sooner I leave you to your business the sooner we get back to work, eh?" His words were tossed over his shoulder as he hurried away.

The assorted butchering tools spread out on the metal tables, the idled night crew in their blood-stained rubber aprons, all served to reinforce Mulhern's feeling of passing through a morgue. He pictured Eamon's naked corpse, chilled ashen gray, stretched out on a metal dissecting table like a dead fish. The picture spurred him to pick up his stride toward the far reaches of the plant.

He was about to retrace his steps at the great sliding doors opening out over the fish dock when he suddenly spun around. One hand reached into the heavy winter coat to rest on his revolver. "Who's that out there?"

An Oriental stepped out from the shadows, an apprehensive smile of submission on his face. The man wore an oil slicker a battered brown fedora, knee-high gumboots, and the stubble of a three-day black beard. He quickly snatched the hat from his head, his round unshaven face a picture of practiced apology. His eyes went to Mulhern's revolver.

"My name is Chuichi Otake." The man stuttered, unsure his name would be enough to appease the towering blue coat hovering over him.

Chuichi Otake was a survivor of two years of contract fishing in the waters of the Gulf of Georgia. He had managed to stay afloat by avoiding Caucasians on the water and conflict with those he couldn't dodge on land with the submissive attitude he was showing Mulhern. He had remained in the shadows on the dock waiting to unload his catch, aware of the perils of a Japanese caught up in a police matter.

"O—what?" Mulhern growled, slipping the revolver back beneath his coat, confident he could throw the little man halfway across the inlet if it came to that. "Spell it," he ordered, producing a notepad from his coat. The Japanese fisherman stuttered out the letters. "O-t-a-k-e."

"What were you hiding from out there?"

"Not hiding," Otake stammered. "That is my boat. October Lady." He indicated the double-ender alongside the plant pier. "I am contract fisherman. Work for Mister Hoopra and packing company."

"Hoopra? Hoopra is it now? How long you been hiding out here?"

"I tie up last night. Unload in morning." Mulhern's interrogation appeared to physically shrink the Japanese as Otake attempted to retreat into the folds of his slicker, the top of his shaved head barely level with the badge on the policeman's chest.

Mulhern lowered his voice and spoke slowly. "Seems I have seen you hanging about before. You have business up on Powell Street?"

Otake rubbed his shaved head. "Get my hair cut, sometimes."

Mulhern nodded, pondering the answer. "Maybe you heard something last night, O'tack, eh? Gun shots?" The words came softly in a voice that carried the message that the wrong answer or tone of voice would mean trouble. Mulhern knew the man was afraid, not because he was being threatened, but perhaps because of something he had seen or heard.

Otake lowered his eyes to study the toes of his rubber boots. "I sleep. Hear nothing," he replied cautiously. There was a brief instant when he thought he read a trace of satisfaction, a softening of the hard set to Mulhern's jaw. The thought passed through his mind that it was almost as if the policeman didn't want to hear anything more.

"You speak fair English."

"I learn English," Otake replied.

"O'taka, O'tak? What's a Jap doing with an Irishman's name?" Mulhern muttered.

"Mister Hoopra told us plant has robbery." Otake was aware it was unwise to say more than he was asked, but the words, seeded in curiosity, came unsolicited. He regretted them the minute they passed his lips.

"Aye. And a policeman's been shot."

"So?" Otake nodded solemnly and sucked a gasp of air through his clenched teeth. "There is much noise. See nothing. Hear nothing." He looked away, avoiding Mulhern's probing eyes.

"Those men in there? You talked to them?"

Otake nodded. "They work all night. Very noisy. Hear only dead fish."

Mulhern penciled the name October Lady into his notebook and turned to leave. He was entering the plant when he turned and came back to stab a finger at the Japanese fisherman's chest. "You wear gloves fishing on that tub of yours? Gloves with the fingers cut off?"

Otake appeared confused. Mulhern raised a fist and wiggled the fingers. "Gloves. You wear gloves fishing?"

Otake guessed at the question and raised his gnarled hands. "No gloves. Gloves no good for fishing, neh?"

Mulhern studied him a moment longer. "Good for you. Best you remember that. Unload your fish, O'tak, then get to hell out of here, PDQ... Understand?"

Chuichi Otake offered an abbreviated bow, replaced his hat on his head and hurried back aboard the October Lady, consciously erasing any thought of what he had seen or heard during the night.

Chapter 7 The Rose of Tralee

The Star of the Sea School building, a three-story red brick structure anchored at the corners by granite blocks, rose alongside a dirt-packed playing field with soccer goal posts on either end. A garage-size, freestanding gymnasium occupied the far corner of the pitch. Joseph was the first of the three Costello boys to attend Star of the Sea under the watchful eyes of the Sisters of the Holy Names. His younger brothers followed at two and three year intervals. Both Michael and Seamus were among those milling around the school's lower level doorway when the bell rang, ending the fifteen-minute afternoon recess. Neither of them saw the black and white police car pull up at the curb. Had they been looking, they would have been surprised to see Father Maurice Lavoie in the front seat alongside their 'Uncle Mulhern.'

The priest wore the black felt hat he wore only when making calls on a bereaved family or to the door of a parish girl planning marriage outside the sanction of the church. Whether he was saying Mass or sprinting over the soccer field with the boys at school, Father Lavoie was more likely to be seen with his unkempt, curly black hair flying about his ears. The sight of the parish priest hustling his short, overweight body back and forth across the soccer pitch, never able to match the speed of the fifth and sixth graders, had for a time denied Father Lavoie the ecclesiastic respect due a priest of Holy Mother Church. But over the years his innate disregard of secular homage, and his unquestionable commitment to church doctrine, had raised the onetime Quebec farm boy's stature to the voice of parish authority.

Maurice Lavoie was the youngest of six sons and three daughters, two of whom had taken holy orders long before their baby brother's life was promised to the church before he left the cradle.

Catching a glimpse of Michael Costello in the crowd at the school-yard door, the priest opened the police car door to call out. Mulhern's heavy arm fell on his shoulder, holding him back. "It's best that we go about this business with a plan," Mulhern cautioned.

The priest stiffened, unaccustomed to being told what to do by a man he had more than once absolved in the secrecy of the Star of the Sea confessional. Father Lavoie was uniquely privy to the sins of the big Irishman and, regardless of Mulhern's badge, he knew the man like no other, having never looked on the policeman as anything but a penitent sinner. "And just what is the plan you have in mind?" he demanded impatiently.

Mulhern, sensing he had overstepped, stammered an apology. "I'm sorry Father. But wouldn't you think it best if we checked in with sister superior before talking to the boys?"

The priest considered a moment without answering, then turned to face the figure slumped in the rear seat of the car. "How are you holding up back there, Joseph?"

"I'm okay, Father." The older Costello brother made as if to sit up in the seat, then slumped back down.

Mulhern had telephoned the rectory with the news of Costello having been shot and asked the priest to accompany him to notify Costello's sons. The two then drove to the neighborhood newspaper shack where Mulhern knew Joseph would be waiting for his afternoon papers. "Someone else can deliver the lad's papers," he reasoned. "Joseph should be with his brothers when we break the news of their father's death."

They discovered Joseph outside the paper shack tossing pennies to a crack in the concrete walk. He was squatting over a patch of sidewalk, so engrossed in the contest he failed to look up until the priest stepped out of the police car. Two older boys involved in the game rose to their feet as Joseph was about to claim their pennies. The priest bent over with an admonishing smile and picked up the coins. "It appears you have won these, Joseph," he said quietly, handing Joseph the coppers.

"Joe, we need you to come with us for awhile," Mulhern announced solemnly. "Let one of these other boys handle your route today." The acting sergeant looked to the teenaged district manager in the door of the paper shack. The manager, certain Joseph was about to be taken to jail, nodded his assurance that the paper route would be taken care of. Joseph's dark eyes searched the two visitors, his questioning glance leaving both the priest and the policeman with little doubt he understood why they had come.

From the day of his birth, Joseph Cormack Costello was different in temperament and physique from the two brothers who came after him. Eamon Costello often found himself studying his firstborn, silently questioning why there was nothing in his son that reflected the Costello physique nor the beauty of his mother. He was certain Eileen Murphy had been a virgin. There had been enough first-night difficulty to testify to that. He finally accepted that there had to have been an unknown relative in the family gene pool, perhaps an Irish gypsy or a shipwrecked Spaniard whose image had reappeared in the seeding of his son.

From his days as a skinny six- or seven- year-old, Joseph was quick-tempered and brave to the point of being foolish. Despite his thin, nervous body and sallow complexion, he would fight anyone of any size at the slightest provocation; his dark deceptively calm eyes masked his short temper. "The lad could end up an assassin or a bishop," Eamon confided to Eileen when they watched their firstborn kneeling at the rail for his first communion. Eileen Costello, having dressed her son in his first suit, bristled at the suggestion. "He's the picture of a perfect saint," she countered.

"Aye, and you best pray the church gets their hands on him before the devil does," Eamon added.

Sister Mary Hildegard seldom missed anything moving in or around Star of the Sea school grounds. The moment the police car pulled up alongside the school, she left the confusion in the yard and briskly headed to the school's main entrance. As Sister Superior, she regarded the school's massive front doors the proper place to receive visitors.

Sister Mary was close to six feet tall and when she moved quickly her body appeared to cant forward, giving her the appearance she was falling forward. This slanted stride propelled her silently over the hallways without a whisper from the rubber-soled, high-top black boots concealed beneath her floor-length cassock. Time after time she startled miscreants in the hallways, catching them by the ear with a reptile-like strike in her iron fingers. It was a move that fostered the belief among the boys that the nun's feet never touched the floor stalking the halls.

"Good morning, Father." Sister Mary shot a curious glance at Mulhern before her eyes fell suspiciously on Joseph lingering behind the priest. Joseph had graduated from under Sister Mary's authority three years earlier, and though no longer a matter of her concern, the nun maintained a mother-like authority over all who passed through her nest. "And what is it that brings the police and the church to our door, Father?" She shot a second suspicious glance at Joseph, driving him even farther behind the priest.

Father Lavoie removed his hat. "We have come to have a word with the Costello boys, Sister."

"Then it might be best if we all step into my office," Sister Mary replied, expecting to hear of some misdeed best kept in confidence. Addressing the priest, she asked, "Should I fetch Seamus and Michael?"

"Please," Mulhern replied. "I need to speak to them together." The nun's gray features revealed little, yet Mulhern could sense her resentment at his assuming authority in the church school.

"You and Joseph wait here, Constable," Sister Mary replied with an obvious chill in her voice. "Father Lavoie and I will gather the others."

Michael Costello was never to forget the pain that was so visible on Father Lavoie's face the moment the priest appeared in the classroom. His warm, vibrant features were contorted into a putty-like, tragic mask, his voice tight with emotion. "Michael. Will you put away your work and come with Sister Mary and me, my son? Sister Mary Margret," he added addressing the nun at the head of the class, "will you have Seamus Costello sent to the office? I believe he is in Sister Francis Clair's class."

Michael was a breath away from confessing he had missed Sunday Mass when he recognized the presence of 'Uncle' Mulhern. He shot a questioning glance at Joseph, who was slouching pale and silent as far removed from Sister Mary Hildegard as the crowded office would permit. Before Michael could blurt out his confession, Constable Mulhern coughed into his huge fist.

"Boys, I bring you sad news." The big policeman paused to dab a large handkerchief over his watery eyes. He stuffed the handkerchief into his pocket, wiped a sleeve over his florid face and wrapped his arms around Michael and Seamus, squeezing the wind out of both boys, momentarily unable to go on.

The priest seized the opening. "My sons." The priest spoke with the same solemn cadence he used in the confessional. "Your father is dead. God has called him to be with Him this very day. For each of you, that means your mother – may God bless and be kind to her—is going to need you as never before. You are now the men of the Costello family. "

Mulhern, having lost the floor, sniffed indignantly. "Your Da has been shot," he announced abruptly. Before Father Lavoie could speak again, Mulhern went on as if he were reading an official proclamation. "Eamon Costello died in the line of duty. And that means your mother is to get his full pension. Of that you can be certain. He was a policeman's policeman. And that's the way he died. No one could ask more of the man." The acting sergeant searched the boys' faces for signs of the pain he was certain the news would bring. He was disappointed.

From the beginning, Michael was unable to accept the story. But a few hours past his Da had popped his head out the bedroom window with an admonishing grin. "Boys, come on now, ease off on the racket out there," he had said softly. Both Michael and Seamus suspected he was still a little tipsy. "Let your old man get some sleep or I'll be coming out there to wrestle the both of you myself." This picture of his Da, suspenders hoisted over his underwear, his red hair disheveled, threatening to wrestle his sons on the grass, remained very much alive in Michael's mind.

Mulhern, startled by the whimsical smile on Michael's face, turned to Joseph only to be met with Joseph's stoic stare concealing whatever he was feeling. Seamus appeared bewildered and it showed in the confusion on his face.

Climbing into the police car for the ride home, Michael squeezed in between his brothers, confident of his secret.

***

The day of the funeral the Costello brothers dressed quietly before dawn. Each wore their Sunday white shirts and dark trousers; Joseph and Seamus the jackets their mother had made years earlier for their confirmations. Eileen Costello had made them both too large, anticipating her boys would take on the stature of their father. Seamus had put on weight and was unable to button his jacket, while Joseph, slim and small for his age, continually hunched his shoulders to keep the coat from falling off his back. Michael, already crowding six feet, had outgrown his jacket and came to the breakfast table in his shirt sleeves when the undertaker's limo driver rang the doorbell.

A mid-morning mist had formed a cold sweat over the limo's windshield; the wiper blades' steady, mesmerizing sweep seemed to command a silence in the car following the funeral Mass. Joseph and Seamus sat on either side of their mother in the rear seat. Michael sat perched on the jump seat facing the rear where he could look back at the long line of trailing police cars. Acting Sergeant Dougal Mulhern was driving the black and white police Plymouth leading the cavalcade up the cemetery drive.

The family limousine stopped beneath the branches of a giant Douglas fir where Inspector Archie McCathie waited in full dress uniform. He took Eileen Costello's arm and led the way over the damp grass to a row of metal folding chairs set out beneath a canopy. The chairs, tilting unsteadily on the bright green rubber grass, glistened wet. Inspector McCathie's boots squeaked on the wet rubber as he wheeled on his heels to take his place among the police ranks. It was beginning to rain, the water dripping off the large black umbrellas of the police pallbearers and running down the fragile aluminum metal awning supports. Joseph brushed his sleeve over the seat of a folding chair for his mother and stood behind the chair.

Eileen had concealed her tears beneath a dark veil attached to her black felt hat. Michael and Seamus sat on the damp chairs on either side of their mother when Father Lavoie began the Latin graveside service. The priest stood sheltered beneath a large blue and white golfing umbrella held by an Italian boy from the Star of the Sea fourth grade. The shivering boy had the look of a child in a Botticelli painting, his large brown eyes searching out Michael for a look of approval. Father Lavoie cast a sprinkling of holy water over Eileen and her sons, then turned to the gaping hole in the earth, to cast the water over the gray casket, where it mingled with the gathered raindrops. The six pallbearers – Mulhern, Dempsey, Donavan and Danny Sweeney among them—stood alongside the casket three to a side. Dempsey handed Eileen a long-stem lily from the Department wreath. She accepted and, leaning over the grave placed the lily among the raindrops and holy water on the coffin lid. At an agreed point in the prayers, the policemen eased the casket into the earth. Father Lavoie then cast a hand full of soil into the grave, the dull rattle of the earth bouncing off the coffin, ending the service. It was raining harder.

On the ride home, Michael continued to smile, despite Joseph's attempt to wipe the smirk off his brother's face with a concealed punch. Eileen Costello saw the punch and raised her veil.

"That's enough Joseph. Michael, you are a brave boy," she said reaching out to pat his knee. "Your mother knows what's behind that smile." For a moment Michael believed she too was aware there was no way his Da could be dead. But before he could be certain, Eileen had lowered her veil to conceal her eyes. Michael was confident that his Da would be waiting for them at the house. He guessed they would all find that he had been getting into the beer Acting Sergeant Mulhern had stacked in the kitchen sink. Eamon Costello had a weakness for beer. Michael only hoped that his Da would be singing. A beer or two was all it would take. Then nobody would be embarrassed about any of this. When Eamon Costello sang the joy in his bright tenor voice filling a room made it hard to be angry. Michael closed his eyes, listening for the ballad that always made his mother smile.

"Oh, the pale moon was rising,
Above the green mountains,
The sun was declining beneath the blue sea...

(The others in the limo pretended not to hear Michael humming along.)

When I strayed with my love
To the pure crystal fountain,
That stands in the beautiful Vale of Tralee..."

Whenever Eamon sang that song Eileen and the boys would begin waltzing around the kitchen.

"For she was lovely and fair
As the rose of summer
Yet 'twas not her beauty alone that won me...
Oooh No 'twas the truth in her eyes ever dawning

That made me love Mary
The Rose of Tralee."

Even as the song faded from his memory, Michael clung to the picture of Eamon Costello snatching his sons up in his powerful arms and dancing down the hall, as alive as any man could be.

***

Smoke from the cigars, supplied by Mulhern, drifted across the ceiling over the living room of the Costello home, the room packed shoulder to shoulder with uniformed and plainclothes policemen. Late arrivals loitered on the porch, others in their cars, all waiting to join the wake. Father Lavoie perched uncomfortably on the sofa beside Eileen Costello acknowledging the line of passing police. Each man took Eileen's hand and offered a respectful nod to the priest, the line working its way toward the kitchen. Occasionally the softly spoken condolences were lost in loud bursts of laughter emanating from the kitchen. Michael stood behind the sofa in his damp trousers, hoping the wet patches in his pants would not be mistaken for his having peed his pants. He was watching the passing faces, waiting for someone to say something that would acknowledge the truth that only he seemed to be aware of. When he tired of waiting, he started up the stairs to the bedroom he shared with Seamus, confident he would find his Da somewhere in the house.

Eamon Costello was seated on the edge of the double bed in the boys' bedroom. His elbows were braced on his knees, his fists supporting his chin in the pensive pose so familiar to his sons. His police tunic was unbuttoned and his uniform hat lay on the bed. Michael remembered his mother preaching that it was bad luck to leave a hat on the bed and reached to pick up the hat. Before he could reach it, his Da laughed, raking his fingers through his curly red hair. "The hat? Michael, that's just nonsense your mother picked up in the Old Country." Michael could see the mischief in his Da's smile and recognized there was a beer or two behind the smile, having seen his father that way so many times. He was certain his Da had already been into Mulhern's beer.

"That's a terrible ruckus the lads are making down there," Eamon said in a quiet voice, almost as if he were afraid to be overheard. "They must be making a mountain of work for your poor Mum, eh? Tell me, did you see that informer Glasheen among them? Was never a drink on the house that one couldn't smell from across a field on a windless day, eh? You remember my telling you how Dougal and I handled the likes of Glasheen in the Old Country, Michael?" His Da laughed softly, the laughter causing the shimmering rainbow over the bed to settle around his head. The pensive look left his face.

"That was long before you were born, Michael." Michael knew all these stories, having heard them more times than he could remember. And it pleased him to hear his Da's remembering once more. They had often spent hours together over Eamon's cherished pictures from the Old Country, admiring the yellowing photographs of his Da in his Irish Royal Constabulary uniform on the streets of Belfast and Derry. "A good force, that was, too," Eamon would insist. "Some of Ireland's finest, until the Brits sent in the Black and Tans. Once that bunch came to Ireland it could cost a man his life wearing the badge. And it was the likes of Glasheen who were pointing a finger at us for the IRA Flying Squads. No Michael. You best keep your eye on that one."

The sound of footsteps on the stairs brought a quiet to the bedroom. Before Michael could speak again, Eamon Costello picked up his hat, lay back on the bed, tucked his hands beneath his head, and with his cap slipping down over his eyes, he slept. A nighttime policeman, he needed his afternoon nap.

Chapter 8 Questionable Vocations

Sister Mary Hildegard paced the gym floor, exorcising the irreverent thoughts flooding her mind; though in the recesses of her heart she was certain her feelings were justified. The black and white numbers on the gymnasium clock indicated thirty-three minutes past two. Father Maurice Lavoie was late, though Sister Mary was aware the clock usually ran a few minutes fast. Fast or slow, this was not the first time the priest had kept her waiting.

The afternoon sunlight slanting through the high windows cast long shadows now stretching across the polished gymnasium floor. Sister Mary calculated that in twenty-seven minutes she would be required to be at her place by the school door overseeing dismissal. She was convinced her presence at the sounding of the bell was the only thing that preserved a semblance of decorum during the student rush to the exits. She flicked her fingers from her brow to her heart and across her breasts and muttered a rapid Hail Mary.

"The man doesn't own a watch," she said aloud, seeking a sense of appeasement in scolding the priest. "He doesn't think of other peoples' duties." She was speaking to the deserted gymnasium, her muttering too soft for anyone to hear. "He's even been late to Mass." In the silence of the empty gym she sighed audibly and cast aside her inbred ecclesiastic restraint. "It's not as if I don't have enough trouble with a Frenchman. I have to wait here for a Frenchman who doesn't own a watch." She shook her head, turned away from the clock and began to pray, hoping prayer would quiet her nerves.

Sister Mary had confided to her nuns earlier that day that Father Lavoie's reviewing the grades of the school's graduating class was a waste of her time, a Jesuit charade. "All his talk of high school scholarships for students interested in a vocation amounts to nothing more than his recruiting paying students for the new Jesuit High School. Why can't he just say so?"

Sister Mary shot an over-the-shoulder look at the clock. To confirm what the wall clock was telling her she slipped a hand into the folds of her habit for her father's pocket watch, his gift on the day of her final vows. The touch of the metal casing in the palm of her hand never failed to awaken the memory of the solemn farmer fishing the watch from his trouser pocket. He had handed it to her as if he were parting with part of himself; the metal still warm, carrying with it the mystery of her father's trouser pocket. There had never been a father-child closeness for any of Charles Kemper's children. For his oldest daughter, there was only the preordained certainty that she would one day be Charlie Kemper's gift to God.

For the past thirty years his watch had rested in the folds of Sister Mary's habit, caressed countless times in moments of frustration, her nervous fingers having worn away the maker's engraving. Some days the watch ran fast a minute or two. Others, when she failed to wind it tight before setting it on the table by her bed, it could lose as much as five minutes a day. Yet whatever time the sturdy black hands indicated, Sister Mary accepted as absolute. Hearing the priest entering the Annex, she made a quick check of the watch. He was twenty minutes late. She let the watch slip heavily into the folds of her habit.

Father Maurice Lavoie was breathing heavily, his face wreathed in an apologetic grin deepening the dimples in his cheeks. He raised his hand in benediction before the nun could speak. "Forgive me, Sister. I know I am late and I am truly sorry. This has not been the best of days for me. I ask you to show a little patience. God will bless you, I promise."

Sister Mary was not in a forgiving state of mind. "We have to be brief, Father. Our meeting was to have been half an hour ago. I have other…" The priest interrupted with a wave of his small, soft hand.

"Have I not confessed? I beg for your forgiveness, Sister," he pleaded, mocking her anger. He glanced up at the clock. "What am I? A few minutes late."

"Closer to thirty," she replied in chilling terms.

"Is there no sin so great that it cannot be forgiven, Sister?" He smiled to humor her, aware there was little humor residing in the lean nun who stood a head taller than him.

"I have dismissal and an after school assembly for the girls' choir at 3:45," she said, the bite in her voice a little less sharp. There were few areas where Sister Mary would have spoken in such a challenging manner to the priest, but in matters of the school they both regarded her as absolute authority. Father Lavoie tried once again to ease her petulance.

"May God bless you with the love of every one of those dear children for all that you do, Sister. But lest we forget, He has also promised to reward a charitable heart, eh? I don't suppose the sisters left us any tea? I haven't had a cup since our morning Mass." His face contorted with a touch of martyrdom. Sister Mary nodded doubtfully before swiftly fixing her school grading papers on the gym table. "Please, don't touch anything while I'm gone." She darted into the gym kitchen with a challenging over-the-shoulder glance.

Sister Mary Hildegard was 53, though until the day he read her age in a medical statement from Dr. Adam Kennedy's office, Father Lavoie had guessed her to be much older. He had seen wisps of white hair — white as gray hair turns white in truly older individuals — escaping beneath her garniture. The sighting cured any thoughts of what she might have looked like more exposed. Such thoughts could lead to a dangerous drift of the imagination for a man living celibate vows. The lean nun with premature osteoporosis hunching her shoulders offered little for sinful speculation. However, when it came to Sister Mary Rose, dwelling on such thoughts was another matter. The dark eyed, young Italian nun had caused the priest considerable penance. Such an image was far from his mind at the appearance of Sister Mary Hildegard bearing a white mug filled with a tepid, amber liquid.

"We were all disappointed in this year's graduates, Father." She handed him the cup, quickly gathering her student papers. "There are only three serious students and all three are Japs."

"Japanese." He corrected softly.

"Yes."

"You were referring to the Wakabayashis?" He suggested.

"As you know, they are all wrapped up in their foreign religion," she countered with an I-told-you-so pinch of her lips.

Father Lavoie detected the nun's note of satisfaction as he sniffed suspiciously over the rim of the tea mug. "The father of those children happens to appear at Mass every now and then," he said between breathing on the tea. "I had hopes for him a few years ago and I continue to pray he will turn to the church one day. You say, Sister, that the Wakabayashi children have done well?" Before Sister Mary could answer, he pressed on. "Who made this tea?"

Sister Mary was intent on ignoring both the priest's lecturing and the disparaging tone of his question. Father Lavoie's forgiving smile faded. "Whoever did," he added with a sour look, "could have improved things with a little hot water, Sister. Tepid tea is tasteless." He plunged his forefinger into the mug to demonstrate. "This is cold."

The nun never looked up, aware that her mentioning the Japanese students had set the priest's thoughts in a direction she hoped to avoid. She caught herself praying she would avoid a lecture on Japanese Catholic converts. "You may not be aware, Sister, that it was the Jesuit Order which first brought the church to the Japanese."

"And the Franciscans," she added without looking up from the graduation papers.

"In 1549, the Basque Jesuit Francis Xavier landed on the Japanese shore with two Jesuit priests and a Japanese interpreter," he said defensively. Following a moment's pause he confessed. "And the Franciscans followed, of course."

The nun shrugged. "What thought have you given to the Henniger boy, Father? Jimmy Henniger is one of our students who has scholarship grades."

Father Lavoie appeared startled. She was right. Jimmy Henniger served Mass five mornings a week and the priest was well aware the boy's angelic features had captured the hearts of the nuns. If Sister Mary detected his silence as his dismissing her suggestion, she wasn't allowing it to temper her enthusiasm. "The boy has real vocational possibilities," the nun persisted, pushing Jimmy Henniger's examination grades into the priest's hands.

Father Lavoie placed Henniger's papers back on the table and reached into his soutane for a yellow pencil and began stirring his tea with the eraser end. For a long moment neither of them spoke, until the nun smiled sarcastically. "Of course, there are the Glasheens. I understand their father is eager to offer those two for vocations." Father Lavoie rolled his eyes heavenward until only the whites showed like two detached golf balls above his cheeks. When they reappeared they were sternly focusing on the nun.

"Sister, I am not giving up on the Wakabayashi boys," the priest sighed, slipping the pencil back into his soutane. "If only the timing was not so controversial. People have become so quick to judge the Japanese. Of course, I understand why. To the uninformed never having lived among them, the Japanese appear clannish and sometimes martially minded."

"Martially minded?"

"Yes. Yet they are a gentle people, especially when they recognize a greater authority. It's their culture. The Japanese accept rules. They will accept what they are told without question when dealing with a voice of authority. That is what makes them such excellent soldiers. It is also why they have proven to be such inspirational martyrs."

"Martyrs?"

"Yes. Martyrs, Sister," the priest replied with sudden irritation, aware Sister Mary was baiting him.

"The Japanese have a history of dying for Christ with courage and faith that has rarely been equaled. Many have died in the manner of the great Saints of Rome. Some were crucified, some burned at the stake, and others died for Christ in deaths that were even more terrifying. Much of today's irreverence of Church doctrine is spoken by those who would have you believe they are merely questioning Papal infallibility. Conversely, I would be willing to wager that our Wakabayashi children have never uttered a challenge to your authority nor to any of your teachings." He paused, giving her time to confirm. When she said nothing, the priest shrugged in condescension. "Of course there are exceptions; that boy Toshio Wakabayashi may be one."

"Sister, you may not be aware that it was I who brought the church to their father," he added. Before she could protest, he hurried on. "I met Isao Wakabayashi in a berry field near Vedder Crossing." The priest smiled evangelically. "He was picking berries."

Sister Mary busied herself with her papers, resigned she was in for a retelling of the story.

"God sent me to that field with a purpose," the priest continued. "Following my early years in Japan, I had set out with the same sense of mission among the Japanese in British Columbia. Wakabayashi may be erratic in accepting Christ, but through him we have his children." Father Lavoie heaved a great sigh. "If only you could have seen the faces of those Japanese the day I first brought them the Word of God, you would understand. It was as if they were hearing divine music for the first time. I was able to speak to them in their own language while telling them of the Japanese martyrs. And I can tell you, Sister, the spirit of Saint Paul Miki was reaching across two hundred years to the soul of each man in that field."

The nun pulled her father's watch from her habit, pointedly studying the time. She was still smarting over the priest's refusal to consider Jimmy Henniger.

"Perhaps the Japs were not so busy spying on us in those days," Sister Mary said, jolting the priest's reverie. "What about the Glasheen boys?"

"You are not serious, Sister?"

"There are many souls called to God, Father," she continued, preaching to his backside. "Christ proclaimed he did not come to—"

Father Lavoie turned irritably. "To save the righteous. Thank you, Sister. I am familiar with all that. But your suggesting the Glasheen boys is out of the question. To encourage Jimmy Henniger or the Glasheen boys would present the Archbishop with problems he would not thank either one of us for." He hesitated, then decided to change course.

"I have another thought, Sister. Are we both overlooking a more likely candidate? What about young Costello? His mother has been praying for years for a vocation for one of her sons."

"Michael?" The nun was unable to suppress a thin smile. "Yes," she agreed tentatively. "Michael would make an excellent religious, Father. Perhaps a cloister Monk. Talks to himself, you know? And he possesses a vivid imagination; what you Jesuits like to refer to as a visible soul. You can almost see it, but you can never tell what is going on inside that head of his. Even as a first grader, he had the quiet, introspective demeanor of a John of the

Cross. Since the death of his father the boy has turned away from almost everyone in school, including his brothers. I used to think he was cut out to be a policeman." She shrugged. "Now he spends entire afternoons in the church."

"Yes," the priest said. "I have seen him praying the Stations of the Cross."

The nun's eyebrows rose skeptically. "More likely talking to himself. Now, the eldest Costello boy? That's the one the church let slip through its fingers." Sister Mary, momentarily put aside their confrontation over Jimmy Henniger and smiled nostalgically. "Joseph was the son the Costello parents were counting on for Holy Orders. Difficult, difficult boy," she muttered. "A born Jesuit. I hear he's living on the wild side now that he's out of school where I could keep an eye on him. But Father, how can you overlook the Henniger boy?"

The priest tried for a conciliatory voice. "We are speaking of vocations, Sister. Jimmy Henniger is just..." he hesitated. The nun's change of attack had caught him off guard and what he was about to say had come too easily to his tongue. He stammered, realizing he had been about to reveal more than he was allowed to reveal. "There are certain traits — certain inclinations, Sister. Jimmy Henniger is in many ways a different boy. In looking at the possibilities for a vocation, we must give great care to examine these, uh, proclivities. Do you understand?" The priest dropped the examination papers on the gym table, attempting to convey with his eyes what he could not say. The school dismissal bell ended the conversation.

Chapter 9 Pink Panties

It was a Sunday, the week before the beginning of the fall school term, the sun drifting in and out from behind a layer of high, thin clouds. A warm Indian summer Chinook breeze played over Jericho Beach, carrying the scent of potatoes frying in the fish and chip stand a quarter of a mile up the shore. Michael Costello, Jimmy Henniger, the Glasheens, and two of the Pappas brothers were pushing driftwood into the surf when Michael began idly skipping rocks over the waves. One of the Pappas boys waded into the surf seeking a better bounce on the stone skippers soon the others stepped in and suddenly they were all up to their knees, splashing in the surf.

Michael glanced down the nearly deserted beach and started for the deep beach grass peeling off his shirt. "Last man in is a Chinaman's uncle!" His shout set off a charge into the tall clumps of summer-dried grass, the six boys tripping over one another stripping off their wet clothes. Jimmy Henniger squatted in the sand, pulling his loose fitting sweater over his head. But for the muscles and his broad shoulders, Jimmy's upper body could have passed for that of a teenage girl. Stripped to the waist his curly black hair gave him the look of a young movie starlet, the nipples on his chest protruding with more form than most pubescent girls. Jimmy kicked his legs in the air and rolling over on his hips wiggled out of his trousers. In that moment a silence fell over the circle of boys in various stages of undress. Jimmy's laughter gave way to an apologetic grin. Without saying a word he raised his bare buttocks out of the sand and began pulling up his trousers to conceal the pink satin bloomers tangled around his ankles. In the sudden quiet the distant radio music playing in the fish and chip stand and a distant cry of an aroused gull carried over the beach sands.

The Pappas brothers didn't own any underwear and appeared less shocked than the others. The Glasheens, mouths agape and their eyes fixed on Jimmy's panties, appeared like wingless cranes in their stained long johns, the one short and heavy, the other lean and tall. The radio music went silent. The sounds of children challenging the chill surf died out as if the entire beach had been struck dumb. There were few among the shocked boys who would dare call Jimmy Henniger a fruit to his face, though the subject had been discussed many times in his absence. At fourteen, Jimmy weighed better than one hundred and eighty pounds and he had a reputation for an uncharacteristic willingness to fight. That alone defied the neighborhood's understanding of those who the boys were inclined to brand as queer.

Jimmy was one of seven or eight Henniger kids, nobody knew for certain how many there were. The day the Henniger family moved into the old Mason house on Third Avenue West, even Jimmy's old man seemed unsure. The Mason place had stood vacant for months when one afternoon the Henniger Ford came into the street weighed down with kids and a chest of drawers laced to the rear tire. The rest of their furniture, chairs and an iron bedstead were fitted over the Ford's running boards. About five o'clock that first day, with the Mason yard filled with kids, Jimmy's emaciated old man came out onto the porch waving his arms.

"Okay," he hollered at the gang milling about the gate. "Supper time. Time for all you neighborhood kids to go on home." The old man remained on the porch, his mouth hanging open, visibly skeptical and suspicious waiting for the crowd to disperse. When no one left, he turned back into the house, sadly shaking his head.

Claude, the older of the Glasheen brothers, a shifty kid who did most of the talking for his younger brother Stanley, was the first to break the silence. "Henniger," he said with theatrical astonishment. "You got them underpants from the wrong end of the clothes line?"

Jimmy flushed and grinned awkwardly while shifting sand through his fingers.

Stanley, a foot taller and weighing thirty or forty pounds more than his older brother, was not so quick with the smart cracks. "Those drawers weren't made for what you got hanging from your ass, Henniger," he muttered, uncertain of his insult.

"Where's your brassiere, Jimmy?" Claude added, supported by his younger brother's bravado. "You got the tits for a brassiere."

Jimmy remained squatting in the tall grass, his eyes lowered, swatting absently at sand fleas. The sight of Jimmy, with his knees drawn up to his chin, was awakening conflicting emotions in Michael, who was standing naked in the grass, his lily-white ass shining like a midnight moon over his sun-brown legs. He was completely unaware of his rising erection.

"Dry up, Glasheen!" he shouted and went splashing into the surf. "Last man in is a Chinaman's ass."

"Chinaman's ass? You said a Chinaman's uncle," Pappas protested, sprinting after him.

"Henniger would probably go for a Chinaman's ass if the Chinaman was wearing those pink panties," Claude Glasheen hollered, picking up the chase.

There wasn't much said on the homeward march. Mostly there was only the squishing of six wet trousers and the occasional "shit" when someone snapped a wet shirt like a whip crack at the boy in front. Jimmy trailed a pace behind the parade, the others dropping off along the way. By the time Michael reached the Costello gate, he and Jimmy were alone in the street. "See you around, Jimmy." Michael smiled, dismissing Jimmy with a slight wave.

Jimmy's large shoulders hunched as if someone had just given him a back whipping. "I don't blame you, Michael." He spoke as if he were confessing a secret.

"Blame me? For what?"

"For not liking me anymore."

Michael forced a laugh. "Forget it, Jimmy. You are talking like a little kid." Jimmy remained anchored at the front gate. "Jimmy?" Michael said. "What you just said reminds me of the song little kids sing: *I don't want to play in your yard; I don't like you anymore.*"

Jimmy nodded. "And I don't blame you, Michael."

Michael broke into a flat unmusical voice:

"You'll be sorry when you see me...

Sliding down our cellar door...?" He forced an easy laugh and delivered a light punch at Jimmy's shoulder.

"You can't holler down our rain barrel,

You can't climb our apple tree...

I don't want to play in your yard...

If you won't be good to me."

"Hell. Go on home, Jimmy. What difference does it make whose pants you got on?" Michael wished they were somewhere other than standing in the street in front of his house. "You should have told those Glasheens to go fuck themselves. You just sat there taking all that shit. I was hoping you would bust one of them. That would have shut them up." Michael sighed wearily. "Everybody knows you are different, Jimmy. Don't you let the Glasheens or anyone else horse you around like that." He was wishing they could drop the whole thing. "Wear your sister's pants if it makes you feel good. It's nobody's damn business."

"I'll always be your friend, Michael," Jimmy whispered. "And I won't forget. I promise." He wiped a sleeve across his cheeks, smearing the tears. "You'll see."

That fall, Jimmy Henniger stopped serving the seven o'clock Mass at the Star of the Sea Church. And he didn't appear to care that whenever someone new showed up in the neighborhood they would get the story of the panties straight from the Glasheens. Years later, to his surprise and pain, Michael would discover Jimmy never did forget his promise.

Chapter 10 Ghosts

Eileen Costello's concern over Michael's behavior following the death of his father had began on the drive home from the cemetery. For a time, she was able to dismiss her worries, attributing his lack of grief to Michael's concealing his emotions, a trait inherited from her husband. Michael had always been different from his brothers, though none of her sons were the boys they were before they buried their father. Seamus and Joseph grew morose, exploding in flashes of anger, while Michael continued to behave as if nothing had changed.

Eileen's concern came to a head late that summer while baking pies for the weekend and keeping an anxious eye on her youngest son. Michael was hunched over the kitchen table, absently tracing his finger over the forget-me-nots on the tablecloth, unmoved by the aroma of the freshly baked pies. It was then she decided it was time to tackle the grief she was sure lay behind all the irreverent smiles. Swiftly working the pastry trimmings between her fingers, she tucked the last of her sliced apples into a pastry pocket. "There. A tart for you, Michael," she said sprinkling a pinch of cinnamon over the apple slices. "It will be waiting here when you come to supper. Now get along out of my kitchen before I trip over your big feet. Get out into the sunshine before you begin looking like you never saw the light of day." She opened the kitchen door to a warm late summer breeze. Michael continued at the table, his chin braced in the palm of his hand.

Eileen Costello tilted her head contemplating her son, though she never liked to see his hair growing down his neck, nor did she approve of his reddish curls growing over his ears. "It's a handsome Irish face you have buried beneath all that red hair," she complained. What she didn't say was that with his hair grown long, Michael was a living picture of Eamon Costello, the boy she had fallen in love with the moment she first set eyes on him. That she kept to herself. Michael resisted a haircut, believing his long hair gave him strength and stimulated his brain. He was also aware that his scraggly hair helped him disguise the awkward, gangling teenager he had become. His mother was on the side of Delilah.

"How many times have I told you I can't stand the look of you with your hair hanging over your face?" She was intent on stirring an argument with the lethargic figure at her table. Michael continued to drag his finger over the forget-me-nots. "You and your brothers behave like wild Indians when you need your haircut," his mother continued, proclaiming a theory that Michael had come to accept. He attributed his long hair as the source of a good number of the sins he took to Friday confession, though he never exposed that theory to Father Lavoie, fearing the French Canadian priest would likely cut his hair right there in the church.

"Maybe when I go to high school, I'll do it your way," Michael grumbled, his self-pity tugging at Eileen's mothering instincts to the point she had to resist the urge to wrap her arms around him.

"What is it that's making you so stubborn about the hair, son?" Her voice softened. "Are you still thinking about your dad? He liked to let his hair grow, though the department was always after him to get it cut."

"No," Michael muttered.

"Then what is it that you can't you tell your mother? You worried about starting high school and leaving Star of the Sea?" She pulled her chair alongside the table and freed the hand propped beneath Michael's chin, cradling it softly in her pastry-cool palm.

"Sister Mary Hildegard says it's time I grow up," he said quietly. "She says if I don't grow up I'm going to end up in hell."

"What on God's green earth would make her say a thing like that?"

"Sister says I can't tell the difference between telling the truth and lying. She says I lie to myself, and that's even worse than lying to other people. I'm not a liar, Mom. I don't lie to anybody."

"That old scarecrow." Eileen's rising indignation brought a flush to her face, her temper screened by the traces of baking flour over her cheeks. Michael shrugged. He had given up talking to anyone about his visits with his Da after nearly ending in a fight trying to convince Joseph and Seamus. Joseph shouted him into silence, hollering that he was acting crazy. Joe wanted to knock some sense into him, though they were both aware Michael had grown too big for Joe to handle.

"You have been acting stupid ever since the funeral," Joe charged. "People think we have a crazy in the family. You saw Dad in the coffin. His eyes were glued shut. His mouth was all puckered up like he was holding his breath. That's because the undertakers glued his jaw shut so his mouth wouldn't hang open. Michael, Dad is dead."

Joseph spun around to face Seamus. "Am I right Seamus?" Seamus nodded half-heartedly without speaking, leading Michael to suspect that he too had been visited. "It's time you quit this talking to Dad. How come I never see him?" Joseph stepped back, measuring how deeply his shouting had penetrated his younger brother's head. "That silver coffin?" He suddenly lowered his voice. "That cost Momma three hundred dollars. Dad is in it, Michael."

Michael was remembering his confrontation with his brother when he looked up into his mother's understanding eyes. He wanted to tell her he had been visiting with his Da that very morning; tell her he had discovered him resting in the shade of the sprawling, fruitless cherry tree by the fence in the back yard. Michael had come onto the porch to pick up the milk when a movement drew his attention to the shaded area beneath the tree. And there was his Da, shirt unbuttoned, his black necktie askew. He lay on his back in the grass, his hands cradling his head, smiling.

"Aah, Michael. I knew it would be you that would be the one comin' for the milk." His Da was twenty or thirty feet from the porch, yet Michael heard every word as clearly as if he had been whispering in his ear. "Come sit a minute with your Da," he said softly, patting the grass with the palm of his hand. "It feels good in the shade on a hot morning, eh?" His Da sighed and the soft rainbow of colors that had surrounded him in the bedroom began shimmering in the shadows of the cherry tree leaves. "Take the load off your feet, Michael. I can't remember it ever being so crazy hot come September."

Michael sat down beside him, feeling strangely peaceful at his father's side. "We miss you, Dad," he said. Eamon Costello replied with a quiet smile, studying him curiously.

"Are you thinking about the priesthood, Michael? Is it a vocation that's troubling you, son?"

Michael shook his head.

"You know that would please your mother no end, eh?"

"You and Mom always said it was Joe who was to be the priest in the family, Da."

"Ahh, but I'm afraid that's not to be, Michael. But a vocation may be something for you, son. It's a good job with steady pay." His father continued to smile, neither of them speaking until the warm wind grew still and the morning sun began to shrink the circle of shade and Michael realized he was alone holding the quart bottle of milk, now grown warm in his hands.

***

It was Seamus who took the story of Michael's miracle to Sister Mary Hildegard a few days before the end of the school term. The nun listened intently, crossed herself, and then with her lips pursed in tight determination spun Seamus by the shoulder propelling him out her office door. "Don't you believe a word of it, Seamus. I'll straighten out that brother of yours before this day is through. You will hear no more of this nonsense."

Sister Mary Hildegard was waiting for Michael at the school door. The nun hissed, cold fury in her voice as she clamped her fingers into his shoulder. "Just you wait one moment, young man." Michael winced beneath the bite of her hard fingers as the nun propelled him at a trot down the hallway. Once behind the frosted glass office door, Sister Mary rolled her eyes heavenward in disbelief. "Now suppose you tell me about this business of your wild ghost stories?" Recognizing there was no answer expected, Michael said nothing. "I am talking about the lies you have been spinning. About your visiting with the ghost of your dear departed father, indeed. Don't you dare deny it, Michael Costello. You know what I'm talking about."

"Yes, Sister."

"And don't give me that 'yes sister' business. I have seen enough of your brothers to know how you Costello boys lie your way out of trouble." Sister Mary rose up on her toes, her deep-set eyes peering into his like hot coals in a black cloud. Michael looked away, his eyes fixed on a lone, grey hair sprouting unattended from her long neck. "You listen to me, young man. Your father didn't deserve to have his son making up lies about his immortal soul. Do you realize what a terrible sin you are committing?" The sister's grip tightened. "You have been lying to your brothers, Michael. What's worse, your lies are desecrating the memory of your father. God has His eye on you, Michael Costello. And God will punish you for this. I want to hear no more of that nonsense about visits from this ghost of your father. Do you understand me?"

Michael nodded silently. The nun glowered a moment before a victorious smile creased her chin and she started him toward the office door. Heading down the hall, Michael sensed her eyes on the back of his neck. It made him feel like a mouse being toyed with by a cat, the bite of her claws still paining his shoulder. Free of the school, he turned quickly for home and had gone no more than a few steps before he caught the scent of his father's Bay Rum. It was a heavy odor that had permeated the Costello house each evening with the appearance of Eamon in uniform, clean-shaven and ready for duty. Michael could feel his Da moving alongside him, stride for stride all the way to the Costello gate. From that day on, he walked home alone in hopes his Da happened to be in the neighborhood.

***

Michael never raised his eyes from the forget-me-nots all through the story of his meeting with Sister Mary. It was as if he had been confessing to an unseen listener, uncertain how he would be heard. She listened without a word. When he finished, she stood up from the kitchen table and slammed her empty pastry pan into the sink.

"So, it's your father, is it? You have been thinking of him all this time. Well that's as it should be, Michael. That old shrew has no business putting her nose into a boy's mourning over his dad." Eileen Costello glared menacingly over the kitchen table, the wooden spoon in her fist ready to deal with anyone daring to harm her child. "Those nuns. I have half a mind..." She let the thought go unspoken and lowered the spoon, struggling to remain calm.

"Aah, you should have known the nuns in the old country, son. We've none like those over here. Some of our dear Irish nuns visited with the departed every day of the week." Eileen wiped her hands on her apron. "If we had stayed in Ireland, you would have been taught by them. They came off the farm right into the convent, sometimes two and three from a family; every last one of them with the look of an angel. And the older they got the more saintly they became, and the more saintly the nun the more she was in touch with those on the other side. It was easy as you please, for them. A boy would never hear our Old Country nuns telling him to turn his back on those coming to him from beyond. You can believe that, Michael." For a moment, the look in her eyes was close to canonizing her youngest son.

Michael looked up with naked hope in his eyes. "It was Seamus who told Sister Mary," he confessed. "Sister told me I should pray for dad's soul and leave him to rest in heaven. But I get to missing him so much and we need him, Momma. I don't want to let him go. I don't want to be without Da. I just can't go on like I never had a Da, can I?"

Eileen drew a deep breath and cradled his head in the soft wattle of her arms. "You don't have to let him go, Michael. And you don't have to listen to that old shrew. It's good you are movin' out of that school. There are some things none of us can explain. We just learn to live with those things we don't understand, even if we have to put up with the likes of Sister Mary. It does no harm, you seeing your dad. That's the way the Lord meant the world to be. It's the devil who messed things up, Michael. It was the devil who closed the curtain on the world where your dad is now. You go on seeing what you please and meeting with your dad if it makes the world any better for you." Her voice dropped secretively. "Your mother does as much whenever I take flowers to his grave. You have heard me talking to your dad out there in the Irish. It's our way of making things right between him and me, Michael." A misty tear filled her hazel eyes. "Your dad left this world in a mess, Michael. Maybe he's sorry now and wants you to know he loves you still."

They sat quietly for a long time, his mother holding Michael's hand while gazing out beyond the kitchen window, lost in thought. The aroma of the pie baking in the oven finally brought her back to the kitchen. She went to the oven and pulled out the tart, juggling it in the folds of her apron.

"There it is. As I promised. You take this out on the porch and let it cool. And Michael, no more of your worrying about the nuns. You will meet new friends and new teachers in high school." She drew him to her bosom once more, cradling his head in her arms. "When you have eaten your tart, why don't you go fishing while the weather's so fine? If your dad were here he would send you on your way. Maybe he'd even go with you. Go on now." She lay a quarter on the kitchen table. "And that's for whatever you fancy."

The midday sun had burned away the last of the morning's scattered clouds exposing a naked blue sky when Michael left the house. He felt the warmth on his back as he headed toward Fraser's Wharf, a fish line tucked in his hip pocket, the scent of the sea fresh on the wind blowing in off the bay.

Chapter 11 Fishing Friends

Kitsilano's salt-water swimming pool was drained for fall cleaning. The pool's sandy bottom lay exposed in winter nakedness except for the deep puddle of brackish seawater beneath the diving board tower. Michael glanced over the empty pool, relieved there would be no more swimming until spring. The summer beach crowds that had invaded Fraser's Wharf were gone. Several times during the past summer he had set out to go fishing only to be turned away from the floating dock by crowds of five- and six-year-old kids fishing from the wharf. Some had been fishing with breadcrumbs for bait on lines of grocery string, many accompanied by their mothers. Michael watched one mother, a giant of a woman who may have been the kid's grandmother, take a wad of chewing gum from her mouth and jam it onto a fish hook. When the gum caught a large shiner, he pocketed his line and turned away.

Michael hesitated on the packed trail above Fraser's Wharf, surveying the empty boat cradles scattered over the upper deck of the boathouse. Satisfied the wharf was deserted, he started down the ramp as Billy Fraser's old man appeared out of nowhere. Michael was aware of old man Fraser's trick of surprising kids who hung out around the wharf. It was his way of letting them know he could be watching at any time.

Lyle Fraser wore baggy bib coveralls that hung like a loose tent over his stooped shoulders. And because he never appeared without his oil-stained baseball cap pulled low, people had no way of knowing if he was gray or bald. When he spoke — which was not often — his words never amounted to much more than a whisper. Mostly, his conversation consisted of a grunt or a nod, with his jaw clamped on the stem of his pipe in the manner of an ancient mariner. Michael imagined Fraser as an old sea dog moving through his shore-bound fleet.

The boathouse owner shuffled out from among the overturned hulls, his perpetual frown softening at the sight of Michael.

"Hello, Mister Fraser. Billy around?"

"No. Billy has been ducking off all day." Fraser cupped his hands over the bowl of his pipe shielding a large metal lighter.

"You wouldn't know," he said between puffs, "anything about ducking off from chores." Puff. "I suppose?"

"I haven't seen Billy, Mister Fraser, if that's what you mean." Michael threw a questioning glance at the vacant wharf. "You think it would be okay for me to fish awhile?"

"I see you got your gear." Fraser's eyes shifted to the twine line protruding from Michael's hip pocket. "You know you don't have to ask to come on this wharf, Mike." He puffed at the pipe until it was going good and paused to savor the smoke. "You're free to come any time. Isn't a day goes by that I don't look out over the bay without remembering you and your dad sittin' out there on the end of the wharf. You were no more than a pup those days. We were pretty good friends, me and that dad of yours."

"Thanks, Mister Fraser." Michael started toward the wharf. "If I see Billy, I'll tell him you are looking for him, okay?" Fraser's grunt implied he wasn't expecting much from that promise.

Fraser's Wharf consisted of a deck of heavy planks attached to large, semi-submerged logs held in place by chains anchored to submerged concrete. Michael chose a piling at the far end of the wharf and allowed his bare feet to dangle out over the shallow water. The tide was running out, the shore end of the floating wharf already resting on the beach. For a time he sat aimlessly, his eye looking out over English Bay, following the inbound afternoon coastal steamers creeping home past Point Atkinson. The Red Funnel Union Steamships carried the mail and city-bound passengers from Bowen Island, Gibson's Landing, Woodfibre and Squamish, and all points up the Howe Sound. Early arrivals came from overnight ports as far north as Alice Lake on the northern tip of Vancouver Island. The black and cream stacked Canadian Pacific Fleet sailed in from Nanaimo and Victoria and up Island ports beyond Campbell River.

Casually, hardly taking his eyes from the distant ships, Michael reached for the hand line in his hip pocket, pricked a moist salmon egg with the barbed end of the hook and dropped the hook and sinker into the water. Slowly, almost imperceptibly, the tide drew his line out from where the silver-sided sea bass sheltered in the shadows of the floating deck. Old Man Fraser's talk of his dad had started his remembering the days of fishing with his father. As a result, he never felt the gentle nibbling on the line that would have told him his bait was gone.

In time, his attention was drawn to a Royal Canadian Air Force flying boat lumbering back and forth across the bay in taxiing exercises, the gray airplane's engine roar sounding the first call of the approaching war. Michael fantasized being at the stick of the flying machine, his head encased in a leather flying helmet, goggles over his eyes. He was in mid-flight, flying west into the setting sun, when a movement off his shoulder brought him back to the reality of the wharf.

His immediate fear was that a mother-led, six-year old had taken up the adjacent space. Without turning his head he managed a sideways glimpse of three strangers settling alongside him on the wharf; they were less than the length of a fishing pole from his perch. A swift over-the-shoulder glance confirmed the intruders were Japanese; a man of fifty or so years, wearing a going-to-church felt fedora, and a woman seated next to him on a metal tackle box. A teenage girl was scooping up a bucket of the seawater. Michael's second glance focused on the man squatting at the edge of the wharf, his shirt sleeves rolled above the elbows, his trousers folded to his knees. Alongside him lay a pair of black leather, low-cut with his balled-up stockings stuffed inside.

When Michael looked again the girl was seated atop a piling, her bare feet dangling over the water. She sensed his stare and turned, their eyes meeting for an instant before she quickly lowered her eyes. Michael's sense of territorial hostility disappeared with the realization these people had come to do some serious fishing.

He continued with his eyes focused on the Royal Canadian Air Force flying boat for an hour or more, ignoring the girl's muted excitement each time she landed a shiner. It dawned on him that he had not caught a single fish.

As the afternoon passed, the changing tide raised a series of languid waves, the late afternoon sun glancing off the surface. The reflection made it difficult for Michael to keep his eyes fixed on the Air Force flying boat and he decided it was time to leave. As he got down from his piling, he noticed that the Japanese woman was watching him intently. The woman turned to the girl, speaking

Japanese. The girl smiled and picked up the coffee tin at her feet and brought it to Michael.

"Hello," she said. The word, cushioned by a trace of accent, rolled softly off her tongue like music. Michael, a head or more taller than she, glanced down into the tin. It was filled with shiners. "Maybe your bait was no good?" she added, almost apologetically.

"I wasn't really fishing," he answered, indicating the flying boat maneuvering a mile out in the bay. "I was watching that airplane. I'm thinking about joining the Air Force one day, if there's a war. Maybe become a pilot." He glanced again at the fish in her coffee can. "You did pretty good."

"My mother would like you to have these. We have too many."

He was about to protest that he only fished for shiners to feed the family cat, but the words stopped before they left his lips. The warm afternoon had raised a fine bead of dew-like sweat across the girl's upper lip, and he had to struggle with an irresistible urge to reach out to brush away the gossamer thread.

"My name is Soju," the girl said. "My mother asks if your name is Costello." Michael caught himself listening for an echo when she spoke his name.

"Yea. That's my name. How did she know that?"

"My mother says you look very much like someone she once knew. She said that if your name was Costello, maybe you could be related to the Costello she knew. My family name is Wakabayashi. Do you know the name?"

"No." His answer appeared to have sealed whatever else she was about to ask.

"I have seen you at Star of the Sea sometimes," the girl explained. "My father works at the school for Father Lavoie." Michael nodded, recalling the clannish groups of Japanese at Star of the Sea. The girl hesitated, unsure whether she should go on. "You start high school next week?"

"Yea, I do."

"Me too. Maybe we will see each other there?" She placed the can of shiners on the wharf and nudged the can toward him with her naked toe. "Do you want these?" It came to him she was offering him a share of her catch. He picked up the can. "Thanks." He wanted to ask her about the Costello her mother knew, but his thoughts were changing so swiftly he was uncertain of what to say to this Japanese girl in her bare feet and shining black hair standing so close.

***

Eileen Costello crinkled her nose as if she were encountering a foul smell. "If you are feeding those to kitty, take them out onto the back porch. They are going to stink up my kitchen."

"No," Michael protested. "I want to see how they taste. The Japs eat them all the time."

His mother sniffed again. "If I cook them, you better eat them," she warned.

Michael watched her lay the fish in the frying pan, sizzling in melted butter. "Smells good," he said encouragingly.

Eileen answered with a negative shake of her head and laid three of the fish on an empty plate and left the room. Michael took an uncertain and curious bite, then lowered the plate to the floor to the impatient cat.

While he was able to forget the oily taste of the shiners, the memory of the Japanese girl wouldn't leave so easily. He was missing something from that moment on the wharf, convinced the girl had been waiting for him to say or do something more. Her mother had known Eamon Costello. Of that he was certain. It was his red hair and his height, so like his father, that led to her asking his name. Why had he been so tongue tied?

***

The day of initiation for the high school ninth graders, Michael prowled the school corridors trying to convince himself that he was merely looking for familiar Star of the Sea faces. He discovered the girl with her back to the wall at the main door, her arms folded over new books. "You made it," he shouted the minute he laid eyes on her. "I was hoping I'd find someone from Star of the Sea. I wanted to tell you the shiners were swell."

"My father eats them sometimes," the girl answered. "But mostly we feed them to our cat." She smiled, leading him to suspect she hadn't believed his lie.

"How come I never saw you on Fraser's Wharf before last Sunday?" he asked changing the subject.

The girl looked down at her shoes. "We used to fish at Steveston on the Fraser River," she said quietly. "My father's friend keeps his fishing boat there." She glanced up briefly and he caught a look of sudden hurt in her eyes. "We live on Third Avenue, near Burrard Street. It's a long way to Steveston. My parents thought we should try a place closer to home. They don't understand very much English." She shrugged with the same shy, almost apologetic innocence that had silenced him on the wharf. "I was embarrassed being with them, afraid I might run into someone from Star of the Sea. Then I saw you there, and it didn't seem to matter anymore." She laughed.

"I used to fish there all the time," Michael confessed.

They stood awkwardly, saying nothing for what seemed an eternity before he blurted the question. "How did your mother know my name?"

"You said your father was a policeman?"

"I don't remember saying that."

"Maybe my mother told me. You know, she worked for years in a hotel on Powell Street?" If that was a question, Michael chose to remain silent. "She worked for a man named Azumo-san who knew all the policemen on Powell. My mother says she used to see this policeman at the hotel. He had red hair like yours and he was tall like you."

"That was my dad."

Chapter 12 Brotherly Love

The sun had taken total command of the open sky through the first week of high school classes. A scattering of sun-dried leaves from the curbside maples and the scorched brown tufts of grass clinging to the school soccer pitch were the only hint summer had ended.

Entering parochial school had been a day of mothers' spit slicking the cowlicks to their babies' brow and a line of uncertain kids in white socks and new shoes quietly awaiting instructions. Michael's first week in high school found him muscling his way into Phair's classroom, squeezing past loud and restless teenaged bodies.

Philip Phair was pretending to be engrossed in a clipboard until the noise level became too loud to ignore. At that point he rose up from his desk to his full six foot six and cast a cold, ominous look over the room. It was a practiced move followed by a sudden hush. In the shuffling quiet, the teacher proceeded to deliberately open each of the three windows lining one side of the room without a word. Then turning to the boys, he smiled menacingly. Philip Phair weighed two hundred and forty hard pounds and was rumored to have played goal for the Canadian Army soccer team. After allowing the silence to settle over the room, he spoke in a soft voice.

"Welcome, gentlemen, to your home room." There followed a long pause. "And may I remind you that this is primarily my room. You, on the other hand, are merely transients, transients who will be staying perhaps for a shorter stay than some of you or your parents have in mind. With that thought in mind, I expect each of you to regard yourselves as guests in my room." The teacher's cold smile faded as his attention went to the boys who had taken it upon themselves to claim seats in the back rows. "I see some of you have apparently taken it upon yourselves to decide where you will sit." Those who had taken seats immediately got to their feet and moved to the back wall. Phair nodded, acknowledging they had done the correct thing.

He glanced down at the clipboard. "Costello?" He barked the name and Michael stepped forward. Phair indicated an open seat near the front of the class. "Another of the Costellos?"

"Yes sir," Michael replied.

"I might have known. Well, you sit there where we can communicate."

"Yes sir."

"Let's hope you are an improvement," Phair muttered.

"Wakabayashi?" The teacher looked to the back of the room.

From among the boys bunched along the wall an arm shot up. Phair's reading spectacles slid down over the bridge of his long nose. "Spell it for me, boy."

"W-a-k-a-b-a-y-a-s-h-i." Toshio Wakabayashi answered, rubbing a fist over his shaven dome as if to erase the confusion of this sudden attention. The teacher checked his clipboard and indicated the vacant desk directly in front of Michael. "Okay, Wakabayashi. You sit in front where I can count on you to be a positive influence on Costello."

Toshio plopped onto the seat attached to Michael's desk. The moment Phair's glance went back to the clipboard Michael's fist shot out with a hammer blow on Wakabayashi's shoulder. The Japanese flinched but uttered no sound. The teacher, either failing to see the punch or choosing to ignore it, went on with the seat assignments.

Phil Phair continued through the first hour until he began recognizing his intimidation was losing its grip over the restless boys. "Okay, gentlemen," he announced, clapping his large hands. "What we need is a little fresh air. Let's see if we can work off some of this excess energy. Maybe we can uncover one or two soccer players in this crowd. Consider this the junior class's first tryout. Outside, on the double," the teacher waved his arms, herding the boys out of the building.

In Michael Costello's mind his territorial confrontation with Toshio Wakabayashi had ended with the punch. The incident was forgotten when he lined up on the soccer pitch at the inside right forward position. Toshio stood quietly on the opposing side at midfield. Had Michael been aware of Toshio on the opposing side, he wouldn't have given a thought to the possibility of what was about to happen.

Phair's whistle blew a shrill blast across the pitch and the ball was taken at center by Stanley Glasheen playing inside right. Stanley took the ball on the run, sprinting downfield, the schoolyard pitch exploding in dust beneath his boots. The opposing center half-started toward Stanley, who sent the ball back with a deft touch off the side of his foot. Michael took the pass sprinting toward the goal with his head down. He never saw the body flying in from his left. Toshio hit him with the force of an artillery shell; the impact sent Michael through the air, a field of shattered stars bursting in his head, to land face down on the packed dirt.

"The Jap blindsided you."

Michael blinked the dust from his eyes and looked up into the moon face of Stanley Glasheen hovering over him. "The Jap blindsided you," Glasheen repeated. Michael's most vivid memory of that moment was of Stanley's wet lips and the fear that he was about to be dribbled on. "I'll fix the little yellow bugger," Glasheen added. Stanley was big for a kid in his early teens and eager to establish the authority his size entitled him in this new world of teenagers.

"No you won't." Michael spit out, struggling to his feet. He caught sight of Wakabayashi indifferently tapping the soccer ball from one foot to the other beyond the circle. Michael swiped his sleeve across the trickle of blood running over his lip and catapulted out of the crowd. His body made contact with Wakabayashi while flying horizontally, the two of them hitting the ground in a lump of squirming legs and arms in a cloud of dust. By the time Phil Phair reached the scene, Michael had Wakabayashi's cropped head cinched in the crux of his arm and was pounding his free fist wherever he could find a piece of the Japanese. What happened next established the teacher's authority with his new class beyond any reasonable doubt. It was also a moment Michael would remember as his one experience in defying gravity.

Phair's arm reached into the mix of the two boys and with a single powerful jerk lifted them from their feet as if they had been autumn leaves caught in a swirl of wind. For an instant Michael continued blindly flailing his arms. It took a moment before either of the fighters recognized they were suspended in air, dangling from Phair's huge fists. The teacher threw back his head, his laughter shaking the two boys like rag dolls.

"So, what have we got here? A couple of tough guys? Just what we needed. Two minutes into our practice and you two have to start World War II." His laughter vanished as suddenly as it had begun. "I've seen better fights in my goldfish bowl."

"He tackled me when I wasn't looking," Michael gasped.

"When you were not looking?" Phair settled the boys on the ground, still gripping their shirts. He turned to Toshio with feigned shock. "Why would you do a thing like that, Wakabayashi? I assume you have been briefed on the Costello rules? It seems nobody is to tackle Costello unless he happens to be looking. Is that it Costello? Those your rules of engagement?" Michael said nothing. "Is there anything else we should be informed of before we play on? Eh?" The teacher's sarcasm was raising Toshio's confidence to the point he began returning Michael's glare. Phair released their shirts. "Nobody takes a swan dive like you did, Costello, unless he is running out of control. You were running like a stork on one wing before this man got near you. Think on that a while, eh?"

"This was supposed to be a practice," Stanley shouted, shouldering his way through the circle toward the teacher. "Nobody said we were playing tackles."

"Dry up and stay out of this, Glasheen," the teacher snapped. "Two tough guys are all I care to handle in one day before I get annoyed. And you don't want to get me annoyed, sonny boy." Stanley slumped back into the crowd.

"The rest of you, back out on the field. West's ball. Free kick at the point of penalty." The teacher shoved the two fighters toward the school building. "You two get to my equipment room and stay there. We will see how far you want to go with this rough stuff when I come in."

The two of them began slouching toward the school building when Michael saw blood trickling from Toshio's nose. "You got blood pouring out your nose, Waka-baby," he whispered triumphantly. Wakabayashi brushed the back of his hand across his upper lip, glanced down at the blood on his hand and sniffed.

"So have you," he said.

"Horseshit." Michael's tongue shot out, tentatively searching his upper lip beneath his swollen nose. The blood tasted salty. "So what?" He put out his tongue again amid a sudden wave of lightheadedness.

Wakabayashi reached for his arm. "What's the matter? You are as white as a sheet."

"Yea? Compared to you, maybe." Michael answered unsteadily.

"That's supposed to be funny?"

Michael stiffened, suddenly aware that Toshio's grip on his arm was all that was keeping him from going down. Anyone witnessing the two of them going up the school steps arm in arm would have taken them for the best of friends.

The wait in the equipment room — Phil Phair had commandeered the dingy dormer space beneath the school eaves as his equipment room — dragged on into the late afternoon. The air was heavy with the smell of damp leather and old sweat, and formed an invisible wall between the two boys. Michael had his finger pressed to his upper lip to stem the nosebleed; Toshio sulked silently in the opposite chair late into the afternoon. It was growing dark in the dormer when Toshio passed him a paper towel.

"It's stopped bleeding," Toshio said.

Michael dabbed the towel to his nose.

"Why did you slug me in class?" Toshio asked.

"You jiggled my ink well," Michael muttered through the paper towel. "Besides, I don't want a Jap who is supposed to be keeping an eye on me." The words coming out of his mouth sounded like Stanley Glasheen, the thought making Michael wince inwardly. "Anyway, a little punch didn't give you the right to blind-side me. So don't get the idea I'm finished with you."

"You scare me," Toshio said with mock terror. "And you can quit hanging onto your nose like you were wounded. I told you, it's not bleeding. Swelling a little, but it's not going anyplace."

"No thanks to you. It feels like it's broken."

Toshio shrugged hopelessly, followed by more silence.

The sun had slipped from the window and the equipment room was filled with deep shadows bordering on total darkness when

Philip Phair appeared in the doorway. He came into the room bouncing a soccer ball and appeared to have forgotten the fighters. Dribbling the ball off his foot he caught it in the air and softly tossed it into a corner barrel. He then stopped in mock astonishment. "Good God. It's you two." He peered into the shadows as if uncertain of what he was seeing. The boys stirred sullenly. "Well? You two had enough time to think through that nonsense you were playing at this afternoon?" No answer. "Then suppose you tell me how you propose to settle this?" Still no answer. "Does that mean each of you still have a few more punches you need to get out of your system? Wakabayashi?"

"No sir."

"Costello?"

"I'm okay."

The teacher retrieved the soccer ball from the corner barrel and began bouncing it off the wall, looking over his shoulder at the boys. "You do know what made you such a target out there today, Costello? I suppose you thought I never saw that punch you threw at this man."

"He jiggled my ink well," Michael said, trapped by the complaint he had leveled at Toshio.

Phil Phair caught the ball off the wall on his forehead and deftly headed it in Michael's direction. "Jiggled your ink well!"

Michael reached out for the ball and missed. "Yea. The Japs are all spies, anyway." Michael was pressing, aware he was sounding more foolish with each utterance.

"And how do you come to that bit of intelligence, Costello?"

Michael got up to retrieve the ball, afraid whatever was about to come out of his mouth would sound foolish. "Stanley Glasheen's old man told Stanley the RCMP is taking the names of all the Japs because they can't be trusted. " Michael was uncomfortable casting his lot with the Glasheens, but it was the best he had at the moment. "I'm not going to let—"

"That's enough, Costello." Phair snatched the ball from his hands and slammed it against the wall. "We don't have to listen to that crap even if you are determined to demonstrate your ignorance."

The teacher turned to Toshio, his temper near explosion. "And what about you, Wakabayashi? You forget you were playing high school soccer when you decided to murder this jerk? You hit Costello like a samurai out to take his head off. That may not be all bad when we play Burnaby. But this was a practice. We were out there to get a breath of fresh air."

Toshio shrugged.

"Okay." The teacher's voice softened. "We have the whole damn world getting ready to go to war and you two want to start one of your own in my class. I didn't like what I saw today and I don't want to see it again. Am I understood?" Both boys nodded submissively. "What does that mean?" the teacher demanded.

"Yes sir," Toshio said.

"Yes sir," Michael added somewhat reluctantly.

The teacher turned to Wakabayashi. "What's this police business Costello is talking about? The alien registration order?"

Toshio nodded. "The Mounties came to our house getting our names." He shrugged, attempting indifference.

"Doesn't sound like anything to get riled up about," Phair suggested. "Nobody said anything about spying, did they?" The teacher looked from Michael to Toshio for an answer. "Except for Costello here repeating garbage he doesn't know anything about."

Toshio, sensing the change in the room, took a worn leather wallet from his pocket and fished out a pink card. "This is what the Mounties gave me. They said I must carry it at all times or I could be arrested. My parents got yellow cards. That's because they were born in Japan. The Japanese call those Yellow Peril cards."

Phair shook his head wearily, stuffed the soccer ball into the equipment basket, and wrapped an arm around Toshio's shoulder.

"Toshio. I had a call from Father Lavoie at Star of Sea the last week. He wanted to talk to me about the kids coming to school here. Said you were a bright kid but a little feisty. You know what that means? Are your family Catholics, Toshio?"

"My dad is half Buddhist and half Catholic, I guess. He works for Father Lavoie. They talk to each other in Japanese. My mother is Shinto."

Phair nodded. "You do know you were being feisty out there, too damn feisty for your own good? A man has to stay calm in times like these. You need to learn that. You can't afford to go around getting sore. Your father's a gardener, isn't he?"

Toshio nodded.

"A Japanese gardener is no threat to the world. And as for you, Costello, you didn't make life any easier for this man today." Michael grunted in reluctant acknowledgement. "Did you ever stop to think he's got enough trouble without you piling on?" Michael nodded more positively. "In that case, after the way you stirred up Glasheen and his friends, you might volunteer to walk home with Toshio today. Right, Costello? You hear what I said?"

"We don't go the same way."

"Today you go the same way or you both sit here while I work over a couple of hours of English lessons."

The two of them went out of the school building together, pausing at the big door to reconnoiter the playgrounds. They were deserted except for a lone kid bouncing a tennis ball off the gym wall. "It's nearly five o'clock," Toshio said. "Everybody has taken off. I don't need you to show me the way home."

"Yea. But Phair is probably watching from the window," Michael replied. "We can go as far as the corner where we will be out of sight."

They reached the corner and Michael turned to step toward home when Stanley Glasheen stepped out from behind the Coca-Cola billboard. Stanley took up a position in the middle of the sidewalk, thirty feet in front of them, as Stanley's older brother Claude appeared, his plump and pimpled face red with excitement, followed by two other kids Michael recognized from the soccer pitch. Stanley, standing hip shot, blocked the sidewalk with the others gathering behind him like support troops. Stanley held an apple in one hand and bit into it with exaggerated nonchalance waiting for Michael and Toshio.

He paused to swallow a lump of apple. "Where in the hell do you think you are going with the Japoo, Costelloo?" He demanded, emphasizing the 'Japoo' and 'Costelloo'. His brother Claude laughed and the two support troops joined in nervously.

Michael took a sideways step, positioning himself alongside Toshio. "Him? He's no Jap," Michael replied.

"He's a Chink?" Glasheen's buddies laughed again.

"Trouble with you, Glasheen, is you are such a bonehead you can't tell a Chink from a Jap," Michael added, making no attempt to hide the fact that he didn't like Stanley.

"Yeah? Well, we're going to teach this Japoo a lesson," Claude, the elder Glasheen, chimed in, blinking through his fogged glasses. "What are you sucking up to him for anyway, Costello? You scared of him?"

Michael ignored him. It was Stanley who had his attention. Stanley was the fighter, not Claude. Stanley closed in, rising up on his toes, his flared trousers anchoring him to the sidewalk like a lamp post. Nature and the Glasheen gene pool had created a fighter's body for Stanley but left him with the fragile courage of a bully. With his free hand, he brushed back the long hank of black hair hanging loose over his forehead. "Yea, you scared of the Japoo, Costelloo?"

"Scared of him? I'm his bodyguard," Michael said quietly. Though he had never been comfortable with the Glasheens he had always tried to avoid fighting Stanley. While Michael was tall, Stanley was big and there was the threat of his dishing out a lot of hurt. Michael was also remembering his nosebleed from the soccer field. A glance at Glasheen's large, bony fists caused the tip of his nose to twitch in anticipation.

"Some bodyguard." Glasheen swiped his hand through his hair once more. His brother stepped off the sidewalk, circling behind. "Better scram out of here, Costelloo." Stanley ordered. "Because we're going to take care of the Japoo."

"Fuck you, Glasheen." Michael's fist came up from somewhere down around his hip and landed on Stanley's open mouth. He could feel the wet lips crush between teeth and knuckles, the impact of the blow shooting pain down his arm into his shoulder. It felt good, like taking a cut with a baseball bat and catching the ball on the sweet spot. Home run. Glasheen's head snapped back, chunks of apple flying from his mouth. At the same moment, Toshio wheeled to face the older Glasheen who was already backing away.

"You bastard." Stanley put his hand to his mouth and looked down at the blood running through his fingers. "What kind of a fucking white man are you, anyway? We were just doing you a God damn favor."

"Don't do me any favors, Stanley, or I'll let you have it again," Michael hissed, up on the balls of his feet, his fists clenched. He wanted to shake the pain out of his hand but was unwilling to reveal how much it hurt. Stanley stepped back. Michael, recognizing his sucker punch had made an impression, pushed Toshio ahead. "Come on. Let's get out of here."

"Prick. Stanley mumbled through his bleeding lips. Michael, flush with the success of his one punch, was tempted to wheel and hit him again, but the thought of getting hit on the nose and Stanley's large fists kept him walking. He was silently congratulating himself for a wise decision when Glasheen's apple core whistled past his ear. He stopped and turned and they stared at one another, neither of them moving.

"Lucky for you that one missed, asshole," Michael sneered, turning Toshio toward Burrard Street.

"Phair was right. They were waiting for me." Toshio grinned once out of range.

"You could have handled them. Stanley is mostly wind, or he woulda flattened me." Michael shook the numbness from his hand. "He's got a head like a rock."

Toshio laughed. "You should know."

"Do you think he's going to tell Phair I hit him? I promised Father Lavoie I wouldn't get mixed up in anymore fights."

"Are you kidding? The Glasheens are already telling themselves that never happened."

Michael laughed and they crossed Burrard Street, making their way beyond the Seaforth Highlanders Armory toward the wooden shacks on Third Avenue. Halfway down the block Toshio stopped at a tall wooden gate. "You coming in?"

Michael hesitated. He had walked Toshio all the way home and was wondering whether the Glasheens would be waiting for him. He looked over the fence beyond the gate. A single-story house with a small covered porch stood beyond a strange yard. Curious, he shrugged casually. It wouldn't hurt to keep the Glasheens waiting. "I guess I could come in for a minute."

He followed Toshio over a path of flat stones through a carefully raked patch of gravel that had been shaped in sweeping patterns around two dwarf pines. The path led to the three front steps where a worn wooden railing led up to the porch. Michael sensed a quiet tranquility in this strange oasis hidden behind the unpainted wooden fence. Toshio pushed off his shoes, placing them on a large stone protruding through the porch deck, and slid open the door. "Coming in?"

"I better not. I got holes in my socks."

Toshio grinned, wiggling his big toe through a hole in his own. Michael kicked off his shoes and followed him through a narrow hallway into a kitchen area. A treadle sewing machine stood against one wall, and beneath the lone kitchen window was a sink suspended from the wall by a single pipe and a metal strap. A small raft of garden vegetables floated in the water beneath the brass tap. At the opposite end of the dimly lit hallway he caught a glimpse of a brightly colored altar bearing a garish portrait of a stoic Japanese on a white horse. The girl from Fraser's Wharf was seated at the table in the kitchen.

"This is my sister, Soju," Toshio said. The girl smiled and said something in Japanese to her brother then in English to Michael. "Hi."

"She says I have found a nice friend," Toshio explained. "She didn't see you sock Glasheen or she wouldn't think you were so nice."

"Now you are also a friend of my brother," Soju added, speaking English.

Toshio shot a questioning glance at Michael.

"We met," Michael explained. "Fishing on Fraser's Wharf." There was an awkward moment when no one seemed to know what to say next. Then all three began talking at once without any of them noticing Soju's mother who appeared in the kitchen doorway. She spoke in Japanese to her daughter.

"You remember my mother," Soju said. "She says she remembers you from the day we met fishing. My mother asks me to tell you that you are welcome in our house." Toshio spoke to his mother in Japanese. She responded with a smile and offered Michael a slight bow.

"Mom is nervous speaking English," Toshio explained. "But she remembers you didn't catch much that day."

Soju exchanged words in Japanese with her mother and they both looked expectantly to Michael. "Our mother asks if you would like to stay and eat with us."

Michael, recalling stories of Japanese eating raw fish, answered quickly. "No. But thanks anyway." He started easing toward the door. "I have to be getting home. Tell your mother I'd like to stay but my mother expects me home for dinner. I'm late already." Yuki Wakabayashi smiled in a way that told him she had understood his every word.

Soju followed Michael onto the porch where he picked up his shoes, attempting to crunch his protruding big toe back into the hole in his sock. The toe refused to retreat. "I just put on whatever happened to be handy." He grinned foolishly, his face colored with confusion.

"You and Toshio were playing soccer today," Soju said. "They told me at school that my brother played too rough."

"You mean his tackling me?"

Soju nodded solemnly and took his shoes from his hand. Their hands touched and Michael's trembled, though he was unsure whether it was his hand or hers that was shaking. "My brother gets angry too quickly," Soju said quietly. "I can tell he is sorry now." She went to one knee, slipping one shoe and then the other over each foot. Seeing him blush, she explained: "This is the Japanese way. You have been a guest in our house."

"Okay," Michael answered, relieved to have his naked toe out of the way. "I hope they told you that your brother and I worked things out." He finished lacing his shoes and started back along the stone path toward the gate. When he turned to look back, Soju smiled from the porch. He didn't want to leave.

BOOK II: Wakabayashi

Chapter 13 The Missionary

Father Maurice Lavoie believed that to those without faith, destiny was a matter of chance tempered with luck. To the nonbeliever, a couple coming together at unpredictable moments in life are no more divinely inspired than two automobiles arriving in an intersection simultaneously. To nonbelievers, accidents are explained by mathematics or traffic engineering statistics. Either the cars crash or, by extraordinary skill, one driver swerves and they pass with nothing more than a frightened look at what might have been.

But in the eyes of the Jesuit priest, destiny was the work of the divine hand of God. To Father Lavoie, who spent an hour or more each night on his knees, God's destiny is what leads to near misses in traffic as well as to good marriages in the church. Yet this concept of destiny would one day be challenged when it came to his dealing with the meeting of Michael Costello and Soju Wakabayashi; it was Father Lavoie who had set the seeds of their destiny long before either of them were born.

***

It began in late June, 1920, the priest's first year serving Star of the Sea Parish. The eight teaching nuns, preparing the 7 a.m. Mass, propped open the church doors to the late spring breeze. They were praying quietly in their woolen habits, grateful for the cool air; their calm, stoic faces concealed their growing irritation at the rapid pace of Father Lavoie's recital of the liturgy. The nuns were in no hurry. Their Morning Mass was the one moment in their day when they could sit quietly and renewed their marriage to God. Sister Mary Hildegard would later complain that the priest read the abbreviated gospel like a man urgently needing to pee.

Except for the nuns and an incessantly yawning altar boy, the church was empty when the priest stopped his hurried recital in mid sentence. His mind had drifted from the liturgy to mentally rehearsing simple greetings in Japanese. Following a long pause, he glanced down to the altar boy in despair. The boy, suddenly fully awake, and recognizing what had happened, whispered the words: "Wash me thoroughly from my iniquity…"

Without raising his eyes to the nuns, the priest picked up his place. "*Amplius lava me ab iniquitate mea et peccato meo munda me.*"

From that point on Father Lavoie continued deliberately, solemnly delivering the Eucharist to the extended tongues of the kneeling nuns. Chastened by his lapse of concentration, he painstakingly cleansed the chalice and raised his arms. "*Ite missa est.*"

"*Deo gratias.*" The words of the nuns followed their retreating young priest as he hurried into the vestry.

***

Father Lavoie had been assigned to Star of the Sea Parish in the fall of 1919 by Bishop Bernard Kemper; the young priest had been offered by the Jesuit Provincial. Bishop Kemper was unsure of what he should do with this Quebec-bred Jesuit who had spent four years out of seminary on a missionary assignment in Japan. The bishop assigned him to Star of the Sea, reasoning there wasn't much even a visiting Jesuit could do to cause problems in an embryonic parish.

During their one interview, the bishop and the young priest might as well have been talking in foreign tongues. Father Lavoie, who spoke fluent Japanese, had acquired a Japanese cadence to his Quebec-French English that was unintelligible to the bishop. Bishop Kemper's heavily Germanic English was equally unintelligible to the priest. At the conclusion of the confusing interview the bishop decided Father Lavoie's missionary zeal was enough to qualify him as a man who might be right for a parish attempting to establish a grade school.

Father Lavoie appeared older than his thirty-six years. His ritual morning straight-razor shave failed to scrape away the dark shadows of a heavy beard; so that he was constantly suspected of having forgotten to shave. He had protruding dark eyes which in moments of frustration he would roll heavenward, leaving two near-blank eyeballs embedded in each cheek. He was five feet six inches tall in his stocking feet and prone to sweat, a fact that contributed to the unpleasant damp handshake he pressed on the bishop on accepting his assignment.

***

The Mass ended, Father Maurice Lavoie retreated to the quiet of the sacristy, shrugged off his vestments, and pushed the altar boy out the side door with a nickel for his service. The priest then stepped up to the dressing table where the sisters had laid out his breakfast porridge — now cold — and toast softened in melted butter. Ignoring the toast, he swallowed several large gulps of the paste-like porridge then, with a passing glance into the full-length mirror, he picked up his breviary and a paper bag containing six early Transparent apples. Drawing himself up before the mirror, he brushed his hands over the folds of his worn cassock as if he were preparing to step out onto a stage. He silently apologized to God for short-changing the sisters and stepped out into the heat of the morning; he had eight minutes to connect with the 8:05 interurban into the Fraser Valley.

On arriving at the track-side station, the priest reached for the boarding stanchion and pulled himself aboard, his breviary in one hand, the bag of apples in the crook of his arm. As he stepped aboard, the bag of apples slipped loose from the crook of his arm; two of his apples bounced beneath the wheels of the interurban. Father Lavoie sighed with anguish, raised his cassock to his knees, and, with a mumbled thanks to God for having saved the four apples in the bag, flopped onto a sun-warmed wicker seat.

The interurban tracks ran south through Shaughnessy Heights, skirting the Shaughnessy Golf and Country Club's rolling fairways, passing within sound and sight of the city mansions built with turn-of-the-century coal and timber fortunes. Beyond the city, the line passed through the crossroads village of Marpole at the mouth of the Fraser River, and stretched through Steveston to New Westminster and the Fraser River Valley.

Father Lavoie began silently rehearsing his Japanese phrases when he felt an urge to turn in his seat and look back into the near empty car. Besides the motorman and an emaciated conductor, there was but a single passenger on the morning tram. Father

Lavoie determined the man's light-blue turban marked him as an East Indian. He was seated in the farthest corner of the car with his eyes closed, his bulky turban rolling to the pitch of the interurban. He wore wash- faded denim coveralls and heavy, toe-scuffed boots. A worker, the priest judged, one of the very souls God was sending him to save. Sensing the priest's intense stare, the East Indian opened his eyes, offered a respectful nod, and spoke what sounded at the other end of the car like 'good morning' in British-accented English. Before Father Lavoie could reply, the man had again closed his eyes in search of sleep.

Obviously a Sikh, Father Lavoie concluded. Difficult conversion, although early Jesuits had made inroads in India. Questions began flooding his thoughts. Was he being summoned to begin his mission on the tram? The possibility kept him perched on the edge of his seat like a hungry bird waiting for a worm, until the man's snoring turned him back to his breviary. After a brief attempt to focus, he leaned back, his face now shaded from the sun, and surrendered to memories of Japan.

A hand on his shoulder brought the priest upright in his seat, squinting into the sunlight. The East Indian stood over him, his gray-flecked beard parted in a dazzling white smile. "We are coming in to Chilliwack," the man said in brisk accented English. "I was worried you would not know we are approaching the end of the line."

Father Lavoie sat up looking out on the passing farmland.

"Chilliwack? Already?" he muttered, groggy from sleep. "Thank you. This is where I get off."

The East Indian continued to smile and was about to turn away.

"I regret I have slept through my chance to speak with you," the priest said.

The heavy beard parted once more. "It is good to rest on a warm day."

Father Lavoie reached into his cassock for his collar, snapped it in place and, gathering his bag of apples and breviary, followed the East Indian onto the station platform. He was disappointed when the man turned with a parting wave and hurried off toward the center of town. Reluctantly accepting his missed opportunity, the priest started along the interurban tracks in the opposite direction, having caught a glimpse of a Japanese crew in a berry field a short distance back. Finding the railroad ties didn't match his short stride, he turned across the open fields, unsure of his direction. After stumbling through pastureland for what seemed a long time, he stopped on a modest rise to mop his brow. There, right before his eyes, were the four Japanese field hands he was seeking. He blinked, wiped the sweat from his eyes, crossed himself, and started toward the crew, confident he was being led by the hand of Saint Ignatius. The heat, the field dirt in his low-cut shoes, and the dust clinging to the skirt of his soutane, were all suddenly forgotten as his thoughts focused on a familiar Japanese greeting. He placed a hand on the top wire of the three loosely strung strands of barbed wire fencing and called out.

"Konichi-wa."

Not a single head rose up. Uncertain of his pronunciation, he called again, louder; his tongue fumbling over his neglected Japanese. "Konichi-wa." This time the man closest to the fence straightened up, lifting his hat to swipe his sleeve over his brow.

"Konichi-wa," the priest called out again. "I am a friend from Hiroshima," he said in hesitant Japanese. The berry picker appeared puzzled. "I come to bring you good news of Jesus Christ …whose spirit dwells among … the Japanese people." Father Lavoie realized he was listening to the sound of his own words, each phrase stumbling off his tongue. He was about to try speaking English when a look of mild surprise appeared on the man's face. Isao Wakabayashi had never seen a Roman Catholic priest. The sight of this one in full-length cassock standing by the berry field fence, speaking Japanese, left him speechless. His curiosity aroused, the Japanese berry picker appeared to be waiting to hear more. He placed his hat back onto his head and answered in Japanese.

"So. What is the news from Nihon?"

Aware he lacked the mellifluous pronunciation of his years in Japan, Father Lavoie smiled uncertainly. "The news I bring you is that the spirit of Jesus Christ is alive and saving souls in all Japan. I am from Hiroshima, where I served Him among the Japanese people." To the priest's ear his Japanese sounded convoluted, yet he pressed on. "Will you rest a moment so that I might tell you of

Jesus in Nihon?" The priest moved higher atop the sun-dried grassy knoll for a preaching vantage, his confidence in his Japanese growing with each sentence.

Wakabayashi braced his hands on his hips, easing the stiffness in his back, and started toward the fence. Father Lavoie braced a shoe on the lower strand of barbed wire, inviting the man to climb through the separated strands. Wakabayashi held his place inside the fence. "You speak Japanese?"

"I have forgotten much," Father Lavoie replied. "It is a beautiful language. Forgive my humble efforts." He produced a yellow apple from his bag and offered it over the fence. "Dozo. This is from the trees of my parish, a springtime apple." Isao accepted the apple, dusted it on his sleeve, and slipped it into his pocket. He then stepped back into the field and, brushing his hands beneath the leaves of the strawberry plants, came up with four large strawberries.

"Dozo," he replied, offering the berries. "Not so big as Nihon berries, but much taste, neh?" Father Lavoie smiled appreciatively.

Wakabayashi finally accepted the priest's invitation and stepped through the wire fence. Squatting in the grass, he took the apple from his pocket, wiped it over his sleeve once more, and began to eat. "I am Isao Wakabayashi. You did not come to pick berries, neh?" The man's face broke into a smile.

"And I am Father Maurice Lavoie, a Roman Catholic priest who has come here to bring you the story of St. Paul Miki, a Japanese saint. Have you heard of him?" The priest was feeling his way. Jesuits had been spreading the word of Christ throughout the Far East for more than 200 years. Wakabayashi's vacant response convinced him he was dealing with a soul in need of salvation. His voice took on a tone of missionary zeal. "St. Paul Miki and the martyrs of Nagasaki were nailed to a cross rather than renounce their Christian faith. They did that so that men like you, Wakabayashi-san, may be freed of sin."

The priest looked down at the strawberries in his hands. With a gesture, something of a toast, he raised the largest to his mouth and bit down, the juice running over his chin. He fumbled for a handkerchief. "Lovely. Lovely berries."

A sudden light breeze over the berry field brought with it a hint of cooler air. Father Lavoie felt certain he was feeling the breath of Ignatius. "All Japanese may rejoice that the Japanese martyrs died as witnesses to their faith in Jesus Christ." As he spoke, he noticed the others were listening.

"The Blessed Anthony Ixida was also a Japanese worker, much like each of you. Ixida-san preached the Word of God in Nagasaki. When he refused to deny Christ, he was burned to death in 1632. The message he preached to the Japanese hundreds of years ago is the same message that I bring to you today. "

One by one the others followed Wakabayashi through the barbed wire, squatting in a half circle in the grass. The priest hesitated, his words momentarily lost in the cry of a distant interurban whistle. He reached into the paper bag and distributed his three remaining apples. The oldest of the crew, a sun-weathered wisp of a man, fished into a pocket for a package of tobacco, which he then passed from man to man. The priest watched the pickers deftly roll their cigarettes, their thick, earth-hardened fingers shaping the paper and tobacco. When they began to smoke, he spread his arms in the form of a man on the cross.

"Your Japanese Saint, Paul Miki, served Christ as a Jesuit lay brother. He prayed at the moment of his death that his blood would fall on all Japanese as fruitful as rain." The tobacco smoke leaked slowly between Wakabayashi's lips, in and out with each breath, as he silently nodded encouragement. Father Lavoie searched the stoic faces for a sign that St. Paul Miki's prayer was reaching their ears. "I have come to you in answer to that prayer."

For a moment, the priest's eyes lingered possessively over the dusty Japanese. He began distributing prayer cards written in Kanji with a color portrait of Mary in a blue robe, then stopped. The circle of Japanese suddenly rose to their feet. Father Lavoie's initial reaction was that they were standing out of reverence for the mother of Jesus before realizing that their attention was centered on something beyond his shoulder. The priest turned to face a middle-aged Japanese standing directly in the line of the afternoon sun. The man wore a high-button, ankle length duster and a brown bowler hat frayed at the brim, the hat giving him the appearance of being even taller than he was. The stranger's eyes were shielded behind green-tinted glasses resting precariously on the bridge of his nose. The priest smiled, assuming he was faced with a fifth convert.

Kenji Azumo had been watching from a distance, uncertain of the priest's authority. "What is this, Wakabayashi-san?" he demanded in Japanese. "Why are you not picking?"

Wakabayashi looked to Father Lavoie.

"These men have allowed me to speak to them of the sacrifice made by the Japanese Christian martyrs." The priest's reply in Japanese startled Azumo. He cautiously accepted a prayer card.

"Dozo," said the priest. "These cards bear the words of a prayer to our Blessed Mary, mother of Jesus." The priest's near-fluent Japanese had the labor contractor scanning the card for evidence of his sectarian authority. Finding no government endorsement, Azumo-san tucked the card into the sleeve of his coat, bowed in token acknowledgement, and uttered a barrage of staccato Japanese, ordering the men back into the field.

The sun was near setting when an exhausted Father Lavoie returned to the Chilliwack station. He was pleased to find the East Indian from the morning tram on a bench in the shade. The man smiled and moved to one side, inviting the priest to share the seat. "We meet once more." The East Indian's glance took in Father Lavoie's dusty soutane. "You have been into the fields?"

"Yes." Father Lavoie settled on the bench and removed his Roman collar. "God's work takes us wherever there is need of His presence." He smiled the smile of martyrs and began wiping the sweat from his neck. "And you?"

The man smiled. "I have been fortunate," he replied his in heavily accented English. "I came looking for a farm and I have found the place I was hoping to find. Now," he smiled, "if I should find someone interested in buying my house in the city?" The subject appeared to interest the priest.

The East Indian's city house turned out to be east of lower Burrard Street, a few short blocks from the Star of the Sea. It was one of a row of sagging wooden frame houses in an area originally housing mostly East Indian wood peddlers. By the time the two men stepped down at the Burrard Street interurban stop, Father Lavoie began fitting the house into his plans for Isao Wakabayashi.

Each week of the summer the priest escaped into the Fraser Valley, rekindling his missionary vocation. The repeated listening to the sins of pubescent boys and frustrated housewives left him feeling futile. He began to suspect that those kneeling in Friday confessional seeking forgiveness were more than willing to exchange five minutes of prayer as a modest price for the rewards of sin. Even his confessional homilies had begun to sound like tired plagiarisms.

"You must not turn your back on Christ by giving in to carnal sins, my son. Self-abuse will possess you. It is a disease. (He stopped short of suggesting it could make a boy blind, a warning he had received at the age of eight). *You must promise God you will surrender to that sin no more."* And in a lighter voice. *"Get out and play ball. Exercise keeps the mind and body from engaging in unnatural habits. And get rid of those magazines beneath your bed. They serve to invite the devil into your thoughts."* At this point the sinner could expect a pause during which the priest's message would hopefully penetrate the mind of the perspiring adolescent. *"Now make a good Act of Contrition and for your penance say two decades of the Rosary each day this week. God bless you, my son. And pray for me."*

Even the steamy bedroom confessions that once fascinated him had taken on a weary similarity. *"And how often do you deny your husband? You say you have spoken to him of your pain? He suggests you do what? No. No. Surely he must be aware there is no procreation in such an act. Conjugal love is the love God seeds in a man and his wife for the creation of a life, a vessel for the soul. What your husband is suggesting is not part of a wife's marriage obligation. Not at all."*

Father Lavoie could never engage in these confessions for any length of time without bringing the session to an abrupt closure. *"Is there anything else you wish to confess?"* Before the penitent could further unburden her soul he would hurriedly conclude with a mild penance. *"Then I absolve you of your sins. Remember me in your prayers. And may God's peace go with you."*

The priest's call to the open sky, to the warmth of the sun on his back, reflected his need to remain in touch with the spirit of Ignatius of Loyola. This true calling is what motivated him to pursue Wakabayashi. The first Monday in September, during the Valley bean harvest, Isao discovered Father Lavoie waiting at the weigh station. They greeted each other like old friends who had accidentally discovered one another, the two of them chatting in Japanese as they boarded the city-bound tram.

"Wakabayashi-san, I have discovered a small house not far from our school," the priest began casually. "This house would present you with the opportunity of starting a business of your own. I have talked to the owner and the house would require very little money."

"What business?" Isao restrained a laugh, choking on his cigarette.

"I have thought this through, Wakabayashi-san. We would start you off working on the school grounds. I am certain there is other garden work for you in the parish as well. You would be free to keep whatever you earn, instead of paying Azumo-san his ten percent."

Wakabayashi silently busied himself dusting the soil from his trousers, appearing more interested in the field dirt on his clothes than buying a house. It wasn't until their tram turned into the Carroll Street terminal and Father Lavoie had given up that Wakabayashi spoke. "Will you show me this house?"

Wakabayashi moved into the East Indian's Third Avenue home the last week in September, and by December Father Lavoie knew he had created a problem. While his Japanese convert did appear dutifully for Sunday's mid-morning Mass, Wakabayashi consistently showed up red-eyed from his weekend drinking. The priest tactfully avoided the subject until a pre-Christmas Sunday when Wakabayashi fell asleep during the Mass, his snoring resounding through the church like the blowing of a shofar. Father Lavoie decided it was time to challenge the Devil.

The priest appeared at Wakabayashi's house the following Monday morning. Isao, flustered by this unexpected visitation, offered him the only chair in the house. "I do not eat here," he apologized, indicating the empty kitchen. "I have only Japanese pickles and cookies, neh?"

"I have not come for breakfast, Wakabayashi-san, and I am not surprised this house has not become a home for you." The priest was speaking in no-nonsense terms. "I am fully aware you have been making your home elsewhere," Father Lavoie shot a judgmental frown at the squatting Japanese. "Yours is an imponderable soul, Wakabayashi-san. You lack morality. We both know that to be true." Wakabayashi nodded agreement, though he had little idea what the priest was saying.

"So long as you continue the life you are leading I hold little hope for your immortal soul, my friend. Frankly, you make it difficult for me to retain you in the service of the church." He was bluffing. Anticipating Isao was about to defend himself, the priest launched into his carefully rehearsed proposal.

"Wakabayashi-san, I have come as your friend. You do regard me as a friend? What is missing from your life, is a wife whose presence would make this a home for you and would keep you from the temptations of Azumo-san's Sun Rise Hotel. A man with your needs should be married. It is time you choose a wife. I can assure you Star of the Sea would welcome your wife as the parish has welcomed you. I am prepared to loan you limited financial support for a journey to Japan to choose a wife." The priest smiled, unaware he was misreading his man.

Wakabayashi continued submissively nodding agreement, his thoughts heading in another direction. *'This priest would deny a rooster the right to crow. What would I do with a woman around my neck? Eating my rice? What if she became sick? Does he think of that? Azumo has women enough without bringing me a mouth to feed.'*

There followed a long silence, Father Lavoie accepting this as his having convinced his gardener.

The following Saturday, while drinking at the Sun Rise with his fisherman friend Otake-san, Isao casually mentioned the priest's proposal and was startled at Otake's enthusiastic endorsement. "A woman of your own would be good, Wakabayashi-san," Otake exclaimed. "She would wash for you. And I could come to your home to eat, neh?"

Isao snorted derisively.

"You would have a woman in your bed every night," Otake-san added with a sly smile. "A woman who would cost you nothing, neh? When you are finished with Azumo's women, you are forgotten as soon as you pay. But a woman of your own, Wakabayashi-san, she would bear you a son to honor your spirit when you die. Listen to the priest." Otake-san clapped his hands enthusiastically. "I will be your baishakunin and arrange a bride for you."

"What does a fisherman know about brides?" Isao grumbled.

"Have I not spoken to you of the beautiful Yuki Nagumo, the daughter of my sister in Tokyo? You pretend you do not remember, neh?" Otake smiled. "I have shown you her pictures. My niece is a healthy woman, Wakabayashi-san. And the Nagumo family prospers in the spice business. You need such a woman, my friend."

Isao grunted, acknowledging he recalled the pictures. "And to how many fishermen on the river have you shown those pictures, eh? Your friends say the Nagumo woman has turned her back on every man you send to her. Now you would send me, because we are friends, neh?" He grinned sarcastically. "Besides, they say the Nagumo woman is too old and she is too cold to keep a man warm at night, eh?"

Otake stammered. "I offer you my service proposing a beautiful bride. Yet you choose to insult me."

Isao slid the half-empty whiskey bottle across the table. "Otake-san, we will not quarrel. You know my family has proposed a bride for me. She is the daughter of a Wakayama citrus farmer." He fumbled for his wallet and produced a creased black and white snapshot. "You can see, the woman is young and strong. She could do much work with me, eh? And she looks warm, eh? Not like the cold stories others tell me of your sister's daughter."

Otake sniffed, cautiously drawing the picture close to his eyes. "And how old do you think this picture is?" He tossed the photograph onto the table. "Ten, fifteen years?"

Wakabayashi smiled. "I have shown this picture to Father Lavoie," he confessed. "The priest tells me this woman would be a perfect match."

Otake rolled his bottom lip disdainfully. "She is too fat," he muttered. "You have never liked fat women."

Isao, regretting he had teased his friend, poured more whiskey into Otake's glass. "Otake-san. I will go to see your sister and her daughter. I think you have already written to them about me?"

"I have," Otake confessed. "I have also sent them the pictures of you that you gave me to send to them. I think you are more interested in my niece than you pretend, Wakabayashi-san. Remember, my baishakunin services are very reasonable."

Chapter 14 Difficult Attraction

Isao Wakabayashi's lingering doubts over having decided to return to Japan for a bride were eventually quieted by the constant badgering of Father Lavoie. Only during his 28-day crossing of the North Pacific Ocean did he wish he had never agreed to the plan. Seemingly endless days and nights of sea sickness had detached his stomach so that he felt certain it had lodged in his throat, where it sat like a used flour sack. By the morning when he first sighted Yokohama on the horizon, he had become a gaunt figure tormented by regret, convinced he had made a terrible mistake.

"You have come to marry a woman you had never seen," an inner voice lectured. *"A fat woman. Otake-san was right. You have no taste for fat women. And she will eat much. Fat women are always hungry. The fishermen on the river say some of these women looking for husbands are diseased. This woman they have arranged for you could bring sickness. Then you would die, Wakabayashi. Or she may nag you to death. Then you will be happy to die."*

For the better part of that morning he entertained the idea of disappearing into the mass of Tokyo humanity, picturing himself wandering the streets, a lost soul. Ultimately, his self pity gave way to consideration of his family honor and he dismissed the plan; his whiskey-inspired promise to Otake-san was long forgotten.

Isao knew the girl waiting for him in Wakayama Prefecture was the favorite child of protective parents. And he was not surprised to discover the parents, her two married sisters and their children, and a brother and his wife all gathered on the Wakayama platform to welcome the prospective husband. The entire family presented the plump, demure bride, as if she were a prized grazing heifer, the moment he stepped off the Wakayama train; the impression continued in Isao's mind. The father, built like his daughter with round, powerful shoulders and a well-developed gut, removed his hat, easing the girl forward with a series of formal, rapid bows. Isao responded less enthusiastically with furtive glances at the proposed bride.

However, when the party arrived at the family's thatched, two-story farmhouse in the center of a modest citrus orchard, Isao's interest in the girl's round, swaying hips began to stir. He was shown his bed in a renovated cow shed alongside the house, the shed boasting a window without glass and only a heavy shutter to shut out the rain. Pleased at being housed alone, Isao presented the father of the bride-to-be with a flat-fifty tin of Canadian Sweet Caporal cigarettes, deciding to leave his intended gift, an imperial quart of rye whiskey, in his bag. However, growing weary of the farmer's boasting of the virtues of his daughter, and incessantly firing questions to which he provided his own speculative answers, Isao went to his luggage for the Canadian whiskey. During the ensuing toasts no-one noticed the late afternoon grow sultry and oppressive, until a clap of thunder shook the house, followed within minutes by a deluge. The farmer, grinning licentiously, tendered his empty glass, proposing a toast to the beauty of his daughter. He then rose unsteadily to his feet, mouthing incomprehensible apologies, picked up the near-empty whiskey bottle and raised it to the light measuring what remained before tucking it beneath his arm and left.

When the rain stopped, leaving the early evening air with a sudden freshness, Isao went to his shed to finish unpacking. He was about to rest when the bride-in-waiting appeared in the doorway. The girl had changed into a summer kimono, the cotton fabric revealing the outline of her robust figure. She was also wearing newly-applied lipstick and a very strong perfume.

"You have painted your mouth with lipstick," Isao smiled, aware his whiskey had relaxed the farmer's vigilance. "But you have no need of such tricks."

The girl shrugged with a note of defiance. "If I am to live in the Land of the Golden Mountains, I must learn the secrets of the women there."

"I have some knowledge of these things," Isao replied. "I could teach you while the others are not here to interfere." He patted the bed invitingly.

"Why don't we walk among the trees where we can be undisturbed," the girl smiled, lowering her head to lead the way out through the tall grass bordering the citrus orchard.

The recent cloudburst lay heavy on the grass quickly soaking Isao's trousers and causing the girl's summer kimono to reveal her saber-like legs. Reaching a shallow gully out of view of the farmhouse, Isao dropped to his knees and pulled the giggling girl into the wet grass, with Isao urgently wrestling his way through some rough romancing. Untying the folds of the girl's kimono, he wiggled his trousers to his knees and attempted to enter her. At the same moment a great flash of lightning lit up the sky, followed by a clap of thunder shaking the earth beneath them. Isao gasped, uttering a painful groan. The girl felt his body go limp. Flushed and confused, she closed her eyes, clinging to him.

"It is too late," he managed to mutter, attempting to free himself, the sudden rain running into his eyes.

"No. Not too late. Not too late. Only nine o'clock," the girl gasped.

"We will try again, later," he grumbled, pulling his soaked trousers over his hips.

The following morning the farmer appeared red-eyed at Isao's door, informing him the prospective husband would be needed at the Wakayama Prefecture Office for the girl's emigration papers. "It is but a brief formality," the farmer explained. "Your bride has already completed her emigration examination." Isao shrugged, his enthusiasm tempered by the lingering resentment of the farmer's consuming the last of his Canadian whiskey.

A two-story, wooden prefecture building doubled as a postal station and headquarters for a detachment of the Wakayama police. An official, his tight fitting-tunic unbuttoned, and his hat tipped casually to the back of his head, made it obvious he was not expecting them. Quickly buttoning up his tunic, the man greeted the farmer and his daughter and Isao with a brief nod, indicating they were to wait in an outer office. The father of the bride bowed profusely and followed his obsequious gesture by offering the official a cigarette from Isao's tin of Canadian Players. The official turned away from the offer and left without speaking.

The morning passed into early afternoon with Isao pacing the tiny reception area, worried that someone had seen him with the girl in the grass. Yet the farmer continued to smile, constantly reassuring him that these official matters have a way of taking all day in Wakayama. At one point, Isao began reviewing his own past; was there a police matter at the Sun Rise Hotel? No. Azumo-san assured him a police friend had taken care of that. Besides, he had been drunk, and there was no way these officials would know that. Yet his concern continued to grow as one Prefecture official after another appeared from the inner office, each regarding the waiting party as if they had overstayed their welcome.

It was when the original prefecture official reappeared dressed as if he were about to lead a parade. Without so much as a perfunctory bow, he indicated a cubicle, positioning himself behind a small desk. After coughing into his fist several times as if the words were stuck in his throat, he declared, "A permit to emigrate is denied." He handed the father of the bride a document from his file. "The woman is infected."

"Infected?" Isao gasped, unsure whether he felt relief or fear, aware that under the Japanese emigration rules, "infected" could mean leprosy, tuberculosis, insanity – or venereal disease.

The farmer's face, flushed from his drinking Isao's whiskey, took on an alarming color. "She is strong. She is healthy," he protested in a hoarse whisper.

"She has the syphilis," the official replied tersely. "Her tests showed she is infected. She cannot be permitted to emigrate."

Isao needed only a glance at the girl's face to grasp what he was hearing and panicked. "You mean I may also be infected with the syphilis?" he blurted, terrified he may have been infected during his amorous fumbling. The prefecture official looked up from his documents.

"If you have copulated with the woman, you should be tested."

"Aah so," Isao mumbled apologetically and started for the door without another word.

Once in the sanctity of his room, he washed his genitals painstakingly and continued through the entire night to search for signs of infection. In the early morning a commotion from the farm house brought him to his door. A neighbor woman was leading the bride-to-be up to the house, the bride's clothes soaked and muddied, her hair falling over her face. The neighbor was excitedly relaying having discovered the girl attempting to drown herself in the shallow irrigation ditch near where she had rolled in the grass with Isao.

In the midst of this confusion Isao saw his opportunity to escape, appearing with his suitcase in hand, wearing his fedora, his suit coat, and the new shirt purchased for the wedding. The porch grew silent, the only sound that of a bird warbling somewhere in a nearby orange tree. Isao, assuming a pose of platonic resignation, waited for the bird to finish.

"I am leaving." He began as if he were reading a biblical text, his eyes apprehensively glancing over the girl's stocky brother and on to the father. The family remained silent. "Your daughter's disease is a sign that has been sent to me by the Catholic Jesus, telling me I am to be like the priest who sent me. There can be no woman for a man who serves Jesus. It is not meant for Wakabayashi to take a wife." He nodded solemnly, trying for an appearance of remorse.

The farmer, having aged and grown smaller overnight, listened stoically, accepting his loss of face. Isao bowed to the girl's weeping mother, and again to her muscular brother, then lifted his suitcase onto his shoulder and started down the road toward the railroad station. Though he listened intently, there was no sound from the gathering at the house.

Isao was on the train to Tokyo by noon, nursing a bottle of warm beer and a sushi lunch box on his lap, enjoying the sun pouring benevolently through the dusty train window. His thoughts turned to the daughter of Otake's sister, and his prospect of spending two nights in Tokyo before sailing. He worried about the costs of a hotel and meals with his remaining money, a problem he had not planned on. These concerns, germinating in the buzz of the warm beer, led him to deciding he would fulfill his promise to view Otake's spinster niece. The visit could provide a place to sleep and an opportunity to explain his new-found resolve to never again consider marriage. He owed Otake-san that much.

Settling on his new plan, Isao bought a second bottle of beer at the next station, and began searching his memory for Otake-san's directions to the Nagumo spice shop.

Chapter 15 Second Thoughts

Isao stepped off the Tokyo train from Wakayama into a city in the grip of a muggy bronze haze; the terminal porters were stripped to the waist, their naked backs glistening in sweat. Isao bought a quart of warm beer from a station vendor and sat for a long time drinking, quietly rehearsing his approach to Otake-san's relatives. He finished the beer and contemplated another before deciding to set out for the Nagumo spice shop with only a vague notion of where he would find them. He remained sober enough to realize that his first objective would be to find Yotsoya Station, the only address given to him by Otake-san.

Reassuring himself of his love for Jesus, he resolved to make it clearly understood that he intended to spend the rest of his life without a wife. Through much of the afternoon he wandered in and out of an endless labyrinth of alleyways before finally stopping at a corner streetcar shelter. Stepping into the shade behind the shelter, he removed his hat, wiped the sleeve of his coat over the sweat in his eyes, and unbuttoned his trousers to pee. He was standing in relief, realizing that he was completely lost and exhausted, when his idle glance swept the nearby alleyways settling on two words printed in Kanji on the station shelter: 'Yotsoya Station.'

Isao blinked and began taking in his surroundings. He was standing at an intersection of three alleyways, each cluttered with a confusion of open shops with merchandise spilling out into the alleyway. Directly in front of where he stood was a scattering of stone-carved lanterns before a stone cutter's open-air quarry. As his glance went further up the alley, he saw a stack of bicycle wheels piled against the opening to a bicycle repair shop. Looking even further up the lane, his eyes went to a worn canvas canopy overhanging a low porch with the words 'Nagumo Spices' written in faded Kanji across the face of the canopy.

Isao stepped out into the roadway, blinking the sweat from his eyes, and realized a woman stood in the shade of the weathered canopy. Reason told him this was the woman in Otake-san's photographs, though he was unable to see clearly through the sweat. This woman appeared taller than in the photographs, too tall to be a desirable Japanese bride. He moved closer, absently buttoning his trousers. The woman wore a blue kitchen kimono beneath a sleeveless shopkeeper's apron, her hair pulled back in traditional Japanese fashion, revealing what Isao took to be a quiet but interesting expression. Though she remained in the shade, he could sense a seductive quality about her that had not been revealed in the photographs. But yes. This was the woman in Otake's pictures, a proud and haughty woman he decided. He realized she had been watching his every move from the moment that he stepped behind the Yotsoya station to pee.

Isao sucked a large breath of polluted air through his teeth and bowed. "Konichiwa." His tongue felt glued to his palate, his greeting sounding more like a guttural cry for help. The woman offered no response. Assuming she had not heard, he set his suitcase on the roadway and bowed again, this time deeply from the waist. "Have I the good fortune to have come to the shop of the family of Hideko Nagumo?" Again, there was no response. Desperate for a sign of recognition, he raised his felt fedora from his head and sweeping it across his chest bowed once more in a move resembling a Paris boulevardier. As his body folded, the umbrella tucked beneath his arm caught the back of his coat, lifting it over his backside, the sweat-stained coat fluttering above his behind like the wings of an injured bird.

Yuki Nagumo bowed almost imperceptibly. "A blackbird. Otake-san has sent us an aging blackbird," she mused. She had recognized him from the moment he began relieving himself, though she could see very little about the apparition in the alley resembling the youthful snapshots sent to her mother. Otake-san's black and white pictures of Isao, yellowing with age, had portrayed a sturdy, self-assured figure in a tightly buttoned single-breasted suit. One of the photos showed him standing with his hand resting possessively on an open-bed Model T Ford truck. The chief resemblance to those pictures was the gray fedora, which Isao was now using to fan the humid air from his face. He coughed and tried once more with what sounded like a plea for help.

"I have come at the invitation of my friend, Otake-san." He was too exhausted to say more, and the woman was now looking down at him as if he were trespassing. His hopes of accommodation quickly fading, Isao picked up his suitcase and was about to start back down the hill when the beaded curtain screening the doorway to the back of the shop flew open. A tiny woman, her face a mass of sundried wrinkles, popped onto the porch like a doll appearing in a Punch and Judy scene.

"Konichiwa." The woman's shrill voice sounded as if it were coming from an injured child. She brushed past the younger woman. "Hi. You have found the shop of Nagumo. You are Wakabayashi-san, neh? From Vancouver, in Canada, neh?" Each word from the old woman came with breathless anticipation of an affirmative answer.

"Hi. I am Isao Wakabayashi."

The tiny woman's face lit up in a wreath of wrinkled delight, her eyes lost in the folds of dried skin.

"Yes. Yes. Wakabayashi-san. We have seen the pictures of you sent by Otake-san." The woman's face was the picture of someone discovering a long-sought treasure. "We have been expecting you."

"So." Isao bowed once more with a doubtful sigh; the daughter's cool reception had left him unsure of his welcome. The old woman pulled aside the beaded curtain to the back of the shop. "Dozo. It is cooler inside. You will come in and have some tea. We have beeru also," she added proudly.

Isao lifted his suitcase onto the porch and climbed the short step to where Yuki Nagumo looked him over with an air of detachment. He bowed briefly in her direction, then brushed through the rustling beads, following the old lady past large burlap sugar sacks into the shadows of a low-ceiling room. The air inside was cool and filled with the friendly scent of hemp and spiced cooking. Yuki followed, brushing past Isao, whose mind was already exploring the possibilities. '*The woman is at least twenty-eight, maybe thirty,*' he thought, his eyes following the tall, slim figure as she moved about the shop. '*She is too old to be much of a prize. The one who would marry her would need a firm hand. Only a fool would fail to see this woman has an obstinate look in her eyes.*' He sniffed audibly, beginning to fantasize Yuki Nagumo's long body stretched demurely on his bed, confident there had been very few offers of marriage.

"So." Isao seated himself atop a sack of raw sugar. "You are aware Otake-san has offered to be my baishakunin?" he asked, blatantly ignoring both accepted protocol and the daughter's indifference.

A startled look crossed the old lady's face and Isao hurriedly apologized. "It is only because my ship sails from Nihon in two days that I speak so frankly." He offered the old lady what he conceived to be his most ingratiating smile. "I have been to Wakayama to be with my family," he added, passing over his failed engagement. "So I have little time for Otake-san's formal services, Nagumo-san." His glance shifted sideways, settling on Yuki. "But your brother has given me pictures of your daughter. Unfortunately, I have left them in my home in Canada as I feared losing them on my long journey." He lied. The unflattering picture of the girl in a school uniform which Otake passed about was tucked in his waterproof wallet.

The old woman nodded her gnarled head, busying herself with the tea and beer without looking at Isao. "So. My brother has also written to us that you are a farmer, neh?" She set a bottle of beer and a glass on a small tray in front of Isao.

"No. Not a farmer," Isao replied reaching for the beer. Ignoring the glass, he put the bottle to his lips, tilted his head and with a series of loud gulps poured half the bottle of warm beer down his parched throat; he gasped and uttered a loud belch. "It is true, I was a farmer. Now I tend the gardens for the Star of the Sea Catholic Church and for people who pray there." He smiled expectantly, hoping for a second bottle of beer.

"The Church is where I have found Jesus Christ, and because I have found Jesus Christ, I have come to Japan to choose a woman as my wife," he announced, pleased with the extemporaneous words emanating from his lips. Isao had not been conscious of this story taking shape in his mind, but Yuki Nagumo was having a strange effect on his thinking. Though still uncertain of how he was to deal with the direction his words were leading him, he felt comfortable with this newly discovered credo and finished the beer. Turning the empty bottle over in his hands longingly, he was about to launch into the tale of how he had turned aside from his whoring ways when the old lady's intervention saved him.

"Wakabayashi-san, our Yuki-chan is a haiku gakko graduate. She was prepared for the university," the old lady said proudly.

"Our daughter is not suited for the work of a farmer's wife." She held up a hand before Isao could protest. "Otake-san may have told you my husband and I have only the one child, Yuki-chan."

Isao nodded, still hoping for a second beer.

"Because we have no son we have trained our daughter in the spice business. Yuki-chan is very good in business."

Isao glanced again at the daughter who was keeping her head lowered modestly but following every word. "Should our daughter's husband become our son, we would train him in our business." The old lady ceased messing with the utensils of the kitchen and faced Isao, determined to be fully understood. "It is a business which has many friends in Tokyo, Wakabayashi-san. My husband is in Hokkaido, his brother attends our business in Sapporo. Like you, my husband's brother has found your Jesus in a Methodist mission in Hokkaido. It is the same Jesus as your Catholic Jesus, neh?"

Isao nodded silently, wary of where this was leading.

"My husband would have no objection to a man who believes in Jesus Christ becoming our son, Wakabayashi-san. You can discuss these matters with my husband when he comes here, neh?" Isao thought the old lady would go no further when she quickly added, "Tonight, you are welcome to stay with us. We will get to know one another better." Catching Isao's concerned glance around the crowded shop, she added: "There is room for a futon for you on the porch beneath the awning, Wakabayashi-san. It will be cooler there now that the sun is gone." Isao rose and bowed profusely. The old lady turned to her daughter. "Bring a basin and towel for Wakabayashi-san," she said.

When he had finished washing, Isao squatted comfortably beside his suitcase, watching Yuki prepare his food. She served him cold fish and slices of fresh cucumbers on a bed of rice in a delicate blue china bowl, along with a modest jug of sake. When he had eaten, she spread the futon on the porch, conscious of Isao's eyes following her every move. Each time she knelt over the bedding she heard his murmuring sigh of approval, her kimono revealing her slender calves and flashes of the pale skin at the nape of her neck.

Yuki rolled back the awning, exposing Isao's futon to the night sky, then with an abbreviated bow left him alone in the evening shadows of the alley. Isao stripped naked and lay atop the futon, welcoming the night air on his body, his gaze fixed on the stars. He was soon dreaming beneath the starlight of a future with the tall, remote Yuki Nagumo.

It was close to midnight — Isao would be forever uncertain whether he was awake or dreaming – when he bolted upright. Someone or something was moving in the shadows of the porch. Isao, soaked in sweat, strained to see into the deep darkness, uncertain whether he had seen a moving silhouette or merely a shadow cast by the moon. His clock had been upside down from the day he sailed from Seattle, resulting in his falling asleep in the daylight hours and sleeping fitfully most nights. Convinced he had been dreaming, he lay back and closed his eyes when suddenly he thought he felt a soft touch on his shoulder. He was wrestling with dreamlike confusion when the shadow appeared to rise up alongside his futon and slip back into the darkness of the shop's interior.

From that moment through the rest of the night he lay fully awake, convincing himself that what he had seen and felt was neither a dream nor a hallucination. Perhaps a visit from a chance burglar? No, he argued. It could only have been Yuki Nagumo. The more the thought teased his mind, the more the possibility excited him. But why had she disappeared so quickly? There was the talk among the fishermen that this relative of Otake-san's was frigid, or worse, strange like some western she-men. Isao had dismissed the thought the instant he laid eyes on her, convinced those stories were fabricated by rejected suitors. Perhaps she is frightened of men? But no. That one does not frighten easily, he assured himself.

By the coming of the first light, Isao was convinced his nocturnal visitor had indeed been Yuki. His conclusion was that she had come to his futon for a bold inspection of his physical assets. He was a 42-year-old suitor. Why shouldn't a woman want to know if a man his age could service her in bed? So, he reasoned with a defiant grunt, the woman requires a good bed partner. Without waiting for the others to rise, he slipped on his trousers and made his way to the wall behind the shop. There he settled on the stoop by the gate, stripped to his undershorts, folded his legs in a Buddha-like pose and waited, his naked shoulders bathed in the morning light. Seated upright with his eyes half closed in a meditative pose, he felt invigorated and virile in the relative cool of the morning. He had not long to wait before Yuki appeared wearing a simple house kimono, her hair falling loosely over her shoulders. She carried a wash basin and a towel. Through lowered eyelids, Isao saw the startled look on her face and smiled inwardly at having shocked her. He remained posing for a moment before he rose to his feet, and turned his back to the shop, and raised both arms over his head. He inhaled deeply, expanding his chest, and launched into a series of vigorous arm waving, knee bending exercises, vigorously demonstrating the workings of all of the exposed parts of his body. "Now you see me, woman. You can see Isao Wakabayashi is fit to please any woman, neh?" He was muttering through his heavy breathing, moving ever more violently while stealing glances over his shoulder at the porch where Yuki had been joined by her mother. The two of them stood as if entranced at what they were witnessing.

At last, breathing heavily with sweat tickling down his belly, he turned to face the two women and was startled to discover he had been performing before a vacant porch. Yuki and her enamel basin were gone along with her mother. Isao, dizzy from exertion and about to collapse on the stoop, caught himself as suddenly the old lady reappeared out of the shop bearing a towel, a basin, a razor and scrubbing sponge.

"Yuki-chan has gone to the bathhouse," she called out in her penetrating, high-pitched voice. "Perhaps you would like to bathe, Wakabayashi-san?" The old lady held out the washing tools. "You will find the Yotsoya Station bath at the top of the hill." Isao slipped down from his perch, eagerly accepting the towel and basin with a hurried bow to the old woman.

Yotsoya Station bathhouse had been in business long before the Nagumo spice shop crowded into the lane of small shops. Over the years, a growing pile of used building material and a tottering stack of discarded wooden crates had all but buried the entrance. Isao explored several gates opening onto the lane without finding the bath, and was beginning to suspect he was being made a fool of. He was about to head back down the lane when a semi-naked old man carrying a basin and towel emerged from beyond the warren of crates. Quickly tracing the man's path through the maze, he discovered the low door to the bathhouse partially screened by a blue fabric curtain. Isao passed beneath the curtain and came face to face with the grizzled bath attendant squatting atop a large overturned wicker basket. A soiled bandana crowned the man's shaved head and a skimpy belly towel sagged from his bulky midsection, exposing what it was intended to conceal. The attendant eyed the stranger suspiciously and slid off his perch, landing heavily on bare feet; he responded to Isao's perfunctory bow with a guttural grunt.

"Aah. So you are the sailor," the attendant smiled sardonically. "The one from America who has come to marry the Nagumo woman, neh?"

Isao bristled. He could accept an ignorant field hand in Azumo's Sun Rise Hotel approaching him with such familiarity, but not this lout and not in Japan. He handed the man the bath money and began to undress.

Undeterred, the attendant hooked up his towel and pinched his chin in a manner indicating he was considering whether or not to share his knowledge of the marriage gossip. Disregarding Isao's lack of interest, he went on. "She is a cool one, that Nagumo woman, neh? She has the body of an eel, a long slippery eel," the attendant mused in a voice directed at no one. Continuing to ignore the attendant's eagerness to gossip, Isao continued to slip out of his trousers.

"Cold as a fish," the old man went on. "I can tell. I see them all."

Isao turned with a disapproving glare that failed to erase the smirk from the attendant's face. "First," Isao said irritably. "I am not from America. I am not a sailor. And I have not proposed to anyone. Is it not enough for you to be wrong three times in one morning? Perhaps the woman appears cool to an old man with a belly that hangs so low he no longer can see if there is anything below to interest a woman?" He turned his back on the attendant without waiting for a reply and began to scrub.

"Ha. So touchy," the attendant grumbled. His lower lip rolled out over his jaw in disapproval. "You should know that I have watched that woman since she was a child this big, neh?" He held a hand thigh high. "I see a woman's secrets when she comes to my bath. Take my advice. Leave that long-legged one to her mother." He shrugged his rounded shoulders, his eyes narrowing as if to emphasize the value of the opinion he was offering. "Many cold women come to Matsuzaki's bath, so? Yet no matter how long a cold woman stays in the bath, no matter how hot the water, her eyes remain cold. That Nagumo-san has the cold eye." The attendant attempted to suck in the soft muscles of his midsection. "Even this," he said tensing his biceps, "cannot change the cold eye. There is nothing except another woman that will warm those cold eyes, neh?"

Isao shook his head sadly, indicating the attendant's exposed crotch beneath the belly towel. The attendant snorted and turned away and Isao eased his hips into the steaming bath. Peering through the steam he could see a small cluster of women, every one of them with their eyes fixed on him. At first he felt it was because he was the only male in the bath, until it became obvious that they had been waiting for him to appear. Quickly he lowered himself to his neck and closed his eyes, the hot water easing the muscles which began aching from his physical demonstration for Yuki and her mother. The magic of the hot water quickly took possession of his mind, his confrontation with the attendant forgotten, as he lay back absorbing the warmth, planning the proposal he would press on the Nagumos. As to someday adopting the Nagumo name? He had already decided he would leave that issue vaguely framed in their discussion. Yuki was past the age of eligibility for a Japanese bride, and he knew he was the final suitor her family would see.

Isao was first out of the bath and found a seat on an overturned crate in the morning sun. When Yuki and her chattering friends appeared he was quick to notice that her hair had been twisted provocatively above her head. The moisture on her damp body set the sheer summer kimono clinging to every curve, revealing the dark shadows at the tips of her tiny breasts. She looked down on him with a faint smile, and he shifted on the crate inviting her to sit. Yuki caught up a corner of her kimono and, turning her face away from the sun, carefully seated herself at his side, avoiding the touch of their bodies.

Yuki Nagumo was 31 and keenly aware of the life awaiting her as a wife in Japan's Meiji culture; 45 years of Emperor Mutsuhito's reign had done little to lift the legacy of matrimonial bondage for middle-class Japanese women. She had spent her early years in studies for entrance to the university, hoping to avoid a marriage. When she completed six years of grammar school she prevailed on her parents to send her to high school in Yokohama City. On the eve of her final university entrance exams, she was struck with influenza and nearly died. The illness caused her to miss the tests that would have sent her on to the university. Both she and her family lost face. Over the next ten years, Yuki buried her dreams by tending the family business. It was her mother who mailed the letters and snapshots to Otake in the Land of the Golden Mountains.

For what seemed to Isao an interminably long silence, neither of them spoke, Yuki calmly oblivious to his heavy breathing. Then she felt him shift so that their hips were touching. "Aah, Nagumo-san," Isao muttered, excited at having caught her in an intimate moment. He rested a hand on her thigh. "We have found each other in the sun, you and I, neh? Yet we do not have much time, Nagumo-san. Your letters have at last brought you a husband, neh?"

Yuki opened her eyes, facing him with a questioning look. "My letters?" Her expression slowly changed to a dream-like smile. She began gently fanning herself with her damp towel.

"So, Nagumo-san. Your dreams have now come to life, neh? It is I who have been in your dreams, like you came into mine last night?" He grinned. "Surely I was not merely dreaming that it was you who came to my futon?"

Yuki raised her arms, adjusting her damp hair, the movement exposing the damp contour of her throat. Isao felt a tumescent surge and slid his hand up her thigh. He was about to make an even bolder move when Mrs. Nagumo suddenly materialized from beyond the stack of water-bottle crates. The old lady was not carrying a basin and it was obvious she was not on her way to bathe. The look she gave Isao instantly told him she was aware of his attempted advances.

"Nagumo-san," Isao exclaimed, swiftly removing his hand. "I have been sharing my dreams with Yuki-san. I have lived alone a long time but now I have discovered how much a woman brightens the morning for a lonely man." Mrs. Nagumo nodded noncommittally and, taking her daughter by the arm, lead them back down the road to the spice shop. Throughout that afternoon Isao sensed his boldness at the bath had offended the Nagumo honor. Yet when he attempted to justify himself by renewing the discussion of marriage, he was met with the mother's noncommittal grunts.

**

Early in the evening of the following day, Isao took up his suitcase and announced that he was about to leave. He carried the case out onto the porch and set it at his feet. He then went into the case for a small Canadian flag on a wooden stick and his last tin of Canadian Sweet Caporal Cigarettes he had been saving for the voyage home. With a solemn bow, he presented the cigarettes to the mother. "Please accept these as my gift to your husband when he returns from Hokkaido. They are a token of my respect and gratitude for your kindness." With each word of his speech, Isao never took his eyes from Yuki. Inhaling deeply through his teeth he handed her the flag.

"It is my hope this flag will lead you to Canada to be my wife." Yuki lowered her eyes, twisting the flag in her fingers. He turned to the mother. "You are aware that Otake-san — who knows me as one knows a brother — supports my proposal. It is because of Otake-san's urging that I have been so bold to propose a marriage."

The old lady studied him as if she were seeing him for the first time.

"You have honored our house, Wakabayashi-san. You can see for yourself, the Nagumo family has a good business. Our ancestors have given us an honorable name, which, we have maintained for many years." She hesitated and he could see she was weighing what she was about to say. "If we had a son, Wakabayashi-san, my husband would not need to worry about the future of our business and our ancestors would be honored and remembered. Should you consider becoming our adopted son, our 'yoshi,' you would be welcomed as the husband of our daughter."

Isao was prepared to hedge. "There is the matter of my older brother whose wife has not yet given him a son. When that time comes, I would be honored to accept the Nagumo name as my own." He began fumbling through his pockets for the crumpled bills of his remaining Japanese currency, intending to encourage the sealing of the arrangement. "Should your daughter come to me, I would be honored to help to pay her passage. Should she not come?" He cast a despondent glance at Yuki. "You could return the money to me in care of Otake-san." He was startled at the stone-like expression on the old lady's face as she heard his offer. "You would honor me," he stammered, suddenly recognizing the insult lay in the appearance of the crumpled bills in his hand.

Without so much as a glance acknowledging the money, the old woman thrust her hands into her kimono sleeves and bowed. Isao attempted to extend the bills toward her, then mumbled his thanks for the lodging and put the bills back into his pocket. With a quick glance at Yuki, he picked up his suitcase and started down the alley toward the streetcar stop, his face hot with anger and shame. He was now aware that in the old lady's eyes his miserably few yen had been seen as an attempt to buy the girl.

"I am not so sure with that one," the old lady said quietly, watching him go. "Wakabayashi-san has the appetite of a man needing a woman, but there is not much else there."

***

Boarding the Yotsoya Station tram, Isao was certain he had found the woman he wanted and was equally certain his blundering had lost her. The more he tried to deny his fantasies of possessing Yuki Nagumo, the more persistently she possessed him. His thoughts constantly slipped back to the mystical moment when he felt the touch of her hand, now certain it was she who had come to him in the night. "Yuki-san. My Yuki-san," he muttered in a mantra that came as close to a prayer as anything he had ever uttered.

Isao closeted himself in his tiny cabin to dig into his suitcase for the waterproof folder. He removed the letters from his family praising the virtues of the Wakayama farmer's daughter. These he crumpled into his pocket. Deeper in the folder he found the photograph of Yuki given to him when Otake-san first proposed his niece. He had hoped the old lady would offer him a more recent picture. She never did. All he possessed was this faded black and white snapshot of a tall, thin girl in a school uniform bearing a faint resemblance to the woman he courted.

Isao's freighter sailed with the Kuroshio, the notorious Black Tide sweeping across the North Pacific to the west coast of North America. The current was called Kuroshio by early Japanese fishermen who sailed to the edge of their known world and never returned. The name reflected the desolation of those left behind.

For days Isao stalked the ship deck, his thoughts filled with Yuki-san wrapped in her damp kimono. In fleeting moments he was able to recapture her rare smile and his hopes flickered until the memory gave way to the fear he would never see her again.

Chuichi Otake, eager to hear if his friend had chosen his niece, took the train from Vancouver to Seattle to meet his ship. Spotting Isao at the Immigration barrier he rushed forward. "Wakabayashi-san. Welcome. We have missed you. What news of my niece? Was she not as I told you? Tell me everything, Wakabayashi-san, everything that—" Isao brushed him aside before Otake could reach for his suitcase.

"What is it you want me to say? To tell you about that woman you claimed wanted to marry me, the woman you said dreamed of coming to the Land of Golden Mountains. She would warm my bed, you said. She would give me sons, you said," he snarled derisively.

"Yes. Yes..." Otake replied uncertainly. "All true, yes?"

"She has turned her back to me. I gave up the strong and beautiful young woman in Wakayama my family arranged for me so that I could propose to your sister's daughter. Just as I promised you, neh? For what? Her family has refused my proposal. I have lost face, Otake-san. I have spent the money loaned to me and I have received only the Nagumo insults. You have cheated me with this woman."

Otake gasped, unable to accept what he was hearing. "You are mistaken, Wakabayashi-san. The Nagumos cannot have refused you. You have been away from Nihon too long to understand Japanese ways. You are from Wakayama, Wakabayashi-san. People arrange marriages differently in Tokyo. A bride's family must appear selective. You came to them a stranger. How could they throw their daughter at you? You will see, my friend," Otake added reassuringly. "Trust me."

"Trust you?" Isao gave an angry laugh. "I am no longer your fool, Otake-san!" As Isao's temper rose his shouting began attracting the stares of a handful of dock workers. "Did I not spend two days with your Nagumos? You have made a fool of me, sending me to a woman more interested in women than she is in any man"

"You are speaking nonsense, Wakabayashi-san. Those are lies you have heard from the Steveston fishermen. That is the talk of fools."

"It is true. At the Yotsoya bathhouse, I was told the woman never looks at a man." Isao was arguing bitterly, attempting to rid himself of the fantasies he had built around Yuki's midnight visit.

"You sulk like a schoolboy, Wakabayashi-san. You have been too long without a woman. You forget the games they play on us, neh? So much the better to have a woman who does not have an eye on every pair of pants that passes by, neh? With a woman such as Nagumo-san, you will know she is not diseased. There will be good news from the Nagumos. You are a good catch, Wakabayashi-san. Give me your suitcase to carry and give the Nagumos time. Their daughter is too old for them to refuse a man such as you." Otake's voice suddenly took on a hint of suspicion. "You did nothing dishonorable with the girl? Your proposal was honorable?"

Isao released his bag and considered mentioning having offered money to the old lady for Yuki's passage. It was a mistake. Why bother explaining? Besides, the old lady — his hope refused to die — did accept his cigarettes. He turned his back on Otake and continued to argue. "You talk much about women, Otake-san, but you know nothing about them. I was wrong listening to you and the Catholic priest. The priest is another who knows nothing about women. Now I have wasted two months when I should have been working and I have spent all my money and have brought nothing but shame on myself."

Otake attempted a burst of laughter, hoping to make light of Isao's fury. "Then why be so upset over one woman, Wakabayashi-san? Azumo has many. We can forget this woman for a while, you and I, neh?"

Isao continued to curse, his temper compounded by the pounding in his head from having mourned over a bottle of Suntory throughout his last day at sea. "Go away, Otake-san. I am through with you and with Azumo's whores as well. You and your women have taken me to hell."

***

Five days following Isao's return from Japan, Otake, having vowed never to set eyes on his friend again, charged through the gate of Wakabayashi's little house off Burrard Street. The two men had barely spoken during their daylong train ride from Seattle. Otake left the train at the White Rock Station, nearer to Steveston, while Isao continued to sleep on the run into the city. They were both convinced that they would never meet again.

Otake, sliding over the stone path, his short steps cautiously navigating the wet stones, discovered the door to the house had been left ajar. Peering inside, he strained to see through the shadows and called out for Isao. There was no reply. He pushed the door open and began down the hall, stopping at the darkened bedroom doorway. A heavy stench of sour whiskey and stale smoke met him before he could reach for the overhead light, which revealed Isao sprawled across the bed, an empty whiskey bottle on the floor. Otake kicked the empty bottle from the bed and pulled his protesting friend into a sitting position with his legs dangling over the edge of the bed.

"Wakabayashi-san. Wake up. It is the middle of the day," Otake shouted, turning his face to avoid Isao's foul breath. He gripped his friend's slack shoulders and began shaking him, Isao's head rolling from side to side as if it were disengaged from his neck. "You are drunk, Wakabayashi-san."

"Go away. I do not want to listen to any more of your shit," Isao mumbled, releasing a second blast of foul breath in Otake's face. Otake turned away, deliberating whether to leave well enough alone before deciding to accept his friend's bad breath and the stinking air that filled the room.

"But you are drunk," Wakabayashi-san. "You must sit up to see what I have brought to you," Otake replied.

Isao opened one eye as if struggling to focus down the sight of a rifle. "What are you doing here?" he grumbled, slowly beginning to question the excitement in Otake's manner. In the whiskey-fogged recesses of his brain he was beginning to question why Otake was in the city away from the river and his boat. Was this not the beginning of the fall salmon run when fishermen earn their living on the river? The thought brought forth a curious grunt as he attempted to balance on the edge of the bed attempting to focus on the envelope Otake was waving beneath his nose.

"This letter is for you, Wakabayashi-san," Otake shouted, toying with a large blue ribbon tied around the envelope. He waved the ribbon beneath Wakabayashi's face, tickling his nose. "This is from the Nagumos. They have sent this to me as your marriage baishakunin so that I would bring it to you. Their letter has been waiting in the post office, but I have been busy on the river, neh? Does your priest know you have returned, Wakabayashi-san?"

"No. He is a fool like you." A flicker of interest brought the first glint of life to Isao's glassy stare, the situation working its way through his throbbing brain.

"It is from your Tokyo family, Wakabayashi-san," Otake shouted excitedly. "You will want to share this letter with your priest who loaned you the money to find a wife, neh?"

The substance of Otake's words were beginning to penetrate Isao's foggy stupor and he lunged for the envelope, falling off the bed. Otake caught him by the arm, holding the envelope tantalizingly beyond his reach. "Aah. You are too drunk to read, Wakabayashi-san. Remember, I am your baishakunin. I will read for you." Otake produced his heavy-rimmed glasses, propped them on the bridge of his nose and, tilting his head to keep the glasses from sliding off his face, cleared his throat ceremoniously. He untied the ribbon, which served no purpose since it had been added as a flourish by Otake himself after having read the letter. Unfolding the letter, he held it at the end of his outstretched arms.

"Please to inform Wakabayashi-san." Otake was reading with the cadence of a town crier. "That is you, Wakabayashi-san," he added before beginning once more in his town crier voice. "Hideko T. Nagumo, father of Yuki Nagumo, accepts the proposal of marriage which Wakabayashi-san has presented for our daughter. The Nagumo family welcomes him to the Nagumo family."

Otake lowered the letter quizzically, the wording of the letter confusing him at this second reading. Isao rolled off the bed, snatching the letter from his hand. "She is coming?" he muttered reverently.

Isao turned the letter over in his hands without attempting to read the words, suddenly aware of what it was he was holding. "The woman is coming to be my wife," he repeated in a voice suddenly unsure. "What is it that now they expect from me, Otake-san?" he asked, undecided whether he should be overjoyed or apprehensive.

"You have won her, Wakabayashi-san," Otake replied reassuringly. "You are the lucky lover, neh?" Otake attempted to reclaim the letter but Isao pulled it away, the two of them jockeying about the tiny bedroom. "Read the rest of the letter," Otake said. "The letter says that you have promised that with the birth of your brother's son you will take the Nagumo name. Nagumo is an honorable name, Wakabayashi-san. You do not need to be afraid of taking the name as your own."

Isao stumbled out of the room, avoiding the fisherman's outstretched arms, the two of them tumbling about like rambunctious schoolboys. "The letter says you have agreed, Wakabayashi-san. It is because you have agreed that you have won the woman, neh?"

Isao's face contracted in a frown of deep concern. "Did you know she is born in the Year of the Sheep?" he demanded ominously. "Women born in the Year of the Sheep are unlucky for me."

"So? That means nothing. Do not think of such foolishness. You must celebrate, Isao Nagumo, neh?" Otake, sensing that surrendering the Wakabayashi name was troubling his friend, was enjoying teasing him with the Nagumo name. If Isao heard him, his thoughts were elsewhere.

"I was born in the Year of the Tiger," Isao muttered. "That is not foolish talk. It is unlucky for the Year of the Tiger to be married to the Year of the Sheep. I have done a thing that is bad luck for me."

"Where is my drink?" Otake demanded. "Or have you poured all the whiskey into your own belly?"

"You are clever, Otake-san," Isao groaned. "You have arranged everything. Now you have arranged to pass your sister's spinster daughter to me so she will be off your hands." Isao continued slowly turning the letter over in his hands. "She is coming to be married to me," he muttered, repeating himself.

Otake picked up the empty whiskey bottle from the floor, holding it up to the light in mock astonishment. "Help yourself," Isao mumbled absently. The bottle was empty. "There is another beneath the bed," he muttered.

Otake rummaged beneath the bed and came up with a partially filled bottle of rye whiskey. He poured a generous measure into two china cups and offered one to Isao.

"I have been drinking too much," Isao said, refusing the cup. "My heart was broken by this woman who now wants to come to marry me. You want me to drink because you have brought me this letter? It is a letter which tells me I am no longer free, neh?" He looked suspiciously at his friend.

"What do you mean by this foolish talk, Wakabayashi-san? You have won. This is the woman who has stolen your heart. Now you pretend you are no longer in love?" Otake said in disbelief.

"You drink, Otake-san," Isao replied with great solemnity. "We are friends again because I am drunk. When I am sober I will see what it is that you have done, neh?"

Otake's laughter exploded. "You joke, Wakabayashi-san. Kumpai." He put the cup of whiskey to his mouth. "You will soon have your woman to clean the smell out of this house. She will cook for us when I come to eat with you. And when you have holes in your pants, she will mend for you, neh?" Otake patted the bed. "And maybe give you some pleasure, Wakabayashi-san. And someday a son."

Isao answered with a doubting frown, masking what little enthusiasm he was feeling. "Maybe this woman will learn what it is to please a man," he answered. "But she has much to learn, Otake-san."

Chapter 16 A Vanishing Dream

The immigration officer, his uniform tunic buttoned tight over a bulging belly, hunched his squat body over a chest-high desk in the Yokohama dock-side immigration shed, pointedly ignoring the approaching couple. Hideko T. Nagumo, tall like his only daughter, and walking with his head tilted slightly to one side as if contemplating an imponderable question, failed to recognize that the official was suffering a severe hangover. Yuki's father, a studious man neither suited for the chores of running a spice business nor inclined to be impressed facing an officer of the Imperial Japanese government, had little interest in the official's bloodshot eyes.

The official had spotted Nagumo and his daughter the moment they stepped through the entrance of the pier gate. Hoping he was not about to be disturbed, he kept his head lowered. Nagumo coughed politely and the official looked up openly measuring the slight, well-dressed man and the equally tall, distant-looking woman at his side. Recognizing a sense of authority in Nagumo's quiet dignity, the immigration official reached for his stiff billed cap.

"Ohio gozaimas." Nagumo bowed. "My name is Nagumo and this is my daughter."

The official slipped off his stool to bow curtly. Yuki remained quiet, having judged the man's resentment of Japanese women who might take it upon themselves to speak without being spoken to. The official had spent the morning processing a succession of mail-order brides sailing on the Fuyu Maru and was in a mood to vent his hangover. Nagumo bowed a second time and handed the man the certified copy of the Nagumo family register. "It is my daughter who is sailing to Vancouver to meet her husband in Canada." The official's red eyes measured Yuki from head to toe with a look that brought a blush to her cheeks.

"Are there no husbands for a woman in Japan?" he asked without expecting a response. He clipped several pages of Nagumo's documents to his ledger and stepped out of his dockside cubicle. "What's this?" he demanded suspiciously over the large wicker basket at Yuki's father's feet.

"My daughter has passage on the Fuyu Maru. The ship will take these goods to her husband," Nagumo answered.

The official shook his head with exaggerated condolence. "So. She has found a man." His finger traced down the page. "This man is Isao Wakabayashi, so?" He slammed a heavy stamp on the cover page of the family document and thrust it at Hideko Nagumo, who handed it to his daughter.

The official stepped back into his shack and threw open a small window overlooking the dock, eager to be rid of their intrusion. "The Fuyu Maru," he barked, pointing a stubby finger toward the far end of the dock. "The ship at the end of Pier Four." He closed the window and went back to holding his head.

Yuki Nagumo looked down the pier, her eyes settling on the black-hulled freighter rocking on the tidal current. Stevedores unloading scrap metal had shifted the ship's ballast, allowing the Fuyu Maru's bow to rise out of the water like a breeching whale. The ship's barnacle-encrusted underbelly awakened Yuki's childhood memories of a beached whale she had watched die on the shore at Shira Hamma. The dying whale lay on its side, its visible eye clouding over as it looked out at the curious onlookers gathered on the sand watching it die. An on-shore breeze slipped boldly beneath Yuki's cotton kimono and her legs began to tremble, though she was uncertain if it was fear or remembering the dying whale that caused her shaking.

Hideko Nagumo bowed once more toward the official's cubicle as Yuki folded her documents, and slipped them into the sleeve of her coat. Her father summoned a dockside porter to hoist his daughter's wicker trunk to his shoulder as together they followed him aboard. Seeing the trunk safely aboard, he turned to his only child in a moment of emotional indecision, neither of them speaking. After a brief, uncertain pause, the father bowed rapidly, turned away and hurried down the gangplank. He paused on the dock to look back at the ship and removed his glasses, making no attempt to hide his tears. Yuki continued waving her small Canadian flag on a wooden stick as he slowly stepped away to be swallowed up into the Yokohama traffic. She had become Isao Wakabayashi's wife that morning in a ceremony with Isao's cousin as the surrogate groom and was suddenly aware that she was no longer of the Nagumo family.

Six mail-order brides sailed with the Fuyu Maru; the other five stood huddled near the bow watching Yuki come aboard. She bowed to each, accepting her share of their uncertainty at leaving the only world they knew. She would learn that each of their stories differed, though each carried a vision of a new life in the Land of the Golden Mountains. One possessed a family portrait of her mother and father and three siblings; the photograph was taken with the departing bride dressed in a rented classic kimono. A stocky, farm-bred girl wearing a country servant kimono with a print scarf about her head wore a locket around her neck containing a picture of her deceased mother. A third clung to a wooden geisha doll. Yuki would later learn the girl had treasured the doll since the day it was given to her as a child, a last link to the family that had sold her into service.

There was one item that linked all five mail-order brides; an item that Yuki was sailing without. It was a flattering snapshot of an unmet husband secreted between the pages of handwritten letters, most of which were composed by professional letter writers. The letters were filled with ephemeral promises of the romantic life awaiting beyond the ocean.

The Fuyu Maru carried a wheelhouse amidship above the passenger cabin. Doorways to the cabin opened onto the deck on either side of the ship. Eight bunk-sized beds were set in two rows of four, each bolted to the deck. The two clouded portholes on each side of the cabin were sealed shut beneath layers of yellowing white paint. An open passageway through the luggage led to a rust-stained sink with a discolored mirror mounted on the bulkhead. Alongside the sink, screened by a torn shoji screen, was a seat-less toilet equipped with a wooden handle flush pump.

The Maru sailed with light ballast, her round belly rolling in the North Pacific swells so badly that all six brides were sick the first day out. Yuki was the first to the open deck, heaving so violently her body felt tied in knots. Losing all fear of the ocean, she could feel her body shrinking beneath the soaked shroud of her cotton summer coat. Yet she stayed at the railing breathing the suffocating umbilical-like stream of coal smoke clinging to the deck.

Near the end of a twenty-eight day passage, the Fuyu Maru, driven at eight knots by her single propeller, was on a heading into the Haro Strait. Yuki remained on deck throughout the day in hopes the wind would scour the stench from her clothes. Rounding Point Grey into Vancouver's inner harbor beneath a canopy of low-flying winter clouds, the greenish-grey walls of the coastal mountains rose up from the shore. These were not the golden mountains of a Japanese emigrant's dream, though the sight took the breath from her empty body. It began to rain.

Yuki survived her ocean crossing by clinging to a fantasy of arriving to a cacophony of celebrating taxicab horns and welcoming bands. It was a vision shaped during the hours she and her mother spent pouring through travel magazines. Her mind pictures featured musicians in scarlet uniforms playing bright brassy horns while arriving passengers at the ship's railing threw ribbons from ship to shore. She sang the words of the Canadian National Anthem, in faltering English during her days at sea. "*Oh Canada, my home and native land.*" These same words were written on the opening page of her diary the day Isao presented her his Canadian flag.

The Fuyu Maru slipped into the inner harbor with the beat of her engine's resolute thumping reduced to the pace of a failing heart. Sailing past the Canadian Pacific Steamship passenger terminal, Yuki saw the ship of her fantasies, the white-hulled Canadian Pacific's Empress of Japan: the ocean liner's name was proclaimed in golden letters beneath the red and gold dragon's head bowsprit. It was the closest she would come to her dreams.

The Fuyu shyly worked her way through the fading light of the late afternoon, waddling through the inner harbor like a fat lady in search of a dance partner. To Yuki's fear-filled image of the unknown, ghost-like figures appeared among the waterfront buildings, lurking ominously for harbor-bound prey. An ancient tugboat, her rubber-tiered snout thrusting up against the ship, nuzzled her toward a pier at the water's edge. It was in that instant while peering through the twilight mist that Yuki Nagumo first set eyes on Constable Eamon Costello. He stood at the edge of the pier, his low-set visor cap shielding much of his face, taller than even the tallest Japanese, a majestic figure in the priestly robes of authority. The twin rows of silver buttons down the front of his uniform greatcoat shone like jewels beneath the dock lights.

An elderly Japanese wearing the black fedora and topcoat of the consular staff appeared under the lights. He hailed the Fuyu Maru's bridge, his words drowned out by the chattering deck winches. Satisfied with the response, he gave a welcoming signal and the gangplank trundled out from the ship deck. Through it all, Yuki remained at the rail too frightened to move, her eyes searching the dimly lit pier for Isao. She was seized by a growing premonition that her Yotsoya magpie had been but a summer dream born of her hopes for a new life. She began to believe she would awaken at any moment and find herself back in Yotsoya Station in the warmth and security of the Nagumo shop. The premonition vanished the minute she stepped onto the gangplank and felt the night wind cut through her damp clothes. The strange man who had looked upon her with such hungry eyes, the man who had courted her in the heat of Yotsoya Station, was near. She could feel his presence.

Isao Wakabayashi was hiding less than thirty yards from the ship's side, furtively poking his head around a partially opened shed door. He snapped at Otake-san's urging him forward. "You think she is so desirable? Then you should marry her, Otake-san!"he snarled.

"I cannot marry my sister's child," Otake answered irritably.

"The pictures you gave me were ten years old, maybe more than ten." Isao charged, stepping back behind the door.

Otake merely shook his head tolerantly, refusing to engage in such talk.

"You grin foolishly," Isao hissed. "It is not you this woman comes to marry, Otake-san. Not you who will care for her if she is sick, neh? What if she has brought the syphilis with her? You think you have done me a service arranging this marriage?"

Otake nodded understandingly and tried again to ease Isao out on to the wharf in view of the freighter.

"Do not push me. It is better I remain where there is no wind. Besides, maybe the woman has not come? Maybe she has changed her mind. Then it would be only you who would be disappointed, Otake-san." Isao grew sullenly quiet, his curiosity drawing him from behind the shed door to scan the disembarking brides struggling down the ship's gangplank, each gripping the railing as if they were walking a dangerous and uncertain path. Suddenly he ducked back behind the door, his face like that of man who has just survived a terrifying accident.

Four weeks at sea had drained the blood from Yuki's flesh and reduced her summer coat to a black shroud. Her crumpled straw hat left her appearing like a drunk in the first stages of recovery from a long binge. Isao was certain he had seen an apparition, a ghost-like resemblance to the woman he remembered. He recognized Yuki as she came down the gangway only because she was taller than the others. "The sailors have made her drunk," Isao whispered, turning a gray face to Otake. "Look yourself," he pleaded, appealing for denial of what his eyes had seen.

At first glance, even Otake was uncertain. Yuki's clothes hung from her body as if she had been fished from the sea.

"What has happened?" Isao demanded, his mind racing in all directions. "Is it the syphilis, Otake-san?" he asked, his memory racing back to his terrifying experience in Wakayama. Unconsciously, he stepped out from behind the door, his total attention captured by the sight of Yuki making her way down the gangplank.

"She has no disease. All Japanese brides have been examined," Otake assured him. "She is sick from the sea. The others are the same. I have seen this before. It is the ocean. It is a long time they are on ship and Japanese fujin become sea-sick. Nagumo-san needs a bath, ofuro. Then she will look better to you. You will see, Wakabayashi-san. You will enjoy your fujin when she is clean, neh?"

Yuki stopped at the foot of the gangplank, her copy of Isao's family register in one hand, his gift of the Canadian flag on a wooden stick in the other. She began nervously twisting the flag stick, failing to notice it was grinding the rain-softened pages of her documents to a pulp. When she glanced down at the disintegrating papers she panicked, terrified she would be ordered back aboard the Fuyu Maru. A crewman, wearing a soiled white jacket, trotted down the gangplank with her wicker chest. The man swept his knitted cap from his head with a slight bow and lay the basket at her feet. Yuki returned the bow, the crewman hesitated expectantly before hurrying back up the gangplank.

Hemmed in by strangers shouting in a language she was unable to understand, Yuki began stepping back toward the wharf's edge. For a moment, she glanced down into the open space between the pilings and gently rocking hull of the Fuyu Maru. The dark surface moved in undulating swells, an oil slick reflecting a rainbow of warm colors on the shifting surface. The chattering deck winches and shouts of stevedores began to fade from her consciousness, giving way to thoughts of Yotsoya Station where she would be free of her damp clothes and this windswept wharf. Familiar faces rose before her mind with the scent of burlap and spices and the acrid smoke from the hibachis in the lane. She was reaching out to that thought when she felt a firm hand taking hold of her arm.

"You are a step too close to the edge there, darlin'."

The voice was gentle, the English words spoken with a trace of the Irish; unintelligible to Yuki. Yet she sensed the authority of the words, her picture of home vanishing beneath the firm hand moving her from the edge. Eamon Costello had all but lifted her from her feet. She looked up into the green eyes of the giant in the greatcoat with the silver buttons as the tired lines in his face creased into a warm smile.

"Things are never so bad as they seem," Eamon said softly. "It's a long drop you would be taking if you were to slip over the edge." Yuki felt a flush of shame, aware that this God-like man had caught a glimpse of her thoughts. He put his hand to her waist and steered her toward the center of the wharf. "You would be giving us a terrible name with your people back home, eh?" Yuki stumbled while attempting a modest bow as an Immigration official stepped between them brusquely taking the crumpled papers from her hands.

Isao quickly stepped back behind the shelter of the shed to make sense of what appeared to be Yuki's confrontation with the police. "Do you think the police are refusing to accept her papers?" he whispered in Otake's ear. The immigration official handed Yuki her papers, nodded to the policeman and stepped away.

Otake came out from behind the shed door waving his hat. "Nagumo-san," he hollered. "We are here. Welcome, Nagumo-san." Isao followed at a cautious distance, offering his bride a perfunctory bow.

"So. You have come," Isao muttered, his face revealing his reluctance to accept what the ocean had delivered. Ignoring her submissive bow, his eyes shifted to the wicker trunk at Yuki's feet. Turning to Otake as if she were not there, he announced. "We will walk to the streetcar."

With that, he made a half turn toward the roadway. Yuki leaned over to lift her trunk. What happened then took place in one swift movement, momentarily stunning them all into silent disbelief. Eamon Costello's large hand appeared from out of the night and in one sweeping motion had lifted Yuki's hand free of the trunk handles.

"Hold on there a minute, Mister," Costello said softly, picking up the trunk as if it were an empty box. Isao, who had already started for the roadway, turned to face the policeman's smile which he momentarily misread. He looked again at the tall policeman holding his wife's trunk. His second glance left no misunderstanding. Isao nodded awkwardly, bowed a token acknowledgement and accepted the trunk. Yuki slipped her hands into her coat sleeves without raising her eyes. She had arrived in the Land of the Golden Mountains, accepting for the moment that for a Japanese woman the world had changed.

***

Yuki sat alone in the near empty streetcar, one seat behind Isao and Otake, who rode side by side without a word passing between them. At the corner of Fourth Avenue and Burrard she followed a step behind the two until they reached the Third Avenue row of fragile, shiplap shacks. By the light from the corner streetlamp she could see that each house facing the road boasted an identical tottering chimney protruding through a canted tar-papered roof. Japanese families had replaced all but one of the East Indian wood peddlers in the shanties east of Burrard.

Isao lead the way to a high-board fence and reached over the wooden gate for the latch, the gate opening to a stone path barely visible in the dark. Leading the way with the confidence of familiarity, Isao stepped up to a covered porch and threw open the door. Yuki, following the two men, hesitated at the door, her eyes searching the dimly lit interior as Isao moved into the house turning on the lights. The naked hall light revealed a single corridor leading to a kitchen containing a black iron stove attached to the crooked metal chimney she had seen protruding through the roof. Alongside the stove a galvanized hot water boiler stood balanced on three iron legs, a block of firewood replacing the fourth missing leg. Between the stove and the boiler, the rust-stained, single-faucet porcelain sink hung precariously from the wall. As her eyes adjusted to the light, she saw beyond a side door an iron bedstead and an unpainted dresser. An open door revealed a bedroom cupboard containing a black rubber slicker and a pair of collapsed gum boots. Isao laid Yuki's trunk in the middle of the kitchen and began nervously rubbing his hands, muttering about the chill and the damp before suddenly remembering Yuki in the doorway.

"Aah. You are cold, Nagumo-san," he said with a trace of a smile. "Come in. Come in. We need a fire, yes?" He spoke in English and, though she was having difficulty following his words, Yuki stepped into the kitchen encouraged by the promise of warmth. She remained silently watching as he put a match to the wood laid out in the stove, sending the pitch roaring in the metal chimney. Isao turned his back to the heat, his face wreathed in a conquering smile.

"Now, Nagumo-san, you will grow warmer, neh?" he said, reverting to Japanese. "You are shaking? It is the ocean in your clothes that makes you cold. Soon we will have hot water for a bath, neh? Ofuro will make you warm again." He laughed nervously, seeing Yuki shrink deeper into the folds of her damp coat. Chuichi Otake, slouched quietly by the kitchen door, chose that moment to cough.

"Otake-san?" Isao turned sharply. "You are still here, neh?" His voice revealed his surprise at discovering his friend still with them.

"Ofuro, neh?" Otake said with a bemused smile. "I told you, Wakabayashi-san, that your fujin will look better after ofuro. But

Wakabayashi-san, just now I heard you speak to your wife and you called her Nagumo-san. No? But she is no longer Nagumo. You forget. I have arranged your marriage and I do not forget. She is your wife, Wakabayashi-san." Otake was enjoying the sudden discomfort on Isao's face. "When you change your name to Nagumo, Wakabayashi-san, then you and your sons will be Nagumos. But now you are both Wakabayashi. So we should celebrate neh? Let's drink to Wakabayashi-san and his wife, neh?"

"So. You come to my house to remind me I must give up my family name, Otake-san? Did you think I had forgotten?" Isao went to a cupboard above the sink and brought out an unopened bottle of rye whiskey. He twisted off the cap with a sideways glance at Yuki as he poured the whiskey into a cup. "You are waiting to drink, Otake-san, yes? There, my fisherman friend. Compi. Drink up. Now it is time for you to go back to your boat."

Otake raised the cup, grinning slyly. "Ofuro," he whispered. "To your hot bath, Wakabayashi-san. Why do you not join me to drink to your new wife? The whiskey will make you ready for ofuro. Then you will thank me, neh?" Both men recognized this entire speech was intended as a reminder of Otake's fee for having arranged the marriage.

Isao forced a thin laugh as he eased Otake down the hall toward the door where he pressed the bottle into Otake's hand. "Take my whiskey with you, Otake-san. Save some for me when I come to the river and we will talk. Now you are letting the cold into my house and my wife is shivering." He laughed once more, the laugh ending in a grunt as he spun Otake out the door with an agility that surprised the fisherman who stumbled to catch himself from falling off the porch. The kitchen grew suddenly silent but for the sound of Otake stumbling down the steps.

Yuki remained at the sink. unable to control her shaking, aware of Isao's eyes fixed on her as if searching for what it was that had aroused his passion at the Yotsoya Station bathhouse. Gradually the picture of her in the thin summer kimono began to emerge from the bedraggled wet figure cowering in the rumpled coat. "Yes. You are cold, Nagumo-san," he said in a thick voice having just discovered her.

"My body will never again be warm," Yuki whispered. "The cold of the ocean has entered my bones forever."

But we will grow warm together. Ofuro will warm your bones." He slipped her coat from her shoulders. "This smells of the ocean." He dropped the coat into the kitchen sink and, taking Yuki by the shoulders, began moving her toward the bedroom, guiding her backward step with his hand on her hip. Yuki closed her eyes, allowing him to push her until the back of her knees came up against the bed. Her quiet sigh of despair only succeeded in exciting him so that his breath came hot and fast on her neck, his callused fingers searching beneath her stockings. When she opened her eyes she was looking up at the ceiling and Isao was on his knees straddling her, pulling at her dress, exposing her hips. She heard the whisper of his leather belt as he whipped it from his trousers.

"I will warm you. This will make you warm again, Nagumo-san." Yuki felt his whiskers against her face as he came down on top of her, the rough texture of his trousers raking her naked legs. Then his flesh touched hers. "It is not good for a woman to be so cold," he gasped.

Chapter 17 Silent Tears

There were no visible tears. Yuki wept dry eyed and silently, the pain sealed within her sense of hopelessness. She had become emotionally dead, her life buried in a world without sunshine, constantly bombarded by a language she had rehearsed and studied but which was spoken by those around her in a manner she could not understand. Isao, sullen and unsatisfied, refused to speak to her in Japanese. "You talk English," he would shout, flushed in anger at her stumbling attempts to comprehend. "You are not in Nihon."

They had been together two weeks, Isao mounting her mechanically each night, and avoiding her during the day, like a territorial cat unwilling to cross the invisible lines separating them. Yuki never ventured from the Third Avenue shack.

The third week following her arrival a parishioner informed Father Maurice Lavoie that the parish gardener had resumed his weekend visits to the Powell Street hotels. The news shocked the priest who immediately decided what was needed to make Isao realize he was a married man was a formal wedding, a ceremony that would eternally bind the couple before God. There could be no Eucharist, of course. No formal Mass. Wakabayashi had not embraced the faith. But something substantial, something blessed by God with more meaning than the mail-order bride nonsense that had allegedly taken place in Japan with a surrogate groom. The man needed a visible wedding ceremony that would have him conforming to the accepted practices of marriage.

Father Lavoie waited his chance, catching Isao on his knees in the flower beds bordering the church. Isao made as if to rise up from his knees, but the priest held out a restraining hand. "No. No. Wakabayashi-san. Stay as you are. No need to interrupt whatever it is you are doing down there. What I have to say will take but a minute."

The priest quickly spelled out his plans for a formal marriage in a voice leaving no room for discussion. "A real wedding ceremony will serve your soul and make the lady you have brought to us proud you have chosen her. I have no intention of pressing the Roman Catholic Church on you or your bride. I understand she is of another faith. A Shinto ceremony will do. She is a Shinto practitioner, I believe. But we will have an official joining, a celebration with vows more fitting in the eyes of God than this long-distance contract that doesn't appear to have had much meaning to you." Father Lavoie concluded with a casual blessing over his kneeling gardener.

Isao struggled to his feet under the priest's authoritative eye.

"But the woman is unhappy," he blurted. "I am preparing for her return to Japan to her family. The Nagumo family needs the woman in the family business." Father Lavoie appeared momentarily dumbstruck as Isao, smiling apologetically, hurried on. "Marriage was a mistake. My friend Otake-san's meddling is to blame. Otake-san's relatives needed a husband for the woman. I had no need of a wife but Otake-san wanted to make marriage arrangements," he added plaintively. "We have made a foolish mistake. The woman will return to her family with no hard feelings, neh? You do not want to bless a foolish mistake, Father Lavoie."

Following a moment of silence, Isao, hoping the story had convinced the priest, made the mistake of talking too much. "Another wedding will not make this dish more tasty for me or the woman." he added. Then, recognizing his flippant attitude had offended the priest, he added hurriedly, "I have much to do to feed myself. A woman eats much. And this woman will not speak English. So, it is best this never happened and she go home." He babbled on. "Marriage was not legal, neh? Only Otake-san insists it was legal. I said to Otake-san that a wedding was not a bill of sale, eh?" Isao was so pleased with his own logic that he failed to see the priest's rising temper. "So now I shall return the goods, neh?"

Father Lavoie exploded, his words shouted through compressed lips. "What absolute nonsense, Wakabayashi-san. You squat there on your knees suggesting your liaison with this woman has been nothing more than a visit to your private brothel. You owe it to this woman to make this marriage succeed. She has come halfway across the world to be your wife. You owe it to me and you owe it to the people of Star of the Sea who advanced you the money for your trip. I will pretend I have never heard this drivel. The parish has a hand in this marriage that you now propose to turn into an immoral bedding of an innocent woman. I have been praying for you, Wakabayashi-san. Praying you will live up to your obligations, praying you will pledge to do so in holy matrimony and remove this offense to God from your mind. And I intend to see to it that you do."

Chapter 18 Ceremony

On the day of the wedding there was a chill in the air, with a blustery wind out of the west herding dark clouds toward the North Shore mountains. Father Lavoie didn't need to see the clouds to know that rain was coming at any moment. He left the rectory following early Saturday Mass swinging his umbrella like a formidable walking stick, rapping the plastic handle on the garden gatepost to summon Isao Wakabayashi out of the house.

"*Ohio gozaimas*, Wakabayashi-san." The priest greeted his protégé with a tolerant smile, choosing to ignore Isao's sullen petulance. Isao answered the Japanese greeting with a curt nod and said nothing. Father Lavoie, determined to keep the day on the best of terms, quickly added his effusive commentary on the weather, speaking Japanese to both Isao and Yuki. Yuki bowed silently, aware that for her to answer the priest in Japanese would upset Isao. Together, the three of them set out along Third Avenue toward the Japanese Language School with Isao ignoring the priest.

Father Lavoie, tapping the sidewalk with his umbrella, stopped to raise his hands in supplication to the ominous clouds. "Wakabayashi-san, I believe God is looking down on you with favor today. I have been praying the rain would hold off until you and your bride are joined in matrimony." The priest sighed condescendingly. "This wedding, even though it is before a Shinto priest, is going to please God, Wakabayashi-san. Keep that in mind."

Isao was thinking only of the celluloid collar biting into his neck; the stiff collar and the jacket were the remnants of what he had worn on his maiden voyage to Canada. He had retrieved them from the mothballs of his trunk out of respect and fear of the priest, but in a gesture of defiance had left the trousers to the suit in the trunk. Instead, he wore a wash-worn pair of blue denim work pants to remind this priest he was sacrificing a full day for this foolish wedding. He was also wearing his gray fedora, a Borsalino that had cost a week's wages, though the moment he felt the first tentative rain drops on his face, the hat came off. By the time they approached the Language School it had begun to rain in earnest.

With Isao walking at the pace of a man traveling his last mile, Father Lavoie raised his umbrella over Yuki.

The Japanese Language School was neither barn nor barracks yet resembled the architectural characteristics of both. Those who viewed the building with passing curiosity were inclined to dismiss the structure with the same disregard commonly assigned to anything made in Japan as simply "Jap junk." The two-story building contained only one floor on a level eight or nine feet above the street. A dozen wooden steps led from the sidewalk to the only doorway which opened onto a row of various sized classrooms. Summer sun had weathered the wooden siding until it took on a patina of silvery gray, the tone softening the building's austere and awkward shape. Kanji letters on a cedar plank over the doorway identified the school for those who could read the Japanese.

Approaching the school, Isao debated with himself over how far he could go in resisting. "I should be at work," he muttered weakly, the first words he had spoken that Saturday morning. "A bad frost is coming. I can feel it." He frowned up at the clouds. "I will lose all my new plants in the frost. My customers will expect that I am to replace them. I have no money for such a loss."

Father Lavoie smiled reassuringly. "Nonsense. There will be time for you to tend to all that. Besides, there is no frost in the rain." Isao shook his head helplessly at the clouds, wondering if he should have mentioned the threat of a flood. Father Lavoie lowered his umbrella, smiled benevolently and, with a gentle pat on Isao's shoulder, turned to leave. He had considered attending the wedding to see things through while remaining well out of the way so as not to lend his Roman collar to a non-Christian ceremony. However, on spotting one or two parish faces among those outside the school, he decided his presence could be misconstrued.

Two other couples were sharing in the Shinto ceremony. Isao recognized one of the bridegrooms, a bandy-legged berry farmer from the Fraser Valley. Isao had picked berries and weeded the fields for the man while working for Azumo. He remembered the farmer as an avaricious cheat who light-weighed his pickers and argued over payment. His bride was a sturdy picture of the farmer's daughter Isao had left in Wakayama. Isao was never fully convinced he escaped the syphilis with that girl, stubbornly steering shy of a visit to a doctor to find out. Seeing the berry farmer's young woman brought a queasy feeling to his already unsettled stomach.

"Wakabayashi-san. You remember me?" The farmer's face lit up. "You picked my berry field, neh?" The man grinned slyly. "Azumo-san told me you would be here. Now you will be married too, neh?" The berry farmer laughed and bowed repeatedly. "I could not believe it was true. I said no. Wakabayashi-san will never marry. Only fools like me who are too old to stay warm at night need to marry, eh?" He turned an appraising eye on Yuki.

"Wakabayashi-san." The farmer leaned closer to whisper in a voice heard by everyone. "You will disappoint Azumo-san's women." The man sucked meaningfully through his teeth, his eyes disappearing in sun-scorched wrinkles. "Your woman does not look strong for work, Wakabayashi-san. She must be good for other things, neh?" He laughed licentiously. Isao turned to view the man's sturdy bride and smiled sympathetically.

"So, now you will no longer need the services of so many berry pickers, neh?" Before the farmer could protest, a third Japanese, a bald, muscular man, his graying whiskers in need of a shave, pushed his way between them. He wore a soiled blue shirt and carried about him the smell of dead fish. His appearance triggered something in Isao's memory, but for a moment he couldn't connect where they had met. Then it came to him. This was the man who had approached him on the pier while waiting for the Fuyu Maru. A fisherman. He boasted he had sailed his trawler from Ucluelet to Vancouver to claim his bride rather than wait for the woman to find her way to his North Coast village.

"So. Are you still nervous, Wakabayashi-san?" The man grinned. "Waiting for your woman you were a school boy wetting his pants, neh?" The fisherman shot an appraising glance at Yuki and nodded approvingly.

Isao bowed and quietly mentioned that he was surprised to see the man still in the city.

"It is because of the Japanese Consulate. I need them. They watch that I am not robbed of my fishing license." The fisherman shrugged his thick shoulders. "What does it matter, all this wedding business? You and I have already taken care of that, neh?" He laughed raucously, twisting his thick neck, inviting Isao to view the blushing girl standing behind his shoulder. He pushed the berry farmer aside for a closer look at Yuki. "Your woman looks thin, Wakabayashi-san." He turned a leering eye at Yuki. "But interesting, very interesting," he said slyly, seeking a fraternal confirmation from Isao.

Chuichi Otake, listening to all this, moved closer to Yuki until he was standing by her side. Whether motivated to defend his niece or to rescue Isao, Otake himself was unsure, he challenged the bigger man. "I am the uncle of Wakabayashi's woman," he said quietly. "I represent her parents." Otake was a man of supple build whose broad shoulders and deep muscled chest were clearly visible beneath his blue denim shirt. His challenge brought a flush to the fisherman's face. For a moment the two men measured one another before the fisherman's scowl gave way to a smile of neglected teeth.

"So, you are Otake-san, the one I am told who has promised us beer, eh? So where is this beer, good friend?" Otake had let it be known that he paid for the pickles, the sushi and the beer to secure his marriage brokerage due him.

There was little about the wedding ceremony that would have satisfied Father Lavoie's hopes of a sanctifying marriage. The Ucluelet fisherman began passing out the beer before the ceremony began, and from that point on the ceremony went downhill. The fisherman ignored much of the proceedings in favor of entertaining Isao with off-color Japanese ballads. No one appeared to care. Isao soon got into the beer himself while engaging in a loud argument with Otake and the Fraser Valley farmer, who had forgotten his young bride in the heat of the discussion. Yuki chose the moment to slip out of the room into the hallway, intent on exploring the vacant classrooms.

The starkness of the building awakened memories of her own school in Yotsoya Station. The rows of narrow desks set tightly up against one another, the soiled window glass, the faint scent of blackboard chalk, even the worn wooden floors spoke of another time and another place.

Yuki wandered the full length of the hallway and was about to return to the main room when she stopped to look into a classroom at the far end of the hallway. The room contained three rows of empty benches facing a small desk and a blackboard upon which were written in chalk familiar kanji letters. It was the elementary grammar she had once dreamt of teaching. She turned, nervously looking back down the empty corridor. Sounds of the wedding party seemed to fade away as she stepped into the classroom, listening for a forgotten voice. Slipping her hands into the sleeves of her kimono, she bowed before the empty desk.

"Nagumo-san. You are late. Our class has been waiting." The voice from the past spoke with affectionate authority.

Yuki bowed once more and slipped onto one of the vacant benches. "Nagumo-san," the voice said quietly. "Come to the front of our class and sing for your sensei." Demurely, Yuki stepped forward, bowed to the desk and turned to face the empty room, her arms folded modestly in her sleeves. In a fragile, childlike voice, she began to sing of her school. As she sang, memories came flooding back and her voice grew more confident. When the song ended she bowed to the empty desk and in a moment of exquisite silence stood once again in the Yotsoya schoolhouse, having passed into a long denied dream. A soft, measured clapping of restrained applause ended the moment.

Startled, Yuki looked up. A tall Japanese wearing a soiled, ankle-length overcoat and a hard bowler hat frayed at the brim stood in the doorway, a faint smile on his face. The man's lips parted revealing a row of large, golden teeth. "That was very good. You sing like a Geisha." The stranger brought his hands together once more in measured applause and offered a tentative bow, as if he were unsure of the stability of his balance. Yuki could feel the blood rushing to her cheeks.

"I am sorry if I have intruded." The man's voice was thin and sharp, as if it were coming from a worn gramophone record. "I came only to learn who was singing such a beautiful song of Nihon. I am Azumo, an acquaintance of the man you have married." He spoke Japanese, the dazzling gold in his smile adding a note of deception to each word.

"I was singing my school song," Yuki stammered uncertainly. "I am ashamed for my foolishness, Azumo-san. When I was young, I had hoped to teach in such a classroom." She cast an apologetic glance around the stark room, placing a hand on her burning cheek. "Please forgive this moment of my foolish memories." She was unable to finish.

"Aah so. I have heard Wakabayashi-san chose a sensei for his woman. In this country many Japanese need to be taught our ways. Even the man you have married forgets he is Japanese."

Yuki nodded submissively without replying.

"Perhaps now you are here, you will sing to Wakabayashi-san. Your songs may help him remember our Japanese ways." For a moment neither of them spoke, Yuki afraid to reveal anything more of herself, while Azumo was judging how much he should speak of his business with her husband.

"Your husband has worked for me before the priest became his friend. Now he has a new friend and a wife so Wakabayashi-san no longer needs Azumo, neh? Wakabayashi-san forgets much." Azumo paused with a look of reflection so that he appeared saddened. "There was a time—" he stopped, aware of a sudden shift in Yuki's eyes and turned to follow her glance. Isao stood behind him.

"Oh ho. Now he comes behind me like a silent tsunami, neh?" Azumo attempted to dismiss his being startled with a thin laugh. "Wakabayashi-san, have you come to rescue your woman from an old man? Did you think I would steal her from you, Wakabayashi-san?" He smiled contemptuously.

The beer flush deepened in Isao's cheeks. "So, you have come to my wedding, Azumo-san. Or is it your farmer friend's wedding that has brought you? Or you are now interested in fishermen as well as farmers?" Isao's slurred voice carried more than a hint of sarcasm. He turned to Yuki. "Azumo-san has many businesses. Now he comes with business for all of us, neh? Do you hope to do business with my wife as well, Azumo-san?"

Azumo ignored the insult. "I was recalling for your woman how you once valued my friendship, Wakabayashi-san." Azumo's lips parted in a cold, glittering smile. "Now my friendship has little to offer, you greet me with insults." The old man shrugged. "You have your own business and now you have your own woman. Maybe you will be hiring Japanese to work for you, neh? Then you will know the pain I feel when you no longer remember our friendship." The two men continued staring at one another without speaking until a burst of loud laughter from the corridor broke the tension.

"That is the fisherman," Isao grumbled. "He is drinking all the beer while we make foolish talk." Azumo continued to smile without moving from the doorway.

"I have no bad feelings for you, Wakabayashi-san. To show you I have no bad feelings, I could find work for this woman of yours." Azumo turned, openly appraising Yuki. "My hotel has need of an honest woman, a Japanese woman who understands something of business, neh? And I have heard that your woman has been trained in business."

Isao let out a deprecating grunt. "Azumo-san believes that if you work for him, you must work for him as long as you breathe. Is that not so, Azumo-san?" He was speaking to Yuki without taking his eyes off of Azumo

"Only so long as one is in my debt," Azumo replied. "Your wife is an honorable woman, Wakabayashi-san, a sensei. She remembers our Japanese ways. I could find honorable work for her. You and I could renew our friendship with such an agreement, Wakabayashi-san."

Yuki grew frightened at what she was hearing, despite Isao's scornful laugh. "Azumo-san, you are not talking about my woman working for you teaching Japanese ways."

"No. But I have honorable work for her. You come to see me at my hotel, Wakabayashi-san. We can discuss the work I have for your woman." Isao nodded suspiciously. The old man stepped out of the doorway and Isao led Yuki back to the wedding party.

Chapter 19 Sun Rise Hotel

Sunday, two days into the New Year, Isao Wakabayashi cautiously worked his way over his frost coated stone path and stumbled onto the porch of his Third Avenue home. It was an hour before dawn. Yuki lay in bed awakened by his fumbling with the door, hoping he would be too drunk or tired to be interested in her. She had not laid eyes on him since he and Otake-san left together Friday night.

"Get up, woman," he called out for her in whiskey slurred Japanese. Yuki remained motionless. He called again, then a third time, each time his voice less resolute, less demanding, a little less certain of her response. After his third call Yuki got up from bed, deliberately adjusting the kitchen smock she wore night and day. Entering the kitchen she found Isao seated at the kitchen table cradling his head in his hands. He looked up at her as if he were seeing a stranger. Yuki could not tell if what she saw in his face was pain or anxiety before deciding it was a look of both.

"Azumo-san has work for you in his hotel," Isao mumbled and slapped the palm of his hand on the table, emphasizing the decision had been made. "You will not have to spend your nights waiting in bed for something that no longer happens, neh? Azumo-san wants you there tonight." Isao grunted, folded his arms across the table and dropped his head onto his arms. "I need tea. Ocha. Bring me ocha before my head falls off." He pushed his chair back from the kitchen table and went to the sink, putting his head beneath the cold running water. Yuki didn't move. He looked up at her, blinking the water from his eyes. "What's the matter with you? You sick again? Make me some ocha."

She continued to look at him, saying nothing.

Slowly, he began to accept that what he was facing was the same disdainful look he saw the first moment she had set eyes on him. It was a look that had made him feel as if he had stepped in dog shit. "Don't look at me as if I have traded you to whore for Azumo-san. The work he has for you is not in his beds." He pushed the dripping wet hair from his face and grunted disdainfully. "There is more money for a woman in one of Azumo's beds than there is in the work he has for you. But

Azumo-san's beds are not for skinny, cold women." He sniffed loudly, attempting to regain the command he felt slipping away. "I myself visited Azumo's hotel last night. Azumo-san and I talked of the honorable work he has for you."

"Honorable?" Yuki repeated without looking up from the stove.

"Yes. It will be as he says. I owe him nothing. I no longer pay him to find work for me. But he is a man who will lie to you when he speaks of me. I warn you, do not listen to his lies." Isao sniffed indignantly. "It is because I will no longer work for him that he speaks of such things about me." He waved a warning finger at her back. "And Azumo-san will see to it that he gets his share of the money he pays you as well." Yuki took a towel from the rack above the stove and began drying his hair.

"Do not worry about the business that takes place at Azumo's hotel," Isao mumbled from beneath the towel. "That old man has friends with the police. In his hotel there is never any trouble. I am not afraid of him and his friends, but it is best not to make him angry. So I have agreed. You will go to work in the Sun Rise Hotel tonight."

"Tonight?" Yuki repeated uncertainly.

"I will take you there myself when you have made me ocha and some food and I have had some sleep. Azumo-san will be waiting for you."

***

In the eyes of the conductor and the three casually interested passengers riding the late Sunday afternoon streetcar, Isao and Yuki Wakabayashi presented a picture of an introverted, stoic, Japanese couple. They sat next to one another while remaining miles apart. Isao's eyes remained partially closed, his face cast in meditative tranquility. Though it was obvious he was not sleeping it was not so obvious that he was nervous and worried. While Yuki's eyes remained downcast, her head was filled with thoughts setting her heart beating wildly. Isao had tried to convince himself of Azumo's promise of honorable work for his wife, but there were doubts about the old man's plans. And he was frightened by the return of defiance in Yuki's eyes.

The streetcar lumbered through the Hastings Street intersection and turned onto Main Street, stopping at Powell, where the Wakabayashi couple stepped down at the empty street corner. The last of the winter daylight laid shadows in each doorway and reflected off the scattered puddles along the curb. Isao hesitated, plagued by last-minute doubts, his eyes following the retreating streetcar as it waddled up Main Street. He shrugged, uncertain of the outcome of what he was about to set in motion. "Come. Azumo-san will be waiting."

The Sun Rise Hotel occupied the middle of the block, a garishly-painted green building opening onto the street through two grimy glass doors. Isao marched purposely up to the door and looked up at the second floor windows as if surveying the site for the first time. "Azumo-san is upstairs," he mumbled. "There is no need for me to go up there with you. It is best he deal with you himself. He says he will treat you honorably. Only when he talks about me will you know he is lying." He cast an uncertain glance at his wife and turned away, leaving Yuki facing the glass doors alone.

The fading daylight reflecting off the glass doorway formed a murky mirror. Yuki started toward the doors and stopped. A tall, Oriental woman looked back at her in the glass. The woman wore an ankle length, black, summer topcoat, her face revealing deep, unfamiliar lines carved by the anxiety of fear and weeks of a meager diet. Only the cleanly drawn facial features and the imperial set of her shoulders reminded her of the woman from Yotsoya Station. She remained facing the glass door for a long time, slowly accepting the reflection of the woman who was so foreign in every way to the world she was about to enter. The thought left her feeling very much alone.

The Sun Rise Hotel boasted 24 rooms in a two-story, turn of the century wooden building. Protruding from the second floor were four bay windows built out over the sidewalk; the windows provided night tenants a vantage point from which they could summon an idle streetwalker. Across the face of the building the hotel's electric sign was made up of a chain of light bulbs which appeared to stutter incoherently between empty light sockets, spelling out the words Sun...ise Htel.

The building's bilious exterior walls leaned shoulder to shoulder with a row of similar frame structures running the length of the block; a barber shop, a grocery store with empty vegetable crates piled to the curb, a fish peddler's shop, two laundries, one on each end of the block, and a single store window where the glass was painted a solid dark green with no announced business. All but the hotel faced the street with drawn blinds in compliance with the city's Sunday closing law. A single red light bulb left burning night and day above the hotel's glass doors lent a unique summons.

Yuki's struggle to come to terms with the woman in the hotel glass door was interrupted when a bleary-eyed Caucasian came staggering out through the doors. The man leaned unsteadily against the building, attempting to focus on this woman in black. He then lurched forward and, to keep from falling, reached for her arm. Yuki shook loose and slipped past his outstretched arms, swiftly pushed aside the double doors and entered the hotel and was immediately struck with the acrid stench of urine. Pressing a sleeve over her nose, she looked about the dimly lit hallway. Two orange light bulbs mounted on wall brackets threw an orange glow over a narrow staircase running up a back wall. Yuki started up the stairs, almost stumbling over a body in the middle of the stairwell, blocking her way. A puddle of urine spread out in a damp shadow beneath the body. Yuki, too frightened to care whether the man was asleep or dead, gasped, unaware of Azumo looking down on her from the railing on the second floor.

"Do not let that one frighten you," he said in his rasping voice, casually dismissing her fear with a wave of his cigarette holder. "That one is a steady worker when he is sober. He will come to borrow my money. You are to tell him to clean up the piss. He will do as you say. Then you can give him a dollar." Azumo pinched his cigarette from the holder, slipped the butt into the pocket of his duster overcoat and disappeared into a second floor utility closet. "Come. Come," he called out when Yuki hesitated on the stairs.

The closet doorway into which the hotel owner had disappeared was partially closed off from the hall by a three-drawer dresser set in the opening where the door had once been. Yuki found Azumo seated behind the dresser in his makeshift office. Azumo removed his bowler hat and began fussing over a small table mirror, his long, thin fingers grooming the loose strands of his gray hair into a center part. He indicated that Yuki was to sit in one of the two straightback chairs.

"She is so very thin," the old man muttered, thinking aloud without turning from the mirror. He reached for a black electric cord dangling from a two-way overhead light socket; the cord connected to the hot plate on the shelf. "Yes. Very thin," he repeated and pulled on the light switch feeding the hot plate coil. Azumo pushed a chair toward Yuki. "Sit. Sit." She accepted the chair without speaking, watching the old man fill a dented metal kettle at the cupboard sink. Azumo reached into the drawer of the dresser and brought out a chipped, blue enamel teapot.

"You will have some kocha with me, Wakabayashi-san. Maybe with a little tea you will sing again, eh?" He laughed the same thin cackle that had so startled her at the school house. "I was pleased to hear you singing of your memories of Japan on your wedding day. You were pretending to be happy. Let us pretend to be happy again. Have some kocha?"

"Dozo," Yuki answered cautiously, unwilling to reveal her thoughts to this sly old man but relieved to be speaking Japanese.

"Please. You make the tea." Azumo indicated the electric plate where the boiling water was rattling the kettle. "Kocha is good for the bowels. Sometimes tea grumbles when it enters an empty stomach but tea will bring warmth to the belly of one who has not much to eat, neh?" he said wisely. Azumo handed Yuki the jar of dried tea. She poured the boiling water into the teapot, inhaling the wisp of steam, hoping to wipe away the memory of the urine stench on the stairs. Azumo went to the drawer of his improvised desk and placed two white china mugs on the dresser. Yuki poured the tea and the old man wrapped both hands around the warm cup. She could no longer see into his eyes.

"Wakabayashi-san has married an honorable Japanese woman. That is good for him and perhaps good for me as well, neh? A woman such as you, even though you are too thin, could make much money in my hotel. But..." he sniffed, dismissing the thought. "I have other work for you." He puckered his thin, dry lips and sipped noisily at the hot tea. "Drink your tea, Wakabayashi-san, it is good for your bowels."

"You will see there is good business in my hotel, even though it is a small hotel. Some business comes to this place late in the night, neh? That is when there is need for my rooms. Yet when I am gone from here I am paid as if the hotel has been empty all night long." He paused to blow on his tea.

"Some come to my hotel who do not need a room for the entire night, neh?" Azumo's eyebrows rose in silent wonder at such a fact. "Sometimes, Wakabayashi-san, they need a room for only one or two hours. Then you will change the towels and the room is rented again. Some nights my rooms are rented two, three times, neh?" At this, he opened his eyes in astonishment. "Yet in the morning, when I come to my hotel, one rent is all I am paid. So now you will count for me how many times my rooms are rented because you are an honorable woman, Wakabayashi-san. I will not be cheated." Azumo paused, giving her an opportunity to confirm his judgment while he rose and slipped into his overcoat.

"You will be paid two dollars each night," he went on, searching through the deep pockets of his coat. "Less my twenty percent," he said, watching closely for a reaction. Yuki's expression never changed. "Twenty percent is what I charge for finding work for you. It is a reasonable sum, neh? Forty cents a night. You keep one dollar and sixty cents." He grinned, his golden teeth flashing in the dimly lit closet, and took a pint whiskey bottle from his coat pocket. Carefully he unscrewed the top and measured the whiskey into what remained of his tea. "Tonight is a good time for you to begin. Sunday the old lady who watches for me likes to go home early. She will show you what to do, though there is very little business Sunday night." He screwed the lid back on the whiskey bottle and slipped it back into his coat. "You will be alone to collect the money tonight. Then I know I will be paid."

Azumo finished his tea, put the empty cup back in the dresser drawer and stepped unsteadily into the hallway. "That one on the stairs stinks. But let him sleep for a while. We do not allow those who do not work to sleep in the hall. When others come to the hotel drunk, you ask the police to take care of them. The police will come by one or two times each night. I have it arranged. They will help you to get rid of those in my hotel who are not welcome and take care of those who do not want to pay, neh?

"When my workers come, they will tell you they work for Azumo-san. You rent them a room even if they have no money to pay. I will collect later. That one on the stairs will be awake soon." Azumo produced a wallet, the leather shining from years of passionate hand care. "I give you one dollar. You give him the dollar when he comes to you, but first he must mop the stairs where he has pissed."

***

Yuki settled into her nights at the Sun Rise Hotel like a child allowing herself to be drawn into a make-believe world, pretending to be something she was not. She concealed her fear of the drunken men by shaking her head as if unable to understand their language. At other times, she adopted a posed authority that swiftly brought the drunks to the incoherent recognition of the role Azumo had vested in her. Through the February nights she propped open the hotel doors, allowing the cold air to purge the hallway, and she learned to close her ears to the shrieks and curses of the unseen violence behind the fragile walls. She learned to identify Azumo's workers and those he sought to be rid of, often summoning the red-headed policeman patrolling the late hours on Powell Street. She also grasped the unspoken understanding between Azumo and the parade of desperately weary Caucasian and Indian women who night after night led transient field hands to her second floor registration desk. Many of their customers were Azumo's workers; quiet, lonely faces, stumbling unsteadily up the stairs in pursuit of the fleeting warmth of a woman's body. The women would emerge from the rooms disheveled, sometimes bruised, and Yuki would share her tea with them and listen to stories she could read in their eyes more clearly than she understood their words.

She fashioned a bed for herself in the second floor utility closet, where she lay awake throughout most nights listening for the sounds of approaching business on the stairs. Isao never again visited the Sun Rise, extending his visits to Otake's boat to two and three days at a time while the house on Third Avenue remained empty.

***

In the autumn of 1924, Yuki Wakabayashi gave birth to Toshio, her first born. The delivery took place in the utility closet with a middle-aged Russian whore in attendance, the whore swearing savagely through the two-hour delivery. One year later, in the same delivery room, she gave birth to a daughter. When Yuki presented Isao with the news that his second child was a girl, he grunted disinterestedly and disappeared aboard Otake's trawler for three days. In his absence, Yuki named her daughter Soju, after her mother, informing Isao on his return the name would reassure the Nagumo family of his intentions to extend the Nagumo name to their children.

Her third child, Tatsuo, followed two years later. Unlike the others, he arrived in the maternity ward of St. Paul's Hospital, at the insistence and expense of Azumo, following a visit to the Sun Rise by an officer of the city health department. The work of Yuki's Russian midwife had drawn the attention of a Powell Street missionary. Suspecting the hotel was being used as an abortion clinic, the Salvationist informed the health authorities. Azumo ordered the Russian whore banned from the hotel.

After the birth of Soju, Yuki grew quietly introspective. To Isao, she appeared to stand taller, her shoulders reflecting an assurance uncommon among Japanese mail-order brides. Unable to deal with a wife he no longer intimidated, he surrendered to their new relationship, giving up his shouting and much of his weekend drinking. At mealtime, he ate what she put before him with quiet acceptance. If Yuki welcomed these changes, she gave no sign.

Each spring, when long days in the fields kept Azumo's workers too spent for forays into the Sun Rise, Yuki took her children on the interurban to the Steveston Cannery docks along the Fraser River estuary where they met the children of Japanese cannery workers and spoke Japanese. When not visiting, she would sit with her three children on the cannery wharf fishing for whatever ventured close to the tidewater dock. At times, when her sons were invited aboard Otake's trawler, Yuki and Soju spent the afternoons foraging among the wild purple beach peas and river grass for river-washed agates. Mother and daughter played like children in the tidal sands until evening, when they would huddle on the wharf over their fishing lines, watching the Pacific Ocean swallow the sun while waiting for Otake-san's return. In those hours, in the warmth of the summer evenings, Yuki painted word pictures of the magic of Yotsoya Station and a Japan that took on a dreamlike beauty in the child's imagination. And for a time, Yuki forgot her disillusions in the Land of the Golden Mountains.

Book III: War

Chapter 20 Changing Tides

In the summer of 1940, following the French armistice with Germany and the Allied forces collapse in Western Europe, Winston Churchill broadcast to the Dominions his apocalyptic entreaty: "*We shall fight on the beaches...We shall fight on the landing grounds...We shall fight in the fields and in the streets...We shall fight in the hills...*" The jingoistic songs of patriotism followed: "*There will Always be an England and England shall be free. If England means as much to you as England means to me...Red, white and blue, what does it mean to you?*"

It had meaning to Michael Costello. His brother Joseph had joined the army in July 1940 and was shipped to England with the First Canadian Division. A year later, his brother Seamus appeared in their mother's kitchen in the uniform of the Seaforth Highlanders Regiment.

***

The afternoon sun scattered diamonds over the wind tossed waves of English Bay. It was a Sunday in late September. Michael Costello stopped on the rise above Fraser's Wharf, looking down on the floating dock. He remained there for a long time watching Soju Wakabayashi, who sat facing out across the bay on the seaward end of the dock. Her legs were draped over a piling, her toes teasing the water; a limp fishing line in her hand floated quietly on the undulating surface. She appeared to be watching the line, her head tilted in childlike expectation. As he watched, Michael knew his thoughts were wrong. He had struggled with a desire beyond his experience to control since the day he turned at the Wakabayashi gate to look back at her on the porch.

Soju had seen him on the path approaching the boathouse and was merely pretending to be concentrating on her fishing. Her pose was to make the gangly redhead believe she was unaware as he came creeping up behind her.

"Fishing inspector. Let's see what you caught!" he barked, seizing her shoulders.

Soju gasped in mock surprise. "Just that," she answered coyly, tilting her head toward the open coffee tin alongside the piling. At the bottom of the tin, staring up at the sky through a glazed eye, lay a ten-inch silver-sided shiner, its body curled to the contour of the can. "I caught that one and I caught a crazy redhead who thinks he can sneak up on people."

"That poor fish looks surprised," Michael said. "Did you ever notice shiners have no eyelids? Even when they are dead, their eyes are wide open. I suppose that's because fish are always looking for the hook in things, eh? Having his eyes open didn't do that old buddy much good, did it?"

"That old buddy?" Soju lifted her chin challengingly. "You make him sound like a friend of yours."

Michael reached for her hand and pulled her to her feet.

"Look. That poor fish in the can and I have a lot in common. What I want to know is what are you going to do with me?" He was smiling as he wrapped her line around the piling and led her into the shadows beneath the boathouse. Hidden from the beach, in the safety of the shadows under the boathouse deck, he put his arms around her waist and kissed her. She came up against him, twisting her hips.

"You better be careful. You might get hooked," she teased.

"We poor fish don't have a chance."

The sunlight through the cracks in the overhead decking painted shadows across the soft tone of Soju's skin. Gently, Michael cupped his hands over the bumps in her sweater and felt her shudder. She pressed her lips to his mouth, as his hands roamed possessively over her body. He had been touching her since their first tentative summer kiss. He tried to speak of love, to say words like Clark Gable or William Powell used when they did their kissing in the Saturday matinee. But the rehearsed words never sounded the same when he touched the soft warmth of her skin. What came from his lips was meaningless stuttering. "Soju. God. You feel good." Now he said nothing as she looked up at him, awkward and exposed, afraid of what was happening and unwilling to make him stop. Michael's hands reached into the soft warmth beneath her sweater, then stopped. His head tilted to the sound of heavy footsteps on the deck above their heads.

"That's Billy Fraser's old man," he whispered, slipping his hands free. He could feel the blood blushing in his cheeks and hoped the shadows beneath the deck would conceal his guilt over what he had been doing. "Come on. We better go see if there is anything on your line. Old Man Fraser will think you fell in."

***

That particular Sunday was also a time of a fear in the Wakabayashi's home. Early that same morning Isao had discovered a page from a 1937 Look magazine fastened to the gatepost outside his garden. The page pictured a baby crying amid the rubble of the Nanjing railroad station following the Japanese massacre of Nanjing. Isao took down the page and was attempting to rub away the "Japs Go Home" scrawled across the gate when Soju came out of the house. Isao did not speak of the picture or of the words he was erasing, but Soju saw the words. They remained with her, buried in the excitement of the moment in the shadows beneath the boathouse deck.

They came into the sunlight hand in hand, hoping to appear as if they had just come onto the wharf. Billy Fraser, working the wharf motor tender through the moorage, was the first to see them. Cupping hands to his mouth, he hollered across the water.

"Michael. I got a deal for you."

Soju released Michael's hand. Billy was so loud and talked so fast he made her nervous.

"Mike? How about you handling the tender awhile? You ran the boat before." Billy's sun-freckled face broke into the pleading smile of a mischievous street urchin. "When I get paid Monday, I'll give you a half a buck." He turned his charm on Soju. "Come on. Take your girlfriend for a ride," he pleaded. Billy stepped out of the red-hulled, double ender, leaving the propeller turning to keep the boat bumping against the wharf.

Before Michael could answer, Billy flipped him the hawser. "I'm just going to be out there for an hour or so, Mike." He rubbed a hand nervously across the bridge of his sun peeled nose and looked out at the mass of sailboats skipping across the bay. "I just want a final shot. Look at them." He waved an arm toward the bay.

Michael glanced out to the boats cavorting like wind tossed daisies over the water. "This is my last chance, Mike. My old man is taking my boat out of the water tonight because we start back to school Monday. Whatd'ya say, pal?"

Michael held the tender against the wharf when he noticed Soju nervously scanning the shore. His eyes followed her glance to the beach below the public swimming pool wall. Soju's mother and two brothers were spread out along the beach turning rocks for sea worms.

"I knew I could count on you, old buddy," Billy urged. "If my old man asks where I have gone, tell him I'm giving a sailing lesson. I'll pay you Monday. I promise."

Before Michael could put the idea to Soju, Billy had hoisted his sail bag to his shoulder and was trotting down the wharf to his Star boat.

"Hold it a minute." Michael sensed Soju's uncertainty, and if she wasn't going along, he wasn't having any of this. Knowing Billy, he also had a good idea that once Billy got under way, it could be dark before he set eyes on him again.

"I won't forget this, old buddy," Billy hollered, pushing off from the wharf without looking back. "Have fun."

"When are you coming back?" Michael hollered, aware it was a meaningless question. Even if Billy heard him, there was no hope of his turning back.

"How about it, Soju?" Michael slipped the hawser around a piling, the tender bumping restlessly against the wharf. "We might as well have some fun."

Soju hesitated, the breeze teasing her black hair and sculpting her clothes to her legs and thighs. God, he thought, she's beautiful. "Come on, Soju. We can pretend we are in the ferry boat business." He reached out to her. "I'll take you anywhere in the world. Over the Channel to LeHavre? Put out for Suez? Close your eyes and Captain Costello will take you to the port of your dreams."

He put an arm around her waist and eased her into the tender, too intent on getting the boat out onto the water to pay attention to her continuing to look back at the beach. He pushed the throttle on the Briggs and Stratton and headed the tender into the wind, the chop spraying their faces.

Soju closed her eyes. "Yokohama. I want to see Yokohama, Michael. Can we go there? I want to see Tokyo, too. My mother has promised to take us to Yokohama and Tokyo. She dreams about the cherry blossoms in the spring and gets homesick for the little streets in Yotsoya Station where my grandmother has a spice shop. When my mother tells us those stories, I wonder if that is where I belong." Soju opened her eyes, ending her vision of a land shaped from Yuki's stories.

"My mother has promised us we will see it for ourselves someday. Michael? Let's go back to the wharf and ask if she will come for a ride in the boat. We can tell her we are pretending to sail to Yokohama and maybe she will tell us her stories. It is like really going there. Okay?" Soju was pleading and he would have heard it if he had not been intent on being alone with her. She read the look on his face. "Michael? What's the matter?"

"Your mother doesn't like us being together, does she, Soju? Neither does your father. I can see it in the way they look at me. Your parents don't trust me. They probably believe I'm not good enough for you because I'm not Japanese. Maybe they are right." He shrugged, releasing her shoulder from his arm and allowing the boat to turn in aimless circles off the beach.

"That's not true, Michael. Mother likes you a lot. She thinks we are too young to be together so much, that's all. She's afraid we are going to do something we shouldn't."

"You mean I'm not Japanese. That's really what you mean, isn't it? If I was Japanese she would be happy. That's it. Isn't it?" He thrust the tender throttle forward, the boat surging into the waves, his thoughts angry and bitter. '*God, why is she so Japanese? She could be from an Indian tribe. Old Lady Kilpatrick in the candy store thinks she's a Capilano Indian or Chinese. Anything but Japanese.*'

"Soju, I wanted to be out here in the boat by ourselves. Just the two of us. " He reached for her waist and felt her stiffen at his touch. "Nobody can see us, Soju."

"I can't go too far from the beach, Michael. My mother needs me to stay close."

"What'n hell for?"

"Because there may be trouble. People might not like them being on the beach."

"What are you talking about?"

"There are people who don't like the Japanese, Michael. You know that. People who think we are spies or something crazy like that. It's the war, I suppose." She was about to tell him about the picture on the Wakabayashi gate, but he interrupted her.

"Your brothers are there with your mother. Let Toshio look after her. Don't you want to be with me?"

"We can never tell what Toshio will do. He gets angry so quickly he could get us into trouble."

"Why don't you just say it? You don't care about us, do you, Soju?" He was steering the boat farther from the shore, the figures along the beach almost beyond sight. "Toshio told me all about the police coming to your house and the identity cards. I suppose that makes you think everyone is against you. But the police are registering lots of people. Your mother has her identity card, right? That's all she needs, war or no war. Nobody can do anything to your brothers or to your mother as long as they have their cards."

"Michael, stop the boat. I want to tell you something that happened this morning," she answered quietly. "There was a picture pasted on our gate of a Chinese baby crying. He was all dirty and burnt. It was a picture taken of Japan's war in China. My family didn't have anything to do with that, but someone put the picture on our gate anyway." She moved free of his arm, unwilling to repeat what she had seen scrawled on the gate. "Yesterday the police went to the river and searched my Uncle Chuichi's boat like he was a criminal. They came and questioned my father again, too. It was the second time they have been to our house." Her voice grew quiet. Michael wanted to kiss away this talk about war, about being Japanese. He wanted to kiss her lips out there in the sunlight before God and the whole world, only everything was coming apart.

"Michael, there was a man at the boathouse watching me when I came onto the wharf," Soju said. "I could tell he wanted to tell me to leave. Then you came along. You don't know what it's like when people look at you as their enemy."

"Soju, that was Stanley Glasheen's old man. Nutty as a fruitcake. Nobody pays attention to Glasheen." Michael attempted to pull her close once more and she pushed him away, her attention fixed on two heavy-set men making their way down the bank toward the shore.

"That's the police." Soju's voice rose above the chatter of the motor. "Those are the men who came to our house to question my father." Michael cut back the throttle, allowing the tender to turn with the wind.

"What makes you think those are the same guys? You can't see that from out here."

"I just know that's them," Soju replied. "I have to go to shore, Michael. Now."

"Christ, Soju. You should have said something about all this in the first place. What do you expect me to do with this tender? I could have told Billy to keep the damn thing if I had known about this. There is a war on, you know." The phrase had popped from his mouth as easily as 'good morning' or 'how-do-you-do'.

There's a war on. The phrase had become a way to deal with everything wrong or unpleasant. Nylons? Sorry. *There's a war on.* Coupons for gasoline? Meat coupons? Coupons for sugar? *There's a war on.* Cancelled ball games, beach patrols, air raid sirens, it was all summed up in those words. He saw the instant pain in Soju's eyes and was sorry the minute the words were out of his mouth.

"I didn't mean that, Soju."

She never heard him, her gaze fixed on the shore. "Michael, please take me in. I'm so sorry." *So sorry.* That too had become a wartime phrase. It appeared in Canadian newspaper cartoons as coming from the mouth of a grinning, large-toothed Japanese soldier. Yet Soju had intended to repeat it just that way, perhaps to emphasize that she was Japanese. Perhaps because she was recalling a day when she felt embarrassed by her mother's apologizing with those words when introducing Soju to Star of the Sea. Yuki, unable to follow the sister superior's rapid English, had bowed apologetically confessing: "So sorry. I do not understand." Soju would have offered Michael the same apologetic bow but for the wind rocking the boat. Instead, she pleaded with him.

"Michael, your father was a policeman. If you told the police my family is on the beach fishing, they will believe you. Will you do that for us, Michael?"

Soju had no way of knowing that Michael's first thought on seeing the police was of his mother's police pension. That was all they had. Those men on the beach were probably RCMP. He was also remembering her words about their searching her uncle's boat and wondering what they found that brought them to the beach. There was also his father's warning that a man who gets in the way of a police investigation is one step from being in trouble. Why had she brought all this on when all he wanted was to enjoy the day, the boat, and their chance to be together? He brought the tender up against the wharf; his hesitation in answering revealed his confusion.

With her question unanswered, Soju stepped onto the wharf and tried once more. "They will believe you, Michael."

"I can't do it, Soju," Michael stammered. "You heard me promise Billy I'd look after the tender. I can't just walk off. People are out there expecting me to bring them ashore." He released his grip on the wharf, allowing the wind to slowly turn the boat back toward the bay.

The afternoon sun had fallen near the horizon and was glancing off the surface. Soju raised a hand shielding her eyes as she watched the boat drift away. When he was well away from shore, Michael looked back and saw her retreating figure scrambling up the bank toward the two policemen. He cut the motor, the tender drifting in the aimless breeze.

***

The moorage was deep in evening shadows with only the wharf deck lights to guide the tender through the anchored fleet when Billy Fraser's star boat came looming out of the twilight. The boat's main sail was down, Billy sailing in on her spinnaker. He stood in the prow gripping the forward stays, his windblown, kinky blonde hair standing on end like a shock of prairie wheat. He looked as if he had been taken from the cover of Puck Magazine. "What a helluva day, Mike," he hollered excitedly.

"You son of a bitch," Michael cursed bringing the tender alongside. "Where the hell have you been?"

"Take it easy, Mike." Billy reached out to catch hold of the tender. "I couldn't give up on that wind. I had her keel out of the water on the last tack. It was unbelievable," he said in a voice alive with exhilaration. "I wouldn't trade today for all the girls in China, even for your Jap sweetheart." Billy laughed and jumped into the tender. "What happened to your gal?"

"The police came and ran her and her family off the beach," Michael snarled.

"Take it easy, Mike. What's got into you? You mean the cops came here?"

"You heard me. I think it was the bloody RCMP." He enunciated each letter as if he were speaking to an idiot.

"You are kidding! They chased away your Jap girl, too?"

"Watch your mouth, Fraser."

"What the hell, she is, isn't she?" Billy snapped back.

Michael glared.

"A Jap?"

"Say that one more time and I'll knock your ass into the water."

"Oh, I'm sorry, Michael." Billy raised his hands in mock fear. "I can't help it if you got hot nuts for whatever you call her. She could be Ubangi, for all I care. Just so long as you think she's okay, that makes her okay with me. You know that." Billy took the tender tiller. "Only you should know, old friend, people don't trust the Japs these days. Nobody has much to do with them except you. And you don't know much about them or about that girl either, except she's got nice cans."

"I'm warning you, Fraser, knock off that Jap stuff. For all I know your old man might have been the one who called the cops when he saw us in the damn tender."

"Get off it, Costello. My old man is more of a Jap-lover than you are. If anybody called the police it was old man Glasheen. He has been hanging around the wharf mouthing off about Japs, taking pictures of the harbor. What did you do, when the cops came?"

Michael turned on him. "What did you expect me to do? Walk off and leave everybody sitting out in the moorage until you decide to sail home? I had the tender on my hands."

"That's bullshit, Mike. You know my old man could have taken over. Anyway, if you ask me, you did the right thing keeping your nose out of it. But don't put the blame on me just because you feel shitty you didn't do anything." Michael winced silently, Billy's words stirring the rotten feeling that had been in his gut since watching Soju running up the bank.

**

Late that Monday afternoon, in the last hour of daylight, Isao Wakabayashi removed his portrait of the Emperor from the Wakabayashi hall shrine. He wrapped it in a blanket, sealed the bundle in an oilcloth raincoat and bound the bundle with a strand of garden hemp. With his fedora set squarely on his head, he and his two sons carried the package to a stand of willows in the brush beneath the Burrard Bridge. None of them spoke as they buried the portrait among the copse of willows. On the walk home Isao wondered if he should have included Soju in what they had done.

Chapter 21 An Unwelcome Caller

Frank Glasheen's gumboot landed with a heavy thud on the bottom step leading to the back porch of the Costello house. Michael felt the porch shudder under the weight of the big man's boot and lowered his book. Glasheen looked up at him with the same flat-toothed grin he had bequeathed to his youngest son. "Startled you, boy."

The fisherman laughed, hooked his free hand into the shoulder strap of his loose-fitting coveralls and started up the steps, bringing with him the mordant odor of dead fish. Michael was unsure whether the smell was a part of Glasheen or emanating from the damp bundle he carried cradled against his chest.

"Caught you reading. I hope you are studying the right stuff, boy." Glasheen didn't wait for an answer, but took a long look down at the open page as he stepped past on his way to the kitchen screen door. Michael harbored his father's distrust of Glasheen and felt a surge of resentment at the man's invasion of his mother's kitchen.

Eileen Costello had caught the sound of Glasheen's voice and stopped with her hands deep in dishwater, listening to his heavy tread on the steps. For a moment, she considered ducking into her bedroom and pretending to be resting, but hesitated, afraid Michael had already given her away.

"Aaah, it's you is it, Frank Glasheen?" She turned from the sink with feigned surprise, wiping her hands in the folds of her apron. "There's never a man comes through that door without so much as a knock that I don't look up expectin' to see Eamon standing there or some poor devil on the run from the Black and Tans."

"The Black and Tans? In the name of God woman, it's time you forgot that old country nonsense. That was better than half a lifetime ago." Glasheen dumped his bundle onto the kitchen table. "That kind of talk will lead you nowhere at all. There's little any of us can do about things that happened yesterday. It's time you started thinking about today. God knows there's plenty for the likes of us to be worrying about, eh?"

Eileen brushed the soapsuds from her naked arms, shifting her glance apprehensively to the bundle on her table. "Maybe so, Frank, but those days are none too easy to forget." She sniffed with a trace of hostility at being lectured by her uninvited visitor, and was pleased to see a flush of resentment on Glasheen's florid face. "And what's that you have brought us, Frank? A fish? It's big enough to be a small whale if a fish it is." Glasheen proudly peeled away the soggy newspaper wrapping, exposing the steel grey carcass of a large salmon. "Mother of God, save us," Eileen Costello sighed with exasperation. "What do you expect me to do with the likes of that? There's just me and the two boys and the cat. Eamon's long dead and Joseph is half the world away."

Glasheen scraped his thumbnail across the carcass, shredding a shower of silver fish scales over the kitchen floor. "Sea lice," he boasted. "Fresh out of the gulf this morning. My guarantee." He wiped his hands across the bib of his coveralls and reached into the bib pocket for a package of cigarette makings. Eileen watched silently as he cupped a cigarette paper between finger and thumb, tapped in a tidy pile of loose tobacco, and rolled a hard round cigarette, sealing it with a quick pass across the tip of his tongue. He grinned as if he had just completed a balancing act, cocked his leg like a man about to fart, and stroked a match across the haunch of his rump. Eileen shook her head in feigned wonder.

Glasheen threw a quick glance through the screen door to where Michael sat with his book in the afternoon sun. Eileen sensed he was planning a move she didn't welcome and stepped to the opposite side of the table, her fists propped on her hips. Glasheen drew deeply on the cigarette, puckered like a man about to whistle, and blew out the match flame in a stream of smoke.

"How is it, Frank, that in the entire Fraser River, you can't bring us a salmon that a mother and her two sons could hope to eat?" Eileen was intent on keeping the talk focused on the fish. Glasheen began easing his way around the table, his raw meat complexion deepening to a shade of purple.

"Eileen." His voice was suddenly soft and coaxing. "I can understand how difficult it can be for a woman such as you, a widow and all. Especially when she's still every pound of her a woman, eh? It's only natural and it's no sin at all. A healthy woman needs a man now and then, to set things regular, eh?"

"Is that so?" she replied with an audible chill in her voice. "And I suppose it's you that's wantin' to be setting things regular, is it, Frank?"

Glasheen coughed smoke into his fist. "No need for you to be embarrassed, girl. You and me, we have known each other far too long for that. You well know it was me who had an eye on you before that redheaded Bogside drink-of-water you ran off with entered the picture. What I'm saying is that a healthy woman has needs that go beyond just getting by in life, eh? Things that require a man's taking care of. It's not just a matter of our being cozy now and then, you understand. I could be here for you whenever you needed me, eh? And you have need of me girl, in more ways than you know." There was a long pause as he began unfolding the newsprint wrapping from the salmon.

"Take that lad of yours out there on the porch. I don't suppose anyone's informed you that your son has been getting thick with a Jap girl, have they? No. I can see by the look on your face you don't know what I'm talkin' about, do you? That's because there is no man about this house to keep that boy going straight. Do you know the Japs have signed a treaty with the Germans and the Italians? No, you don't. Well, it's been on the news today. Neither you nor your Jap-loving Priest Lavoie can see what's taking place right beneath your noses. But I'll tell you this. You better be worrying about what those Japs are doing to that boy of yours."

"What's this you are saying about Michael and a Jap girl?" Eileen was immediately sorry she asked.

"He's sneakin' about with a Jap girl, that's what." Glasheen pinched the burning ember of his cigarette and slipped the butt into the cuff of his coveralls. Eileen reached for her purse, hoping the business of the fish would distract him from moving closer.

"What do you mean, he's sneakin' about? Don't talk to me in riddles, Frank Glasheen." she demanded.

"Your boy is gone sweet on a Jap girl. That's what I mean."

"My Michael?"

"Your Michael." Glasheen nodded slyly. "I ought not to show you this, you being so damn huffy. But you seem to be interested in seeing for yourself, dear girl." He saw the undecided expression on her face. "I'm going to show you sumthin', okay?" Glasheen reached into his coveralls as if he were about to produce a rabbit from a hat and fished an envelope from deep in the bib. He held the envelope for a moment as if deciding whether to go further, and then began to deal a series of snapshots onto the kitchen table, never taking his eyes off of Eileen Costello, all the while smirking like a man laying down a winning poker hand. Eileen spoke not a word watching the pictures fall. One after another he laid them across the table. Michael's angular figure was photographed facing away from the camera, but there was no mistaking it was her son. His hair down to his shoulders betrayed him as clearly as his stooping, teenager's apology for his long body. He had an arm around the waist of an Oriental girl; that much she could see plainly. In one of the pictures their heads touched, forehead to forehead, as if they were leaning on one another.

"Where on God's green earth did you come by these?" she asked quietly. "If that were Seamus or Joe, I'd not be so surprised. But Michael?" Eileen shook her head in disbelief. "And it is Michael, I can see that."

Glasheen stepped around the table in pursuit of the surrender he thought he detected in her voice. "Japs don't live like white people, Eileen. If there were one last salmon swimming up the Fraser River it would be the Jap who would gaff it out of the water. There's not a fisherman on the river will tell you anything different. We have no way of tellin' how many of them that Jap-loving priest of yours has encouraged to come over here. What we ought to be doing is shipping the bunch of 'em back to Tojo, pretty damn quick. I have been told we have better than twenty thousand Japs right here in our laps in B.C."

Glasheen sniffed indifferently, indicating the fish on the table as he tucked the photos back into his coveralls. "That's a choice King. I'll let you have it for less than fifteen cents a pound. Better than twenty pounds of salmon there. It's yours for a dollar and a half. I'd be insulting you if I said anything less. I'm cutting the price in half in memory of your Eamon. I would do as much for him if he were alive, Eileen."

Eileen Costello's thoughts were still with the snapshots while she absently counted out the coins from her purse. Glasheen's photographs had set a series of pictures passing before her mind's eye, images of Michael in his baptismal white skirt, gazing up at her in the days she nursed him at her breasts. The boy was blessed with the deep green eyes of his father, eyes that made her a slave to his slightest whimper. She thought of the nights she had sat listening to his rehearsing his catechism for confirmation. She, not his father, walked with him hand in hand to his first day at Star of the Sea. And now these pictures. A boy, more nearly a man, arm in arm with a girl, a Japanese girl. She marveled at how tall he appeared next to the girl. She had never paid much attention to how he had grown. Must be nearly as tall as his father, she thought, a good head and shoulders taller than the girl. Suddenly, the images flooding her mind vanished with her startled gasp.

Frank Glasheen, misreading the distant look in her eyes, placed a comforting hand beneath the cheek of her rump. "You know, Eileen," he whispered. "I have considered you one of my own ever since Eamon's died. I've always felt the embers of our friendship ready to burst into flame. We need only to give it a chance, eh?" She stiffened, backing away and laying a hand on a steel frying pan.

"I'd give up on those burning embers if I were you, Frank Glasheen," she hissed. "Take your money. It buys the fish. There's nothing else being peddled in this house."

Glasheen stuffed his hands into his coveralls, his voice rising. "And that's the thanks I get for bringing you information that could save that boy out there from serious trouble?" His voice dropped and he spoke with a threatening coolness. "You are the last woman I'd expect to be indifferent to that son of yours bein' with a Jap woman, Eileen Costello."

She put the money on the table. "Exactly what is that supposed to mean, Frank?" The fisherman's color grew darker, his frustration releasing his temper.

"Mark my word, lady. That boy is old enough to land in serious trouble. Oriental women don't have the morals of the likes of you and me. And you should know about that." Glasheen, recognizing nothing was coming his way, lashed out. "There won't be these easy answers coming from you once that boy gets a taste for that kind of woman. Instead of his sniffing after a Jap, you'd do well to have him keeping tabs on his Jap friends for the good of the country."

"An informer? Is that what you want, Frank?" Eileen knew how to strike back. "Maybe you think I have forgotten whose informing it was that chased my Eamon out of Belfast? You of all people should be the one to understand that we have had enough of informers in this house."

The fisherman's eyes narrowed. "Don't let that sharp tongue of yours cut your own throat, woman. Maybe you should remember that there's a police department pension keeping a roof over your head. Maybe the doings of that man of yours and his pal Mulhern wouldn't sit too well if the right people were informed, eh? Remember that when you start blathering things you know nothing about."

"There's never a thing Dougal Mulhern or Eamon Costello ever did that they need apologize for," she answered with a sudden trace of uncertainty. "Eamon and Dougal both were working with Chief Inspector McCathie when they served the RIC. You know that." The mention of McCathie's name appeared to take some of the fire out of the fisherman, who shrugged indifferently and began gathering his coins from the table.

"Believe what you like, girl. But there's people keeping track of anyone thick with the Japs." Glasheen leaned his long body across the table, his face so close she could taste the tobacco on his breath. "That boy out there is messin' with trouble."

Chapter 22 December 7, 1941

Wind-swept white caps danced like dabs of cream-colored coffee on the silt brown Fraser River, slapping up against the hull of Chuichi Otake's 26-foot double ender, each wave hitting the hull without rhythm or pace. To Otake, the October Lady was speaking a whispered caress, for he was openly in love with his boat. Every sound was an intimate message spoken to no other.

Otake had wanted to name his boat the October Maru, October was the month of his birthday and the month he took possession of her; Maru because he was proud of being a Japanese fisherman working his own boat on the river. Morgan Hoople was quick to change his mind.

The fish packing plant had advanced most of the boat's six hundred dollar purchase price and Hoople had personally sponsored Otake's loan. While it was Hoople's practice to make an occasional dockside visit to the company-sponsored fleet, he made a special visit the day Otake took possession of the boat anticipating his Japanese protégé's gratitude. It took Hoople the blink of a startled eye to catch the word Maru alongside the bow.

"Maru? What the hell kind of name is that?" Hoople demanded with his fists braced on his hips.

"All Japanese ships are Maru," Otake blindly replied, his explanation momentarily striking the cannery manager dumb.

"October Maru?" Hoople repeated as if he had not heard correctly.

"October is also the month of—" Otake began to explain before Hoople cut him off.

"You paint Maru on that boat and I can name half a dozen fishermen who are going to put a hole in her before she's twenty-four hours on the water. What's more," Hoople added, intending to end the discussion, "the company has not advanced you money to buy a boat that is going to the bottom before you deliver a fish. And I can't see you paying off the loan working for two bits an hour in the packing plant. You won't live that long, Otake. So, you can forget that Maru business, right here and right now."

Hoople saw the joy fading from Otake's face and his voice softened. "There's nothing wrong with calling her October," he offered with a hint of conciliation. "October is a good month; happens to be my wife's birthday in October. She's a Scorpio, you know. What's more, the fall salmon runs into October, and that's also the month of your birthday, you say. I'm okay with October. But not that Maru business." He shook his head sadly. "Name her the October Lady. That sounds just as good and October Lady is not going to give anyone the idea the Japanese navy has invaded the Fraser River. What do you say?"

Hoople had no idea his suggestion would transform the little double ender into Otake's lover, yet from that day the Japanese fisherman openly set out to romance his boat. There were nights on the river when fishermen swore they could hear him serenading his October Lady in Japanese. Others told of seeing his shadowy figure dancing about the tiny cabin by lantern light.

Otake's life on the river was never easy, even without the Maru painted on the boat's bow. Japanese boats were a threat to anyone believing in a white man's exclusive rights to fish. Boats sailed over Otake's nets, sometimes bumping up against the October Lady in the dark. More often than not he would find the fleet blocking his way to the cannery docks for hours. His romancing his boat made things worse.

***

It was a gray Sunday morning, the sky over the Fraser River Delta shrouded beneath banks of threatening clouds. Wind off the Gulf carried a sharp chill and the threat of snow. From the Steveston docks one could look south to the snow-dusted foothills of Washington's Mount Baker. Otake had invited Isao Wakabayashi and his family aboard that day so he could discuss the troubles he was having with the October Lady's balky single-cylinder Vivian Marine engine. The engine, a gas fueled lump of cast iron set in the belly of the double ender, was painted green, the paint burnt black where the head gasket had burst on Otake's last run up the river. He had managed to coax and cajole the wheezing motor to the wharf despite almost losing consciousness from the fumes.

"What do you think, Wakabayashi-san?" Otake held up the broken gasket with a look one would reserve for a misbehaving child. "Only a week ago, I gave her a new gasket. Now she has done this again. You think she is too tired to fish?" Isao peered over Otake's shoulder at the open cylinder and grunted disgustedly.

"You talk crazy about your boat, Otake-san." Isao slapped his open palm on the dismantled engine block. "The engine needs a gasket and a file to smooth the engine block so the gasket seals." Isao straightened up to look out the cabin window to where Yuki and Soju were fishing over the stern. The two of them were hunkered down next to the bulkhead, shielded from the wind. Each held short lines draped over the bulkhead. Isao pushed open the window. "There are no fish," he shouted. Yuki merely turned her head and nodded.

"There is a real woman, Otake-san." Isao closed the window. "Like your engine, she is trouble and needs to be smoothed down sometimes, neh? You are lucky you have only an engine to deal with." He shook his head wisely, his words softened with a trace of a smile. "You should try dealing with a real woman. Your engine cannot make you feel like shit just by looking at you, neh?" Isao picked up the broken gasket and studied the engine block. "Anyway, you are lucky, Otake-san." He was letting his mouth ramble in a manner Otake had seldom heard from his friend.

Isao had left home before dawn, sleepless with worry, hoping to find reassurance to ease the fears in his head that began the day the Royal Canadian Mounted Police came to his door. His footsteps lead him to the church. Father Lavoie insisted Star of the Sea remained open night and day so that a troubled soul would never be denied a visit to the Blessed Sacrament. Isao couldn't remember when he last encountered the priest, but decided he would wait through the seven o'clock Mass to talk.

Alone in the darkened church, he sat in the shadows, uncertain whether or not to pray. And if he did pray, he wondered: what would he ask of this Christian God? Maybe, if this Jesus was there on the altar as Father Lavoie claimed, He would listen. He needed someone who would listen.

A couple with three children, the young ones still half asleep, appeared for the early Mass. A few minutes later the nuns from the school arrived and then an elderly woman who, if she had noticed

Isao, soon forgot him in the intensity of her prayers. Isao recognized the Henniger boy when he came out of the sacristy to light the altar candles. Once the Mass began, others began drifting in like an incoming tide, one or two turning to smile at the Japanese gardener.

Father Lavoie chose that Sunday morning to preach of loyalty and patriotism in the face of the fear they all faced with the war in Europe going badly. When he finished, Isao decided this was not the time to take his fears to the priest and left before communion, deciding instead to accept Otake's invitation to bring Yuki and the children to the river.

By nine o'clock the clouds were breaking in the west and Otake, seeking to ease the gloom that came aboard with Isao, opened the pilot window and called to Yuki. "Come inside where it is warm, Yuki-san. Have some kocha with us, neh?" Neither Yuki nor Soju could hear what he was saying, his words lost in the wind. Their attention was fixed on a flight of snow geese passing beneath the clouds. Otake shouted again. "Kocha, Yuki-san. Come have some tea." He raised the metal teakettle to the cabin window.

Yuki saw the kettle. Unwilling to turn away from the geese, she pointed to the clouds and called out, "The birds." The sight of geese, flying in tight formation, lit up her face with the excitement of a child. "They are flying south. That means we will have an early spring, Otake-san." Otake looked up, filled with a quiet longing at the sight of the freedom of the flock, and closed the window.

Yuki tied down their fishing lines and the two of them gathered around the dismantled engine with Isao and his two sons. Otake turned down the kerosene stove, rubbing his hands over the tiny blue flame. "We will have tea and a little music, neh?" He poured the hot water into the teapot, then leaned over the engine to switch on the battery radio. "Isao-san does not believe my October Lady's engine is broken. But I have been working her too hard. I know she is temperamental," he explained earnestly. "Twice this month she has burst her gasket." He turned to Yuki. "Does a woman get too tired to work, Yuki-san? Do you think my October Lady is tired?" He turned the broken gasket over in his hands as if he were asking her to examine a broken limb.

"I know nothing about engines, Otake-san," Yuki replied, speaking Japanese. "But I do know women get tired. Sometimes when given rest, they get well again. Sometimes it is something more than being tired."

The radio began to warm up, the static filling the cabin, smothering Isao's muttered comment. The static stopped and in the sudden quiet a voice out of the small speaker came thin, high pitched and nervous, as if it were calling through a distant storm.

"We interrupt this program to bring you a special news bulletin. The Japanese have attacked Pearl Harbor by air. President Roosevelt has just announced the attack was also made on all naval and military activities on..." The voice drowned out in a wave of static. Those paralyzed in the cabin swayed silently with the movement of the boat. Only their vacant faces revealed the shock the words had left. Otake was the first to move, reaching over the dismantled engine to fine-tune the receiver. The static rose louder, then faded, and the voice returned.

"Early this morning..." the announcer's voice paused as if the man himself was unable to believe what he was reading. "Early this morning the Japanese attacked the United States fleet at Pearl Harbor."

There was more, delivered in solemn, static-filled words followed by an interlude of heavy, religious organ music. The music took Isao back to the morning Mass and Father Lavoie's homily. He wondered if the priest had seen his Japanese gardener in the back of the church and what the priest could have said to him to set his mind at peace. In the long silence, Isao's mind went again to the police visits to his home and the answers they demanded. *'What is your religion? Are you a Shinto believer? Do you believe the Emperor of Japan is a God? What is the purpose of your frequent visits to Japanese freighters calling into the Port of Vancouver? What Japanese publications do you receive?'* For the hundredth time, he wondered what it was he answered that made them come back a second time to take his fingerprints. Now, they would come to take him to prison, he was certain.

Otake's thoughts were of his October Lady and his fishing rights on the river. The police had boarded his boat earlier that week.

Yuki, looking across the dismantled engine, watched her husband press his fists to his temples attempting to block out the radio, which was repeating the news bulletin. "This cannot be so!" Isao shouted into the face of the radio speaker.

"We are at war with Japan," Otake muttered, his voice subdued with apprehension, unaware his "we" had unconsciously chosen sides against Japan and the Imperial Sun God ruler.

Isao pushed his way toward the cabin door to escape the news. "How do we know what that radio says is true? Such words must come on official paper. Who is it that speaks these things? The radio spreads false rumors like a disease on the wind." Isao was aware he was babbling, but couldn't stop. "One cannot believe a radio. When I see these things written on paper, then maybe I would believe. There can be no war. That is only a fishing boat radio full of bad noises," He shouted, turning to shake his fist at the glowing receiver tubes.

"That was the government radio," Otake said quietly. "There is no mistake, Wakabayashi-san." He followed Isao out onto the deck of the pier, the two of them looking down the wharf for signs of war. Other Japanese fishermen were appearing in two's and three's, emerging from the fishing fleet like stunned bees escaping a smoked hive. "Look. They have all heard. It is true," Otake said. "Japan has attacked the United States at Pearl Harbor."

"If such a thing is true, it will be a short war," Isao muttered, suddenly searching for reassurance. "A short war to straighten things out, neh? Then there will be peace. Things will be better for us after a short war, Otake-san. Better on the river for you. Better in my work, neh?" His attempted confidence was answered with a doubtful nod.

"Only a short war, then peace," Otake repeated, attempting to give weight to Isao's promise.

***

"Since the unprovoked and dastardly attack on Pearl Harbor, a state of war has existed between the United States and Japan..."
Roosevelt's Harvard drawl, drawn out hard and cold, was a recurring nightmare haunting Toshio Wakabayashi all night. He

listened to each rebroadcast of the speech, his shoulder to the Wakabayashi Philco, his ear next to the speaker fabric, hoping for a hint of reconciliation. There was nothing. The President's declaration of war had all but dismissed the short-war promise his father was repeating over and over.

Isao Wakabayashi began drinking Sunday afternoon and by Monday his words were stumbling with the coherence of a man recovering from a blow to the head. "Things will be better with an honorable truce. Japan will sue for peace." In Toshio's mind, there was only the American President's final pledge: *"We will gain the eventual triumph, so help us God."*

***

December seventh passed slowly for Michael Costello. He stayed listening to the living room radio with his mother throughout the day and into the evening. Eileen Costello never took her eyes from her son, praying his brooding was because of the news. Early in their marriage she had ceased trying to penetrate those moods with her husband, but she had no intention of surrendering to Michael's morose behavior. Late in the afternoon, when they would normally be sitting down to Sunday dinner, she brought him a cold beef sandwich. In the evening, she turned the radio dial. "I think we have had enough of that today, son. Let's see if we can still catch Amos and Andy." Michael answered by getting up and going to his room.

Monday, December 8, a bitter-cold morning, Michael left his bed with the world-changing words of the American President, Franklin Delano Roosevelt, echoing through his mind. *"Yesterday. December seventh, nineteen forty-one. A date which will live in infamy. The United States of America was suddenly and deliberately attacked by air and sea forces of Japan..."*

Michael ran his head under the kitchen cold-water tap, raked his fingers through his hair and slipped quietly out the back door, determined to make things right with Soju. They had spoken several times since the Sunday at the wharf. They even walked home from high school together. But the unspoken distance of that day remained. Now he was heading to the corner of Second

Avenue and Burrard Street to wait for her to appear for school. Walking through the pre-dawn dark, he searched for the words to make her understand how the memory of that day had left him ashamed.

When he arrived at the Wakabayashi gate, an overnight rain was turning to sleet mixed with large flakes of wet snow. Isao Wakabayashi's truck was parked alongside the house loaded with winter prunings, assuring him they were inside.

For the next hour he paced the unpaved roadway, the wet snow melting down his neck. By the time the morning turned to daylight, his feet had grown numb. He was about to leave when he detected a movement beyond the sculpted pine trees and reached over the gate, intending to lift the latch. Isao, his grey fedora on his head and dressed only in his long underwear, which was tucked into knee high rubber boots, stepped into the pathway. His face was puffy and swollen, his eyes filled with streaks of tiny ruptured veins. The damp shadows on the shoulders of his underwear revealed where the morning snow had melted. Michael realized he had been watching from beyond the trees for some time. When Isao spoke, his face was so close that his whiskey breath polluted the cold morning air.

"What you want here? Soju not home." Isao waved his arm in the direction of Burrard Street. "You go away now."

Michael, momentarily speechless, managed to stammer, "Where is she?"

Isao shook his head, his lips pinched tight. "Soju not home anymore." His all-night drinking slurred his words so that Michael was unable to understand. A sudden gust of wind sent snowflakes dancing about their heads. To an observer they could have been figures in a snow-filled crystal ball. Isao's head ached, the blood pulsing in his temples. He was about to be sick. "You go," he repeated less forcefully.

"I'm here to talk to Soju," Michael said. For a moment he considered forcing his way through the gate. He was big enough. Even if it meant he had to scuffle with the smaller man. Toshio, watching from a window, could see the confrontation coming and stepped out the front door, his coat over his head like a cape, the empty sleeves flying in the wind.

"Why are you hanging around here, Costello?" he demanded.

"I came to talk to your sister."

Toshio turned to his father and spoke Japanese. The old man released his grip on the gate, grunted a brief answer and went into the house, looking very old and beaten.

Roosevelt's declaration of war had drained the boldness from Toshio and softened his attempt to bully Michael. "My father already told you, it's no good you being here. He doesn't want you seeing Soju anymore. So you better beat it, Mike. There's no point in hanging around bothering my sister."

"To hell with you, Toshio. I want to hear that from Soju. Where is she?" Michael's readiness to fight had its effect on Toshio, and what he said next was almost pleading.

"My parents are aliens, Mike. The RCMP is already rounding up Japanese

Toshio shook his head. "Mike, my father is acting like he's sore at you but it's only because he is scared shitless. Your hanging around my sister is making things worse for us. My old man is already on a police list as a dangerous alien and a troublemaker. Now he's drinking again and telling everybody Japan is going to win the war. Shit." Toshio held his breath trying to contain his exasperation. "It's like he wants us all to go to jail. He goes on with that crap about the Emperor of Japan being the hundred-and-twenty-fourth human descendant of Amaterasu Omikami. How do you think that sounds to the RCMP? What's worse, the cops have a Japanese guy taking everything he says to the RCMP, word for word. The Mounties don't give a shit that he is nothing more than a scared drunk. All they know is that he's talking trouble. Christ, when he gets going like that he sounds like a spy to me. He doesn't listen when he's drinking."

Michael shuffled his feet in the slush, searching for words to sway Toshio, and recalled Philip Phair's reassurance. "Why would anyone worry about your dad? He's just a gardener."

"Yea. We heard that one before, didn't we? And Christ was a carpenter. Look what happened to him." Toshio attempted to blink back a sudden flood of tears. "My father actually believes the only chance we have coming out of this in one piece is if Japan wins the war." He sniffed derisively. "For all he knows, if Japan wins they'll probably shoot us for being Canadians."

Isao reappeared on the porch wearing a rubber slicker over his underwear. Toshio looked back at him and dropped his voice. "Look at him. Does he look dangerous? I'll tell you how dangerous he is. He keeps a rosary hanging on our Shinto shrine. Says Jesus was the same spirit that came to Japan as the Sun God. Christ and the Sun God, the same man, they just came at different times as different people." Toshio tried a thin burst of laughter. "Wait until he tries that on Father Lavoie. We'll all end up in jail."

Michael stamped his feet to beat the numbness from his toes. "How about your mother, Tosh? Can't she talk to him?"

"She cries every time I turn on the radio and she hears that Roosevelt talking. All she talks about is that it's time for us all to go back to Japan." Toshio brushed his hand through the snow settling on his closely cropped hair. "Japan? Shit. I hardly understand the language. Besides, there's something else you might as well know, Costello. My mother believes you are a part of the reason the cops are after us. Some of them knew your old man and they don't like you hanging around a Japanese girl. My mother knows that for a fact."

"Horseshit, Tosh. Nobody gives a hoot about a couple of kids. If you think by saying that you are going to get me to take off, you are wrong. I am not leaving until I see Soju."

"Leave her alone, Mike, please. She doesn't want to see you. You don't know what it's like now. Soju and I went to the Blue Owl yesterday to get out of the house for a Coke. There's a sign on the door. No Japs. Soju read it and cried. We have been told there is a sign like that on the ticket window at the Kits Theater too. Japs, Mike. Soju and me, we are Japs." Toshio blinked back his tears. A movement near the house caught their attention. Soju was coming toward the gate, a knitted stocking cap pulled down over her ears, her coat turned up around her chin, the wet snow settling on her shoulders like angel feathers. From the porch, Isao called out to her in Japanese, then turned and went back into the house.

"My father was reminding me I have to be back before dark," she explained. "There is a curfew for Japanese." She opened the gate. For a moment Toshio's eyes seemed to hold her at the gate before he turned and followed his father into the house. Michael put his arm around her waist, noticing for the first time how tiny she was.

They started down Third Avenue, their heads bent into the wind, Michael holding her next to his body in the shelter of his arm. He had forgotten his freezing toes and the dampness in his clothes. At Third and Burrard Street they stopped at a copse of freshly cut fir trees stacked against a two-by-four frame. Hand-scrawled red letters painted on a board alongside the trees announced: "Xmas Trees for Sale." A sallow-faced young man, a woolen scarf wrapped over his ears, was shaking the snow from a tall Noble Fir.

"How about it?" he asked, shaking the tree. "Take it home for two bucks. You won't get this kind of a tree in a couple days." Snow on the branches made the trees look as if they were dressed for Christmas.

"We won't have a Christmas tree this year," Soju said, looking up at Michael. "We always have one. My dad usually brings us a tree. It's something he picked up from Father Lavoie, I guess."

Michael signaled the man with the tree. "Maybe later," he said and the man smiled, setting the tree back among the others.

"I like Christmas," Soju said as they started across Burrard toward the beach. "I have been knitting you a hat like mine for your Christmas present." She mischievously tugged her cap down until it almost covered her eyes. "If you are good, you may get something to keep your ears warm. Do you still have holes in your socks, Michael? Maybe I should knit you socks instead?"

"Soju. I want to talk about us."

She went on as if she didn't want to hear. "My father says we may not even be here for Christmas this year. So I better get busy and finish the hat or you may not get anything." She squeezed his arm playfully and they continued toward the beach through the falling snow.

When they came in sight of Fraser's Wharf, they looked out over the water. The dark clouds in the west were lifting, revealing a mystical, lavender light between the ocean and the sky.

"That's the sun trying to get through," Michael said. "It has already gone down but seeing us together, it hates to leave the day behind."

"It goes down early this time of year," Soju answered.

"Out there in Yokohama, where you wanted us to sail that day, the sun is probably just coming up. Remember?"

Soju squeezed his arm harder, not wanting to look back.

"I was stupid," he answered. "And I was afraid."

They arrived above the wharf at a spot where the path dropped down and was shielded by the shoreline brush from the wind. Michael brought her into his arms and felt her body go limp. "Soju, why don't we get married?"

"We are too young," she whispered, their breath mingling in the cold air. "Kids can't get married. Not without their parents' consent. Your mother would stop us. Mine too."

"Not if you were pregnant. If you were going to have our baby we wouldn't be too young."

"But I am not. Anyway, your mother and Father Lavoie…" He put his lips on hers, erasing the thought from her mind.

"My mother wouldn't stop us if there was a baby about to be born outside the church. I know her, Soju." He was trying to make it sound real, the words tumbling from his lips onto hers, vaporizing in meaningless cotton puffs in the cold air. Her answer startled him.

"We have never even done it, Michael." He felt her shiver in his arms and kissed her again, holding her tighter as he gently began steering her toward the shelter of the boathouse where the nest of the winter-stored sailboats rested on leggy cradles across the open deck. He shook the snow from the canvas tarp covering the cockpit of a Star boat and held it for Soju to crawl beneath. She curled up in the cockpit on a dry canvas sail bag and he pulled the tarp over them, shutting out the remaining light.

There were no words. They were both stumbling blindly into something neither of them understood. She lay motionless, like a lamb frozen in fear, as he struggled to raise her hips, his hands tugging at her cotton underpants. "Michael," She gasped, catching her breath at the touch of his cold hand moving up her leg.

"Help me, Soju. I want to put it in..." She reached up with her mouth and stopped the words, swiftly slipping out of her underpants and opening herself to him. "Be gentle, Michael. Please be—" Her voice broke into a sharp gasp and he felt her cheek, suddenly wet with warm tears. He was taking her, defying his mother, defying the church, denying the existence of everything that would keep him from the warm, softness yielding beneath him.

"Oh God, Soju, I'm in you," he whispered.

***

It was dark when Michael left Soju at the Wakabayashi gate, the puddles of wet snow on the stone walk barely visible. She ran from the gate, her coat and sweater soaked to her skin, splashing through the puddles without looking back. Stopping in the doorway to the kitchen she faced her entire family: Toshio, Tatsuo, her mother, and Isao, all silently demanding an explanation. Soju met her mother's eyes with a fleeting glance and looked away, her heart thumping as if it would burst.

Yuki got up from the table and set a bowl of rice and fish before the vacant chair. "You are late," she said quietly. "You knew about the curfew?" Soju burst into tears, shrinking from the doorway, afraid to speak for fear of what might come from her lips.

"What's the matter? What happened?" Toshio demanded, jumping to his feet. "You are soaked. What has he done to you, Soju?" Toshio couldn't tell if the look she gave him was a look of fear or loathing before she suddenly turned away from the room. For a long time nobody spoke, the brittle ticking of the Swiss cuckoo clock in the hall and the muffled sounds of Soju's sobbing filling the quiet of the house.

Toshio finally looked to his mother with the anger of despair. "What the hell happened to her?"

"It is all right," Yuki assured him. "Soju is a good girl."

As the night came on, silence continued to envelope the house, the wooden bird chirping in and out of the cuckoo clock marking the mechanical passing of the hours.

Chapter 23 Detained

The family was still seated at the kitchen table when the wooden bird in the clock startled them with the announcement that it was about to chirp nine times. As if in answer to the bird's call, the family heard a truck engine come to a stop in the road. "Shush," Isao whispered. They heard heavy footsteps on the porch, followed by a pounding on the door. In the brief glances passing over the kitchen table, the Wakabayashi family knew that their world was about to change forever.

The family had been quietly waiting through the evening with the uncertainty one awaits a jury verdict, knowing it is coming, hoping without hope for a verdict that would mean freedom. Yuki saw the fear in Isao's eyes and resisted the urge to reach out to him. Soju reappeared in the kitchen doorway as Toshio started to his feet in a surge of territorial hostility. Before he took a step, Yuki grasped his arm, urging him back onto the chair. The pounding shook the door a second time; Isao, passed his leather billfold, containing 78 dollars, beneath the kitchen table to Toshio. He then solemnly glanced around the room, the fear passing from his eyes as quickly as it had appeared. It was as if he were seeing those around him for the first or the last time. In that moment his shoulders drew back, and in Yuki's eyes her husband appeared to grow taller. Isao got up from the table, deliberately removed his hat from the wall hook, placed it on his head, and opened the door.

Two large men in dark overcoats came through the open door shoulder to shoulder, the taller of the two demanding: "Isao Wakabayashi?" Before Isao could answer, the two moved into the hallway, forcing him against the wall. Beyond their large bodies, in the light flooding out from the door, Isao caught a glimpse of several others crowding the steps. One of the two men put a hand on Isao's chest and with his free hand flashed a badge close to his face, demanding a second time: "Isao Wakabayashi?"

"I am Wakabayashi," Isao replied, his voice steady and calm.

"RCMP," the man barked. "You are being detained by the authority of the British Columbia Security Commission." Isao felt the last vestige of his fear leaving his body, giving way to a tolerant sense of resignation as if aware the life he had known had been taken from him. In that moment, the details of his house, so much of it crafted by his hand, suddenly took on an ephemeral quality. His dime-size garden of gravel and pine, Soju's drying overcoat above the stove filling the kitchen with the scent of warm, wet wool, the driftwood door handles he had polished by hand; all suddenly appeared unreal, as if conjured in a dream. His children, his wife, all were part of this vanishing dream. He reached up to remove his hat.

"Leave the hat on, buddy. You are coming with us." The policeman stepped back.

"I will get some things," Isao replied calmly.

"You don't need anything tonight. Come along with us just as you are." The man pushed Isao out the door into the hands of those on the porch.

Toshio jumped from his chair. "What are you taking my father for? He's just a gardener, for crying out loud."

The second policeman, a thick-set man with Oriental eyes and swept-back black hair, took hold of Toshio's shirt with a gloved hand, twisting the shirt in his fist until the buttons began to pop onto the floor. "Don't you go getting out of line, kid."

"I'm his son. That's my father."

"So get back in the kitchen when you are told. Now." He shoved Toshio, sending him stumbling back.

"What is he supposed to have done?" Toshio protested.

The man's Asiatic eyes narrowed. "I am not warning you again, sonny." There was menace in each word. Yuki came up behind her son and spoke Japanese. "Toshio. Do as they say." From the slight change in the man's expression, she recognized he had understood her.

"He is a boy. He is still in school," she continued in Japanese.

The policeman, his bulky body looming large over Toshio, paused before moving past him into the kitchen without answering. He stopped in the hallway at the space on the wall where Isao had removed the portrait of the Emperor. The man's gloved finger traced the light imprint on the wall. "Where is the Emperor?" he demanded, speaking fluent Japanese.

"It was a family shrine," Yuki replied in Japanese. "We took it down."

"Shinto?"

"Yes."

"You people practice that shit in this house?"

"Sometimes, yes."

"It's a military religion." He continued speaking Japanese. "Teaches you people you are going to rule the world, neh? Had your Hirohito hanging up there, didn't you? Sitting on a white horse lookin' like he crapped his pants? That's all Shinto shit. You worship him like he's a God." He turned to the man who had flashed the badge in Isao's face and continued in English. "They tried to pedal that Hirohito crap in Manchuria. Want you to believe they got God on their side so's they can do whatever they damn well please."

"My father is more Roman Catholic than Shinto," Toshio protested. "Ask Father Lavoie at Star of the Sea."

"Uh-huh. And where was it you had the picture of the Pope hanging on the wall, eh?" The man answered in English for the benefit of his partner. "Where are the weapons in this house? Where's your swords? Explosives? Cameras?" he demanded briskly.

Toshio's eyes looked about with confusion. "There are no weapons."

The man quickly separated the top half of the Philco radio from the speaker, jerking the connecting cord from the wall. Toshio was about to confess Soju had a folding Kodak camera when he saw the man already had the camera.

"Can't you tell us where you are taking my father?" Toshio pleaded, his voice betraying his sense of defeat.

The policeman was about to go out the door when he turned to Yuki, and spoke in Japanese: "He is to be held in the Immigration Detention Center. Nothing is going to happen to him. You can ask about him there in the morning." Yuki detected a note of regret in his voice.

Yuki and her children stood on the porch, oblivious to the chill wind gusting rudely through the open door, watching the tail light of the police truck disappear into the night; each of them harbored the fraudulent hope that Isao would reappear, unapologetic, his gray hat set determinedly on his head. Perhaps the police would realize they had made a mistake. If not a mistake, then they had taken Isao for questioning and more fingerprinting. Even the truck that had carried him away seemed unreal, lurching into the night like a Conestoga wagon on rubber tires.

***

Six other Japanese were huddled in the absolute darkness beneath the truck's canvas tarpaulin when Isao tumbled aboard. His body landed up against an unseen passenger and he quickly apologized in Japanese, certain that whomever he had landed on was Japanese. The truck's clashing gears drowned out the reply.

Isao wore only a shirt and the work trousers he had worn during the day, immediately regretting that he had not taken his heavy woolen Mackinaw from the hall. A passing street lamp offered a flash of light beneath the truck canvas, giving him his first glimpse of the man he had landed on. It was the Shinto priest, the man who had presided at his wedding. The priest was bundled in an overcoat, with his legs folded beneath him. A second flash of light revealed the priest resembling a roosting bird staring vacantly into the dark, neither seeing nor caring.

The lurching truck slowed at each intersection, the gears clashing in the hands of an inexperienced driver. The moment gave Isao a passing glimpse of the others beneath the canvas. One was a round-face Japanese who crouched on an opposite bench as if he were about to spring out of the truck. He wore a felt hat similar to Isao's and a suit jacket with a tie-less shirt buttoned to the neck. *'That one has dressed as if he were going to a wedding,'* Isao mused. *'He must have been waiting for the police.'* He found himself wondering what this frightened man did to be so certain the police were coming for him.

As his eyes began to penetrate the dark Isao was able to make out the faces in the far reaches of the truck. A grizzled dwarf of a man Isao was certain he had seen before sat braced against the rear. Another street corner and a passing light and he saw that it was the Powell Street barber, his arms folded defiantly as if oblivious to his surroundings. Isao had last seen the old man through the barber shop window wearing his green eyeshade and barber smock, and recalled this was the man who had shaved Toshio's head after Toshio had been the target of a stranger shouting 'Jap go home.' To Isao's surprise, Toshio had arrived home bald and angry, his shaved head a statement of defiance. Isao was silently pleased but with talk of war and the threat of a Japanese invasion, realized the old barber had not done his son a favor.

Isao resented the barber, who once spotted him leaving the Sun Rise Hotel following a night-long visit. In Isao's mind, the old man had looked at him with contempt, though Isao had never attributed his own guilt in what he imagined. Now, in the close confines of the police truck he tempered his tongue, worried a confrontation with the barber could fracture the fragile sense of security among the others facing uncertainty. In time, he would reevaluate his opinion.

The Immigration Detention Center rose over the harbor, a monument of institutional architecture. The building had served for years as the house of detention for ship-jumping Lascars, Fijians, and others from East Asian ports. The prisoner's truck, for all aboard realized that was what they were, turned sharply into the shore-side ramp, the turn tossing Isao into a tangle of arms and legs. Isao was the first to extricate himself, managing to climb over the others to look out through a parting in the canvas. He was greeted by a burst of blinding light and a sound resembling a series of hedge clippers snapping in unison. It took a moment before he could see past the lights to discover the six rifles aimed at his chest.

"Put those fucking weapons down before somebody gets shot," hollered a voice from beyond the lights. "And cut the damn lights." The lights wavered, then swept aside, coming to rest in a glistening half moon on the wet pavement. Isao squeezed further out from beneath the canvas. The policeman who had backed him against the wall stepped into the light.

"You boys can save your heroics for the Krauts," he shouted at the riflemen. "There's not going to be any trouble here tonight." He looked up at Isao with a grin bordering on humor. "They are kids, most of 'em nervous as hell and handling a rifle for the first time in their lives. So take it easy and do what you are told." He glanced at the clipboard in his hand.

"Okay. You, Wakabayashi. Climb down out of there and empty your pockets into one of those envelopes by the door." Isao lowered himself to the pavement and followed the policeman's light to a tall metal door where a white dispensary table held a stack of manila envelopes. He emptied his pockets into an envelope, one item at a time. "Hustle it up," the detective barked. "We don't have all night." Isao calmly slipped his glasses and its leather case into the envelope along with his brass pocket watch. His worn notepad followed. He went through his pockets once more and pulled out his handkerchief and a chewing gum wrapper folded over a pocket of tiny brown seeds.

"You can keep all that crap," the policeman muttered. "Where's your money? That's what goes into the envelope. Nobody is going to steal anything tonight." He tapped the table with the butt of his flashlight. "Come on, come on." Isao deliberately turned his trouser pockets inside out. "Don't be a smart ass," the policeman warned ominously. Turning to the heads peering out from the truck canvas, he called out. "Any of you birds don't have any money, say so. We might even take your word for it."

"I have no money," Isao said quietly.

"You can keep your specs and all that other crap. Just watch your attitude," the policeman growled. Isao retrieved his glasses, his notebook, and the gum wrapper containing the seeds, and went on through the open door. The policeman focused his light on the typewritten sheet. "Tanaka? Which of you is Takayoshi Tanaka?"

"I am Takayoshi Tanaka." The barber leaned out of the truck tapping his chest.

"Okay, Baldy. Climb down." Isao glanced back from the doorway, remembering the conspiracy of silence his friend Otake whispered about. "There are men on the fish dock who say the barber is a Japanese Imperial Navy admiral," Otake had whispered. "Do you think it is true, Wakabayashi-san? Fishermen know these things, neh?" Isao had thought so little of the rumor he had shrugged off the question without bothering to speculate. Besides, Toshio told him the barber was a Japanese seaman who fled Japan in 1894 to escape the Sino-Japanese War. Toshio said the barber was one of the early immigrants who seeded the stories of a Land of the Golden Mountains. Now, witnessing the old man's indifference with the loaded rifles pointed at his chest, Isao was less certain.

Once beyond the doorway, Isao was directed to a wire gate blocking the corridor, where he stopped awaiting instructions. Suddenly a guttural voice hollered his name. "Wakabayashi-san." The voice spoke Japanese. "So, they have arrested the nervous berry picker?" Isao strained to see beyond the gate. "Did the police arrest you so they could be with your pretty woman, Wakabayashi-san? Where is your woman tonight, berry picker?"

A door opened beyond the wire mesh casting a light into the shadows, revealing the Ucluelet fisherman, unshaven, his fingers clutching a wire cage door. Before Isao could answer, a restraining hand settled on his arm.

"That one is drunk, Wakabayashi-san," the barber spoke quietly in Isao's ear. "Pay no attention. It is not good to quarrel in front of the hakujin." The old man spoke with an authority that surprised Isao. "They have put him with us to quarrel," he said. "You know that I see everything at the Sun Rise Hotel. What he wants you to believe is not true."

Chapter 24 Internment

Toshio remained in a simmering rage, cursing the departed policemen, then turning his anger on his father. "Why did he keep up his crazy preaching of a Japanese victory? He knew he was daring the RCMP to arrest him. Why did he spread his crazy theory to Azumo-san? Azumo was never a friend of the Wakabayashis not since the day the police closed the Sun Rise Hotel for a year." Toshio repeated this to all who would listen. Adding to his anger was the realization that as the first-born son, he had become the family's 'shotainushi'; so it was now up to him to decide what they were to do. The prospect appeared hopeless.

In the hours following Isao's arrest, Toshio watched as the family silently drifted in and out of the kitchen, their expectant glances awaiting his plan. At one point Soju took her father's woolen sweater from the hook in the hall and quietly slipped it over her older brother's shoulders. Toshio leapt to his feet. "What did you do that for?" he shouted. "That's father's sweater." The anger of fear in his voice backed Soju away, clutching the sweater. "Put it back," he shouted. Toshio took a deep breath and, with a pained smile, announced: "I'm going to see Father Lavoie in the morning. The priest will know what to tell the police. They will listen to a priest and send our father home." He smiled uncertainly at Soju. "He will be happy you didn't give me his sweater."

Toshio never wandered far from the kitchen throughout that night, getting up from his chair every hour to pace the hallway. Occasionally he would stop to stare at the emasculated radio as if expecting it to magically come to life.

The morning was still dark when he started for the door. Soju, who had been watching him through his night-long vigil, appeared in his path. Before she could speak, he touched a finger to his lips. "Let them sleep," he whispered, and stepped out into the rain.

***

The Civil Defense order requiring that all headlights be tapped, so that only a horizontal slit of light could be seen, created a moving field of Oriental eyes prowling the pre-dawn traffic.

Dodging the oncoming cars, Toshio had the feeling he was being pursued by a hostile invasion. He felt his first moment of reassurance on seeing a light in the window of Michael Costello's home. Cupping his hands to the living room window, he cautiously twisted the mechanical doorbell crank, wincing at the harsh ring sounding through the house. Within a minute, Michael's head appeared in the opening, his eyes caked with sleepy dust. "Toshio?" he mumbled, still half asleep.

Before Toshio could answer, Michael's mother appeared, hovering over her son's shoulder, her hair in a halo of knotted rags. "What is it, Michael?" she demanded. Seeing Toshio in his father's gardening slicker, her thoughts went to Frank Glasheen's photographs of the Japanese girl with her son. "What in the Lord's name does that boy want with you at this time of the morning?"

"It's Toshio, Momma." Michael stepped out onto the porch rubbing his knuckle into his eyes, and attempted to pull the door behind him. Eileen Costello resisted.

"I can see who it is," she snapped. "Tell him to come back at a decent hour. You'll catch your death standing there in your pajamas." She put her head out through the open door to face Toshio. "Go home, boy."

Michael pulled the door shut behind him, closing her out. "What's up, Toshio?"

Toshio found himself suddenly hating the sight of this safe son of a policeman. "The police came to our house last night," he said, trying for a voice of confidence that wasn't there. "They took my old man away. I thought maybe you would know about what they are going to do with him."

"How would I know that?"

"You are a cop's son. Even though your old man is dead, I figured they would tell you," Toshio replied. His words about Michael's father being dead had startled his friend.

"You are crazy, Toshio."

"My old man warned us that this was going to happen," Toshio said. "And he was right. There's a Japanese guy feeding the police crazy stories about him being a Japanese spy." Toshio's voice quivered. "And you were the one who told me I was full of shit when I said the cops were out to get us."

"I never said that," Michael said indignantly.

"But that's what you thought."

Michael let that pass. "What's happened to Soju? Where is she?" Michael noticed Toshio's shivering, revealing how the night had drained much of the feistiness out of his friend.

"She's at home," Toshio said, his lips beginning to tremble, aware that his angry attitude was not coming off the way he intended. "Anyway," he added, "my mother says you are the reason the cops are after us because your old man's police pals don't like seeing you with a Japanese girl, Michael."

"That's bullshit, Toshio. Nobody gives a hoot about two kids. The cops are probably out picking up all kinds of Japanese. Christ, Japan has bombed the American navy in Hawaii. What did you expect? People are scared there's going to be an invasion." The despair in Toshio's eyes made Michael sorry he said that.

"Pearl Harbor wasn't my old man," Toshio said, suddenly subdued. "You know that."

"Tosh, I know your dad hasn't done anything wrong. All the cops care about is that he's Japanese."

"He told us that if there was trouble I should go to Father Lavoie, Mike. That's where I'm going. You want to come?"

"Now?"

"My dad is in jail. He's been there all night. He has nothing but the shirt he had on to keep him warm. I'm wearing his slicker. He's probably freezing."

***

Toshio waited while Michael threw on an overcoat and boots, and together they went marching across the Star of the Sea school grounds. They had gone only a minute or two when they ran on into Father Lavoie headed toward the church for early Mass. The priest carried his large black umbrella warding off the wind-driven rain. His free arm was looped through a Christmas holly wreath. Jimmy Henniger trailed a step behind in the shelter of the umbrella. Father Lavoie waved his umbrella, in theatrical astonishment.

"And what is this I see? A minor Christmas miracle? Michael Costello and Toshio Wakabayashi? And they are on their way to join Jimmy and me and the good sisters at Mass? Boys, tell me I am not deceived. It's the Christmas spirit. Right? " The priest's eyebrows rose hopefully before quickly giving way to a defeated sigh. "No. This looks more like trouble. I can't imagine anything else bringing you two out in the rain at this time of morning. So tell me, before we all drown out here. What are you two up to?"

"We are not in trouble, Father. It's Toshio's dad," Michael said, irritated at the priest's mocking tone. "The Mounted Police came to the Wakabayashi house last night and took him away."

"In a truck with a bunch of other Japanese," Toshio added.

"Isao?" the priest repeated incredulously. "Isao Wakabayashi?"

"About nine o'clock," Toshio answered, nervously rubbing his fist over his shaved head. "My Dad said I should come tell you. He said you would know what to do."

"Your dad told you to come to me? Did he say what he wanted me to do?" The priest left the question unanswered and lowered his umbrella, exposing himself to the full force of the rain. "Of course, you did the right thing, Toshio. Absolutely. But we must all stay calm." Father Lavoie handed the holly wreath to Jimmy Henniger, who was getting wet now that the priest was no longer providing his shield. Father Lavoie began speaking like a man talking to himself.

"There is a war on. Things have changed after what happened Sunday. The Japanese did join the Axis. They have declared war on us as well, I believe." Then, suddenly addressing the boys, he shook his head. "People do desperate things in time of war, Toshio. Look at what's happened to our troops from Quebec, eh?" The stern scowl on the priest's face brightened at the thought of the analogy. "The French Canadian soldiers have refused to volunteer for overseas service. People are now calling them Zombies. They are boys, just like you two, good Canadian Catholics. They believe their place is at home, protecting Canada. England expects Canadian boys to jump whenever the Empire calls for help."

Father Lavoie, failing to recognize his analogy wasn't working, was about to ramble on. "Why should French Can—"

"What about my dad?" Toshio blurted.

Father Lavoie sniffed loudly. "What I am saying, Toshio, is that your father is not the only one feeling the injustice of war." He raised his umbrella and drew Toshio into the shelter out of the rain. "It's also quite possible the police are picking up these Japanese men for their own protection. You said there were others? Your father is a man with a mind of his own, Toshio. He did choose to associate with questionable friends like that bunch at the Sun Rise Hotel."

Toshio twisted away from the umbrella, glaring at the priest.

"There's nothing for you to worry about, Toshio. Nobody is going to harm your dad as long as he is in custody. He is probably enjoying breakfast, right this minute," the priest added reassuringly. "The thing for you and Michael to do is come along to the church and say a Rosary for the swift return of your father." The priest's face broke into what he felt was a confidence-inspiring smile. "God has a way of letting things like this happen now and then. It's God's way of getting our attention." The priest smiled in gentle reprimand. "And Toshio, neither you nor your father have been paying very much attention to God lately."

Toshio stepped back, unleashing a staccato of Japanese.

Father Lavoie's round face blanched. "Toshio." The priest fumbled for words, his shoulders drawn back indignantly. "Christ died for you, Toshio. You must never speak His name like that again. It is not for us to know the mystery of God's ways, no matter how disappointed we may be. Isaiah 55, verse eight and nine: *For my thoughts are not your thoughts, nor are your ways my ways, says the Lord. As high as the heavens are above the earth, so high are my ways above your ways and my thoughts above your thoughts.* We know only that He loves us no matter what befalls us. Your talking like that could land your soul in hell, Toshio. It certainly won't help your father. Don't think for one minute that because you say such things in Japanese that it is any less offensive to God."

Toshio muttered a muffled curse, turned and stomped off across the schoolyard with Michael hurrying after him.

"What in hell did you say to him, Toshio?"

Toshio kept on without turning, his lips buttoned in anger.

"For God's sake, Toshio, what have you done?" Michael demanded, dog trotting to keep up.

"I told him he was full of shit."

"You must have said more than that."

"I told him what he could do with his Rosaries. What did you expect? You heard him. He wants me to believe that Jesus Christ sent those cops to pull my old man from the supper table because he hasn't been getting to Mass? Christ almighty, Michael." Toshio's sarcasm began to lose its defiant bite. "That fat priest wants me to believe that his God started the whole damn war just to get my old man to church. My father has been pulling weeds for him since before I was born. He's hardly ever charged him a nickel. Now my old man is up to his ass in trouble and that windbag says he ought to go to church more often. Pray the Rosary? That's sure as hell not going to do my old man a lot of good, sitting in the clink without a coat, half frozen to death. I have to do something on my own." Toshio continued to stride off the school grounds, Michael protesting at his heels.

"Toshio. You have got to remember Father Lavoie is a priest. Priests go to God for everything. Father Lavoie would rather say a Rosary for your dad than talk to the King of England about him. It's what he does for a living. You have got to go back there and tell him you are sorry. Your dad needs his help."

"Yea? What's he going to do? Light a candle?" Toshio stopped, turning to challenge Michael. "I'm going to the Detention Center. You do what you have to do, Mike. I'm going to find my old man and see if they will let me give him this coat."

"You are making things worse, Toshio. You are angry and that's the wrong way to handle this."

"What do you know about it? Your old man's dead. How did you handle that, Michael? Even your brothers say you went crazy." Toshio knew he should not have said that but it made him feel better to see the hurt in Michael's face. "Shit, Michael. Go on home. Go to church. Say the Rosary. Do something that won't get you into trouble."

"I'm going with you," Michael muttered. "But we are only making more trouble for your family."

Toshio set a fast pace over the Burrard Bridge, never uttering a word until they crested the hill and looked down at the Immigration Detention Center in the distance. "Cheesus," Toshio said softly at the sight of the massive grey building rising out of the waterfront mist. "The place even looks like a prison."

Michael nodded in uncertain resignation. "We have come this far. Might as well go down there and see what's going on." The doubt was in his voice as he silently prayed Toshio would turn away, even as Toshio started down the hill.

Drawing closer, they could make out a group of six or seven Japanese women in the rain on the Burrard Street side of the building. Michael recognized Soju among them. "Is that your sister?" he said seizing Toshio's arm.

"God, she must be soaked," Toshio replied.

The night had aged Soju; the rain pasting her hair flat to her skull accentuated her broad cheeks and Oriental eyes. She looked like a picture of a turn-of-the-century West Coast Indian woman Michael recalled seeing on the wall of the Fourth Avenue Public Library. She looked so much like the woman in the picture he remembered, Soju could have been her granddaughter. Mrs. Kilpatrick, the old lady who owned the confectionary store on Fourth Avenue, mistook Soju as one of the Capilano Indian Reservation kids. Mrs. Kilpatrick gave her one-cent candies because she liked the Indian people. He doubted she would have given candy to a Japanese kid. Besides, nobody was arresting Indians. Why couldn't Soju be an Indian? Conflicting thoughts of Indian and Japanese spies were piling up in Michael's head.

"What is she doing with those women?" he muttered in disbelief. "I thought she was at home with your mother."

As he talked, Soju broke away from the Japanese women and began hurrying toward them. She arrived breathless and reached for Michael's hand as if she were grasping a lifeline. "Oh Michael, I have been wishing you would come," she said.

"What are you doing here?" he demanded. "Toshio said you were at home. Why…"

"What am I doing? Toshio must have told you. They have our father locked up in there. These women have their husbands and their fathers and their sons locked in that building like criminals.

We are here to see them. To at least talk to them. If the police see us out here maybe they will let them go. It sounds crazy, I know. But Michael, we have to do something. Some of these women say the men are going to be sent to a concentration camp as prisoners of war. The police already suspect my father is a spy. You know he's not a spy, Michael. He's scared and confused. That's why I'm so glad you came. You know him. You are the one person who can tell them he's not a spy and they would believe you." Michael sighed helplessly.

Soju, sensing his thoughts, stepped back, her hands releasing his.

"I wish I could help, Soju. But I'm nobody. These guys wouldn't even know who my dad was. They are not going to believe a kid anyway. Come on Soju, we need to get out of here. Go some place where we can talk. Standing here in the rain doesn't make sense for anybody." He was silently praying they could escape this sidewalk, wishing he could turn back the clock to the summer days on the wharf with Soju's toes dangling over the water. She was his that summer; now she was Japanese and the police had arrested her father.

It was raining harder, the wind driving the rain in sweeping sheets across the pavement. "Soju. I tried telling Toshio. This is not doing your dad any good. These women are only making things worse. The police have their orders." He hesitated, aware what he was about to say was going to hurt. "You must understand, Soju. People are afraid. There could be an invasion here any day. For all the police know there are Japanese battleships off the coast this very minute." The hurt in Soju's eyes told him that he had said too much and said it badly.

"But my father hasn't done anything to anyone," she said with a bitterness he had never heard from her. "He was born in Japan. Is that a crime?" She was unable to hold back the tears appearing in large, crystal drops on her cheeks. "How do I get you to understand, Michael? All this is happening to us because of that man Azumo who owns the hotel. It is Azumo who is telling lies to the police about my father. He's the one spreading his lies to other Japanese and they believe him because he's with the police. My father and Otake-san did visit Japanese freighters when they came here. They went to drink Japanese beer with the crew and to read the Tokyo newspapers." Soju bit down on her trembling lip. "Old Tokyo newspapers, Michael."

Michael wanted to touch the crystal tears running down her cheeks, to tell her that none of that mattered. Not the police. Not the war. Not some old Jap with a grudge. The words never came.

Soju sniffed back her tears. "A long time ago, when my mother came to this country, she went to work for Azumo in his hotel. There was trouble. My mother would never talk about it, but the police closed down Azumo's hotel. He blamed my mother for that."

Michael, unable to deal with the pain in her eyes, turned away to look up at the tiny Detention Center windows. "At least we know he's safe in there," he mumbled. "Nothing this guy Azumo can do to him now."

"Michael," Soju said, brusquely clearing the tears from her face with the back of her hand. "Your father was a police hero. Maybe there is someone among these policemen who will remember him—" She broke off, her attention suddenly shifting.

"Never mind. You better go, Michael." He followed her gaze to the nearby ramp. Three plain-clothed policemen were starting up toward them.

"I'm not leaving without you, Soju."

"Michael, my mother believes that our seeing each other only brings more trouble for my family. I see that now. And I am asking you to please go before you make things worse."

"You don't mean that, Soju."

"Just go," she pleaded and turned back toward the Japanese women on the sidewalk in the rain.

***

Isao Wakabayashi's time in the Detention Center passed swiftly for the first few months, marked by rumors of Japanese victories circulating with the arrival of each new detainee. Japan's Imperial Navy sank the British battleships HMS Prince of Wales and HMS Repulse three days after Pearl Harbor. That gave the detainees all the encouragement they needed to listen to Isao's short-war theory. The fall of Hong Kong to Japan following a seventeen-day siege only added to Isao's confidence in predicting a Japanese victory. However, when the rumors of the collapse of Hong Kong, which was garrisoned by Canada's Winnipeg Grenadiers, began to filter in with reports of Canadian soldiers being executed, the mood inside the detention center changed abruptly.

The rumor of Singapore's surrender to the Japanese reached the detainees not long after, followed by word of the Japanese conquest of Manila and the Philippines, and the Japanese bombing of Australia. By February there were rumors of the Japanese Imperial Fleet battering the Americans in the Battle of the Java Sea. This latest information arrived in the person of a Japanese mortician who had a tendency to deliver his news in a near whisper so that his listeners were forced to sit with an ear close to his lips. Isao became so certain that peace was but weeks away that he began detailing plans for the spring gardening season, confident he would be free in time to handle the spring pruning. His detailed notepad outlined April as a time for removing the winter wrappings from delicate azaleas and newly planted Japanese maples. That would also be his window for thatching lawns. Meticulously he listed his customers, reinstating those who had told him they no longer needed his services. He would take Toshio and Tatsuo from school for a week to help with the flowerbed plantings and the early spring mowing.

But March passed swiftly into April, when the word of General Doolittle's April 18 bombing raid on Tokyo reached the Detention Center, and Isao experienced the first pang of doubt. The Japanese landing in the Aleutian Islands, on June 6, was quickly tempered by word of the Imperial fleet losing four carriers in the Battle for Midway. Though the war had changed beyond his ability to comprehend, Isao continued adjusting his gardening schedule and preaching a negotiated peace to a doubting audience.

Isao had dressed and was sitting on the edge of his bunk, readjusting his work timetable when the soldiers came down the corridor rattling the cell doors and hollering: "Time to go. On your feet." Isao's handwritten calendar told him it was the 10th of June. The ramp doors swung open and the guards began herding the detainees into the first rays of the morning sunlight. For a passing moment, Isao felt as if the sun was offering an invitation to freedom. It took but a quick glance up the ramp through the cordon of khaki-clad police to banish all thoughts of freedom.

From the ranks of parading prisoners came a voice Isao recognized as belonging to a boyish-faced cannery worker who had listened attentively to his theories of a quick peace. "Are we going home?" the young man asked uncertainly.

He was immediately answered by a humorless guffaw from a nearby guard. "Home?" the guard demanded incredulously. "Here we've been up half the night arranging a lovely, long train ride for you buggers and now you ask if you are going home?"

Isao folded his gardening plans and slipped them into his pocket, the fresh breeze off the waterfront a painful reminder of his early spring mornings in the Kerrisdale gardens. For a moment he allowed his mind to entertain the thought that Yuki may have gotten wind of the move. He searched for a sign of his wife among the crowd of curious office workers gathered on the Burrard Street corner to watch the column of Japanese coming out of the Detention Center. A newspaper photographer, wielding a heavy Graflex, scurried alongside the column, firing off flash bulbs.

A short, overweight man wearing an expensive topcoat, his gray hair stirring in the morning breeze, shouted at the parade. "Take the Japs to hell out'a here and don't bring them back." The man began clapping his hands in an attempt to lead the sidewalk gawkers in applause. The office workers moved off, leaving him clapping alone.

The detainees were marched into and through the Canadian Pacific Rail Road Terminal then down a long flight of open stairs to the trackside. There they were ordered aboard a string of reactivated Trans Continental day coaches. Isao sat next to a window and began struggling with the lowered shade. "You there," a uniformed policeman at the end of the car barked at him. "Take your hands off that blind. Windows are to remain covered until the train is out of the city. The rest of you," he called out, "leave those windows as they are."

Isao lowered the blind and went into his pocket for his gardening schedule. The coaches were cool and suddenly very quiet, the air heavy with the scent of decay. As he sat studying the notes, he began deliberately drawing a line through each scheduled item, most of which were soon crossed out. When he came to the last page, the end of his spring planning, he folded each page and ripped it into paper shreds, the torn pieces falling to the car floor like dying petals. The rumors circulating through the Detention Center for the past weeks were true, though Isao remained unaware that he was among the first shipment of Japanese detainees being sent to the prisoner of war compound at Angler, Ontario. There would be no gardens there.

As the train lurched with a clash of couplings and began to move, Isao looked to the rear of the car. The policeman was gone, allowing him to raise the blind enough to permit a lookout through the soiled glass. For a few minutes he saw only standing freight cars flashing past as the train gathered speed. The train passed through a grassy draw and in an instant — so brief that he later questioned if it was but a trick of his mind – he saw her. Yuki, standing in the knee deep grass, his two sons and Soju at her side, was waving frantically.

Through the coming months of monotonous confinement in Angler, Isao would return to his doubts, questioning again if what he had seen was a trick of his imagination. Yet he continued returning to the picture over and over again of his family waving blindly at the passing train.

Chapter 25 Orders

Michael returned to high school for the spring semester to complete his junior year following an empty Christmas season that had dragged on like a painful dental appointment. He wore his Christmas sweater for the first day of class in an effort to please his mother, though he was growing so fast it was already a size too small. While convinced his days with Soju were beyond repair, he surveyed the chattering juniors, and realized there were no Japanese kids. It was as if Pat Tanaka had never played on the soccer team, though Pat had been their best goal scorer since the ninth grade. There had never been anyone who pitched like Toshio Wakabayashi did when they won the inter-school softball championship at Jesuit High. Though their pictures as school scholastic champions remained posted on the hall bulletin board, it was as if there had never been a Tanaka, a Kisawa, a Matsushima, or a Wakabayashi. The Japanese had become a missing page from the high school yearbook and Soju had vanished with them.

Michael attempted to act as if nothing was missing from his life. After all, he had convinced himself, Soju had turned away from him in the rain at the Detention Center. It was Soju who had pleaded with him to leave her alone and accused him as the cause of her father's arrest. Intent on reinforcing this sense of being abandoned, he silently repeated her words during his days of sullen silence. He went days without shaving, and when he ate it was disinterestedly and only at his mother's insistence. For a time, he even tried resurrecting his visits with his father, yet even there found himself alone.

But by the end of February, swallowing what remained of his pride, he found himself heading toward the Wakabayashi's front gate. What remained of the previous autumn's leaves danced in the warm Chinook Wind along the unpaved road skirting Third Avenue. Isao Wakabayashi's groomed garden had been invaded by tufts of weeds and crabgrass; the sagging gate hung aimlessly from a single hinge. Undecided, he hesitated at the gate when suddenly Toshio appeared at the front door. "What are you doing here?" he called out.

"I have to see Soju," Michael opened the gate and walked up to the house.

"It's not a good idea for you to be seen talking to any of us. Look at this and decide if you want to hang around." Toshio unfolded a paper in his hands and passed it to Michael. The opening lines read:

"Every person of the Japanese race shall be at his usual place of residence each day before sunset and shall remain there until sunrise the following day.

No person of the Japanese race shall have in his possession or use any motor vehicle, camera, radio receiving set, firearm ammunition or explosive."

The bulletin was signed by the minister of justice.

"That's the law, Mike. You still want to talk to your Japanese girlfriend? The Mounties are probably coming to arrest us any minute. You don't want to be here when they come. I remember that day the cops chased us off the beach," he added deliberately. "You weren't so hot to talk to my sister then."

"She told you about that?" Michael felt the shame rush to his face. "I'd do about anything if I could have that day over again, Toshio. I have been ashamed ever since. I guess I was scared. Maybe just stupid. There were things in my head that day that I can't deny are scaring me right now, things you don't know anything about. But they don't change how I feel about Soju." He shrugged. "I don't have any excuse, Tosh. But I have got to see your sister, now more than ever." Toshio folded his document, and turned back into the house without answering. At that moment, as if in answer to Michael's pleading, Soju appeared at the door. Seeing one another, they hesitated a moment before he took her in his arms. Together they started down the street towards Fraser's Warf.

A week later, Michael arrived home from school and casually picked up the afternoon newspaper from the porch. The front page headline started his hands shaking. 'Japs Rounded Up.' On the front page a Provincial Police detachment was pictured herding Japanese into the Exhibition Park Animal Pavilion. Slowly, as if he were disengaging an unexploded bomb, he unfolded the paper. Below the fold a picture showed a line of impounded Japanese cars and trucks. Far down the line was the open-box Ford belonging to Soju's father. On the inside pages photographs of seized Japanese fishing boats topped a story detailing the government- ordered evacuation of all Japanese from the West Coast. Those interred were to be held in the livestock barns at Exhibition Park, awaiting relocation to camps in the Interior. Michael put the paper onto the table and left the house.

Michael felt a wave of helplessness on reading the sign posted to the front door that read: 'To Let'. Someone had imposed the letter 'I' in dung-colored mud in the center of the word so that it read: 'To-I-Let." A fluttering fragment of soiled towel hanging from the clothes line was the only evidence the Wakabayashis had ever lived there.

Michael was about to turn away when a shrill voice brought him up short. "Hey you! What you lookin' for?" A pimple-faced young man, not much more than a boy himself, stepped down from the porch and stumbled, his clipboard flying through the air. "Shit," he swore, landing in the gravel, glaring up at Michael as if he had been tripped. "What's your business here?" he demanded.

"I'm looking for my friends. They live here." Michael picked up the fallen clipboard; the man snatched it from his hand as if it contained war secrets.

"Is that so? Well, nobody lives here. But you probably knew that already, eh?" The man brushed his trousers while eyeing Michael skeptically. "You know you are trespassing, eh? This is government property. The British Columbia Security Commission seized this place and you got no business prowling around here looking for so-called friends. Now get your ass out'a here before I call the cops."

Michael sensed the man was mostly bluster and ignored the threat. "All I am asking is where the Wakabayashis are? Why can't you at least answer my question? What's happened to them?"

"I told you, there ain't nobody living here and there won't be until somebody gets that stinking pile of shit out of the kitchen." He glared at Michael with open suspicion. "Some smart-ass has taken a dump in the middle of the kitchen floor. But you wouldn't know anything about that, I suppose?"

"No. And I can tell you that the Wakabayashis wouldn't do anything like that either."

The man accepted the look of disgust on Michael's face as evidence he spoke the truth. "I didn't say your friends crapped in there," he said. "But some son-of-a-bitch did." His blustering voice suddenly eased. He glanced at his clipboard.

"You are looking for the Japs who lived here, eh?" He began leafing through the pages on the board. "All I can tell you is, if the damn trains are still running, that bunch, the Wakabay-what-ever you call 'em, could be on their way to Hope or Slocan or maybe even fucking Moooo-se Jaaaw." The man laughed contemptuously at the pain on Michael's face.

"Come on kid. It ain't the end of the world. I hear they got a bunch of Japs locked up in the horse barns out at Exhibition Park. Your pals may still be out there," he added. "Plenty of shit for 'em out there, eh?" Michael failed to smile. "You need a sense of humor, kid. There's a war on and I got work to do. You want to do your bit and clean up that kitchen? Make it fit for real Canadians to call home? We got Bohunks comin' in from the Prairies to work in the shipyards, and they have no place to live. We got soldiers knocking up their girlfriends before they ship out. None of 'em got a place to live. How about it? Even a dump like this could look like home to some people once we get rid of the turd in the kitchen." Michael shook his head without answering and turned away.

Chapter 26 Confessions

Eileen Costello had been standing behind the living room curtains for the better part of an hour, watching and waiting for Michael when he stepped over the knee high front gate. She held her breath without moving, praying to Mary Mother of God that she was completely hidden behind the curtain as she listened to his footsteps on the porch. Through the patterns in the stiff lace she watched him come in the front door and start up the stairs to his room. She had rehearsed the confrontation she was determined to have with her son, only now she hesitated. Listening to the sounds of his moving about upstairs she heard the toilet flush followed by the door closing to Michael's bedroom. There was the soft thump of his shoes landing beside the bed, then all went quiet. Swiftly, almost furtively, she genuflected before the icon of Jesus with the bleeding heart in the front hall, and with a deep, resolute breath, started up the stairs.

As the door to his room opened quietly, Michael sat up with a start, expecting to see his father in the doorway. Eileen Costello could see the disappointment on his face as he fell back on the bed.

"Michael," she began in a tentative voice. "Is this a good time for you and me to have a talk?" Michael sighed with a look that made her regret having opened his door without knocking. "I thought you might be sleeping," she explained. "I was just intending to peek in to see…" Michael said nothing to ease her confusion. "Michael?" She was stammering, intimidated by his disparaging look that seemed to silently demand: 'What do you want now'. Eileen had lived with that look from Eamon Costello, a look that warned: 'I'd just as soon walk out of this house as listen to you.'

She stiffened, reminding herself this was not her husband. "Michael. I'm tired of watching you moping about the house. I want to know what it is that's bothering you. I just hope it doesn't have anything to do with that Japanese girl. Does it?" She was as close as she dared to challenge him without revealing that she had seen Frank Glasheen's photos. Michael turned his face to the wall. "It isn't healthy for a boy your age to be carrying on this way," she added, mustering a note of parental authority. "You won't be finishing high school, much less be given consideration for seminary, if you keep on like this." She sat on the edge of his bed as lightly as she could and placed a hand possessively on his shoulder, speaking softly. "If it's that girl, she belongs with her own people, son. She's going to meet one of her own kind in one of those camps. Dougal Mulhern says the government has built brand-new homes for them in the Interior."

"I intend to marry her," Michael muttered defiantly into his pillow. For an instant, his mother was tempted to laugh, to tousle his hair and tell him how foolish he sounded. Had it been Seamus or even Joseph she might have done just that. The temperament of his father in this son caused her to check her tongue.

"You are not even out of high school," she protested.

"I'm eighteen in November, and when I am," he added turning to face her, "I'm joining up. And if Soju will have me, I am going to marry her before I go overseas."

Eileen felt the wind burst through her lips. It was all she could do to catch her breath, the bed suddenly wobbling unsteadily beneath her. She steadied herself with a hand on the headboard and stood up. Recovering enough to trust her voice she attempted to speak as if she were comforting someone in mourning. "Have you spoken with the girl about this, son? Or to her parents? Remember, they are Japs, and..." The word escaped without thought, bearing an ugly, heavy sound. "Japanese. I meant to say Japanese. I don't resent those people, Michael. But, I don't imagine Japanese mothers welcome white boys running off with their teenage daughters more than I do their daughters running off with my son." She forced a high-pitched, nervous laugh.

"Soju is better than I am," Michael said, turning from his pillow. "She would never have behaved toward me the way I have treated her. Twice she asked for my help. She asked me to say one word on behalf of her father. I turned my back on her, because I was afraid, mother. I was afraid of people like you who call her a Jap. I was afraid of Chief Mulhern and his police friends. Afraid they might take away your police pension if I told them they were wrong about her father. All I had to do was say one good thing. The Wakabayashis are good people. Instead, I gave myself a million crazy reasons to turn *my* back on her when she needed me. I am a coward, mother, and I am ashamed of myself."

"Exactly what was it she asked you to do, Michael?" Eileen dropped heavily onto the bed, suddenly frightened by what she was hearing; visions of Frank Glasheen's jingoistic warnings flashed in her mind. This was her son these foreigners were dragging into their dangerous business. She began to imagine a story that was turning her stomach in knots. "Michael, you are not trying to tell me you have been involved in anything serious with this girl. I mean, have you?"

He answered without speaking a word, the look in his eyes an unspoken answer that made his mother clap a hand over mouth. "My God, Michael! No." Their eyes continued challenging one another, the truth not only self-evident but confirmed in his resolute, defiant stare. The silence was interrupted by the sound of Seamus's boots on the stairs.

"Michael," his mother whispered hurriedly. "That girl is gone now. It's over. And you have to finish school. If you are telling me what I think you are telling me, you must go talk to Father Lavoie. Michael?" Righteousness made her bold. "I am asking you. Have you been to confession?"

"No."

"Then you must go, son. For the sake of your immortal soul and for your mother who would rather spend eternity in hell than be in heaven one minute without her sons. You must go."

"Chief Mulhern said Soju has been sent to some place in the Interior. Sandon, I think. Anyway, that's where I'm going." He got up from the bed as Seamus appeared in the doorway.

The minute he entered the room, Seamus, who shared a bed and secrets with his younger brother, sensed what was happening. He wore his new Seaforth Highlanders uniform and looked taller and older than his 19 years. The army tunic buttoned tightly across his chest, the Highlanders' white puttees wrapped around the tops of his big black boots, and the wedge tartan cap changed everything about Seamus. He was even encouraging a pale, tobacco-colored mustache that struggled for recognition across his upper lip to reinforce his role as the man of the house. He read the look of despair on his mother's face.

"Uh-no." Seamus shot a humorous glance at his younger brother. "You told her? Right? About the girl?"

"Sort of."

"Everything?"

Michael shrugged.

Eileen Costello braced her hands on her hips, "Seamus. You knew about this business and never told me?" Seamus raised his eyebrows in mock fear and turned to his brother.

"Come on, kid. It's time both of us got out of here for a while. I'll treat you to a movie. Let Betty Grable's legs take your mind off that heartache of yours."

Chapter 27 A Call for Help

Chuichi Otake had a premonition that his love affair with the October Lady was coming to an end long before the morning when the battery radio static cleared long enough to hear the words of the Japanese attack on Pearl Harbor. His fears had grown with each new trouble. The engine head gasket bursting on the Vivian Marine, the most recent, was followed by the Canadian Coast Guard rounding up all the northern Japanese fishing boats from the coastal waters. Working as far north as the Naas River, the northern fishing fleet was taken under tow in a three-day convoy to the mouth of the Fraser River. Under the authority of the Canadian Navy, Otake's wooden-hulled double ender was impounded ten days following the Pearl Harbor bombing. By June, a good number of that fishing fleet lay off the banks of the Fraser estuary, some floundering in the shore mud like a pod of beached whales. Otake's October Lady lay on the outer edge of the fleet, her stained under-belly resting on the riverbed at each low tide.

The morning of June 18, 1942, a day with a stiff wind riffling the mud-brown river, Chief Constable Dougal Mulhern looked out over the water. He eased his large body out of the rear of the police car and shook his head sadly at the sight of the crippled fleet. "It's a damn shame, Dempsey," he growled, turning to his uniformed driver. "Look at that mess. A strong tide and this damn wind could blow the lot into the Gulf."

Mulhern began scanning the outer edges of the flotilla for the man he was to meet when he caught sight of the khaki-colored uniform of the Mounted Policeman waving from the outer edges of the flotilla. The man was a stranger to the chief constable, who liked to believe he knew every man in the local detachment. "Must be one of those inter-agency birds brought in to tell us how to do our business," he muttered.

"For the love of Jeeesus, Dempsey," he asked the driver. "What's that lunatic wavin' his arms about? You don't suppose he expects me to go out there?" Mulhern dreaded the thought of venturing out across the tilting fleet, some of which lay partially submerged in pools of shallow river water. Dempsey nodded with a dubious shake of his head but said nothing. For a long moment the chief refused to move, his jaw clamped, defiantly staring out at the man. Finally, muttering what sounded to Dempsey like a prayer, he started toward the boat nearest the shore with a confession. "Keep a sharp eye on me, Dempsey. I can't swim a stroke."

"Neither can I," Dempsey replied, momentarily refusing to follow. "The two of us would go down like stones."

"Aaah, then God forgive us for being the fools we are," the chief answered. With one arm locked in the arm of his driver, Mulhern began maneuvering the two of them from one boat deck to the next.

The RCMP sergeant, clutching the mast of a boat rocking at the outer reaches of the flotilla, kept urging them on. "It's safe enough, chief," he shouted. "The water is no more than waist deep if you stay out of the pools."

"I have half a mind to give that bugger a taste of his bloody waist deep pools," Mulhern muttered, each step of his heavy body sending the bilge water beneath him sloshing ominously in the bowels of the boat underfoot. "Did you ever set eyes on such a god-awful mess, Dempsey? And that madman out there waving his arms like he was chasing a fart from church," he cursed, his grip tightening shamelessly on Constable Donavan Dempsey's arm. "It's the devil himself that's calling us to a watery grave, Dempsey. This is like crossing the River Styx in a leaky canoe. I swear I can feel the grieving souls of the bloody Jap fishermen we stole these boats from sloshing around underfoot. We have no business with this nonsense, Dempsey," he said. "It's as plain as the wind in my ear." Dempsey swiped the nervous sweat from his face. He wasn't listening.

The RCMP sergeant released his grip on the mast to offer a hand to the tottering policemen as they lunged onto the deck of the October Lady. "Walker. Sergeant Barry Walker, special investigations. I am on assignment with the Vancouver Detachment." The chief, still clinging to Dempsey, ignored the man's outstretched hand. The October Lady was floating in some six feet of river with a foot of mud-brown water sloshing in her bilge. The anger of fear put a bite in Mulhern's reply.

"I just hope to God you have a decent reason for getting us out here? Why the hell we couldn't do this ashore is beyond me." He let go of Dempsey's arm and raised his shoulders imperiously to his full six-foot-six stature. The Mounted Policeman grinned in triumph, too pleased with himself to catch the temper in Mulhern's voice. Mulhern was quick to note the man's gray hair beneath the stiff peak of his RCMP hat, his clean-shaven jaw and the parade-bright brass buttons of his tunic. Too damn spic and span for a full duty man, Mulhern judged, pegging Walker as one of those the RCMP had commissioned out of retirement. He had no trouble taking an Irishman's instant dislike to the sergeant's British-army styled mustache.

"Chief, we needed you out here because we want you to be as committed to this investigation of ours as we are. It is important that you see what our investigation has uncovered." He was speaking in a crisp command voice as if he were lecturing a recruit. "These boats may look a little weather beaten, but the government intends to get them out fishing again by fall. This time under the hands of real Canadians," he announced proudly.

"Real Canadians, is it?" the chief added innocently. "I seem to recall a monument in Stanley Park that says that out of 196 British Columbia Japs who volunteered for the Great War of 1914 to 1918, there were 145 killed or wounded. Real Canadians? They gave the Military Medal of Bravery to that fellow, Sergeant Masumi Misui, in 1917," Mulhern added with continuing innocence. "It had something to do with Vimey Ridge, if I remember. Real Canadians, you say?"

"That was another time, and another war," the sergeant answered coldly.

"It was indeed," Mulhern grumbled. "And by the way things are going, we could well lose this one."

The RCMP sergeant looked visibly shocked. "Surely, you don't believe that, chief? So long as we do our jobs, there isn't a doubt we will win." The sergeant's tone came as close to a reprimand as he dared, suddenly aware he was close to touching off Mulhern's temper.

Sergeant Barry Walker, Mulhern would later learn, was indeed a thirty-five years service RCMP constable called out of retirement and given his stripes at the beginning of the war. His every word rang with the authority of a man who has never had any. As if to demonstrate his new-found authority, the sergeant lifted his shining, mud-caked boot and slammed it against the October Lady's wheelhouse door. The door flung open, torn loose from the door frame.

"What'd you do that for?" Mulhern asked incredulously. "You ruined the bloody door. All you had to do..." He sighed shaking his head in open disgust.

"We are going to have to rework these boats from bow to stern, chief. A new door is the least of our challenges, eh? Besides, it gives a man a good feeling to take a kick at anything that smacks of the Japs. Right?" The chief cast a look of despair at Dempsey. "Technically, these boats still belong to the Japs," the Mounted policeman added. "Repairs come out of the owners' reimbursements, if there are any. "Now chief, I want you to take a look below." It was becoming apparent to Mulhern the sergeant had lost sight of the fact he was addressing the city's top police officer. "See for yourself the dirty work that's been going on."

Mulhern peered into the wheelhouse of the October Lady. A burnt pan containing what appeared to be a crusted circle of rice rested on a rusting kerosene stove. Barely visible in the shadows of the cabin he made out a tightly bound bundle of clothing tucked under the helm. Parts of the dismantled engine and what remained of a shattered radio receiver lay scattered over the single bunk.

"You see?" the sergeant exclaimed triumphantly. "That's a radio transmitter you are looking at down there. We suspect this boat was being used to carry on communication with Jap submarines off shore."

Mulhern's eyebrows rose, his face a mask of courteous sympathy. "What I'm seeing, sergeant, is the remains of a dismantled single cylinder engine, a pot of moldy rice on a cold stove, and a pile of junk. That junk may once have been some kind of radio receiver. But if what I see there was ever anything more than that, I'll swallow the buttons off this bloody tunic, so help me God. Don't you think, man, if there was ever a transmitter aboard any of these tubs, it would have been at the bottom long before you got here? Even you must know there's hardly enough juice put out by that one lung kicker to run a flashlight, much less some kind of transmitter. Furthermore, constable," — he smiled with his intentional slip — "if the beggar who manned this tub had nerve enough to sail her a hundred miles off shore to hook up with a Japanese submarine, then you and I and the Yanks are in for a helluva war. Any man brave enough to do that would have no fear of dying. And that would make him a damn sight more dangerous than most of us, you can be damn sure."

"Best you get one thing straight right now, constable." The chief's voice took on the cold tone of command that had carried him through the ranks. "I've no interest in sending my men rummaging through these waterlogged fishing boats, sorting through bundles of underwear, looking for espionage. You can think what you like about my lack of patriotism. We are not about to be doing your work."

The sergeant's face flushed. "It's sergeant, Chief. Sergeant Barry Walker. And you might like to know we have an informant, who works right here on the docks, who has brought us hard evidence proving the owner of this vessel was in continual contact with Japanese seamen calling into Vancouver. What's more, our informant has helped us uncover an extensive file of coastal navigation charts aboard these boats as well as photographic evidence of Japanese strategic intelligence gathering; the details I'm not at liberty to discuss."

"Strategic intelligence? And coastal charts, you say?" The chief looked to his driver with mock concern. "What do you think of that, Dempsey? That's strategic intelligence, the sergeant is talking about," he said softly. "Now I'm no marine expert, Sergeant, but even I can tell you that any man can buy charts covering the entire British Columbia coast, fathom for fathom in any ship chandler's office from here to Hong Kong or in any other major port in the world. British Columbia harbor charts are on file in every shipping company that ever sailed a ship into Vancouver. Now I'll say it as clearly as I know how so that there won't be any misunderstanding. I don't have enough men to keep the pimps and thieves from working Pender Street. I can't keep a lid on the Prairie Bohunks peddling bootleg poison in the shipyards. I don't have enough men on the force to arrest the cheats selling phony ration coupons on street corners. And I sure as hell don't have men to go looking for Japanese spies among these fishermen. Is that understood?"

Mulhern dusted his ham-like hands together. "I have heard it all, including stories of Japanese admirals working as Powell Street barbers. What in hell an admiral can hope to achieve in a barbershop is beyond this simple policeman. And fishing boats feeding herring to enemy submarines?" The chief pushed back his cap and rubbed his head before gripping Dempsey's arm and turning the two of them toward the shore. He was about to step off the deck when his eye caught the name printed alongside the stern of the vessel.

"This is the October Lady," he exclaimed with the wonder of a man discovering an old friend in an unexpected place. "Damn it, Dempsey. I know the man who owns this boat. Known him for years." He turned to the RCMP sergeant. "Sergeant. You say the man who owns this boat is a spy?" The chief gave a derisive burst of laughter. "That would be a man by the name of Otake. Otake has been cooperating with us for years. Practically a member of the Vancouver department. Spying for the Emperor of Japan?" He smiled sympathetically. "You have just kicked the hell out of the wrong boat."

The sergeant's aging skin began to color, the thin red veins rising beneath his cheeks. "This investigation has Ministry of Defense priority, Chief," he snapped. "Frankly, I assure you there are authorities who will be disappointed to hear of your attitude."

Mulhern wheeled. "My attitude? Listen to me, constable," he said, again intentionally demoting the sergeant. "I was walking Powell Street keeping an eye on these people when you were scattering horse dung in the bush. These fishermen have never been troublemakers. They kept their noses damn clean. Most risked their necks just putting a boat on the water. To a man, they walked softly just to keep their lines from being cut and their nets from being torn apart. Their biggest mistake was working their tails off alongside men who figured the river owed them a living."

The chief turned to leave again, almost bumping chest to chest against a lanky stranger wearing bib overalls and a steel Tommy helmet. The sergeant's expression assumed an immediate I-told-you-so smile as he reached to accept the man's outstretched hand.

"Well, Chief. Let me introduce you to Frank Glasheen. Frank is our informant on the river."

"Informer?" the chief's eyes stripped Glasheen as he would a suspect under interrogation.

"Glasheen, Civil Defense." Glasheen saluted, snapping off his identity with military briskness. Mulhern ignored his extended hand. He had seen that flat-toothed grin before, the recollection stirring a note of caution as he searched his memory.

"Glasheen?" The chief repeated cautiously. Glasheen continued to offer his hand, assuming the chief had failed to see it in the first place. "Haven't I run into you or that name somewhere? Aaah, yes. You were an acquaintance of Eamon Costello's." The chief's voice grew cold as his recollections began to fall into place. "Didn't I see you at the Costello home the day of the funeral?" Glasheen's confident smile began to fade. He whipped a wooden match over the haunch of his coveralls, lit a cigarette, coolly inhaling a long drag.

"Sure, I knew Eamon Costello, if that's what you are saying," he answered casually. "I call on the widow, now and then." This he said with a subtle grin as if he were letting Mulhern in on a secret.

"I seem to remember," Mulhern replied dryly.

Glasheen was beginning to catch the chill in the chief's reply and added hastily. "I look out for the lady now and then. Out of friendship to the deceased, so to speak. We go all the way back to the Old Country, Costello and me. I know the family quite well. Her sons, now, that's another story."

"The sons? Then it was your work I saw. The photographs? Michael Costello with the Japanese girl? It's you that's been taking those pictures of the young ones?" Detective Vigna had spotted the Costello name in the RCMP report and had brought the photos to Mulhern.

Glasheen began working his cigarette back and forth over his lip. "You might say I have been keeping an eye on things, yes. We can't expect the sergeant's people to cover everything without civilian support. Can we, sergeant?" Glasheen offered his flat-tooth grin to the RCMP sergeant, searching for an endorsement. "That wasn't just any Jap girl we caught the Costello boy messin' with," he said. "That girl's old man has been locked up, a prisoner-of-war. But you'd know that already, Chief, if you saw my report."

Mulhern was beginning to feel queasy, the rising river rocking the boat beneath his feet. His temper had the blood pounding in his head. He began very softly, speaking in a dangerously tolerant tone. "What you may not be aware of, Glasheen, is that two of the Costello boys are in the army. One of them is overseas, likely fighting the Germans while we stand here gabbing. The other is in the Seaforth Highland Regiment. And that's his baby brother, Michael, you have been photographing, the boy in your pictures with the Japanese girl. He is from a good Roman Catholic family. His mother and I believe he is likely on his way to becoming a priest." The chief's voice lost its restraint as he turned to the RCMP sergeant.

"I'll be leaving you and your informer here to continue your investigation, sergeant," he said with cutting sarcasm. "You can call headquarters if there's anything else we can help you with. And I suggest you tell your informer here to get his head out of his arse and stop wasting his time and ours photographing children." The chief bowed his great neck ominously, willing to charge at the least provocation.

***

By the time Mulhern set foot on the riverbank he was near blind with the tension throbbing in his temples. He dropped heavily into the back seat of the police Buick, signaling the policeman at the wheel with a weary wave of his hand. "Get us the hell out of here, Dempsey. Those damn fools have given me a bejesus of a pain in the ass." Dempsey turned the car onto Granville Street. "Take us to Kitsilano. I have a stop to make to see Eamon Costello's widow. You know the house."

The chief leaned back and closed his eyes, wondering if what he had just seen and heard had anything to do with Eileen Costello's begging him to stop by. He had forgotten the promise until he ran into Glasheen. The car rumbled over the Granville Street car tracks, each thump of the tires on the metal rails jolting the pain behind his eyes. He tried to recall the snapshots Detective Sergeant Vigna had laid out before him. Michael cozy with the Jap girl. He remembered that. If his mother saw those, and Mulhern was convinced Glasheen had seen to it she had, the pictures would have been enough to account for the anxiety in her voice.

The chief slumped into the depths of his greatcoat and with a series of deep sighs attempted to rid himself of his queasy stomach. As always whenever he became involved with Eamon's kin, his thoughts began to drift back to the night Eamon died, a night he had spent years trying to forget. He would keep an eye out for Michael. That was one thing he could still do for the love of Eamon. For now, though, he had to deal with Eileen Costello's call for help.

***

Chief Mulhern's massive body seemed to crowd everything out of the compact Costello living room. He waved aside Eileen's attempt to lift the heavy greatcoat from his shoulders. "No, no. I can stay only for a minute or two. It would take me half the day to fasten the buttons," he protested, collapsing heavily into Eamon's leather chair. The chief's practiced eye searched the living room for traces of his old friend as he gripped the leather arms of the chair, feeling Eamon's presence in the soft scent of the worn leather. His glance went to the ornate floor-stand ashtray alongside the chair. Mulhern once owned one just like it. Eamon had admired the thing in a Pender Street pawn shop. When the shop owner told him to take it as a gift, Eamon refused unless the pawn broker could come up with one for Mulhern as well. He did, and Eamon delivered it in a brand-new box with the large, ember glass bowl wrapped in tissue. Mulhern smiled recalling the pain on the pawnbroker's face when the man realized Costello's none too subtle suggestion was going to cost him double. Mulhern's wife wouldn't have the thing in the house and, though he never mentioned it to Eamon, she donated the ashtray to the Knights of Columbus rummage sale.

"I see you have a new photo of your boys." The chief indicated the softly muted color portrait of the three Costello boys on the mantle above the fireplace, with Joseph in his khaki uniform.

"I had them sit together before Joseph left," Eileen replied proudly. Facing the boys from the opposite end of the mantle was an early picture of Eileen in an ebony frame. It was taken when she was in her late teens or early twenties, her eyes gazing off into her future, her stiff-back pose and the heavy crucifix at her bosom testifying to her Irish morality. It took but a quick glance for the chief to tell the picture had been taken in a portrait studio in the old country, probably Derry where she grew up. That pose was common back then. The photographer would fasten a brace to the subject's back to square the shoulders and to help tilt the chin, allowing the camera to capture that far-away look. You could see the same pose almost every day in the newspaper obituary columns. Mulhern sensed he had seen this picture of Eileen before, only something about it appeared out of place. Then it came to him. There had been another half to the portrait; the half with Eamon standing equally straight behind his wife's chair. Mulhern leaned forward, examining the portrait closely. There was the man's hand on her shoulder. The rest of Eamon had been cropped out of the picture.

"Aah, Mother of Mercy, it's a relief to sit," the chief sighed.

Eileen watched him settle deeper into the chair, then with a nod of approval she hurried from the room, calling over her shoulder from the kitchen. "Have you had a difficult day, Dougal?" She was back carrying a mug of whiskey and hot water before he could answer. "It's a touch of Tullamore Dew, Dougal. Eamon's whiskey. It's a chilly day out there; you'll need something to warm the cockles of your heart." Mulhern's hands closed eagerly around the mug. "Seeing you there in Eamon's chair, you in your uniform and all, it's like turning back the hands of time," she said.

"You always had a knack for understanding a man's needs, Eileen," the chief said, taking an appreciative, loud sip of the hot whiskey. So much of the Irish crept back into his talk when he was with his own. Mulhern had trained his tongue to harden his soft brogue until it could pass for the clipped protestant Irish, a manner of speaking more acceptable at City Hall as well as among the

Scottish Presbyterians making up the core of the force. "And how are the boys? Soon it'll be Seamus that's off to the war, I suppose?"

"That's true," she said pensively. "Then I'll have only Michael here at home."

Eileen's lips pinched nervously. She had begun to suspect the chief was beating around the bush. He knew of Seamus' orders. They had talked about it in detail on the telephone. This hashing over things was a game her Eamon had played. It was an old country way for men to deal with women, dancing about with a lot of meaningless jabber to avoid getting down to serious talk. Well, she could play at that as long as he liked if it made the man happy putting her on like that. So be it. She smiled, concealing her impatience while Mulhern continued to sip the whiskey. Finally, his eyes came up over the edge of the mug and he peered quizzically across the living room.

"Well. Get on with it. What is it that's got you so fussed up?"

"It's good of you to come, Dougal. It's Michael. I'm worried about the boy. It seems he thinks he's serious about a Japanese girl." Eileen spoke as if she were revealing her son had been stricken with a terminal disease. Mulhern's quizzical gaze bore into her, his nose never far from the lip of the whiskey cup, his grey eyes revealing nothing.

"Izzat so," he replied softly. "You know the Japanese are all gone from here, Eileen. They have been shipped away from the coast. Whoever this girl of Michael's is, you can relax. She's not about to be seeing the lad for some time, eh."

"Dougal, the boy is seventeen, going on eighteen." Eileen Costello was determined not to be brushed aside by this reassurance. "And it wouldn't sit well with him if he knew I was asking you to take a hand in his affairs. He's much like his father that way."

"That I understand," the chief answered solemnly. "Getting to be a difficult lad, is he?"

"It's not that I'm holding any negative memories of Eamon, may God rest his soul. It's only..." She hesitated, struggling with what she wanted to say and wanting to say it right. "This girl is Japanese, Dougal, and I must confess, in some ways she seems to have been good for him. It's because of her that Michael took to bathing two or three times a week. That hasn't happened since she's been gone."

Eileen began twisting her hands nervously. "When you see him, Dougal, you will know what I mean. He's taken to wearing his hair slicked down like his dad. Looking at him I can't believe how much he's taking on so many of the ways of his father."

"A girl can change a man," the chief said carefully.

Eileen's voice dropped to a whisper. "Dougal. He's as much as told me he's been up to serious business with this girl. Now he says he intends to marry her."

The chief lowered the cup with a look of surprise. "Does he now? That would be a kettle of fish, wouldn't it? What with you and Father Lavoie praying the lad has a calling."

"If not the priesthood, Dougal, then God willing, Michael could someday be taking up with a girl like your Juanita. You know how Eamon would have had a song to sing about that."

"Ahh," the chief muttered. "There's nothing would please me more. I've always had a place in my heart for Michael. But this business of fallin' in love, dear lady," he said, shaking his ponderous head. "That's much like being called to a vocation. There's a voice that's speaking to a man when he is smitten by a woman, a voice only those in love can hear. It's best to leave such things up to the Almighty. Isn't that right, now?" The chief swallowed the last of his hot whiskey and shifted in the chair, positioning himself to rise up.

"Dougal, I know the girl's family has been relocated." Eileen rushed her words, seeing he was about to leave. "Michael told me. Her family is probably in one of those internment camps in the Interior. He is talking of taking the train up there to see her. To marry her." Her voice began to crack, adding a helpless plea to her words. "You know I would accept the girl and do my best to love her. But it's a decent girl Michael needs. I wouldn't know what to feed this one, her being Japanese and all. And those Orientals all look so, so foreign," she added, her voice suddenly charged with morality.

The chief replied with a slight nod, hoping that would suffice.

"I'd feel like a chicken that had hatched a duckling with a girl like that in the family," Eileen went on. "For my sake, Dougal. For Eamon's. You can stop the boy from doing something he's going to regret the rest of his life. Michael is a child in these things. When he's older and has a chance to know himself, then he can be thinking about women and I won't be meddling."

The chief squared his shoulders, heaved himself to his feet, and handed her the empty mug, his silver-buttoned greatcoat hovering over her. "There's a war on, Eileen. Boys grow up fast in wartime. It's not like our day in the Old Country. You are asking me to interfere with a man's life."

"It's my baby's life," she snapped.

Mulhern studied her anxious face for a moment before he fumbled in his coat for a small, leather-bound notebook. "And what's this girl's name?" He wrote Soju's name in large print. "And the camp, do you know the name of the camp?"

"Somewhere near a place called Slocan or Kaslo, I think."

The chief considered what he had written with a long, contemplative hum. "It happens I have had some police matters with an RCMP sergeant concerning the Japanese. This morning as a matter of fact. Maybe, just maybe mind, the Mounties could manage something, though the man I met today wasn't too pleased with the send-off I gave him. Strange you're calling me today. By the by, I met a Mister Glasheen while I was attending to some police business on the river. You remember him, do you?" The chief didn't miss the rush of color to her face.

"I buy fish from him," she replied coldly.

Mulhern considered pressing the matter a little farther, but her response had told him all he cared to know. She had seen the pictures. He stepped closer and placed a heavy arm around her shoulder. "Where have all the years gone, dear girl? Seems only yesterday your Eamon was telling me how happy he was with me makin' acting sergeant and all. Acting sergeant, mind," he said, marveling at the thought of how far he had risen in the force. Eileen could see by the look in his eyes that his thoughts were of another time. "Eamon was close to making detective himself. But you know all that. The department gave you his badge because of his dyin' in the line of duty, retired it forever, eh." The chief twisted the visor of his hat in his hands, tears glistening in the corners of his eyes. He leaned forward and kissed her cheek.

"And I am forever grateful to you for all of that, Dougal," Eileen whispered. "For the pension and for whatever else you did to spare the boys and myself." The hard, bitter look returned to her eyes. "Did you know he bought her a ring, Dougal? I found it when I was putting the rosary in his pocket. It was in a small, velvet box. So I opened it and then put it back in his pocket, sayin' nothing about it, thinking it was for me. After a few days, I asked him. 'And who was the ring for, Eamon?' I said. He looked at me with those green eyes that told you he was lying before he opened his mouth. 'The ring that was in your pocket the other day?' I said. He blushed. It was easy to catch him blushing with his sad, pale face. He said it was a ring that had been stolen. Police property, he said. He was returning it to the owner. But I could tell. It was for her." Eileen made no effort to keep the pain from her voice.

"And you, Dougal Mulhern," she said, stepping back a pace, leaving her whispering tale like something best forgotten, "May Mary the Mother of God protect you from the temptations of the street. I pray that for you, day by day."

Chapter 28 A Questionable Arrival

Soju Wakabayashi blinked, blinded by the light flooding the cabin, momentarily unable to free her thoughts from the last vestiges of a restless sleep. She was unaware that she had awakened to one of the rare moments of winter sunshine in the Sandon Japanese Resettlement Camp. This early sunlight, stealthily creeping through the trees like a Peeping Tom, would disappear long before all but the very early risers could claim to having witnessed its passing. Soju sat up into a world bathed in surreal light, her mind suspended somewhere between dying and dreaming. The thought passed her mind that she had frozen during the night and the bright light surrounding her was being cast by Michael's unseen angels come to carry her from the drafty mining shack.

Tentatively she shifted her legs beneath the coarse institutional blanket, slowly confirming each detail of the cabin: the knots in the rough lumber, the rusted nail heads, and the naked two-by-fours reaching like fragile limbs from the floor to the steeply canted roof. Gradually accepting that she was still among the living, she became aware of the overnight snowfall blanketing Sandon beneath a pristine coverlet. Gingerly, she placed a hand on her swollen belly in search of the life beneath the taut skin and was answered by a reassuring surge beneath her fingers.

Yuki Wakabayashi turned over in the bed and opened her eyes. "Is it time?" she asked softly in Japanese. In the hard light of the morning her mother appeared so very tired and old.

"No. Go back to sleep," Soju whispered, pushing her feet out from their shared cover.

Yuki turned to the wall, her muted reply buried in the covers.

Soju sat up placing her naked foot on the floor, the icy boards sending a shocking chill up her legs, challenging the fragile warmth where the baby began to stir. She pulled a blanket from over the rafters, and, with the blanket clutched to her shoulders, went to the cabin window. Their night-long breathing had formed leaf-like etchings of frost on the glass. Soju marveled at the infinite patience of the one who created such perfect images, only to have them vanish with the first breath of warmth from the cabin stove.

Placing her lips close to the window, she breathed on the frosted glass. A small, clear circle appeared in the frost. With the tip of her finger she rubbed the melting frost, creating a clear eye to the outside world. Beyond the cabin porch she could see the pattern of the roadway buried in snow, the indentation twisting toward the village like the trail of a giant worm. Though it was still early for the baby, she was satisfied the snow was not so deep that she couldn't manage when it came her time.

Soju remained at the window, warming her hands between her thighs, the touch of her cold fingers bringing memories of Michael's searching touch in their nest on Fraser's Wharf. She closed her eyes recalling the warmth of his breath on her neck and shuddered at the thought of his mysterious coming in to her with his whispering promise to be with her forever. She conjured a vision of his plunging through the knee-deep snow, stumbling eagerly in his rush to her cabin. He would be shouting and laughing, tumbling head long into the snow, his face alive with excitement at seeing her at the window. It was an image that gave way to doubt as she reminded herself Michael might not know where to find her. She often wondered if she had been right in not writing to him. He had seemed so distant when they last... Her thoughts were lost in the need to light the fire.

Soju moved awkwardly beneath the army blanket, stuffing paper and small pieces of wood into the cold stove. She was so engrossed in her thoughts of composing the letter she would write Michael that she failed to catch the sound of footsteps on the cabin porch. Someone stamping the snow from their boots brought her head up sharply, poised over the unlit stove like a doe frozen at the crack of a twig. Soju pulled the blanket to her throat and lifted the latch, cautiously opening the door wide enough to see out onto the porch. The winter-chapped face of the camp nurse appeared in the narrow opening. She was bundled in a long, blue overcoat with a red-lined cape over her shoulders. A heavy, blue scarf covered her throat to her ears, and a starched, white nursing dickey sat perched atop her closely cropped red hair.

"Good morning, Soju." The nurse stepped forward, smiling expectantly, intending to slip through the partially open door. When Soju failed to step back from the door, the nurse's smile vanished. "Well. I'm glad to see you are up and around, Soju. We have been worried about you. You didn't show up at the infirmary for your appointment yesterday. With all the snow, I thought we better come and make sure things are okay."

An unshaven camp attendant who had been standing out of sight appeared at the nurse's side. The man wore an army greatcoat, his thick neck tucked deep in the collar, his bare head protruding like that of a large brown turtle. "Nurse Kelley here has come through all this snow just to check up on you. She don't want anything to happen to you and that baby of yours, eh?" The man shouted, as if by raising his voice he could penetrate Soju's stoic stare. The nurse produced a government form from the folds of her cape.

"Did you keep your copy of your appointment schedule, Soju? The one I gave to you last week? It was for eight o'clock yesterday morning," she said. "Didn't you bother to read it?"

"I am sorry. I didn't think I needed to come unless things changed. I will come this morning, if that's all right," Soju replied. "I have to start the fire for my mother now. Then I will come." She attempted to close the cabin door to shut out the freezing draft. The camp attendant's hand held it open. He shouldered the nurse aside with a loud voice.

"Let me handle this, Kelley. You have to know how to get through to these people. They don't understand your fancy English. Pretend they do, but no way." He shook his ponderous head, addressing the nurse as if Soju were not present. "When you have dealt with as many of 'em as I have, you will get the hang of it." He turned to Soju, attempting a paternal smile that succeeded in transforming his menacing blue-bearded face into a grinning gargoyle.

"You don't want trouble with that baby now, do you, eh? Nurse Kelley here is the one who decides when you go to the clinic, in Slocan, eh? She don't want you having your kid out in the snow, eh? Now you come with us, okay?" Soju looked helplessly past the man to the nurse.

"I will come. But first, I have to—"

"See," the man interrupted impatiently, turning to the nurse. "They just don't get it. Talkin' plain English goes right over their heads." He moved closer to the narrow door opening and broke into Pidgin English. "You under standee, eh? Go? Have baby in hospital. Okay?" He began rocking an imaginary baby in his empty arms. "You savvy? Chop chop. Come now."

Soju closed the door.

***

The blazing wood-burning heater filled the infirmary cabin with hot air, heavy with the smell of disinfectant and difficult to breathe. Soju sat on a straight-back chair near the door hoping to catch a breath of outside air. She worried that her breathing the disinfectant would harm the baby in her womb. As she waited, she appeared to be studying the small puddle taking shape from the snow melting at her feet; she began drawing circles with the toe of her boot in the puddle. After a time, a tiny, grey haired Japanese woman, her back bent so badly she appeared about to fall with each step, came out from behind the muslin screen of the clinic. The woman stopped and attempted to bow to Soju with little more than a movement of her head. She said something in Japanese that Soju was unable to hear and left as the red-haired nurse appeared from behind the screen.

"Well. I see you finally made it."

"I'm sorry I'm late," Soju said quietly.

"At least you are here." The nurse forced a fixed smile and drew up a chair, moving closer until they were sitting knee to knee. She took Soju's hands in her own and began in a nurse-knows—better voice. "Now there's one thing you and I have to get settled today, young lady. We need to keep our camp clinic records straight. You understand? That means you have got to tell me who did this. We can't have any more of your head-shaking bull. I need to have the name." She reached out and patted Soju's swollen abdomen. "So, who's the daddy who put this baby in there?"

Soju's eyes cut to her boots where the puddle was spreading across the linoleum floor. "Well?" the nurse insisted. "Who?" Soju didn't answer and the nurse attempted a casual laugh that revealed more frustration than good nature. "Why do I get the feeling this baby is going to come as a big surprise to some loverboy, eh? One of those Japanese boys working in the road camps? Is that it?" Soju continued to trace her boot through the growing puddle. "Listen. We can arrange to have this guy, whomever he is, brought to Slocan. He can be here with you when his baby comes, Soju. That would make things better for all of us, wouldn't it?"

Soju's attention shifted to a loose button dangling precipitously from where her belly split her overcoat.

"Soju." The nurse's voice softened. "That's such a pretty name. Did they name you after your mother?" Soju looked up, silently shaking her head.

"No. Soju is my grandmother's name."

"That's nice, but Soju, nobody wants to see a kid your age go through this business all alone. Having a baby is no picnic." The nurse waited for a response before going on quietly. "The RCMP tells me your dad is in detention back East. Are you afraid of his finding out about this?"

"He is at Angler Camp in Ontario," Soju said quietly. "They think he is a spy." She twisted the loose button between her fingers without looking up. "He is not a spy."

"Okay. But now let's talk about the man who made you pregnant. Where is he, Soju?" Soju gripped the loose button and tore it off and slipped it into her coat pocket. "The RCMP says you have two brothers in the road camps. Is this…"

Soju interrupted before the nurse could finish. "The father of my baby is not in the road camps."

"Then he is in Angler? Is that it?"

"No."

"Why are you making this so difficult for me, Soju? The government requires that we register both parents, especially in a case like yours. You are only seventeen." Soju turned again to stirring the puddle on the floor with the toe of her boot. The nurse sighed. "Well, we can come back to this later. Right now, you get into a gown and climb up on the table behind the screen. I need to see how things are coming along."

"I would tell you," Soju said, her voice coming from behind the screen. "But he does not know."

The nurse attempted to answer as if she really didn't care. "Then why don't we just give him the good news?" She peered around the screen and bit her lip at the sight of the tears running down Soju's face. "Oh, kid. I know it's rough. I'm sorry. You just take it easy, okay? Everything is going to be fine." She helped Soju onto the table and took her knees in her cold hands. "I can tell you this, kid. You are damn near ready. This will all be over before we know it, sweetheart."

Soju's water broke three days later while she stood frightened in the melting snow, her arms loaded with cabin firewood. A camp truck carried her to the Slocan clinic where she delivered a six-pound, eight-ounce girl into the hands of Nurse Mary Kelley; the baby slipped free at 7:50 a.m., ten minutes before the nursing shifts were to change. The arrival brought an immediate hush to the room, followed by Nurse Kelley's loud whisper: "Goddamn it. That does it."

The assisting nurse, a tall, rangy middle-aged woman with tied-back graying hair, her dark skin evidence of her Indian heritage, held the baby up in a flannel swaddling blanket. A coating of slick mucous over the baby's head failed to mask the matted crown of ginger-colored hair. "Whoever was the daddy of this tyke, was no Jap, Kelley."

Nurse Kelley took the baby. "Christ, I was afraid of this," she muttered. Soju reached out feebly for the wailing baby. "No, no, sweetheart. You just take it easy. We have to clean her up before you get your hands on her. There's plenty of time." She held the child tantalizingly just out of reach. "And before we go any farther, you are going to tell me who the daddy is, isn't that right? Look at that hair. He's a white man, isn't he?"

Soju nodded weakly.

"Honey. Did some bugger force himself on you? You have got to tell us."

"Kelley, have a heart," the assisting nurse whispered, failing to conceal her words beneath her breath. "The kid has just had a baby. Quit working her over as if you were the bloody RCMP."

"I'm trying to help her, for God's sake," Kelley snapped. "You saw her mother sitting out there on the hall bench when you came on last night? That old lady has been there all night long. Wait until she gets a look at her daughter's redheaded baby. Orientals can be just as touchy about who knocks up their kids as anybody.

Maybe more. If this baby was all Japanese, that's one thing. We could deal with one of those little buggers on the road crews up by New Denver. Not this." She turned the baby over in her large hands and pursed her lips. "You, my little redheaded doll, are going to require some explaining. Yes, sir. And by God, your momma is going to have to tell us who put you in there, eh?"

The tall assisting nurse took the baby and stepped away from the delivery table. "They say these Japanese girls are trained never to say no," she suggested. "This kid probably thought it was good manners to let some bugger have it. Still, the baby is a cute little tyke, isn't she?" She put her face close to the baby's wrinkled nose. "Oh, I'd like to take you home with me, you beautiful china doll. Nobody would ever know you were a Jap if you were mine, sweetie. You think I could keep her, Kelley?"

Soju lay forgotten, her eyes closed, tears forming damp shadows on the sheets bunched beneath her head.

***

Toshio arrived at the Slocan clinic as the fading daylight formed long shadows over the mud-stained snow. Nurse Kelley had been watching for him since sending a message to the road camp two days ago. She knew who he was on sight, and remained poised on the hard waiting room chair by the clinic doors, watching his slipping and sliding over the ice-crusted snow. Toshio, flailing his arms to keep his balance with each step, cursed silently. Kelley crushed her cigarette in the fire bucket by her chair and stood up to study him when he reached the clinic steps. The sight of him started her questioning her decision in sending for Soju's brother.

Toshio's trousers were tucked into knee-high rubber boots and his worn windbreaker, zippered up to the neck, was bulging and deformed by the several layers of sweaters. Months in the road camp had left him with a heavy black beard and his hair growing wildly and unkempt down his neck beneath a knit cap. Finding his first firm footing on the bottom step, Toshio looked up into Nurse Kelley's critical eye. Sensing her obvious hostility, he tried to smile; the two of them studied one another, with Toshio on the steps and nurse Kelly glaring out through the door glass. Toshio pulled off his cap and lowered his head in the slightest show of submission. Nurse Kelley opened the door.

"You Soju's brother?" She said it like she didn't want to believe her own words. "Wakabayashi?"

"Yes. I am Toshio—"

Before he could finish, Nurse Kelley interrupted, barring the way with her arms folded across her breast. "You sure as hell don't look like someone I'd choose to turn to if I was in a jam."

"In a jam?"

"Your sister. They told you, she's had a baby?"

"Yes."

"Well, she's waiting for you. You will find her at the end of the hall, last door on the right." The nurse's eyebrows rose skeptically as she stepped aside to avoid contamination. "And don't you touch that baby until you wash. And don't get too close to your sister."

Toshio repeated his abbreviated bow and started down the hall, hesitating at the partially opened last doorway. He eased the door open. The room was in semi darkness.

"Soju?" he said softly, peering through the afternoon shadows. "Soju?" he repeated.

"Toshio?" Soju rose up on one elbow and spoke his name as if she had discovered someone resurrected from the dead. "Is that really you, Toshio?"

"Hi." He stepped into the room. "You expecting someone else?" He approached the bed, his whiskers parting in a nervous smile. Soju saw his eyes go to the soft bundle in the crook of her arm. "So. Is that it?" He nodded uncertainly, indicating the baby. "God. Why do they look like that when they are new? Looks as if it's in pain. Is it okay?" He stepped around the foot of the bed, taking care to position himself a step away from the baby. The baby winced and let out a smothered cry.

Soju frowned, unsure whether her brother was nervous or being unkind. "You have never seen a new baby before, Toshio. They all look different at first. What you see is her spirit getting used to its place in her tiny body."

Toshio's expression softened, giving way to a look of helpless wonder. "Yea? So, does it have all its fingers and toes? All the parts in the right places?" Soju merely smiled, sensing he was nervous and saying stupid things hoping to ease the tension in the room. "Well. What are you going to call it, anyway?"

"She. This is your niece, Toshio. And her name is Yuki." Soju searched her brother's face for approval, then peeled away more of the swaddling cloth to offer him a better look. "Don't be angry, Toshio. She doesn't deserve that. Be angry with me. But don't be angry with the baby. She needs you to love her. Do you think she is beautiful?"

"You gave her Momma's name," he replied quietly.

"Uh-huh. But for her Canadian friends, she will be Mary. After the Queen. Yuki Mary. She can take her choice which name she wants to use."

"The Queen of England? You're naming her after the Queen of England?" Toshio surrendered to a sudden urge to reach out and extended his little finger into the baby's fist. "How's your Irish boyfriend going to like that idea? The Queen of England?"

Soju blushed. "You knew this would happen, didn't you, Toshio? You tried to make him go away."

"No, I didn't know this would happen. If I did suspect this was what he was after, I damn well would have made him keep the hell away from you. Momma had an idea what was going on. She wanted to send you to Japan to stay with the Nagumos. Only it was too late by then with the war going to hell. How are you going to explain this to Poppa? Have you thought about what he is going to say when he learns he has a redheaded hakujin granddaughter?" Toshio cautiously pulled back the blanket. The baby's tiny hand remained clinging to his finger. "I suppose Momma has seen her? Seen that hair? What did she say?"

"She loves the baby like it was her very own," Soju said. "She came and held her and sang to her like she sang to us when we were kids on the wharf at Steveston. Nurse Kelley sent Momma back to Sandon. Kelley said she was driving the nurses crazy wanting to wrap the baby like they do in Japan."

"What did Momma say about the red hair?"

"Toshio, she just loves the baby. She didn't say anything except how beautiful she is. Do you want to hold her, Toshio?"

Toshio wiggled his finger free of the baby's fist. "No. Not right now. I just came in from camp," he answered quickly. "They got us living in boxcars out there. I haven't had a bath in a month of Sundays. Your nurse doesn't want the kid catching my germs. But tell me, what does Michael have to say about this?" Soju busied herself tucking the blanket around the baby. "Soju? Answer me. You have told him, haven't you?" Soju looked away, her eyes cast down. "Aww Christ, Soju. You are not telling me he doesn't know? You haven't told him, have you?"

"No. I don't want to tell him. Not right away, Toshio. Not yet."

"That's not right, Soju. The guy has a right to know. It's his baby. He's responsible. He is an Irish Catholic. His family is going to want a baptism and a priest, the whole business once they find out. You don't know those people like I know them. I have been in their house. They are different from you and me. Really different. He's not going to marry anybody who isn't a Roman Catholic, either. So you better get used to that. There's even a big picture of Jesus with His heart hanging out of his chest in their front hall. That isn't anything like Poppa hanging that picture of the Emperor on our Shinto shrine to remind him of Japan, either. Michael's family is really serious about everybody being Roman Catholic. His mother is going to climb the wall when she learns about this."

Toshio looked down at the baby and once again slipped his finger into the tiny fist as a sign that he wasn't really as upset as he sounded. "What did you tell the hospital? Whose name did they put on the birth certificate?"

"She is Yuki Wakabayashi," Soju said quietly. "Michael has not given us his name. So she has mine." Toshio was about to ask how Michael could give his name when he didn't even know he had a baby. But he had heard the touch of defiance in his sister's voice and merely sighed. The baby gurgled, a tiny spit bubble popping out between her lips, and he quickly withdrew his finger. At that moment Nurse Kelley turned on the overhead light, putting an immediate end to the baby's romancing her uncle.

"I see you two have found each other. That's nice," she said briskly, taking the baby from Soju's arms. "So," she said, measuring Toshio with hard, uncompromising eyes. "Did you wash?"

"Yeah," Toshio lied.

Kelley cast a swift glance at his hands. "Well, uncle, just to be sure, do it again and do it right this time at that sink in the corner. Then I'm going to show you how to double up as a surrogate poppa to your niece. Go on. Wash." She sniffed. "This one is going to smell sweet for awhile, Mister Wakabayashi. And if you start doing these chores early, you will hardly even notice when things begin to change."

Toshio slept on the bench in the clinic corridor that night. In the morning the two nurses watched through the hospital storm windows as brother and sister picked their way through the puddles of brown water formed by the melting snow. Toshio carried the baby. "What a perfect picture," the relief nurse sighed. "If it wasn't for the kid's ginger-colored hair, you and I could pretend we are standing here watching a nice Jap couple hitting the road with their brand new Jap baby."

Chapter 29 The Land of Golden Mountains

Soju unbuttoned her coat, cradling the baby to her breast, and moved closer to the stove, her hips so close she could feel the heat through her heavy woolen coat. She was trying to bring the baby into the circle of warmth, her thoughts far from the bare walls and cold drafts sweeping through the cabin. She was paying no attention to Toshio's meaningless lecture on how to stack the green alder firewood.

"Hey." Her brother looked up impatiently. "Any day now they are sending me back to the road camp and you are going to have to do this yourself. Pay a little attention or you are going to be damn cold. This wet wood won't burn, Soju."

His sister answered with a non-committal nod and removed the lid from the stove, exposing the kettle to the open flame. She moved to the other side of the stove where she could hold the baby closer to the kettle, hoping the thin puff of steam would ease the child's breathing.

Toshio frowned irritably and poked a piece of green firewood at the stove as if he were scolding a child. "If you don't learn how to dry this wood it won't burn." Soju smiled apologetically and his voice softened. "When summer comes I'll try to get back here and cut a load in time for the wood to dry in the sun."

"When summer comes?"

Toshio shrugged. "We don't know how long they are going to keep us locked up like this." He began explaining again about the wood and was interrupted by someone on the cabin steps. He shot a questioning glance at his sister, placed his finger to his lips and went to the window. Two mounted policemen stood at the door bundled in hip-length coats, the flaps of their fur caps pulled down over their ears. They spotted him peeking out. "Open up," one of them barked, pulling off his gloves to pound on the door. Toshio went to the door and held it ajar.

"You Wakabayashi?" The taller of the two pushed his cap back off his brow, revealing a lean face with deep-set eyes and a hawkish nose. He had the look of a bird of prey.

"I am Toshio Wakabayashi."

"Good. I'm Corporal Stan Murdock, officer in charge of the Sandon RCMP detachment." The policeman spoke with a deliberate, word-at-a-time cadence as if his lines were being read from an official document.

Toshio's expressionless response concealed his thought. '*This guy thinks I can't understand English.*'

"And this here is Constable Dave Sorensen." The short, thick-set man at his side smiled faintly, acknowledging his presence. From his place shielded by the cabin door, Toshio could see only Sorensen's dimpled chin and very little else of the face buried beneath his fur-trimmed hat. Toshio later learned Sorensen was a six-month recruit who had recently been rejected for an army commission. A university graduate, Sorensen was having difficulty adjusting to serving in the remote posting.

The corporal pulled an official-looking notebook from his coat pocket and thumbed through the pages without looking up at Toshio. "You are from the New Denver road camp. Correct?"

"I have a pass." Toshio began to fumble for his wallet.

"That is not necessary. We are aware of all that. We are here to see you on a matter concerning your father, Isao Wakabayashi."

"What's happened?"

"You are aware he's being held in detention at Angler, Ontario," the corporal said. Sorensen's head bobbed affirmatively without saying anything.

"Please." Toshio held the door open wider for the two men to come inside. "My sister's baby has a cold. We are trying to keep the place warm. Come in and let me shut the door." The corporal ignored the invitation.

"This won't take a minute," Constable Sorensen said apologetically. "And we want you to know, nothing has happened to your father."

Corporal Murdock turned with a cold frown to silence the university graduate.

"What we need to talk to you about is another matter," Sorensen added blithely.

The baby's coughing seemed to distract Murdock and he stretched his long neck to peer over Toshio's shoulder into the cabin. "That your kid?" Toshio detected a note of innocence in the corporal's question that warned him to answer cautiously.

"No. That's my sister's baby." He turned to Soju hovering next to the stove. "I'm the uncle. The baby is only a few weeks old."

The corporal sniffed a wet drop from the tip of his nose and quickly reverted to his official proclamation cadence, causing Toshio to become even more nervous. "The Slocan clinic has filed a report stating they have no record of the father of that child. The mother is a minor and that presents several problems." At that moment Yuki slipped out from under the army blanket where she had been all but hidden and took the baby from Soju to huddle with her beneath the blanket.

"It is only a problem if you were planning on keeping the baby," the fat Sorensen injected. "Your sister is what? Fifteen, sixteen years old?" He shook his head woefully, causing the hood of his hat to fall back, revealing his baby face.

"What Sorensen here is trying to tell you is that this is a matter that has to be cleared up. Your sister is an underaged girl, a minor. "

Toshio stammered, struggling to remain calm. "You are not going to take her baby from her."

"Maybe not," the corporal replied. "We don't know anything about how you people handle these things. Foreign cultures don't always behave in ways that conform to a more civilized society. I served in the Kootneys where we have the Dukhabors to deal with. They have different ideas about things like that. But I can tell you this much, if you intend to keep that baby it's not going to belong to your sister. That just won't fly."

Toshio's eyes cut to the constable and then back to the corporal, searching for the proposition he sensed coming.

"Sorensen here is a college man." The corporal smiled condescendingly at Sorensen. "And he has come up with a thought that could solve your problem and ours. Suppose the clinic was to report that your mother was the one who gave birth to that baby?" The corporal glanced again at the notepad. "Your mother is Yuki Wakabayashi, right? And that's her with the kid on the bed, isn't it?" He smiled at Yuki, who was watching warily from where she held the baby in the blanket. "Good evening, Miss," the corporal called out across the cabin. "Looks to me as if the baby belongs to her anyway. What do you think, Sorensen?"

"That's the way it's got to be," Sorensen answered. "These people have enough trouble without adding a police investigation to the mix."

"The baby's name is Yuki Wakabayashi," Soju offered anxiously. The policemen exchanged satisfied glances.

"Well then, let's just have our report state matters that way and avoid a lot of trouble for everyone. There's a war on, you know." Sorensen beamed at the acceptance of his solution.

"Now that we have taken care of that, there is the matter of your father," the corporal said. "You will be glad to hear there is a possibility of his being released from Angler detention. How does that sound?"

"What does the baby have to do with my father being released?" Toshio asked.

"Nothing. Nothing at all. But until we solved this problem with the baby, we were going to have to keep you here to investigate the birth of that baby to an unwed teenager," the corporal replied with exaggerated patience. "You need to understand, the government is considering releasing your father on the condition this entire family joins him and establishes residence in Ontario. You must agree to make no attempt to return to the West Coast. Should you fail to accept those terms, Isao Wakabayashi will remain in confinement and we will go ahead with our investigation of this teenage girl being knocked up by someone unknown." The threat in the corporal's sharp words was unmistakable.

Toshio turned to Soju, but before they could do more than exchange a questioning glance, the corporal continued in a reasoning manner. "It's dangerous for Japanese out on the West Coast. Back East, people are not so hostile toward you people."

"What about our home in Vancouver?" Toshio demanded. "And my brother Tatsuo? He's on the road crew at New Denver."

"My detachment has no jurisdiction in matters pertaining to your British Columbia property. That's B.C. Security Commission business. You will have to write to Austin Taylor's Security Commission. It's out of our hands. All you need to consider now is that Constable Sorensen here and I can and will get your brother on a train east. What you must decide is whether or not you want your father released from detention. The government is prepared to re-classify him and provide your transportation to join him in Ontario. But you are to remain there, permanently. You. Your brother. Your sister. Your mother. And that baby."

"Permanently?" Toshio's hand was frozen on the door handle but he wasn't in a hurry to accept the terms, suspecting that Soju's baby was somehow the pawn behind this offer.

"That may mean you only have to stay put for the duration of the war," Sorensen chimed in. "Once we win the war you could probably go wherever you like."

"How long do we have to decide?"

The corporal stretched a bony wrist free of his heavy coat sleeve to glance at his watch. "Talk it over as long as you like. Constable Sorensen and I will be here to put you on an east-bound train at six in the morning." He pushed his fur hat back down over his eyebrows, signaling the matter closed.

"Tomorrow?" Toshio frowned.

But the two police officers were already picking their way over the path their footsteps had broken in the deep snow. Toshio couldn't tell whether they heard or didn't care to answer. He braced his back against the closed door, as if by holding his body to the door he was keeping the world at bay. "I hope to God those buggers freeze to death in their bloody fur coats. They sure as hell didn't care about freezing us."

When he finally abandoned the door he began poking at the struggling flames in the stove, mulling over the meaning of the surprise visit. "I don't buy their story. Releasing dad and shipping us back east has something to do with you having a baby in this camp, Soju. You have got to write Michael and tell him what happened, now."

"I would write, Toshio, but I can't," Soju pleaded. "You know the camp censors read every letter. If I told him about our baby it would be like my trying to talk in whispers with those policemen listening to every word. I could get Michael in trouble."

"So what?" Toshio took his sister's two hands in his and held them hard. "Listen to me. It was Michael who got you into this trouble. For all we know he may be the reason we are out here in the middle of nowhere with the police telling us we can never go home again. Soju. Write the letter. I'll get it mailed. Nobody is going to read it but Michael. I promise."

"Can I wait until Christmas, Toshio?" She was pleading, uncertain whether to share her dream. "Maybe," she whispered, "he will come to Sandon at Christmas." She blushed, aware she was revealing a prayer she had shared only with God.

"Soju. You don't really expect." Toshio checked his words, aware that what he was about to say would crush what remained of her dreams. "We are going to have to decide right now if we are going to go along with their deal to get Poppa from that prison camp. I don't think it's going to do any good me trying to tell those Mounties to wait until Christmas because you are hoping your boyfriend might show up." He shook his head sympathetically. "Come on, Soju. Write to Michael tonight and leave the rest to me."

The two of them had forgotten Yuki struggling to follow their English from where she huddled on the edge of the bed rocking the baby. "Shikata-nai," she said softly.

Toshio wheeled to face her, straining to maintain a civil voice. Hurriedly, in a burst of staccato Japanese, he repeated the details of the police visit.

"Shikata-nai," Yuki repeated quietly.

"Shikata-nai? Bullshit," Toshio shouted. "They take our house, and you give us shikata-nai. What do you mean, it can't be helped? They put Poppa in a prisoner of war camp and we watch the train take him away. Was that shikata-nai?" He kicked his carefully stacked pile of fuel, sending firewood tumbling across the cabin floor. "Every time they come after us, everything they do to us, its shikata-nai. That's Japanese bullshit, Momma. Soju and Tatsuo and I were born in this country. We are as Canadian as those Mounties or anyone else. What right does anyone have telling us we can't go home? Shikata-nai, my ass." He snatched up his hat and slammed out the door.

***

Later that night Toshio reported to the RCMP station that they would be ready to leave in the morning. He then sheepishly slipped back into the cabin to curl up on his bed with his face to the wall. Yuki put the supper away and went on packing her remaining pieces of china into a folded blanket. She took the hemp cord from the rafters where it held the partitioning blanket and bound the bundle into a manageable satchel. Across the cabin, Soju propped a frozen ink bottle against the stovepipe, adding a few drops of water from the kettle.

The cabin was very still when she heard the distant children's voices and moved closer to the window. At first, the window resisted her attempt to press it open, then gave way, allowing the voices to carry clearly through the brisk night air. Japanese camp children, some not much younger than she, were caroling. Soju wrapped the baby in her coat and raised her to the open window so that she too could hear the singing.

"Oh, little town of Bethlehem,
How still we see thee lie..."

Leaving the window ajar, Soju returned the baby to her mother and began to write.

"Dear Michael. Soon it will be Christmas in this place in the mountains. The snow here is dry and fluffy and makes pillows on the branches so that the trees look like paintings on a Christmas card. Since I last saw you, we have had a baby girl. She was born here in the camp infirmary. Her Japanese name is Yuki and her second name is Mary for her Canadian friends to call her, if she wishes. The baby's hair is dark but in the morning light, when I brush her, I can see the evening sunset in every strand. She is very beautiful and she is a good baby."

She put down the pen and went back to the window, straining to catch the words of the fading carol.

"Above thy deep and dreamless sleep,
The silent stars go by.
Yet in the dark streets shineth,
The everlasting light..."

She closed the window, and with the singing in her thoughts, began to write again. *"We are being moved in the morning to Toronto, Ontario, to be with my father. I will miss the beauty of the* snow and the mountains of the Kootenays, but it is very cold here for the baby. When night comes and I am nursing her, I look into her eyes. They are so much like yours that I feel I am looking at you. I tell her about you. I believe she understands how much I miss you.

"I am afraid of being in Ontario, Michael. It is such a long way for my dreams to travel. Toshio says he will mail this letter for me. Perhaps you will receive it and write to me? The police have told us we can receive our mail in care of the Young Women's Christian Association on Yonge Street in Toronto.

"It is nighttime in our camp now and I can hear the children singing Christmas carols in the snow. It must have been a night like this in Bethlehem when Jesus was born, far from home in a bed that was not his own." She paused, recalling the voices now faint in the distance, and she wrote across the bottom of the page.

"The hopes and fears of all the years,
Are met in Thee tonight.
Soju."

**

The cold grew intense through the night, clouds of icy fog blowing across the camp driving dust-like mounds of ice beneath the cabin door. The Wakabayashis spent the early morning hours listening for the police truck until the headlights appeared, searching their way through the swirling snow. Corporal Murdock stepped out of the truck, leaving Constable Sorensen in the cab, thrumming the engine, the truck belching dumpling-like exhaust clouds into the wind.

"Time to get this show on the road," the corporal hollered.

It was too cold to hate, too cold for anything other than fear of the wind. Toshio grasped Yuki's blanket bundle in one arm and a hamper of clothing in the other.

Soju appeared in the cabin doorway silhouetted against the cabin light.

"Sorensen. Get your ass out of the truck and give the girl a hand," Murdock ordered when Soju hesitated in the open doorway. She looked back into the cabin, her eyes seeing with the camera-like clarity that comes when one is seeing that which they will never see again. The naked beds stripped of their mattresses like pieces of abstract sculpture, the rusted springs clinging to skeletal frames. A worn broom leaning in the corner at rest, having scattered dust over the floor for the last time. Toshio's firewood remained stacked close to the dying fire in futile defiance of the cold. Soju felt a pain pass through her body, aware she was leaving more than an empty miner's shack. She was leaving her last link to her Third Avenue home, her childhood at Star of the Sea, her memories of Fraser's Wharf, and her prayers that Michael might one day come to find her. These dreams were seeded and kept alive in the desolate cabin.

Constable Sorensen, reading something of her thoughts, spoke as if consoling a dying friend. "It's hard to let go, but you have a train to catch to a better place, young lady."

The corporal hollered through the wind at Yuki. "You get into the cab with the baby. Make room for Sorensen." Turning to Toshio and Soju, he grinned malevolently. "You two can hold down the luggage." He reached into the bed of the truck for a canvas tarpaulin. "Cover yourselves. Don't want to be unloading a couple of icicles." Toshio and Soju scrambled over the baggage into the truck bed and the truck lurched forward, tracing its tracks in the snow to the main road. Toshio, sulking his way through his guilt from the night before, began cursing the cold as he struggled to build Soju a sheltered nest beneath the canvas.

Snow crusted Toshio's black beard and ice clung to his coat and trousers by the time Corporal Murdock brought the truck alongside the Valley Railroad Station. Toshio had managed to shield Soju beneath the tarp so that she had escaped the wind, though the feeling in her toes was gone. Constable Sorensen offered a hand for Toshio to climb down. "You look damn near frozen, kid," Sorensen said, fumbling though his jacket pocket for the government travel voucher. He slapped Toshio across the back in an awkward goodwill gesture that sent a shock down Toshio's spine. "I can only guess at how you look at all this. But I'm willing to bet you are sure as hell going to be a lot warmer where you are going than I will be in this forsaken hole, eh? I wish your family luck," he said with an attempt to smile.

"God or bad luck?" Toshio answered, as if to reinforce his bitterness.

Sorensen looked confused, then grinned. "Hell. Good luck, kid. Lots of it. All you Japs have had more than your share of the other kind." Toshio was about to answer when the corporal stepped between them and their attempt at friendship passed.

***

Late that afternoon the family boarded an ornate Colonial railroad carriage drawn up on a side track by the station. The car was unattached and gave the appearance of having been left standing by a passing train a century ago. The carriage was painted pea soup green with faded yellow trimming all but buried beneath endless miles of track dust. Yard workers had wiped small circles in the dirt to reveal the brighter green and golden letters of the car's glory days. The carriage – it had been in first-class service at the turn-of-the-century — had been resurrected for wartime duty like so many old and retired people and machines. The plush seats smelled of tobacco smoke, the smell dominating the cold odor of carbolic disinfectant. A broad-bellied iron heater squatted at one end of the car, surrounded by a litter of cigarette butts, a crumpled Players Cigarette carton, and withered orange peelings. A half-filled bucket of coal seemed to add to the debris.

"Stinks in here like a public toilet," Toshio grimaced, dropping the luggage into the aisle. He pushed the toe of his boot into an opening in the flooring where the carpet was patched with bright green linoleum. Soju adjusted the blanket around the baby and laid the sleeping child on a seat next to Yuki.

"This wreck must have been a hundred years in the barn," Toshio muttered.

"What are you complaining about, son?" A high-pitched voice fired back, seemingly from out of nowhere. "This is a troop train that was good enough to carry our boys to two wars. Don't you think that makes it good enough for the likes of you travelling on a free ticket?" The red-faced little man, in his mid sixties, perhaps older, wore a slightly frayed, tight-fitting, blue serge suit with brass buttons. His well-worn wicker cap, the solid visor tilted back exposing heavy, gray eyebrows, marked him for a conductor, probably retired.

"The Mounties give you your vouchers?" he demanded.

Toshio handed the man the travel vouchers. He was tempted to defend his opinion of the car but thought better of it and said nothing.

"I hear the government is shipping you people out of British Columbia, eh." It was a matter-of-fact statement spoken without malice.

"That's the way it looks," Toshio replied.

"Did I hear you say you didn't care for the smell of my car?"

"It's the disinfectant," Toshio admitted.

"You would rather have the germs, I suppose? Just what that baby on the seat needs, eh?"

"No. It's just that it smells like a public toilet."

"This old car has been around a good many years, young fella. She's been away for awhile. A little mould got into things. Besides, you'll have her all to yourselves all the way to Calgary." He scanned the vouchers. "I don't suppose I have to tell you there's a war on, do I?"

"We heard," Toshio replied dryly. The old man's preaching was beginning to wear thin.

"We will move the car out of here within the hour, then hook you on to the Calgary train. You should be rolling by eight. You can get some heat going in the fire, warm the car up a bit." The conductor fished into his vest and pulled out a large, shiny railroad watch. Without looking up from the watch, he asked; "Bring anything to eat?"

"Didn't have time," Toshio replied dejectedly.

The conductor turned to Soju and the baby with a hint of a smile, punched the vouchers and handed the stubs back to Toshio. "There's no food service between here and Calgary, you know," he said with a warning frown at Toshio, then left.

The conductor was gone only a short while before he reappeared carrying a large, brown paper bag. Toshio braced for another confrontation. The little man thrust him the bag.

"There's a sandwich in there for each of you and half a dozen hard-boiled eggs. People have got to eat. Not fancy, but I suspect you will be glad of it by the time you get to Calgary." He looked again at Soju cradling the baby in her arms, with the same hint of a smile, then turned and officiously paced the full length of the car, inspecting each seat exactly as he had over years of mainline service. With a touch to the bill of his cap, he stepped down to the trackside platform. They never saw him again.

Soju's head fell back on the headrest and she closed her eyes with her hand resting possessively on the sleeping baby. She was thinking of the sunlight on the waves of English Bay, seeking the kind of warmth only favorite memories can deliver. She listened again for Michael stealthily approaching to startle her. His hands closed over her eyes. "Guess who?"

She smiled. "Mussolini?"

The rail car shuddered, bringing a flutter to her eyes; she lost touch with her dream and sat up. There was a moment when she caught a glimpse of the trackside shacks sliding past the window before the effects of the long day claimed her once more and she slept. When she awoke the car was in darkness, a flickering light in the ceiling casting shuddering shadows over the seats. Soju attempted to peer into the night beyond the window and saw only her faint reflection in the glass. She lifted the sleeping baby to her cheek, both of them appearing in the glass. "See, Michael. This is your beautiful baby," she whispered. "Aren't you proud of her?"

Her stirring awoke Toshio. He sat up in the seat across the aisle.

"Go back to sleep. You need to rest," he said gently. "If you get sick, who's going to look after your baby?"

"But I want to stay awake to see Banff and the Banff hotel," Soju protested. "The King and Queen of England slept there."

"This train doesn't go through Banff," Toshio lied. Soju chose not to hear him.

"Do you remember when they came to Vancouver, Toshio?

"Who?"

"The King and Queen. Before the war? They came along Point Grey Road in a big open car, remember? I wore a kimono with the kids from the Japanese Language School. Don't you remember? Momma was the only one who believed me when I told her the King waved to me. He did, Toshio. He truly did."

"The King was falling asleep when they drove past me," Toshio mumbled. "Hundreds and hundreds of kids were out there, Soju. Maybe thousands. You think the King even saw one little Japanese kid?"

"At Japanese Language School they gave us a Union Jack. I waved it hard and the King looked right at me. I know he waved at me, I saw him, Toshio."

"Okay, he waved," Toshio yawned, too tired to talk. "Now go back to sleep." He reached out across the aisle, and to her surprise, lifted the sleeping baby from her arms.

When Soju awoke again the train was passing through the foothills of the Rocky Mountains coming down into the high plains of Alberta, where the land lay drenched in a bronze morning light as far as her eye could see. In Sandon there had been the endless ranks of the Selkirk and Purcell Mountains, mountains that rose in Soju's mind like prison walls guarding the long valley. Looking out over the prairie, she watched the sun rising majestically from the low hills. The scene brought back the images she had formed around her mother's stories of the Land of the Golden Mountains. She turned to Toshio, her voice full of wonder at the sight.

"Toshio, do you think this is what they saw when the early Japanese spoke of a Land of Golden Mountains."

Toshio nodded.

"Did we go through Banff?" she asked eagerly. "You promised you would wake me."

"You were tired," he answered, not wanting to lie again. "You'll see Banff when we go back home. It will look even better then. Maybe we will get off and stay a few days. How about that?"

"Are they ever going let us go home, Toshio?"

"You are damn right they are. When this war is over, nobody is going to care where we go. Did you write the letter?" Soju searched the seat beneath the baby blanket and withdrew the envelope.

"There is no stamp," she warned, tentatively passing the envelope into his hands, aware they were conspiring to break the law.

Toshio grinned and brought his wallet from his pocket. He had the look of a magician about to produce a rabbit. Dipping his fingers into the worn leather folder he carefully withdrew six three-cent stamps bearing the exposed head of King George VI. "I knew these would be valuable one day. I saved them ever since we left home. I'll see your letter gets in the mail when we change trains in Calgary."

"What if you are caught?"

"So what? Are they going to send me back to New Denver?" He shrugged indifferently. "Listen, Soju. We are Canadian citizens. Don't ever forget that. We can write letters like anybody else." He smiled wickedly. "I'd just like to be there to see the look on Michael's face when he opens this."

Chapter 30 Confession

The Teutonic Christ, His sweat-soaked hair tumbling over a bleeding brow, His ribs protruding through the drawn skin of his narrow chest, looked down from the wooden cross at Michael Costello. Michael had been kneeling by the flickering light of the votive candles at the feet of the alabaster Jesus for more than an hour, his knees grown numb on the marble altar steps. He welcomed the pain. Perhaps if he suffered enough it would help to placate this Jesus to whom he had come for forgiveness. He was aware that the contrition expected of him, the confession the church required for the absolution of his sins, would be a lie. His only hope was that Jesus, this man who loved Mary Magdalene, would understand.

During the second hour on his knees he lost all sense of time, continually turning from the altar to glance over his shoulder at the single line of Friday penitents. The line remained unchanged from when he first entered the church. The sight seeded his hope that there would be someone in that line who would be unloading even more mortal sins than his own. The red light over the cubicle went out and the green light lit up. A woman, her shoulders bent as if weary from the burden of serious sinning, wisps of gray hair falling loose from beneath her shawl, stepped into the velvet curtain screening the booth. Ten minutes passed and he looked again. Could she still be in there? For the first time that afternoon he glanced at his watch. He became so absorbed in imagining the sins of the woman he momentarily forgot his own. *'Over-the fence gossip? She looked the type. An apple lifted from a neighbor's yard or jar of peanut butter from the Safeway? No. More likely it was something kinky. Old ladies keep dogs for things like that.'* He tried to push these thoughts from his mind, convinced that whatever the old woman's sins might be, they would sound like the works of an angel compared to what he was there to confess.

He shifted his weight on the altar step and turned again in time to see the woman shuffling directly toward him, a faint trace of a smile on her face. She glanced at Michael and knelt alongside him, raising her hands in prayer, her face suddenly drawn in a pained frown as if recalling a sin she had failed to leave in the confessional. When she finished praying, she turned to Michael with a smile filled with sympathy, leaving him certain she had glimpsed into his sordid soul.

By late afternoon the sunlight that had been painting the rows of empty pews in the heavenly colors of the stained glass windows began to fade. Michael's thoughts turned to his mother, whose incessant coercion had brought him to his knees. "You must get right with God, Michael," she insisted. "Things will all work out for the better once your soul is made clean. If a car should hit you today with you in a state of mortal sin, you would go to hell forever. I couldn't live a day in heaven knowing one of my sons was in hell."

Eileen Costello had been herding her sons to the confessional with that story since the day of their first communions. Michael's first confession had him stumbling through a recital of his repeated masturbations — a sin that seemed of such magnitude it reduced all others to the inconsequential — until Father Lavoie grew impatient. "Yes. Yes. What else?" It was only after weeks of visits to the cloistered secrecy with the priest that Joseph, sensing the burden of Michael's guilt, convinced him there were many similar deeds constantly being reported through the muslin curtain. It was then that he developed his inventory of venial, less-than-deadly sins to be recited each Friday until he was confessing with the rhyme and cadence of a teenage nursery rhyme. Over time, he came to accept that he was merely one of the soiled Friday crowd seeking weekly absolutions; his confession a ritual like the Costello Saturday night bath demanded of him and his brothers. "Doesn't matter whether you need a bath or not, no boys of mine are going a week without a scrubbing," Eileen Costello insisted, scrubbing all three with a pumice stone and a bar of Fels Naptha laundry soap long past the appearance of their puberty.

Over time, even Father Lavoie's assignment of penance had become predictable. Three or four Our Fathers. A decade of the Rosary, more often than not followed with suggestions on how to make things right with God by making things right with mother. The seasoned Jesuit behind the screen never did express much concern over how many times Michael had been abusing himself so that sometime around his eleventh year, he began forgetting to mention the sun-bathing magazines and the pictures of corpulent nude women tucked beneath his mattress.

Dusk was settling over the church when the last person in the line of penitents — a middle-aged man wearing a rumpled brown suit and in need of a shave — ducked in to the confessional. After a very brief time behind the curtain, he popped out, heading for the church side door, hurrying to leave behind whatever it was he had revealed to the priest. Michael inhaled deeply, held his breath, and with an audible sigh rose on aching legs. The early evening shadows softened by the light from the vigil candles cast a calm over the empty church. Through the afternoon the sounds of shuffling feet, coughing, and the rattle of penitent coins falling into the metal candle bank had been a constant reminder of the afternoon penitents.

Michael drew the curtain aside and plunged into the darkness as if he was going under water, not knowing if he would ever surface. The day-long sessions of confined breathing had filled the confessional booth with the heavy odor of geriatric cosmetics and stale breath. Fixing his eyes on the thin muslin curtain he saw the shadowy outline of Father Lavoie's face so close to the screen he could hear the priest's deep nasal breathing. Michel went down on his aching knees, attempting to block out the presence of the priest hunching impatiently beyond the screen. Michael thought: *'If only it were really Jesus Christ in there, an all-loving Jesus who made wine for the wedding party, who let them bathe his head in precious oils, who dined with the tax collectors. That Jesus would understand.'* He wasn't so hopeful about Father Lavoie.

Michael silently crossed himself and waited, the stillness broken only by the priest's heavy breathing.

"Yes?"

Michael's image of a forgiving Jesus vanished at the sound of the French-Canadian voice.

As he had hoped, he detected a note of impatience in the priest's hurry-it-up tone of voice. Michael had waited through the entire afternoon counting on Father Maurice Lavoie being eager to be out of there. He was about to launch into his confession when the priest discharged a powerful blast into his handkerchief.

"Bless you," Michael uttered.

"What's that?" the priest demanded.

Michael gathered himself once more, attempting to conjure the image of Jesus listening beyond the screen.

"Bless me, Father, for I have sinned," he whispered. A long pause. "I can't remember when I made my last confession, Father."

"What's that? Speak up."

"I said, I can't remember when I made my last confession."

"None of us can ignore God indefinitely, my son." The priest's voice betrayed a weariness that had set in around mid-afternoon, listening to the endless infamy of his parish. Michael caught the tone and immediately prepared to launch into his rehearsed litany of routine sins. Swearing. Masturbation. Immoral Thoughts. He had them all on the tip of his tongue, sins Father Lavoie would accept without much fuss. His plan, carefully rehearsed during his hours at the altar rail, was to ease in to a casual mention of his mortal sin at the very end, a mere afterthought. He had mentally scripted the whole confession, confident the weary priest would not be listening too closely.

"Father, I have been fornicating." The words came blurting out as if they were the boast of the devil. The asthmatic breathing on the other side of the screen stopped, followed by a collapsed sigh.

"How many times have you done this?"

"I don't know, Father."

"Two? Three? How many do you think?" The priest's voice was brittle, impatient.

"About that, Father."

"The same girl?"

"Yes, Father."

"How old are you?" Michael's hopes soared. Father Lavoie had baptized him, knew his age to the day. The screen, perhaps the catch in his voice, had concealed his identity. He immediately began answering in an artificially deep voice.

"Seventeen, Father."

"How long have you been doing this?"

A pause while he silently recounted the days. "Quite a long time, Father."

"And you have stopped now?"

"She's gone away," he whispered.

"But you are sorry? You do know what you were doing was wrong? You realize that you are in a state of mortal sin." Silence. "Did you never think of denying this sin for the love of Christ?"

"No, Father."

"You come to Mass to proclaim your love of God, yet you give in to this terrible sin knowing it pains Christ? Pains Him more than the nails pained Him on the cross? These sins are your nails being driven into the body of Christ. When you commit this sin you are paining Christ that much."

"Yes, Father."

A long, silent pause.

"What about the girl? Are you aware of what you have done to the soul of this girl?"

"She's not a Catholic, Father."

"Don't think that because she is not Catholic she won't have to pay for her sins." Michael could hear the priest's growing irritation and began to fidget nervously. He was suddenly worried the old lady who had looked into his soul at the altar may have returned to the church to complete her confession and could be overhearing the priest as his voice grew louder. "That doesn't excuse you or her. Do you understand?"

"I want to marry her, Father. I love her," Michael whispered.

"Seventeen-year-olds don't make sound marriages. Besides your being too young, you said the girl is not Catholic. I want you to promise God in good conscience that you will not see this girl alone again." Silence. "Did you hear me?"

"She's gone away, Father."

"Never mind that. You must promise God that you will never again commit this sin or I cannot give you absolution. Do you promise?"

"I don't know. Father, I want to see her again. I think she needs me."

"And how about your mother who has no husband to help her? Doesn't she need you?" The words instantly shattered Michael's illusion of anonymity. "You have committed a most grievous sin."

Another long silence filled the close air of the confessional, broken only by the heavy breathing, now on both sides of the screen. Silence was Father Lavoie's technique for giving the sinner time to ponder the gravity of what he had confessed. When he had first begun going to confessions, Michael believed that pause was the priest's conferring with Jesus on what to do with the sinner. When the priest spoke again it was with a voice of conciliation.

"The greater the sin, my son, the greater is the rejoicing in the heart of Christ at our repentance. Christ died so that you may be forgiven. You must pray for His strength whenever you are tempted with this sin. He will aid you in denying the devil and these temptations the devil puts before us. Examine your heart. Expose this selfishness for what it is, the devil's carnal call to hell and damnation. Let your thoughts of Christ fill your heart and leave no room for these desires. You have allowed lust to endanger your immortal soul and the soul of this girl. Now let me hear you make a good Act of Contrition, then go out into the Church and recite the Sorrowful Mysteries of the Holy Rosary. As you meditate on the sorrow you have caused in the heart of Christ, make firm your resolve to love God and put an end to this sin." The priest's voice dropped to a sanctified pitch. "Ego te absolve. In nomine Patris et Filii et Spiritus Sancti."

The muttering of the priest's parting prayers trailed after Michael as he stepped out of the confessional, relieved to see there was no sign of the old lady. He was very much aware he had made no promise. Even as Father Lavoie's absolution was lifting the sins from his soul, his thoughts had been far from the sanctity of the confessional. Soju was somewhere in the mountains, and he was unwilling to turn from her, even for Jesus.

Chapter 31 The Last Stop

Toshio, Soju, and Yuki Wakabayashi remained awake in their seats through much of the day and late into the night, their train rushing east through the Prairies, then winding through the barren moonlit tundra of Northern Ontario. They wore their coats all the while, their baggage tucked beneath their seats, each harboring the silent knowledge that whatever remained of their lives on the West Coast had been left at the foot of the Selkirk Mountains. From time to time, as the train rounded curves, they could catch a glimpse of the engine, breaching steam like a triumphant long-distance racer, plunging headlong across the frozen landscape.

Long before the train began easing into Toronto's Union Station, Soju stood with her baby in her arms in the vestibule between cars, near frantic to be free of the train. As the train braked to a stop, she hurriedly stepped down, her foot slipping from under her on the ice-covered step. As she went down, she released the baby from her falling body. Toshio, one step behind, dropped the luggage and lunged forward, snatching the child out of mid air; Soju landed hard on the ice.

"You okay, Soju?" he cried, seeing his sister sprawled on the platform.

"Give me a minute," she gasped, looking up with a pained smile. "Thank God you can catch."

"Best infielder Star of the Sea ever had," her brother grinned, holding the baby close to his chest. "Did you break anything?"

Before Soju could answer, a heavy-set man, the shadow of a two-day beard over his chin, stepped down from the adjoining car. Toshio had seen the man on the train, suspecting he was a plainclothes Canadian Pacific Railroad cop or RCMP. The man lifted Soju to her feet.

"Damn slippery," he said. "Somebody better get salt on this platform." He held her arm, momentarily steadying her on her feet before heading into the station without another word.

"You think he's worried we are going to sue the railroad, or was that our watchful Mounted Police?" Toshio muttered.

"I'm just relieved he didn't arrest me for loitering on the platform," Soju said with a relieved grin.

The vastness of the Union Station rotunda stopped them before they had moved more than three steps inside, dumb-struck by the sight of the cathedral-like station crowded with a moving mass of humanity. The baby began to cry. Soju laid her bundle at her feet and, taking the baby from Toshio, placed her lips close to the child's ear and began to croon softly in Japanese.

A year of camp supervision had conditioned the Wakabayashis to wait for orders before moving, so they continued to wait, mesmerized by the monotone speakers echoing off the vaulted ceilings. They had lost track of time when a tall stranger, who wore a black fedora tilted rakishly to one side, stepped directly in front of Toshio. Before Toshio could step back the man offered his hand.

"I'll bet you are the Wake-a-bay-ash-ee family." The man's round face broke into a shy grin "Right?"

"Wakabayashi." Toshio repeated the name cautiously, worried for a moment that he was about to be embraced by the stranger. "I am Toshio Wakabayashi."

"Great." The man whipped off his hat, revealing a mop of unruly blonde hair, which immediately flopped down over his forehead. He brushed the hair aside, his smile growing more confident. "That's one for me then. I was guessing it was you. I guess you didn't see me standing right behind you. I was afraid to ask until I heard the lady singing to the baby in Japanese. I said to myself, that must be the Waka—bee-yash-ees. You were singing in Japanese, weren't you?" He turned his smile on Soju, who nodded somewhat uncertainly. "I don't speak Japanese," the man added hurriedly. "And we don't often get the chance to hear anyone speaking Japanese in Toronto. There are not that many Japanese people here." He hesitated, fearing his confession may have offended. "But the song and the words sounded so beautiful. Your singing and the melancholy sound made me think of Cio Cio-san from Madame Butterfly. You know, when she was waiting for her Lieutenant Pinkerton to return…" He broke off, recognizing that Soju was merely nodding out of politeness.

"Well now, am I to understand that you three are the entire Waka-bee-yash ees family?" The man glanced at the meager pile of luggage. "And this is everything. Your entire luggage?"

"Wakabayashi," Toshio repeated, enunciating slowly. "This is my mother and my sister." He thought it wise to leave the baby unidentified, uncertain how much he should reveal to this stranger in the worn, double-breasted overcoat offering them his innocent grin. "They told us my brother Tatsuo will be coming on another train."

"Wonderful. I'm sorry, I should have explained. I am Philip Murphy. And I am here to welcome you to Toronto. And if you will permit me, I'm going to help you on your way, so to speak." The man's spectacles were beginning to fog up in the heat of the terminal. Turning to Soju he removed the glasses to wipe them in a crumpled soiled handkerchief, squinting as he spoke. "I am a Jesuit brother. Most people, at least those who work with me, call me Phil. Brother Phil, if you happen to be more comfortable with that. It is up to you." He shrugged, continuing his smile, which Soju noticed added life to his pale features. "I am assigned to Catholic Charities." He turned his sleeve, pointing to the white armband bearing the initials C.C. and clapped his hands enthusiastically. "And now, if you will permit me, Catholic Charities would like to start off by treating each of you to a good breakfast, and that includes the wee one there." He focused his smile on the baby. "I imagine after two days on the train you are all eager to get going? I hear the train doesn't serve breakfast the morning the Transcontinental arrives in Toronto. Is that right?"

"Breakfast?" Toshio was about to tell him about the hard-boiled eggs and the loaf of sliced bread he bought at the Calgary Station, but Murphy's attention had shifted to the scattered luggage.

"In that case," Murphy went on enthusiastically. "What do you say we gather up your stuff and be on our way?" He reset his glasses on the bridge of his nose and surveyed the assortment of belongings on the station floor and reached for Yuki's blanket bundle of china. "Allow me to help you with some of this."

"That's breakable," Toshio said nervously, snatching the bundle. "Why do you want to help us, anyway? We are not Catholics."

"That doesn't really matter much," Murphy replied. "Our Provincial House received a telegram from British Columbia informing us of your coming. Though chances are there would have been somebody here from C.C. regardless of whether or not your Jesuit friends sent us the wire. C.C. has people like me at the station every day meeting relatives of service personnel, displaced persons, and people like you being moved around because of the war." He grinned boyishly. "Catholicism is not a prerequisite." He picked up Yuki's hamper and began herding the Wakabayashis toward the street. "Come on. Our baby is beginning to fret. We'll get the restaurant to heat some milk. Boy or girl?"

"Girl," Soju replied, tightening her arms about her baby, still undecided about this man whose quick smile reminded her so much of Michael.

Brother Murphy led them out of the Union Station and over a pedestrian path cut in the snow across Front Street. "I understand you know a Jesuit, Father Lavoie?" He spoke over his shoulder in bantering conversation as he picked his way over the snow.

Toshio answered with a noncommittal nod. "My dad worked for him."

"Well, it was Father Lavoie who sent us the telegram informing us of your coming. As I understand things, your father will be joining you here in Ontario. Is that right?" Brother Murphy stopped at the curb to offering a steadying hand to Soju. "Father Lavoie's message indicated all this was arranged by the Vancouver RCMP. Right?" The questions were coming too fast for Toshio and he said nothing. "This old world gets smaller by the day, doesn't it?" the brother went on happily.

"Do you know where my father is right now?" Toshio asked.

"I'm not certain," Murphy replied. "But we were told he'd be relocated around Niagara Falls, to work in the orchards there. I will get the details for you once we get you straightened around. You asked about your brother? "

"Tatsuo has been in the road camps in British Columbia," Toshio replied.

"Well, when he arrives, I can arrange transportation for all of you to Niagara. You are free to go on your own of course, though it might be better for the young lady here to look for work in Toronto. There are several Japanese women sewing in a parachute factory here. Even a domestic position might be better for a girl than working in the orchards. C.C. can help should she decide that's best."

"What about our travel permits?" Toshio asked.

"There are no travel permits in Ontario." Murphy removed his hat, pushing his fingers through his untrimmed hair. A tiny transparent drop had formed at the tip of his nose. He sniffed loudly and it disappeared. "In Ontario, you can go where you please." He pointed to the cafe doorway. "Lord, I hope I'm not catching cold in this wind. How about this place? Then we can go over your plans."

It was all happening too quickly for Soju. In a few short moments this stranger had taken command of their lives. Even Toshio was trotting submissively at his heels. The baby had stopped crying, seemingly reassured by the man's soft-spoken confidence. There was gentleness in Brother Murphy's eyes that made it easy to feel secure, and she decided she would like him and trust him.

Chapter 32 Dead Letters

The envelope arrived at the Costello house four days before Christmas, the address spelled out in a round, schoolgirl hand. Eileen Costello had been standing behind the lace curtain — as she did each day — watching for the postman making his way up the path to her front steps. She knew the postman by name and in the summer months often came out of the house to meet him by the low-slung front gate. But this was Christmas and it was wet and cold; besides, she didn't want to appear too eager for what he might or might not bring. George Walker, the overweight, door-to-door postman, was ready for retirement. He served the Costello route with such punctuality that Eileen was able to time when he would appear almost to the minute, his bag over his shoulder, sorting letters with a proprietary curiosity. Eileen had baked him a rum-soaked Christmas cake, now sitting on the hall table wrapped in Christmas foil. Walker would have to wait for that until Boxing Day. This day she was looking for a letter or a card from Joseph. He had been gone so long without a line.

The moment the envelope slipped through the letter slot her glance picked up the schoolgirl handwriting and she froze, her eyes fixed on the envelope at her feet. After a long moment, during which she attempted to deny what her instincts were telling her, she picked up the envelope and held it up to the daylight streaming through the opaque glass in the front door. The post mark read Calgary, Alberta. The address, Michael Costello, 2145 West York Street, Vancouver, B. C. Driven by an intense sense of matriarchal protection, she slipped her fingernail beneath the flap, testing the seal. It held. She turned the envelope over in her hands several times before turning to the portrait of Jesus with the bleeding heart and prayed briefly for forgiveness for her thoughts. She then went into the living room, leaving the bulk of the Christmas mail on the hall floor, and dropped the unopened envelope into the green Chinese vase alongside the fireplace.

Chapter 33 Juanita

In her early years, Juanita Mulhern's sandy-colored hair grew in tight, kinky curls and the freckles reigned boldly across the bridge of her nose. She lived as a member of the Costello family, having arrived when she was four carrying a small, black kewpie doll wrapped in a blanket. The Costello boys had watched her standing in the rain outside their house alongside her father's patrol car, stubbornly refusing to budge, the rain flattening her hair in ever tighter curls. "It's Little Orphan Annie," Joseph Costello quipped, looking down on the scene from an upstairs window with his two brothers. The three of them watched their mother hurry out to the curb and wrap her arms around Juanita, holding her close for a long time in the rain. When they came into the house, she told her sons Juanita's mother was under the weather and Juanita would be sleeping in Michael's room for a while. Michael would sleep with Seamus.

Later the Costello boys heard Juanita's story of how she watched through the rain running down her bedroom window as two ambulance attendants wheeled her mother from their home. Colleen Mulhern's wasted body barely created a ripple beneath the sheets. She died in the tuberculosis ward of the General Hospital three weeks later.

For Eileen Costello it was as if she had been sent the daughter she had prayed for through the birth of each of her sons, and from that morning there was never a moment when Juanita was a stranger in the house. There were photographs in the Costello family album of Juanita naked, floundering hip and thigh, in the Saturday night tub with Michael and Seamus. Juanita took her first communion in a crisp white frock alongside Michael wearing his first suit and tie. Even Michael's early reputation for being ready to fight had a lot to do with Juanita being on his side.

She was ten when she returned home to live with her father. After that, she moved through the years at a quicker pace than the Costello boys, leaving Michael and Seamus in corduroy pants and playground sweatshirts as she began appearing in silk stockings and high-heeled shoes. They would see her now and then walking arm and arm with older boys, including Stanley Glasheen's older brother Claude. But it was only Michael who had the nerve to tease her from a distance, and after a spell even that seemed to have lost its appeal.

Michael had not seen Juanita since the day she accompanied Chief Mulhern to say farewell to Joseph when his regiment boarded the train to war. Oh, they exchanged distant smiles when passing in the halls of the high school and during the occasional Sundays when they would nod to one another on the church steps. But Juanita had become a stranger in the Costello house, as if a sister had gone off to college and forgotten the way home. Michael never saw her coming the day she stepped back into his life.

He was walking home from the Star of the Sea late that Friday afternoon following his reconciliation with Father Lavoie. Neither his reciting the Sorrowful Mysteries of the Rosary nor Father Lavoie's absolution had turned him from his plans to find Soju. He was so caught up in the confession of love and regret he would pledge to Soju that he never heard the big, green Hudson sedan roll up alongside the curb.

"Costello." Juanita's sharp voice spun him around. "Get your head out of your bum before you get run over." She leaned across the front seat of the car with the teasing grin he remembered well. Michael's recollection of Soju coming to him through the snow along the Wakabayashi garden path vanished from his mind. "What's the matter kiddo? You look as if you are seeing a ghost," Juanita laughed, delighted at having startled him.

"Mulhern?" Michael muttered, momentarily annoyed at having his dream invaded. Juanita's hair, once a crown of tight curls, lay in soft, copper waves off her face and her freckles lay buried beneath a cosmetic veneer. She wore a camel-hair overcoat thrown loosely over her shoulders with a silk scarf knotted in a large bow at her neck. When she got out of the car he saw she was wearing wartime silk stockings that curved up over shapely calves from her spike-heeled shoes. He stammered, a slow smile crossing his face. "I thought for a minute I was being hustled by a movie star, Mulhern."

"That kind of talk will get you whatever your little heart has in mind, Costello," she grinned.

Michael, embarrassed at having overdone his compliment, quickly replied: "What's with all the face paint? You in love, little girl?"

"Since when did you begin noticing girls wearing lipstick, Costello?" Juanita puckered her painted lips mischievously.

He shook his head. "You always were too fast for me, Mulhern."

"Was I now? Well, I'm here to see that you don't forget that." She walked over to him and locked her arm through his with an infectious grin beaming up at him like a light in the darkness of his December afternoon. "Besides, what do you care whether or not I am in love, Costello? There doesn't seem to be much point in a girl waiting around for you. Though I heard you can't stay out of trouble without me."

"You were good, Mulhern, I'll give you that." Michael shook loose of her arm and took a horsing-around boxing stance. "But one punch and you went down like a wet bird."

"It never happened. I may have played a bit soft for the likes of you." Juanita danced a step away with her fists at the ready. "But you never dared mess with me, did you now? Come on, and I'll give you the old one two."

Michael couldn't hold back his laughter and pulled her to him, wrapping his arm over her shoulder. He felt comfortable with her next to him, and for the first time since the day he walked away from Soju he was feeling good about himself.

"You come to visit Mum?"

"And you," Juanita said. "I have been informed by the Chief of Police himself that you may be in need of my feminine charms." She laughed a short, throw-away laugh that seemed to ridicule the dark thoughts that had been filling his mind. "My Pop hinted that if I don't get back into the picture, you could go chasing off after somebody else. It isn't true, is it Michael? Until just now, I was sure the old man was pulling my leg. But when I saw you moping along the sidewalk like a man headed for the grave, I said to myself: *Juanita, there's something going on with your guy.* She attempted to run her fingers through his hair.

"And what's this? Slickum in your hair?" She made a pretense of sniffing behind his ear. "He smells sweet, too. I'm beginning to see what the chief was getting at, Costello. Now, if you could just get rid of that stinky sweater and those terrible pants. Who knows? Maybe a nice girl like me could go for you, huh. Honest to God, Mike, you dress like you are still a sixth-grade kid chasing around the playground." Michael surrendered with a shake of his head.

"So tell me about this hot romance of yours, Costello." She punched him playfully on the arm. "What happened between you and your Miss Tojo of 1942, or whatever her name was?" Juanita was quick to catch his sudden mood change. "Ouch. I touched a nerve?" She pulled a face mocking his dour look. "Okay. I'm sorry. But I'm just saying I'm sorry so's you won't look so injured. Don't expect me to be sorry that the cops moved the dame out of my territory. And you are my territory, Michael. You know that. Even though I may let you trifle with some Japanese gal, it doesn't mean you can go getting any ideas."

To Eileen's eyes the picture of Juanita Mulhern coming through her kitchen door with her arm locked possessively around Michael's waist was a far cry from the freckle-faced child she remembered. She was facing a woman who was gazing up at her son with a possessive, this-is-my-man look in her eyes that momentarily took the breath out of Michael's mother.

"Look who nearly ran over me, Mom. And she's driving Chief Mulhern's Hudson," Michael announced. "I'll bet she doesn't even have a driver's license. Do you, Mulhern?"

Eileen Costello wiped her hands in her apron and reached out to take Juanita in her arms. "Where have you been, child? How long has it been? Christmas last? You will stay to supper with us?" She threw a questioning glance at Michael. "Michael, have you told her Seamus is about to go overseas any day now? They are sending his regiment to Kingston, Ontario, I think. He hopes to go from there to join up with the Canadian First Division and be with his brother Joseph. This may be the last chance for all of us to have supper together, you and the two boys. Will you stay, Juanita?"

"Okay, I'm staying." Juanita slipped out of her coat and tossed it to Michael. "Your son here never told me about Seamus, mother Costello. It was the chief who sent me. He issued a summons to be served on every Costello I could find. Our chief constable says those Costello's still in town on Christmas day are to appear at our house for Christmas dinner. Two o'clock. Come early if you like. Dad says it's been too long since we have all been together. Besides, I need to get my hooks into this wandering Romeo of yours." She added a gentle punch at Michael's biceps. "You still intend on marrying me, right, Michael?" Juanita's teasing brought the blood to Michael's face. "Look at him blush, mother Costello. I suppose he's about to deny he ever proposed?" She grimaced with exaggerated pain. "To think this is the boy who begged me to run away with him. Who promised we would ride wild horses across the prairies together and live like Indians in a tent. And don't you dare deny it, Michael Costello."

Michael shifted uncomfortably, attempting to dismiss the subject with an awkward grin.

"And I'm your witness to every word." Seamus had quietly appeared in the kitchen doorway, a bemused grin on his face. Michael instantly saw the glaze in his brother's eyes and hoped the others wouldn't pick up on the signs that Seamus had been drinking. Michael had seen that slightly bewildered, happy-go-lucky expression before, a look he'd become accustomed to seeing in his father in years past. Seamus was taking on many of Eamon Costello's ways, including singing Irish ballads in a voice reminiscent of his father. The whiskey glow in his cheeks was only a little less obvious inheritance.

Seamus wore his Seaforth Highlanders regimental battle dress, the tunic tightly buttoned across his chest, the high-top black boots shined and topped with white puttees. *He looks so much older*, Michael thought, *even a little dangerous*.

"I was there and heard him promise to marry you, Mulhern. Heard it all with my own ears." Seamus raised his eyebrows in a challenging look at his younger brother. "And if he's getting cold feet, you just give old Seamus the nod and you will find me ready and willing." With that he strode into the kitchen and lifted Juanita off her feet, holding her effortlessly high in the air while he kissed her on the mouth. "My God, little girl, you have grown into a full-blown woman, eh?"

"Seamus. Put her down," Eileen demanded petulantly. "You'll break the child's bones tossing her about like that."

"See. What did I tell you?" Juanita cried triumphantly from where she was cradled in Seamus' outstretched hands. "Your bother remembers, Michael. You are trying to weasel out of it."

There was a touch of wicked mischief in her tease, almost as if she were reading Michael's mind. Michael was in fact remembering and the memory caused him to fidget nervously, worried how far her teasing would go. Juanita had made it easy for him not to take their childhood games to confession. "We are only playing a game," she had insisted in the shadows of the Costello garage. "Father Lavoie would think you were silly telling him. There's no sin in make believe."

Watching her swish her narrow hips provocatively about the kitchen, Michael was remembering the brazen little girl peeling off her sweater to show off the swelling, pink buds on her chest. "Touch them, Michael. Touch them if you want to."

Michael went to the sink and turned on the tap, unable to deal with her resurrecting their mischief. He plunged his hands beneath the running water and raked his fingers through his wet hair.

Seamus set a brown paper bag on the kitchen table and ceremoniously lifted a partially consumed bottle of Seagram's rye whiskey from its folds. "Anybody here feel like joining me in a little celebration?" Without waiting for an answer he laid out four water glasses and poured a generous finger of whiskey into each. "I propose a toast to young love, wherever we find it, eh kids?" He winked at Michael. "And if anybody doesn't want to drink to love, then we can drink to my shipping out tomorrow." The silence that followed his announcement sucked the air out of the kitchen.

"Tomorrow?" Eileen's lips barely moved as she repeated the word.

"Yep. Christmas in Kingston. We finish our training there until we ship overseas. You showed up just in time, Mulhern," he said, his words whiskey soft and touched with sentiment.

"But it's only been a week or two since they put you on notice," Eileen protested. Seamus shrugged and hugged her with one arm, raising his glass in the other.

"To my brothers," Michael answered in a serious voice, lifting his glass. "May God watch over them both and bring them home to us." He downed the whiskey and felt it explode in his chest. Eileen sipped her whiskey but it failed to restore the color to her face. What Michael said next seemed at first to pass over her head without her having heard.

Michael coughed. "I have an announcement to make as well, Mom. This is a good time to tell you something that's been on my mind. I won't be here for Christmas either. I was worried about you being alone. Now that the Mulherns are going to be looking out for you, everything is falling into place." He smiled nervously.

"What will be falling into place?" Eileen's question was something of an abstract denial, her thoughts still mixed up with Seamus' leaving.

"I intend to make a Christmas retreat with the Jesuits at St. Michael's in Spokane," Michael answered. "I'll be gone for a week." Eileen's vision had always been that one of her sons would end up serving Mass in a nearby parish, somewhere close so she could iron and launder his vestments and be a mother forever. It was a dream she often shared with the boys. "But the Jesuits," she muttered uncertainly. "I would never see you with the Jesuits. They send those Jesuits everywhere, Africa and China."

"Mother, there's not much chance of my ending up a Jesuit, even if I should decide I have a vocation. You know I don't have the grades. Besides, I couldn't take the twelve years to final vows. I just want to do this retreat." Eileen nodded in silent approval, aware her son had just come from his confession with Father Lavoie. Juanita's tipped-back chair slammed to the floor with a bang and she was on her feet in Michael's face in a flash.

"What's this? You, thinking of spending your life as a Jesuit? Give us a break, Michael. Don't believe a word of it, mother Costello. Excuse me, but I know this guy. He's just—"

"I didn't say I was making a commitment to anything," Michael added hurriedly. "I'm not a candidate. All those academic and spiritual examinations are not for me." He was talking too fast, hoping to shut out the questions he could see coming and wishing he had left Juanita at the curb. "I couldn't get through all that, even if I wanted to."

"He's been talking to Father Lavoie today," Eileen explained cautiously. She could sense her son's nervousness and she was suddenly afraid that Juanita's skepticism would lead to Michael confessing the reason he needed time with the Jesuits. "Maybe we better let things be," she said, forcing an understanding smile. Juanita wasn't ready to let go.

"Michael. You are not trying to tell us that Father Lavoie put this idea in your head without ever talking to your mother?"

"No. For crying out loud! Father Lavoie had nothing to do with this. I'm going on my own, using money from my university fund." Michael spoke with an attempt at indignation; the whiskey burning in his belly added confidence to his lies. Besides, he reasoned, they would all discover the truth soon enough. What difference did it make how far he stretched things? "I won't be going to university until after the war anyhow," he added.

Juanita downed the last of her whiskey and, raising the empty glass up to his nose, eyed him suspiciously. "Those Jesuits will get you up at four in the morning with their mea culpa and you will never escape." She shook her head, the tight curls suddenly reappearing where the beauty parlor had carefully worked to flatten them out. She turned to Eileen, her face flush with the confrontation. "You see what this man comes up with the minute a girl reminds him he's promised to marry her. I'm insulted. He's telling me he would rather become celibate than keep his promise."

Seamus drained the remainder of the whiskey bottle over the four glasses, evenly dividing the Seagram's.

"We all knew that someday this was coming for Mike," he said, raising his glass with a wink at Michael. "Get it out of your system, little brother. Go for it."

***

Eileen Costello wrapped cold chicken and pickles in wax paper and placed the package in a brown paper bag while her son slipped into his raincoat. She tucked the bag beneath his arm, believing his cool behavior was merely Michael's way of handling his emotions over his leaving her alone at Christmas. Michael mumbled a harried thanks for the food, avoiding his mother's apprehensive frown.

"By suppertime you will be happy to have it," she said. "And Michael, don't be worrying about me. Just remember to say a

Rosary for your father at St. Michael's. And say one for each of your brothers." Her voice dropped apologetically. "And if you find the time, it would be nice if you could say one for me as well."

With that, she took him by the arm and led him into the front hall and pulled him to his knees before the portrait of Jesus with the bleeding heart. "Pray with me, son." She closed her eyes.

Michael balked. "Mother. I'm running out of time. I promise to pray on the train. You are going to make me miss my train."

"Michael, God will always see to it that a son who takes time to pray with his mother will travel safely."

"Hail Mary, full of grace, the Lord is with Thee. Blessed art Thou among women and blessed is the fruit of Thy womb Jesus."

There was a perceptible pause while Michael struggled with whether he should put aside his lies and tell her everything. He was surprised he felt so little guilt and responded weakly.

"Holy Mary, mother of God, pray for us sinners now and at the hour of our death."

"Watch over my sons," Eileen Costello prayed. "Wherever they may be." Struggling to her knees she announced: "Michael, I am coming to see you off on the train."

"No," Michael insisted. "It's raining and cold. The streetcars will be packed with Christmas shoppers. You wouldn't get home for hours. Besides, I don't want to be looking out the train window at you bawling on the station platform."

His mother sighed, disappointed but comforted by the thought she may be making this gift of her youngest son to God.

Chapter 34 Deceit in Sandon

A sharp wind whipped the powdered snow through the Sandon valley that morning. Two hundred miles to the west, ocean clouds were enveloping Vancouver in a somnolent pre-Christmas Season when Michael Costello left home. He walked at an even, unhurried pace, his collar turned up against the rain, occasionally glancing over his shoulder, uncertain in his lies, worried that his mother or Juanita, or more likely Chief Mulhern, had failed to swallow his story of a Jesuit retreat.

Michael explained he would catch the morning Great Northern to Seattle for a connection to Spokane and St. Michael's; he left the details intentionally vague in case Juanita carried the story to her father. The policeman in Mulhern would see through the itinerary in an instant. Michael's plan was to mingle with the Great Northern passengers boarding the Seattle train until the last minute before departure. He would then slip out of the terminal and walk through downtown Vancouver to the Canadian Pacific Railroad Station and wait for the night train that would take him to the Kootneys and Soju.

Unable to shake his fear that, given the time, Juanita or her father would see through his lies, his uneasiness increased the minute he entered the Great Northern Terminal. The crux of his worry was the chief. The old fox could appear out of the crowd at any minute with his know-it-all grin having trapped him in his lie.

Michael loitered at the Great Northern magazine stand until the call for the Daylight boarding for Bellingham, Snohomish, Everett and Seattle, then fell in with the passengers moving toward the standing train. Stepping around the last car, he crossed the tracks and sprinted across the open rail yard. If this was a crazy dream, he told himself, it was a dream that promised to take him to Soju.

On reaching the Main Street sidewalk, he slowed to a brisk walking pace, catching his breath at each intersection until he faced the Canadian Pacific Terminal, and hesitated inside the main doors, reconnoitering the rotunda. In the far reaches of the deserted terminal a lone broom pusher loitered near the magazine stand. The entire row of ticket cages was vacant but for one where a middle-aged blonde sat, looked out from behind the wire mesh cage like a yellow-feathered bird. Michael waited, watching the woman nervously probe the nest of her bleached blonde hair with the pointed end of a pencil, before deciding to approach.

"Ticket to Slocan," he said too loudly, placing four ten dollar bills on the counter. The woman didn't answer. "Slocan," he repeated.

"You said that. I'm not deaf. You want one way?" The woman's eyes cut to his four ten dollar bills. She pushed one of them back at him. "One way is twenty six dollars."

"On second thought, make that a return ticket."

The woman retrieved the other ten, looking at him as if she was about to call for the police.

"Coach?"

"Yes, please."

"That's thirty-eight dollars return." She meticulously folded and punched his ticket, reached into the counter drawer for a two-dollar bill, and slid the two dollars and the ticket beneath the cage window. Michael picked up the ticket and in his hurry to get away started off without his change. When he turned back to the cage the two-dollar bill was gone.

"My change. I gave you four tens and I had two dollars in change." The woman gave him a long, blank stare, then casually opened the cash drawer and placed the two-dollar bill on the counter without a word.

It was still mid-morning, with the entire rotunda all but deserted, when Michael chose a bench partially concealed behind a dying, spindly Christmas tree, certain the woman in the ticket window was following his every move. Once behind the tall fir he dropped onto the bench in his rain-soaked clothes, engulfed by the pungent scent of the drying fir needles. He drew a low branch to his nose, seeking memories of a distant Christmas and his father.

***

Eamon Costello, the night-long stubble of ginger whiskers bristling his chin, threw open the front door and hollered into the house. "It's Christmas morning. Michael. Seamus. Joe. Come kiss your tired old Da." Michael smiled, recalling his father's plaintiff plea. Eamon Costello had stood as tall as a tree himself. "Your old Da has been out all the night keeping the streets safe for that old gasper, Santa Claus. He got here all right, did he? Well it was thanks to your Da, eh."

"Eamon." Eileen called out from the kitchen. "Get in out of the cold before the boys catch pneumonia with all your gabbing at the door." His dad ignored her with a broad grin and reached out to Michael and Seamus. "Come on boys, Da needs a hug. That's all the Christmas I'm askin'." Scooping Michael into one arm, he snatched up Seamus in the other. Joseph hung back. "Come on, Joe. No lad's too old to kiss his dad." And the four of them, arms around one another, wrestled and hugged their way through the front hall, Eamon's whiskey voice carrying the joy of Christmas through the house.

***

An off-key trumpet echoed through the train station, ending Michael's day dreaming. He looked down at the fir tree needles pressed between his fingers, the remnants of a Christmas already past as a second horn began awkwardly working its way through the scales. A third and then another joined in until the rotunda echoed with discordant brass. The terminal began filling with people and by the main doors a band of Salvation Army players began feeling its way into "Joy to the World." At the first sound of the carol, three Salvation Sisters came working their way toward the Christmas tree, baskets in hand, singing as they came. Two obviously beer-befuddled teenage boys in loose fitting army uniforms followed behind, shaking the hands of those who fed the Salvation baskets.

"The Lord has Come... Let Earth Receive Her King..." The Salvation horns blew more confidently, picking up the brave voices of the bonnet-bound singers. *"Let Every Heart... Prepare Him Room... And Heaven and Nature Sing. And Heaven and Nature Sing..."*

Their singing gave new life to Michael's plans. If Soju would have him, he would marry her in Sandon or wherever he found her. There was a war on. A priest would make allowances for that. If not, then these Salvation people would do. He hoped the band was headed for Sandon and began to form mind pictures of the Salvation ladies singing at a wedding beneath a tall Christmas tree covered in snow. His heart felt light and the warmth returned to his hands and feet as the band marched past, he dropped the two dollars from his ticket change into their basket and shook the hands of the two tipsy soldiers.

"Headed home for Christmas, sonny?" The railroad cop had quietly come up behind Michael's bench. The man wore tan trousers with a blue policeman's jacket and badge. He had a long, cadaver face that bore a deep scar from his cheek to his neck, the scar adding a skeptical twist to his smile. Momentarily startled, Michael recalled his father's warning. "Policemen don't ask questions just to be friendly. A man with something to hide, should be careful how he answers."

"No. I'm headed for Spokane." Michael wanted to bite his tongue the moment the words were spoken. The lies his mother had accepted would make no sense to a Canadian Pacific railroad cop familiar with the CPR routes. He tried to remember if he had said anything about Spokane to the woman in the ticket cage, suspecting she had called this cop.

"Spokane?" the cop repeated.

"Traveling to Nelson first," Michael added hurriedly. "I'm going to a seminary. On a Christmas retreat. With the Jesuits." He could hear his father laughing. *'How many times do you have to be told, men convict themselves answering questions nobody asked?'* Michael silently scolded himself. *'The guy asked if you were going home for Christmas. You told him. Now shut up.'*

A puzzled look passed briefly over the policeman's face, then the broken smile reappeared. Michael saw the next question coming. Why Spokane on the CPR? But before either of them could say anything, the terminal speakers blared out the boarding call for the Kettle Valley train. The railroad cop looked up at the bank of speakers as if he were being called away. "That your train?"

"Yeah."

"Then you better get going." Before Michael could react, the cop reached over the bench and picked up his suitcase. It contained nothing but a sweater, one change of underwear, his toothbrush and a razor rattling inside. "Traveling light?" The cop raised the suitcase with questioning frown.

Michael forced a smile and accepted the bag, now all but certain he was facing Chief Mulhern's man. Juanita must have told the chief. She had seen through the seminary story from the beginning. His dad's old pal had sent this cop to let him know they were on to him. He had made a mistake asking the chief to help locate the Wakabayashi family, claiming he merely wanted to write to his friend Toshio. Sure, and you expected him to believe that as well? Now this railroad cop, with a dead man's grin on his face, was probably going to make him miss the train.

"Nelson, you said?"

"Yeah."

The public address was repeating the boarding call and the rail cop fell in behind Michael as he started toward the gate behind the two tipsy teenaged soldiers. Michael last saw the cop leaning over the rail, watching him boarding the train.

By the time he made it to his car the two soldiers were sprawled over the plush seats, their legs stretched across the aisle. Stepping over their legs, he slid his suitcase beneath a seat next to a window and peeled off his damp raincoat, suddenly remembering that he had left the bag of chicken and pickles on the terminal bench. For a short time, he remained half-awake, barely conscious of the screaming crossing signals flashing past, the train charging into the darkness through the Fraser River Valley. Feeling warm for the first time since leaving home, he closed his eyes to the whispering mantra of the track and slept.

When he awoke the first thing he saw was a cherubic smile on a chubby face that would have been at home on a Christmas card. "It's time to wake up son. Slocan coming up." The round, cheery-faced conductor was gently shaking his shoulder. Michael bolted upright.

"What's the time?"

The conductor pulled on a chain hanging at his waist anchored to the pocket watch in his vest. It was a gesture of habit. Without glancing at the watch he answered. "Four in the morning. Right on time." He continued to smile on Michael with paternal concern.

"Those two soldier boys are sleeping and they have a ways to go," he whispered. " Let's not wake 'em." Michael turned to the window and peered into the darkness. He could feel the train slowing down.

"Where did you say we are?"

"Slocan." The conductor shook his head apologetically. "Hated to wake you, son. But this is where you want to get off."

Michael looked around at the soldiers buried beneath their army great-coats, their arms and legs entwined like four-legged frogs and for an instant wished he could stay aboard in the warmth of the train. He reached for his suitcase and, slipping his arms into the sleeves of his raincoat, staggered to his feet.

Before the screech of the brake pads died out the conductor swung down from the car and with surprising agility dropped a small step stool by the track. It all happened in one practiced motion, holding up a hand for Michael, taking the suitcase from his hand with the other. "Have a good night, lad," he said, quickly handing back the bag with his cheery smile and then, in less time than it took to say goodnight, he scooped up his step stool and was gone. Michael stood watching the train slipping quietly into the dark, the trailing red light vanishing in the night.

A blast of iron-fisted night air, colder and darker than anything he had ever felt, seized him instantly, snatching the breath from his lungs and chasing the last vestige of sleep from his brain. A path outlined in the snow led to a building with wind-driven snow piled up against the wall, the word "Slocan" clearly visible above the snow. With his body cringing for warmth within his light coat, Michael started up the path and stopped, aware of a movement among the shadows. Straining to see beyond the light he stepped closer to the edge of the path. A Provincial Policeman stepped into the light, his fur collar turned up around his face. The policeman studied Michael while slowly slapping his large leather gloves against the thigh of his britches in the manner of a man bringing his dog to heel.

"Expecting somebody to meet your train, young fella?" The policeman's voice came muffled through the thick fur collar.

"No," Michael answered, straining to see the man's eyes.

The policeman's pouter pigeon chest beneath the tightly buttoned coat and his thin, spindly tight leggings made him appear top heavy. He tipped back his hat to reveal the mildly curious expression common to a policeman at work. "You are not dressed for this kind of weather, kid." Before Michael could think of an answer, the policeman turned with a shrug and started back into the building. Michael trailed after him in time to see him enter the men's toilet.

Alone in the empty station, Michael scanned the buff-colored walls and the empty oak benches, realizing he had no idea where he was or how to get to Sandon from Slocan. A large poster advertising a mountain lodge somewhere in the snow-capped mountains showed a Canadian Pacific locomotive rushing through a mountain pass. An unattended smoke stand locked behind a metal screen at one end of the station offered no help. Michael decided to wait, listening for the toilet to flush. After fifteen minutes he left his case on a waiting-room bench and followed the policeman into the toilet, a long, narrow room with two wall-mounted urinals and two toilet cubicles. The cold air smelled of urine and chemicals.

"Hello in there?" Michael peered at the policeman's boots beneath the cubicle door. A toilet flushed.

"I wonder if you could tell me how a person gets to Sandon from here?"

"The Internment Camp?" The voice answered from behind the door. The toilet flushed again and the policeman came out buttoning his coat over a ragged True Detective magazine tucked into his belt. "That's a hell of a place for anyone to be going at this time of year. It's Christmas."

"I'm going there to be with some friends."

"There's nobody there but Japs locked up for the duration, for Christ sake. Couple of white men left over from the mines and the RCMP, but that's it." The policeman studied Michael with a puzzled look. "Japs don't make much of Christmas, do they?" He spoke while busying himself with the buttons on his heavy winter jacket, then turned to Michael with renewed interest. "You are going to freeze your knockers off up there in those clothes, kid." Michael shrugged. The policeman sighed sympathetically. "I guess

I can give you a lift into New Denver. You stand a chance of catching a ride from there to Sandon." He shook his head silently as if to discourage the idea. "There is a trucker there who hauls into Sandon." He pulled his fur cap down over his ears. "That's avalanche country. Lots of snow on that road," he added, recognizing his warnings were having little effect. "One hell of a place to be spending Christmas, that's all I can say."

***

Michael rode the police pickup into Kaslo through clouds of swirling dust-like snow beneath an overcast sky that seemed to promise more on the way. The policeman pulled up alongside a dual wheel, two-ton International dump truck outside a storefront café. A canvas tarpaulin covered the truck's dump bed, the outline of the loaded freight bulging beneath a coating of new snow. The truck was old, with large patches of rust visible around the doors. One side of the engine cowling was missing, revealing an engine blackened beneath years of grease and oil. A sleepy-eyed, long-hair dog rose up in the cab and put its head out the open window from the passenger side of the truck.

"That's old Charlie Grafton's rig. He's never far from that dog of his. You will find him around here someplace. Probably eating in the café." The policeman rolled down the pickup window. "Charlie does most of the hauling into Sandon. Looks as if he is either loaded to go or just come back from there. Anyway, he is your best bet, kid."

Michael stepped out of the pickup as the policeman flipped on the truck siren, sending a brief wail over the deserted roadway, and quickly drove off grinning mischievously.

A wiry little man with a two-day stubble of grey beard instantly appeared, hurrying out of the coffee shop chewing on the remainder of his food. "What in hell was that all about?" he demanded, having spotted Michael sitting on the running board of the truck. "And who in hell are you?" The man held a half-eaten donut in one hand and a paper-wrapped package in the other hand.

"My name is Michael Costello," Michael answered, getting to his feet. "I am looking for a ride into Sandon. The Provincial

Policeman told me the man who owns this truck would be the only way I had of getting there."

The little man worked a toothpick from one side of his mouth. "You like dogs?"

"Sure. I suppose," Michael answered. "Are you Charlie Grafton?"

"How come you got my name?"

"The policeman told me."

Grafton opened the truck door and the dog, a long-limbed cross between a collie and several other breeds, climbed painfully down from the cab and began nosing into the package hanging from the old man's hand.

"It'll cost you two dollars," the trucker said, measuring Michael with ice-blue eyes that were partially screened behind his perpetual squint. "I guess if Cecil set you on my truck you ain't running from the law. You don't have a mind to rob me or anything like that?" Grafton never glanced down at the dog while allowing the paper package in his hand to unfold. The dog — repeating a long-practiced trick — shoved its nose into the paper and put his teeth into what looked to be the remnants of a meat sandwich.

Michael counted out two one-dollar bills. "When do we leave?"

Grafton spat the toothpick onto the ground. "In a hurry, ain't you? Can't get started until Junior here finishes his sandwich. You are going to share the seat with Junior. Best we let him eat first so's he won't have a mind to be taking a bite out of you." The old man laughed, revealing several missing teeth. He reached into the cab of the truck. "Here," he tossed a canvas jacket to Michael. "Put that on. The day's not going to get much better" The dog bolted down the remains of the sandwich, eyeing the new passenger warily. "Next to my truck, Junior there is my most reliable friend," Grafton said climbing into the cab. "He don't really bite. Like me, he don't have enough teeth to do much biting even if he had a mind to. But he's old and he farts a lot. You'll just have to put up with it." He placed an affectionate pat on the dog's head. "Ready to go, old boy? Climb in kid."

Charlie Grafton steered the rattling International over an endlessly winding road, skirting sheer shoulder drops made treacherous by thin coatings of snow and ice. Each time Michael felt the tires lose their grip in the ruts in the snow Grafton would curse through pursed lips. "God damn," and slam the transmission from gear to gear, pulling the International back onto the middle of the road. "Hang on kid; don't want to lose my paying passenger."

They had been crawling through what seemed to Michael to be endless hours with only the yellowish headlight beams revealing a few feet of roadway when Charlie Grafton brought the truck to a stop atop a slight rise in the road. He threw open the driver-side door and the dog leapt out into the snow.

"Junior's got as much right to piss as you and me," Grafton said, unbuttoning his trousers to join the dog. "Can't get this damn dingle berry of mine workin' worth a damn in the cold. " He was talking to Michael over his shoulder, waiting for his pee to flow, leaving the engine idling as if he was giving the old truck a chance to catch a breather. "At least old Junior is safe out here taking a leak. I'm sure as hell not turning him loose in Sandon. He could end up in somebody's chop suey. I hear Japs love dog meat. You ever hear that?"

Michael rubbed his fist over the frosted windshield, his eyes following the headlight glow down the road. "No. Raw fish. Some of them eat raw fish. I never heard of anyone eating dogs."

Charlie Grafton gave up trying to pee, looked up into the truck and grinned. "What's the matter? You disappointed? What'd you expect, kid? The bright lights of Chilliwack?"

"What do you mean?" Michael rubbed his sleeve over the windshield, clearing a hole in the icy glass. The pale beams from the headlights stretched out over a short section of the road. At the outer edge of the light he could see the outline of several shacks tucked into the snow at the edge of the road.

"You are lookin' at Sandon, kid," Grafton chuckled as he climbed back into the cab. "Now you can tell your grandkids you made it to Sandon, B.C., when it was full of Japs."

The dog leapt back into the cab, shaking the snow from his hide before settling down next to Michael. Grafton released the brake and the truck began rolling down the hill between the ruts in the snow like a hound on the scent. Human shadows, muffled in scarves and battered hats, moved in and out of the truck's trembling headlight beams. Grafton eased the truck off the road into a clearing scooped out of the snow.

"This is the end of the line kid," Grafton announced, climbing down from the cab. He walked to the front of the truck to open the steaming radiator cap. "You say you are lookin' for some Jap friend of yours?" He swore and dropped the hot radiator cap into the snow. "Well, this place is full of 'em. I hope you know which one you are after. Like they say, they all look alike, eh." He began beating his arms against his chest and stopped long enough to point to a shack leaning into the side of the hill. "That there's the district RCMP office. The Mounties keep tabs on everyone in the camp. None of 'em moves without the Mounties' say so. Best you ask them about your friends." He pulled back his coat sleeve searching for his watch. "It's now going on six, kid. I'm out of this load in about two hours and heading back. You can ride along for another two bucks. Junior here seems to like you okay. You can keep each other warm."

"Thanks." Michael began to peel off the canvas jacket. "I think I will be staying."

Grafton shook his head. "Wait and see what the Mounties say before you make up your mind. I got a feeling you are going to be lookin' for a way out of here later today. Whether it's today or tomorrow, I'm probably going to be the one who hauls you out of here. You can hang on to the coat 'til then."

The door to the RCMP office faced a shallow wooden deck sheltered beneath an overhanging corrugated roof, the entire building capped beneath two feet of crusted snow. A pair of narrow windows flanking the door looked out onto the road, casting an orange light over the snow. Michael had the feeling he was about to enter a cottage crafted from a Christmas fairy tale. He stepped onto the porch and looked in the window. Two policemen sat facing one another from either side of a single desk. One was reading a Vancouver newspaper beneath a gooseneck desk lamp. The other sat with his chair tipped back, his hands folded over the belly of his open tunic, his eyes closed. Both looked up at the sound of Michael stamping the snow from his shoes.

"Hi."

The awakened policeman let his chair come to rest on all four legs. "Shut the bloody door."

"Sorry." Michael quickly stepped inside, drawing the door shut behind him. "I just came in with Charlie Grafton. He said I should come to see you guys for some help."

Michael recognized the trick when neither policeman spoke. Let the suspect talk and what he says can be used against him. Another lesson from Eamon Costello. But Michael had always been comfortable around policemen, unaware that his friendly smile was regarded as presumptuous to the man who had put down the paper.

"I'm looking for some Japanese friends of mine who are here in the encampment."

The lean, angular man with the newspaper pushed back his chair pensively, sizing up the lanky teenager wearing an ill-fitting fur collar canvas jacket two or three sizes too small.

"And just who are these friends you are looking for, young fella?" The policeman got up out of his chair and started toward the office counter. Michael took note of the two stripes on each sleeve of his uniform shirt.

"They are from Vancouver. The Wakabayashis?"

"Japanese, you say?" the corporal replied with a note of curiosity. "Wakabayashi? You sure they weren't Swedish with a name like that?" He grinned a patronizing smile and turned to the short, heavy-set policeman at the desk who had been sleeping. "Sorensen here could probably help you if they were Swedes." The corporal opened a drawer at the counter and brought out a manila file folder and repeated the name. "Wakabayashi? Let's see what we got here."

It occurred to Michael that it was odd, or perhaps just fortunate, that the corporal was able to produce the Wakabayashi file so readily. The thought passed quickly.

"And what did you say your name was?" the corporal asked innocently.

Another police trick Michael recognized. He hadn't said his name but answered quickly. "Michael Costello."

"And you do have a permit to be here, Michael?"

The thought flashed through Michael's mind that maybe the folder was something else. Maybe that folder was a listing of those with permits. "Nobody told me about permits," he answered.

"Then you either didn't ask or you weren't listening when told," the corporal replied coldly. "This is an internment camp under the jurisdiction of the British Columbia Security Commission. Civilians are required to have authorization before coming in here."

Michael stammered, then fell back on his father. "Look. I'm a friend of Chief Constable Dougal Mulhern in Vancouver. He's the one who told me my friends were here. My dad served with Chief Mulhern on the Vancouver force." He was tempted to add that his dad was killed in the line of duty, but had never played that card, not even with Soju. He let the thought pass.

The corporal looked to his partner. "Mulhern? Sorensen, do we know a Chief Mulhern in Vancouver?"

The man who had been sleeping answered with a ponderous shake of his head.

"What about Costello? That name mean anything to you, Sorensen? You are the one who spent half your life going to college in the city."

"Nope. Can't say it does. But I have heard of Chief Mulhern."

Sorensen untangled his legs from beneath his chair and came up and set his elbows on the counter, his fists propped beneath his chin, his eyes on Michael with a look of exaggerated suspicion. "Any particular member of this Wakabayashi bunch you happen to be interested in, Michael?"

"Soju Wakabayashi. She's the girl I'm going to marry if she will have me. That's why I came. I was hoping we could get married right here in Sandon before I go back to Vancouver to enlist." Michael grinned sheepishly and fished a palm-size velvet-covered box from his coat pocket. "She's getting this for Christmas."

The corporal took the box and flipped open the lid. Michael could only marvel at how the sixty-dollar diamond looked so tiny in the large-boned hands of the Mounted Policeman. The corporal lifted the ring out of the box.

"Well, well. Look at this, Sorensen." He handed the ring to the second policeman and swung open the hip-high wooden office gate, inviting Michael to pass into the inner space. "Come on in and sit down a minute, young fella. Let's see if we can't get you straightened around. I'm Corporal Jack Murdock. This officer here is Constable Dave Sorensen. Sorensen is a Vancouver boy. Went to the university there, didn't you, Sorensen."

Sorensen smiled. "How about a cup of tea, kid? You look as if you could use something hot. A man can lose a lot of body heat running around up here without a hat."

The corporal pushed a chair toward Michael. "You said your dad's name was Costello. Costello what?"

"Eamon Costello. He was about to be promoted to detective when..." Michael stopped.

The corporal's brow contracted, forming a series of wrinkles as if he were searching his memory. "When what?"

"He was shot," Michel added quietly.

The corporal shook his head. "Must have been a long time ago. I never heard of him."

Michael tried to mask his disappointment with a glance at the second policeman, who gave no sign of remembering. "Well, anyway," Michael continued. "Soju Wakabayashi and I have been going together for a couple of years."

"Hell, you're not much more than a kid right now, are you? What, fifteen? Sixteen?" the corporal said.

Michael inhaled, rising to his full six feet three inches. "I'm eighteen."

Corporal Murdock pressed the ring back into the velvet box and handed it back. He turned to Sorensen. "You go ahead and tell the kid, Sorensen."

"Tell me what?" Michael's voice revealed his sudden anxiety.

"You are the officer in charge," Sorensen shrugged.

The corporal released a long, weary sigh. "Well kid, it's like this. Your friends are no longer in Sandon. That's the case in a nutshell. You are a day late. That entire Wakabayashi clan shipped out of here a couple of days ago to join their old man in Ontario."

Constable Sorensen set a mug of tea in front of Michael. "Milk? Sugar?" Michael was too stunned to answer.

"And your Soju?" The corporal spoke her name sarcastically. "She must be some gal. Soju got married right here in camp the day before they shipped out. Married one of her own from one of the road camps. They left together, one happy family." The corporal turned up the palms of his hands in a gesture of helplessness and looked to Sorensen for confirmation.

"That's a fact," Sorensen added. "They had a regular wedding party. Rice flying through the air, the whole Magillicuddy. You would think with them being Japanese they would be eating the rice, not throwing it at one another, eh?" He waited for a laugh, his face visibly disappointed when it didn't come.

"Anyway," Corporal Murdock added, "you can bet they are not having much of a honeymoon travelling coach seats to Calgary, then two days and two nights from Calgary to Toronto sitting up all the way. What lovin' that guy gets, he is going to have to get it standing up. Sorensen and I gave them their tickets and put them on the train."

Michael put the ring box into his coat pocket, unwilling to accept what he was hearing. The corporal attempted a sympathetic smile that came off with more sarcasm than he intended. "Look. You hang on to that ring, kid. Some day there's going to be a nice Canadian girl comes along and you got the ring right there, handy to pop the question. These Jap women are not like Canadian girls. You should always count on them doing something sneaky, like running off with this other fella and all the time leading you along. Look what they did at Pearl Harbor. How'd you like to be hitched to someone that did a thing like that?"

"Soju's Canadian," Michael answered with quiet defiance.

"That may be. But it doesn't change what we have been telling you happened right here in camp now, does it? Those people have different ways of looking at things, kid. You didn't have any idea she was going to marry this other guy. Else you wouldn't have come running up here with that ring and all. And what happens? She stiffs you. Drink your tea. You look colder than the balls on a moose. Best thing for you to do right now is high-tail it on home. There's no need for anybody to know you were even here."

Michael was about to ask how she had looked, wanted to know the name of the Japanese she married. His thoughts ran through the names of the Japanese guy from school, then decided he really didn't want to know.

"Was there a forwarding address?" He hated the sound of his helplessness. Neither policeman bothered to answer. He wanted to ask if he could see where she had lived, to retrieve some trace of her having been there, something he could build a memory around. Before he could speak, the corporal wrapped a long arm around his shoulder.

"Finish your tea, young fella. Sorensen here will walk you over to Grafton's truck. He'll be pulling out in an hour or so. Take my word, the sooner you forget this Wakababy dame, the better off you are going to be. Right, Sorensen?"

Outside, the wind had swept away the clouds and a sunlight bathed the snow in a soft light. From somewhere through the trees Michael caught the sound of children's voices on the crisp air. They were singing Christmas carols.

Chapter 35 Lost

Wilting poinsettias and a small copse of dying Christmas trees surrounded the Star of the Sea manger scene. A pink plastic doll representing the newborn Christ looked up from a patch of scattered straw; the scene reminded Michael of his lost Christmas. Since his ignominious return from Sandon he had come to the church each morning to escape the reproachful silence of his mother. There, he would sit for hours quietly returning the sorrowful gaze of the crucified Christ suspended above the altar. The second day of the New Year following the morning Mass he became aware he was being watched from behind the sacristy door. From his days of serving Mass Michael was aware of the peepholes in the door that were all but invisible from the pews. The priest used the holes to count heads before Mass and note those who failed to appear for their Sunday obligation.

Michael decided to make it obvious he was aware of being observed, openly staring at the door. After a few minutes it opened and Father Lavoie stepped out. The priest genuflected before the tabernacle, paused for what appeared to be a hurried prayer on one knee, and then turned with a look of feigned surprise.

"Michael Costello." Father Lavoie's voice echoed through the empty church. "God truly works in wondrous ways. I have been wanting to have a talk with you ever since your trip."

Michael suspected his mother had revealed every detail of his Sandon lies, though he was momentarily grateful Father Lavoie chose to refer to his deceit as his trip.

"If it is Soju Wakabayashi you want to talk to me about, Father, I have already said all I am going to say." His words came out defiantly, as if he were telling the world to get off his back. Smiling benevolently, Father Lavoie came shuffling toward the back of the church.

"No, Michael. That's not it at all." The priest eased his bulky body onto the pew. "We need to spend a few minutes together so that I can talk about something more important. What I have been hoping is that we could have a talk about your relationship to God. These past few days I believe I have been watching someone who has lost his meaning in life."

Without pausing for an answer, or perhaps it was to avoid an argument, the priest hurried on. "I hesitate to say this Michael, but you appear to be so buried in self pity that you have lost sight of God."

Michael stood up to leave. The priest placed a warm, thick hand on his knee. "Michael, please. That is not all I have to say. I also believe the Holy Spirit is reaching out to you. God chooses our moments of great disappointment to lead us to the vibrant life that comes to all who serve Him. What is required on our part is a willingness to hear His call and answer: 'Here I am Lord. Do with me what you will.' Michael, few of us are born priests. For many of us it is our individual determination that leads to ordination. Callings such as my own are born through our prayers and the prayers of our parents and loved ones. But you, Michael, I believe, have a true calling from God. Your mother told me you were considering seminary after the death of your father."

A parish woman, one of the volunteers who came to the church each morning to launder and iron the vestments and altar linens, appeared at the sacristy door. She was about to call out to the priest, thought better of it and stepped back out of sight.

"It's true, I thought about seminary," Michael admitted sullenly. "So did my brothers. I know it would make mother happy after everything that has happened. But my ideas of God would have a tough time in the seminary." Michael yielded to the pressure of the priest's hand and eased back in the pew.

"Is that because you have been unable to understand why you have been hurt so badly by the death of your father? Or what happened with this girl, this Japanese?"

Michael groaned irritably. "Why do people pretend to listen to what I say, then try to tell me what I really mean? What happened between Soju and me has nothing to do with how I feel about God. And my dad is with me, now more than anyone knows."

"I am sorry, Michael. Tell me what it is about your thoughts that would be in conflict in seminary."

Michael sighed wearily, debating whether or not to get up and leave. "For one thing, you should know that I am not here every day praying for anything. I just want to be left alone. I don't know the God you say is calling me." The priest's benevolent expression changed. "I'm sorry, Father. It's just that I sometimes have the feeling that I'm the only one who really knows God and the God I know is not the same God that you and the sisters teach us is keeping score on everything we do." Michael paused, uncertain whether to go on.

"Yes." The priest's voice contained a note of uncertainty. "Please. I asked to hear."

"I believe there are times when I see God in the sunlight on the waves off of Fraser's Wharf. I know I saw Him often in my father's smile, and I still see Him in the photographs of my dad laughing with me in his arms. I understand why people climb to the top of a mountain, Father, because that is where they find their God. I believe the Indians' dancing brings the God they know to their fire. Their God loves them to dance; it's a prayer He understands. God spoke to the Jews from a burning bush when He told Moses to carve His Commandments in the stones. Mister Hyslop, the Star of the Sea choirmaster, told me that if I listened, I could hear God in the music of Mozart. I have listened and I have heard Him." Michael shrugged, suddenly uncomfortable with how much he was revealing of himself. "I'm sorry, but that's the way it is with me, Father. I once found God in a blueberry patch."

Father Lavoie continued to nod, though Michael sensed somewhat skeptically.

"I was lying on my back in the grass looking up through the bushes at the big, ripe blueberries. And I knew that if God ever existed in a form he wanted me to see, He was there, in those sweet blueberries. I don't suppose the sisters ever found God in a blueberry patch and I have an idea what they would say if I told them I did." Michael smiled at the futility of what he was trying to put into words.

"Father, I don't come to Mass because it is a sin if I don't show up. I can't believe God condemns me to hell if I stay in bed on a Sunday morning. I have never confessed that as a sin. Lots of good people sleep in Sunday morning. That's a working man's free time. How many times did my dad get to sleep on a Sunday without worrying whether he was missing Mass? I miss a lot of Sundays. So did my father, and I know he's not in hell. Sometimes I am at Mass just so I won't have to argue with my mother." Michael was surprised to see the trace of humor in the priest's eyes. "And yet there are times, Father," he added turning to the altar, "when I'm sitting here and I know He is here with me in His church. It's a good feeling. He listens."

"In the tabernacle?" the priest suggested. "You find Christ in the Eucharist?"

Michael shrugged. "It's something like when I visit with my dad." He was struggling with thoughts he had never shared and was beginning to hold back. "We don't say much, we just sit or walk together for awhile. Anyway, I don't think someone with these feelings would be acceptable in seminary, Father." He gave a quick, deprecating smile. "I know I didn't win your Jesuit scholarship, did I?"

The priest nodded knowingly. "And those thoughts have been going through your mind all the time you have been sitting here in the back of the church?"

"This has been one of my good days."

The priest's smile broadened. "Michael, I believe that in your own way you have truly found Him."

"I suppose sooner or later God is found by everyone whether they go looking for Him or not, Father. My dad used to tell me he talked to God nights when he was cold or when he was afraid. He was afraid sometimes, he told me so. You do know my mother always thought it would be my brother Joe who would end up being the priest in the family. Then Joe joined the army. He wrote us not to worry about him; that God was looking out for him over there. Then my mother prayed Seamus would be the one." He laughed a short chuckle shaking his head. "Seamus would probably tell you he's not the one. For Seamus, heaven would be any place with Juanita Mulhern in his arms."

"And you, Michael?" The priest paused. "Our hearts were made for you, O God, and they will not rest until they rest in you. Does that not speak for you?"

"That speaks for St. Augustine. Those were his words," Michael said quietly.

"That's right. And St. Augustine's experience is not unlike your own. Would you like me to hear your confession?"

"No. I have some things to do this afternoon. I'm taking my army medical today. If the army takes me, I'll keep looking for God on my own terms, Father. If they turn me down, then maybe I'll come looking for Him on yours."

The priest struggled to his feet, placing his hand on Michael's shoulder. "Take my yoke upon you, and learn from me, for I am meek and lowly in heart, and ye shall find rest unto your souls. For my yoke is easy, and my burden is light." Father Maurice Lavoie was certain he was witnessing the birth of a priest.

Chapter 36 An Engaging Meeting

Murray Goldberg operated his business out of a third floor office in the red brick Dominion Bank Building on East Hastings Street where he showed his diamonds behind a frosted glass door. The glass concealed a web of iron bars designed to deter a forced entry. Michael pressed the electric doorbell alongside the name plate. "M.C. Goldberg. Wholesale Jeweler." The buzzer was followed by a soft click unlocking the door. Goldberg, a thick-set man of late middle age, his head bowed beneath a tilted desk lamp, looked up from his chair behind the heavy, oak table that was jammed up against a chest-high service counter topped with a sheet of yellow-brown linoleum. Beyond the counter, the back wall was entirely taken up with a double-door steel filing cabinet. Michael fingered the box in his pocket containing Soju's engagement ring.

Goldberg got up from his chair and came to the counter. "What can I do you for, young man?" He smiled, pleased with his play on words.

Michael was surprised to see how Goldberg had aged. The man's chin, once visible in the wattle at his throat, now vanished into his neck which had become a mass of wrinkled flesh. The strands of black, wiry hair, formerly stretched over the top of his head, were now reduced to a single, carefully placed curl that had survived the years. He had known about Murray Goldberg since he was ten years old, yet wasn't surprised when Goldberg acted as if they were meeting for the first time. It had been that way when he came before Christmas to buy the ring for his run to Soju in Sandon. That's when Goldberg first confessed to a short memory.

"Hello, Mister Goldberg. Remember me?"

"Remember you? How should I remember you? People come here every day. I don't keep track of everyone comes in that door," the jeweler had protested.

Michael had been tempted to tell him that he remembered every detail of the day they first met more than five years ago. It was the day that Eamon Costello first confided in his youngest son, man to man.

***

Michael and his father rode the number 12 streetcar downtown together that day, an unusual father-and-son togetherness day. It seemed unusual because Eamon Costello wore his uniform, something he didn't like to do, especially on his day off.

Michael's father was in a chatty mood that Saturday, explaining in somewhat convoluted terms a policeman's responsibilities in taking care of people who take care of a policeman. "It's a community obligation," he said, continuing his reasoning right up to the moment they entered Murray Goldberg's frosted-glass doorway. Eamon indicated a folding metal chair in front of the high counter. "Now you just sit there and you might learn a thing or two. And be quiet while your Da does some business with Mister Goldberg."

Goldberg, his mouth filled with a large sugar pastry, brushed his hands on his trousers, licked the sugar from his lips and set what remained of the pastry on the counter, beaming like a man discovering a long lost son. Michael watched as he lifted the narrow gate at the end of the counter, inviting Eamon to step inside. Together they went to the steel filing cabinet, and the jeweler, with the reverence of a priest at the tabernacle, began spinning the combination dial. "And how's things going for you at the station?" he asked over his shoulder. "What are your chances of being promoted off the night beat, Eamon? I hear tell there's a desk sergeant promotion in the wings."

"That's not for me," Eamon replied. "However, if the right thing comes along, I'll think about it. Detective, maybe."

"Making detective? Would that be a burglary detail detective, Eamon?" Murray Goldberg nodded wisely and swung open the steel cabinet door.

"Phew. You keeping a body in there?" Eamon backed away from the cabinet, holding his nose as immediately the tiny office was filled with a smell of decay.

"I have to clean that out," Goldberg answered. "It's cheese. The old lady packs me a lunch and I never get time to eat the cheese."

"Smells like somebody died."

Goldberg nodded apologetically and began pulling trays from the cabinet.

The two of them then huddled at the open cabinet door, Eamon turning from time to time to cast an uneasy glance at his youngest son. When he came out from behind the counter he greeted Michael with a guilty grin. "Come along, son. Our business is finished here. And I trust you will always remember, Michael, our business is strictly between you and me," he added sternly. "You understand?"

"Sure dad," Michael pledged.

The answer pleased his father, who suddenly felt encouraged to take him deeper into his confidence. "This," he said, his voice dropping to a near whisper, "is by way of a little gift for a good friend." He opened a small leather bag and brought out a ring with a single green stone. "It's for a friend, just a friend mind. But I don't think your mother would understand. Women are funny when it comes to other women, Michael. Remember that. It will help you get along in the world."

***

The jeweler's memory was equally blank when Michael came to return the ring. "Remember you? How should I remember you? I don't keep track of who comes in that door," the jeweler protested. "You say you bought a ring, ok. So what?"

Michael handed him the ring box.

"I don't remember this ring," Goldberg said, quickly snapping the lid shut and pushing the box back across the counter. "How am I supposed to tell where you bought it? Rings come and go in this place. I got an eye and I remember the ones I sell. Not this one." The jeweler leaned his elbows on the counter. "One thing, I'll tell you. That's not my box." He eyed the box suspiciously. Michael was waiting for the jeweler to examine the ring with his jeweler's eyepiece as he had the day he sold the ring.

"When I bought the ring you told me the cut and the clarity of the stone was outstanding," Michael protested weakly.

"I'll give you twenty dollars," Goldberg said curtly. "What we are looking at here is a used diamond." His welcoming smile vanished. "As a favor to your old man, eh? You say he was a policeman? Okay, I'll take your word for it." He tapped a thick finger on the lid of the box. "Nobody wants to give a girl a second-hand engagement ring, kid. That may well be a perfectly good stone, but it's bad luck. Didn't work for you, did it?" The jeweler shrugged, sweeping his hands free of the box as if it contained something contagious. "Twenty is all I can go. You took all the romance out of that ring, kid."

Michael was about to remind the jeweler that the ring had been a sixty dollar, single cut diamond two weeks ago, remind him that Goldberg had scolded him: 'Don't be a skinflint. If the girl is worth the rest of your life, she's worth a sixty-dollar ring. Am I right?'

"I'll take the twenty," Michael muttered sullenly. Goldberg reached into his pocket for a roll of bills and counted out two fives and ten ones.

It was one o'clock when Michael left the East Hastings Street building for the Seaforth Armory. He lingered on the street corner, recounting and folding his money, his pocket feeling empty without the ring box. He resolved to make this day his new beginning, no matter what the outcome. With a full hour before his army medical, he decided on the long walk to the Seaforth Armory along the shore past English Bay and across the Burrard Bridge. He had reached the middle of the bridge when he stopped to look out over the inlet. Below, a scattering of sailboats out of Fraser's moorage were cavorting across the bay, awakening his memories of Soju and that day when she asked him to speak to the police. Regrets were very much in his mind as he leaned over the concrete railing looking down at the water, hating the person he was that day. How easy it would be. One leg over the railing. Then let go. Falling with the air rushing past his face. There would be one fleeting moment when he could look up at the bridge and see the steel girders flashing past and hear the thunder of the traffic overhead.

At that moment a distant movement turned his glance toward the Pacific Street entrance to the bridge. A woman was half trotting in her rush toward him. She wore an ankle-length raincoat that was making it difficult to run. A small man, who appeared physically impaired, was struggling to keep pace. The woman saw Michael look up and began waving her arms as she ran.

"Good God," Michael realized, stunned that she had somehow read his thoughts. Quickly, he waved back at the couple and began to hurry off the southern slope of the bridge toward the Armory. When he looked back, the couple had slowed and the woman waved back. He felt embarrassed, unable to rid himself of the dark thoughts she had somehow perceived.

Chapter 37 Decision Time

Looking back, Michael couldn't understand why he had not recognized that his arrival at the Seaforth Armory had been predetermined before he ever walked through the thirty-foot double doors. Passing into the vast, open rotunda drill floor, the first person to greet him was a sergeant seated at portable picnic table set up with folding chairs. The sergeant, his chest medals testifying to service in the First World War, looked up with a questioning smile. "Good afternoon, young man," he said. "And what can the army do for you?"

"I came to enlist," Michael replied. "Is this where I sign up?"

"It is indeed. Take a seat, young fella," the sergeant said indicating a folding chair. He then laid a printed form on the table and handed Michael a pen. "Just answer a few of these questions and we will see what we can do."

"Well lad," the sergeant took a hurried glance at Michael's signature when he finished the form, "so you want to be a soldier?" He sniffed his tobacco-stained mustache into his nostrils. "Well then, follow me." He rose from his chair, threw back his shoulders, brought his heels together with a loud clap, and barked a marching order. "Head high, lad. Shoulders back. Smartly now. Follow me."

Michael shrugged, assuming the sergeant's performance was to give the man the appearance of an active-duty soldier. Still, he found himself following along with short skipping strides to keep in step across the Amory.

On reaching a cluster of muslin screens set up in a series of cubicles, the sergeant slammed his heels together once more and looked down at Michael's single-page document. "Michael Daniel Costello. Correct?" The sergeant's grey eyes scanned Michael from head to toe as if he were judging a new colt. "Good lad. Make a fine soldier, son. Make us all proud, eh? Now step in there and strip down."

"All the way?"

"A man has nothing to hide from the army, lad." The sergeant took one step back from the muslin divider, wheeled and marched off, his boots landing with a resounding clap across the concrete floor.

Michael removed his shoes and began unbuttoning his shirt when his curiosity drew him to peek out beyond the screened cubicle. Four naked men stood lined up facing a similar picnic table, this one occupied by an officer wearing a white cotton smock over his khakis. A lean, sickly-looking corporal slouched to one side. Michael finished undressing and took up a place at the end of the line with his clothes bundled beneath his arm. One after another the line of pale bodies came up to the desk, their arms dangling awkwardly from their sides as if searching for a pocket. Each went through a series of coughing, arm waving, and bend-over examinations before being escorted to an adjoining screened cubicle.

"Costello?" The corporal barked, glancing down at Michael's paper. Michael stepped forward.

The officer behind the desk looked up. "You in a hurry to get out of here, kid?"

"No, sir."

"Then why the hell are you hanging on to your civvies?" The officer gave the corporal an exasperated glance. "This man thinks the army is out of uniforms."

The corporal sniggered and put the form Michael had filled out onto the desk. The officer glanced at the page, then reached for a second folder on his desk. He scanned them both side by side, then laid them to one side with a half smile. "I guess that's the way it is. Corporal, escort this man to Major Henderson. You can go ahead and get dressed, young fellow."

"What's that mean?" Michael stammered.

The officer handed Michael's form and the second folder to the corporal. "Follow Corporal Smuts. He'll take you to Major Henderson. Next?" A gangly teenager with the pallor of a corpse stepped up to the desk.

"Just a minute," Michael protested. "You haven't even examined me. Does this mean I'm in or out?"

His question went unanswered as the corporal placed a hand on his shoulder and steered him back out into the corridor. Michael's confidence was swiftly eroding as he unrolled his trousers, intent on continuing his protest with his pants on.

He was balancing on one foot with one leg in his underwear, struggling to regain his dignity, when Jimmy Henniger stepped out from behind an adjoining screen. Jimmy was buck-naked, clutching a manila envelope over his groin. "I thought I heard a familiar voice. My God, I was right. It's Michael Costello."

"Jimmy. What the hell are you doing here?"

Michael was so intent on trying to ignore the great white expanse of Jimmy's pudding-soft belly as he bent to retrieve his clothes, that the obvious answer never occurred to him. Michael had seen Jimmy around the church from time to time, but after that day at the beach Jimmy had taken to mostly hanging out in the company of his sisters. Michael couldn't help wondering if he had worn his sister's pants for his army medical. *The army would probably turn down a guy wearing ladies underwear. Good dodge to get out of being called up?* He tried to put the thought aside.

"You here to join the army, Jimmy?"

"Not if I can help it." Jimmy's answer came with a deprecating grimace. He lowered the manila envelope and offered his free hand to Michael; the move exposed his surprisingly tiny jewels. "Only reason I came is that the newspaper said that old fart Mackenzie King is going to give us a compulsory conscription law. I'm not waiting to be conscripted. I figured that once they get a look at me they won't want me anyway and I can go on about my business. You know I'm not the military type, Michael." He smiled, raising his eyebrows mischievously, and stepped closer to whisper. "I expect to be rejected."

"Is that what you really want, Jimmy?"

"Well," Jimmy smiled apologetically. "I don't want anyone thinking I'm a slacker. I mean, if I tried to enlist and they turn me down, people will know I'm patriotic."

Michael nodded understandingly, yet there was a note in Jimmy's explanation that didn't ring true. He was startled by the sudden realization that Jimmy Henniger really wanted to be in the Army, wanted to be a Seaforth Highlander. Maybe it was the kilts. Then he recalled that Jimmy had never dodged a fight with anyone, and that would include Hitler.

"Sure, Jimmy. I wish you good luck, whatever it is you really want to happen." For a minute, Michael was afraid Jimmy was about to hug him and was grateful he had managed to get his underwear pulled up.

"Thanks, Michael. Whatever happens, let's pray you and I don't end up permanent neighbors in Flanders Field. You know, where poppies grow, row on row?" Jimmy tried to laugh, his smile ending in a long, sorrowful sigh. "Poppies never were my favorite."

The medical officer was already studying Jimmy's file when Michael turned to press his case. "You still here? I ordered you to follow Smuts." The sickly corporal reappeared and with an impatient nod indicated Michael was to follow.

At an office door at the end of the corridor the corporal knocked, opened the door and stepped aside for Michael to pass. An overweight Major Henderson, his long hair flowing over the top of his shirt collar, much too long for army hair, looked up from his desk. The corporal saluted and marched away, bringing a touch of amusement to the major's smile.

"That's Corporal Smuts. Wants you to believe he is related to the great South African General," the major said softly. "Sit down, son." It was more by way of an invitation than a command. The major sighed wearily, combing his fingers through his hair. Michael hesitated –he was still wearing only his underwear — studying the cold surface of the wooden chair. "The chair is okay, son. You can't catch anything from a chair." The major glanced at the folder on the desk and set it to one side.

"You might as well get dressed. I am sorry, but I guess you have figured by now that the army can't take you in the current draft." He smiled sympathetically, a smile Michael immediately resented. "This war is just getting started, Costello. Wait until you are nineteen, then come on in and see us again."

"What's nineteen got to do with it?" Michael demanded. "Eighteen is the enlistment age. Eighteen is the age you took my brother."

"The decision isn't mine, son. The order came down from regimental command. Believe me, it has nothing to do with whether or not you would make a good soldier. I see you have a couple of brothers in the army?"

"That's right."

"Well, it seems there's some who think that two of you is enough for now. Frankly, you'd make a better soldier than a lot of these men we are taking in today. Look at me. I'm a lawyer, for crying out loud. A criminal defense practice. A boy like you could run circles around an old man like me in a battle. The army is going to need plenty of young studs like you to do the fighting for the rest of us stay-at-home boys before this war is over."

The major opened a green tin box of Export cigarettes and held it out across the table. "Have a smoke? I don't want you taking this personally, son. It's not the end of the world, believe me. Just think about all the dollies out there who are going to need some attention on the home front. Bless 'em all, the long and the short and the tall, eh?" The major, unaware he was hitting on the wrong theme at the wrong time, broke in to song. "Bless 'em all. Bless all the sergeants and their horny ones." He laughed, a coughing smoker's laugh. Michael refused the cigarette. The major helped himself. "Consider today a reprieve, Costello." He flashed a large flame cigarette lighter beneath his cigarette. "Figure today is the day that the army commuted your sentence, okay? You could consider yourself the first client I have gotten off since I left the court." He laughed again, spewing smoke across the folding table.

Michael muttered a curt thank you, hurriedly stepped into his trousers and left. Passing the recruiting desk and the silver-haired sergeant, he never turned his head.

He crossed Burrard Street through the oncoming traffic, daring the cars to run him down, ignoring the horns and screeching tires. He was heading into the Blue Owl Café. The No Japs Allowed sign had been removed from the window a few days after Pearl Harbor. He never saw the Mulhern Hudson parked in a slot next to the building. Juanita Mulhern, watching him crossing Burrard Street, decided to wait until he was inside the cafe. She came up quietly behind him and slipped onto the adjacent counter stool.

The Blue Owl had grown seedy since the advent of war, the red plastic counter stools were cracked and torn, the large, multi-colored jukebox dimmed with an 'out of order' sign over the coin slot. Recruits and old line soldiers from the Armory had carved their goodbyes into the counter and in the wooden panels separating the booths. *"Stan Holland. Here for his last Coke.*

December 6, 1939." And on the counter in front of Michael, carved into a crudely-shaped valentine. *"Sidney Williams – Peggy Ribchester, January 6, 1940".* Even the heavy-set waitress waiting impatiently for Michael's order had her name carved in the counter as a result of a short-term romance.

"What's up, big boy?" Juanita whispered in his ear. "The army turn you down?" Michael spun on his stool. Juanita tilted her head, her pouting lips close to his chin, looking up into his face like an artful child playing for a soda. "My poor baby." She had startled him, but discovering her there beside him seemed to revive his spirit.

"What are you doing here, Mulhern? I heard you were selling Victory bonds on a downtown street corner."

"Then you heard right. Ten to noon every morning. I'm on the corner of Dunsmuir and Granville. Me and a Great Dane named Butch. Butch, that's a dog that is damn near as tall as I am. And I'm pleased to say that so far Butch hasn't done anything nasty."

"Nasty?"

"Like pee on my shoes, or worse. Can you imagine if he had to go? Right there in the middle of Granville Street? My God. What a pile!"

Michael grinned. "What's a dog got to do with selling Victory bonds?"

"People stop to pat the dog. He's so big they feel brave just putting their hands on him. Some take his picture. Some even take mine. Then I say 'Hello. How would you like to buy a twenty-five-dollar Victory Bond? If you don't, Butch here might bite your bum.' That's all there is to it. I'm irresistible. So's the dog. Now how about buying me a Coke? Or do I go fetch Butch to convince you?" Her hazel eyes danced with mischief.

Michael ordered two Cokes.

"So. The army wouldn't take you, huh? But you still have Juanita, you know."

"What gave you the idea they wouldn't take me?"

Juanita's eyebrows rose helplessly. "I could tell by watching you trying to commit suicide crossing the street. Besides, the chief told me they wouldn't. He said they wouldn't take you without the consent of your mother because they already have Seamus and

Joseph." Juanita stirred the ice in her Coke without looking up. "I got a hunch the chief also shared that opinion with the recruiting officer."

"Damn. When are people going to quit trying to live my life?" Michael smothered a burst of angry words in a sigh of resignation. "I suppose he sent you here to make me feel better? To make sure I didn't jump off a bridge? Is that it? There was a couple up on the Burrard Bridge that thought I was going to do just that awhile ago."

"Uh-uh. Though, watching you crossing Burrard, you didn't act as if you gave a damn, either. But the chief had nothing to do with my being here. I came 'cause I'm worried, kiddo. I didn't want you getting the idea there was anything really wrong with you." Michael turned to take a good look at her. Her freckles were showing beneath the makeup. "Because there isn't, pumpkin. You know that, don't you?"

"Isn't what?"

"Anything much wrong with you. At least there isn't anything Juanita can't cure. Come on. Take me downtown and buy me a beer. We can cry together and you can tell me how beautiful I am."

***

Juanita drove the Hudson as if she were disciplining a fractious horse, a very powerful horse. Gripping the steering wheel with both tiny hands she stamped down on the gas pedal, roaring the engine defiantly, cast a mischievous grin over at Michael to reassure she had him firmly committed, then spun the car out of the Blue Owl parking lot.

Michael glanced back at the gravel rooster tail in their wake. "Cheesus, Mulhern. Turn on your headlights and ease off. " He was clutching the door handle so hard his knuckles hurt.

Juanita laughed and set the headlights glowing meaninglessly in the grey dusk of late afternoon. The Hudson came down off the Burrard Bridge and shot through the red traffic light at Pacific Street. Michael threw his arms over his face. "God almighty," he shouted. "You went right through that red light."

"What do you mean?" She wrinkled her nose in a mask of feigned indignation. "I'll have you know, I don't have one single ticket on my record."

"Then your old man is fixing tickets."

"Uhmm," she replied with a smile that admitted the truth. "Don't we all enjoy a little of that now and then, Michael?" she said, bumping the car against the curb alongside the entrance to the Georgia Hotel beer parlor. "So what's all your bitching about? Here we are. Safe and sound and we made it fifteen minutes before closing time." Michael came around to her side of the car and opened the door, relieved to have his feet on the pavement. Juanita laced an arm through his and steered him down the steps into the basement-level beer parlor.

Shadows cast by a series of sickly yellow wall-mounted lanterns all but hid the near empty Ladies section. There were no windows and in the dim light the puddles of spilt beer glistened on the black marble tabletops. Juanita led the way past a scattering of disinterested late afternoon drinkers and waved at the waiter. "Six in the corner, Barney." She steered Michael to a dark corner. "That's my table in the corner."

The waiter swiped a soiled towel over the tabletop and set down six glasses of beer. "Ten minutes to closing, folks," he said, reminding them of the British Columbia law mandating hotels stop serving beer between six and eight o'clock, the government's means of sending afternoon drinkers home for supper.

"Barney will give us a few minutes beyond six if we have beer on the table, won't cha, Barney?" Juanita winked at the waiter. "Pay the man, Michael. Think we can handle six in eight minutes?"

"You drink three quick beers and I'm walking home," Michael grumbled.

He was beginning to be caught up in the game, excited by her teasing. He caught himself watching the provocative movement of her tiny breasts beneath her blouse as she waved her arms in animated chatter. Juanita was aware of his watching. He lifted his first beer, swallowed half the glass in a series of gulps and licked the foam from his lip.

"So what's up with you, Mulhern? Why are you giving me that look? Has it anything to do with what I have been hearing about you and Stanley Glasheen?"

"Stanley? You mean his brother," Juanita said coyly. "Claude is the mover in that family. But that's yesterday's news. I'm more interested in you, right now. You still thinking of becoming a priest? You know I used to think that was all bullshit. I was the only person who suspected you were just running off after that Jap girl. Now you are trying to join the army? What the hell are you up to, Costello?"

Michael picked up a second beer and attempted to turn the conversation. "What's the matter, Mulhern? It's not like you to be changing the subject when we are talking about your boyfriends."

"Boyfriends? If I started telling you about my boyfriends, you'd probably take that as an excuse to pick a fight with someone. You were always ready to start something, Michael, and not too good at finishing." Michael smiled and said nothing, content to see the return of her mischievous smile.

"You may be right," he admitted quietly. "Maybe I should forget worrying about boyfriends and girlfriends and haul myself off to the Jesuits and learn to pray. I could pray for a gentle heart, no more fighting, and a good man for you, Mulhern. How's that sound?"

"Shitty. You got it wrong, Michael. Without me, you never were much. I'm your guardian angel. And frankly, this religious talk of yours, angels aside, is bullshit. You go to the Jesuits you won't be seeing the likes of me, ever. You couldn't live with that, kiddo. Reading pious books every night. Thinking of me doing you know what. Getting to bed by nine-thirty. Alone. And wondering who I'm in bed with. Jesuit vows? Let's see." She raised three fingers. "That's Poverty. Obedience. Chastity. I heard somewhere they even wear upper bathing suits to go swimming and they cover their arms with long sleeves when washing the dishes so's they don't get the hots looking at each other's arms. Michael," Juanita shook her curls, leaned across the table and kissed him on the lips, "how about that?" Michael smiled and wiped his lips with the back of his hand.

The waiter gathered the last of the empty glasses and swiped the table with a towel. "Time to go folks."

The beer had left a silly grin on Michael's face when he took Juanita by the elbow and lifted her to her feet. She came up eagerly, fitting snugly beneath his shoulder. "Come on, Angel-face," he said. "Before your friend Barney here throws us out into the street like the bums we are. You can fill me in on the details of celibate life in the car. How come you know so much about the Jesuits all of a sudden, anyway?"

"Because I care. I really do care, Michael. You know Stanley Glasheen is doing it."

"Doing what?"

"The priesthood. He's going into a Dominican seminary somewhere back East, Montreal, I think. He took a hard look at the Jesuits."

"Stanley Glasheen? Are you serious?" Michael felt a moment of being cheated by the news. "He must be trying to get out of being conscripted." Juanita's frown made him regret having said that.

"Is that you talking, Michael? Or is it a jealous little boy?"

"You're right. Who'n hell am I to be making cracks like that? Can't even say something decent about a guy who... Oh, to hell." He laughed, rejoicing in the beer and the warmth of her tiny body next to his, stumbling up the stairs to the sidewalk. He pulled her to him and felt her tiny, firm breast under his hand, the touch chasing all thoughts of celibacy from his mind.

"You are the only saint in my life, Michael Costello," she sighed sliding under the steering wheel.

Juanita drove slowly through the dinner-hour traffic, back over the Burrard Bridge and west past the Kitsilano swimming pool. She was following the shoreline toward Point Grey, finally bringing the car to a stop on the sand at Spanish Banks. Early evening shadows enveloped the beach, the last of the daylight swiftly fading beyond Point Grey. From the shore, they could see the line of shrouded automobile headlights tracing the traffic patterns on the West Vancouver shore.

"Look at those headlights," Michael said, indicating the moving traffic lights in the dusk. "That's some blackout. Makes a swell target for a Jap battleship barrage." The nearness of the beach, his mention of war, and the thought of a Japanese invasion brought his mind to Soju. For an instant, he pictured the summer wind teasing her black hair, her deep brown eyes alive with excitement.

Juanita turned off the headlights and faced him in the soft light from the instrument panel. "Hey. Wake up. I have to pee, Michael." She sounded tipsy.

"Not in the car, I hope."

She leaned across the seat and slid a hand inside his shirt. "Wanna watch? You used to want to watch, Michael."

"I told you that beer would make you goofy. You drank it too fast." He took her hand from beneath his shirt. "It's cold and dark out there on the beach. Why don't you just pee in my pocket?" She kissed him, warm and wet on his mouth, then jumped out of the car.

"Come on, Mike. Stand guard, in case." She called out over her shoulder and broke into a run over the sand toward the water's edge. He got out of the car and began chasing the sound of her laughter, laughing himself, the wind whipping through his open shirt. He felt the soft dry sand slip from beneath his shoes as he ran, almost tripping over her, the two of them stumbling forward in a heap on the sand.

"Christ, Mike. I'm going to wet my pants," she gasped.

He ran his hand up the inside of her thigh, searching the warmth between her legs. "You don't have any on." She began fumbling at the zipper of his pants.

"Do it, Mike," she whispered. "I know you want to." He pushed his hands through the sand beneath her naked hips. "Oh, God, you are huge," she said, her voice breathless and harsh, her tiny hands leading him into the warmth between her legs. The sand and the cold air on his buttocks and her rapid, hot breath beneath him receded and he was once again clutching the hard-chested, naked little girl in the Costello garage, pressing his thing, erect and hard as a stick against the hairless, mysterious crack in her crotch. Juanita. Ten, eleven-year-old Juanita was demanding again and again. "Like it, Mike? Like it? I won't tell. It's just pretending." Then the sick, empty feeling as his soul left him as she stroked him until he went soft with a strange twisting deep inside. Just pretending. Pretending. Only now he had her hips in his hands and was deep inside her, holding her and filling her over and over again, the sound of her high pitched gasp rising above the sand.

"Oh God, Michael." Juanita's breath burst loose as she pushed her free arm straight up into the air, reaching for the stars. "Don't come out, not yet, Mike."

He looked down, his face touching hers, feeling alive and filled with life. Her mouth opened, soft and warm. He kissed her and let her tongue search blindly through his mouth, seeking to claim whatever he had left to give. "We have to get out of here," he whispered.

She wrapped both arms around him. "No."

"You said you had to pee"

"I forgot."

***

Juanita marched Michael into Eileen Costello's kitchen hand in hand, her hips swaying with the swagger of a victorious prizefighter. "Mother Costello," she announced before Michael's mother had the time to dust her hands in her apron. Michael heard the triumph in her voice and knew she was about to say something he would regret. "We want you to be the first to know." Juanita's eyes flashed possessively over Michael, as if she had just allowed him to get up off the canvas. "I landed him." The words struck a body blow to Michael's midsection.

"You what?" Eileen's eyes went from her son to Juanita clinging to Michael's hand, beaming triumphantly.

Michael quickly freed his hand and turned to the kitchen sideboard where a small stack of mail lay unopened. Confused, his mother stopped wiping her hands and burst into tears. She reached out and took Juanita in her arms.

"Is it true? Is what I think I'm hearing really true, child? Michael has asked you to marry him? You are both so young, but..." There was a hint of uncertainty in her voice and when Michael continued to silently probe through the mail, she stepped back, holding Juanita at arms' length. "Michael?" she demanded suspiciously. "Say something."

"It's not going to be right away, mother Costello," Juanita added hurriedly. "Like you said, we are young. But we have come a long way down the road. Haven't we, lover?"

"She's pulling your leg," Michael grumbled without looking up from the mail. "Why do you want to get her all upset, Mulhern? Mother, you know this girl is never going to make up her mind who she wants. One minute it's Seamus. Then it's me or one of the Glasheens. Juanita's target changes day to day. Was there any mail from Joe or Seamus?"

Juanita braced her hands on her hips indignantly. "What are you saying, Michael Costello? The next thing you'll be telling me you don't love me anymore."

Michael shook his head, silently offering his mother a hopeless shrug.

"Maybe he just needs a little time, child," Eileen suggested. "I'm afraid we have to let that one do things in his own crazy way. Why anyone would want him is beyond me."

"It's just a matter of time," Juanita said with an injured tilt of her nose. She punched Michael's back, making a game of his uneasiness. "You do intend to make an honest woman of me, pumpkin?" He blushed uneasily. "What can we do with these men, mother Costello? One minute they are sweet talking us into their arms, then they get cold feet when we ask them to say out loud all the mush they whisper in our ear." Eileen Costello turned back to the sink with a sympathetic smile.

***

Michael rose quietly before dawn the next day, splashed cold water over his face at the kitchen sink and looked up at his reflection in the window glass. He pinched his unshaven cheek, convinced his reflection bore visible traces of the licentious coward Juanita had discovered in him. Nothing in the character of the face suggested a candidate for a Roman collar. But neither was he willing to be a married man, at least not a man married to Juanita. Finally he accepted that he was without identity. It was an interesting face, he assured himself, but lacking maturity. At the sound of his mother stirring in her bedroom, he stepped away from the sink and slipped out the kitchen door without a sound.

Father Lavoie was raising the host before a half dozen early morning communicants when Michael arrived at Star of the Sea Church. He did not come forward for communion but waited near the back of the church until the Mass was finished.

Chapter 38 The Novice

Michael stepped off the bus at the Texaco Station at the junction of the Valley Highway and the Yamhill County township road. The half-filled gasoline hand pumps offered orange colored gasoline at twenty five cents a gallon for farmers with wartime gas ration coupons. He remained long after the Greyhound had pulled away, surveying the seminary hill from the roadside bus stop before picking up his bag to climb the dirt road to the hilltop seminary. Mid-way to the top he stopped to catch his breath and look back toward the crossroads town of Sheridan and the winding highway running through the heart of the Yamhill River Valley. His eyes took in the scattering of the valley's scrub farms, some boasting a grazing cow or a band of sheep feeding on meager pasture land. The Greyhound had passed the weathered farmhouses, giving him a close view of the road-side graveyards of cannibalized trucks and rusting automobiles. Up ahead, looming over the hillside orchards, the Jesuit Novitiate's tar-coated concrete walls rose up from the summit, its arms outstretched as if the building itself were reaching out to him.

The grim late-winter scene that day was softened by a hint of early spring with the late afternoon sun glowing timidly over the land. After a pause, mixed with his reluctance to step away from the setting sun, Michael stepped through the seminary entrance. Finding himself alone in the hallway — he could hear the distant sound of someone repeating Latin phrases — he began exploring the high-ceiling chapel. The dimly lit, oblong, windowless room filled with shadows created a quick spasm of regret, which he quickly attributed to the chilly chapel air. "This," he acknowledged, speaking to himself in quiet voice, "is the beginning of your life-long retreat from all the disappointments of secular life."

Most Sheridan farmers and gyppo loggers in the valley looked with suspicion on the Jesuits and that strange building they occupied on the hill. Old timers recalled the days when the place was known as Paradise Farm, the name chosen by the original owner, a strange man who sold the acreage to the priests. The frugality of the landscape atop a remote hillside free of surrounding distractions presented the Jesuits with an appealing site for the teaching of Ignatius' spiritual disciplines.

Chapter 39 Separation

The bus was to leave at two o'clock. The weather blowing in off Lake Ontario was forcing downtown offices and department stores to early closings. Wind-driven snow swirling through the canyons of Toronto's Younge Street drove people from the street into doorways and lobbies. When Soju stepped out of the shelter of the bus terminal to the waiting blue bus, she carried her baby in the blanket given to her at the Sandon clinic; she was struggling to hold back her tears as she handed the child to Yuki. Following Tatsuo's arrival earlier that morning, the family had decided to head to Niagara Falls as soon as possible to prepare for Isao's arrival. Soju hugged her brothers, bowed to her mother, and stood waving at the departing bus for a long while after it had disappeared into the swirling snow. There was no one on the curb to hear her softly spoken cry. 'Oh Michael, if you were only here, you would hold me now and we would cry.'

By the time Soju turned away from the terminal for the 3 p.m. domestic job interview arranged by Brother Murphy, the streetcars were jammed with homebound shoppers and office workers escaping the storm. Soju boarded the Eglington streetcar near the bus terminal and was quickly pressed by those crowding into the car onto the rear platform. The car managed to reach the outer edges of the downtown by rolling past crowds at street corner stops until the motorman was forced to allow passengers off. As more passengers crammed aboard, Soju struggled to hold her place on the rear exit platform and found herself faced by a large, red-faced woman using an armload of packages as a battering ram. The woman thrust her way to rear the door by shouting at Soju.

"God dammit. Get out of my way." All that Soju could remember happening, as a blast of hot garlic breath struck her in the face, was the woman lunging for the automatic door. What she later realized was that the woman's charge had carried her into street and sent Soju sprawling onto the trackside snow.

For a moment the door remained open. Soju scrambled to her feet, ignoring the pneumatic signal warning the door was about to close. In a moment of desperation, she stuck her arm into the closing door as the car began to move. For a few quick steps she managed to run alongside the car with her arm in the door before falling on the hard snow between the tracks. When she got to her feet she did not know where she was. A clock in the window of a corner deli said it was 2:45 p.m. She would be late for her three o'clock appointment and her arm ached.

Deciding to continue along the streetcar tracks she started off in the blind hope of finding the address listed in Brother Murphy's note. Michael had always preached to her that everyone should believe in miracles. "If you don't believe, miracles can never happen, " he had said.

After plodding on past several car stops, Soju turned away from the car tracks and began wandering through the side streets in the quiet of the falling snow. She was becoming confused and her arm was throbbing when she decided to give up and find her way back to the car line. It was in that moment, at a sweeping curve in the road, when the miracle Michael had promised happened. A stone gateway stanchion, partially buried beneath a cap of fresh snow, revealed a polished brass plate bearing the street name and the number she had been seeking. Soju took Brother Murphy's note from her pocket, checked the number, then brushed her numbed fingers across the brass plate to be certain of what she was seeing.

She had seen big houses. Her father tended sprawling lawns larger than the expanse of snow covering the hillside rising before her. But never had she seen a house as imposing as the grey stone mansion rising against the dark sky at the top of the driveway. Satisfied she had found the right house, she started up the drive between rows of naked sycamores, their dark, bare branches slick with ice.

She hesitated again, checking the Jesuit brother's note for the third time, before entering the cave-like alcove over the massive doorway. "This will introduce you to the Callahans," Brother Murphy had written. "They have registered with Catholic Charities for a live-in domestic."

There was a meaningful message beneath Murphy's post script to the introduction. "Soju, you have never spoken about being the mother of the child. Many young girls find themselves in this situation in time of war. But, should your mother take the baby to

Niagara, your work in the Callahan home would go a long way toward getting your family back on their feet."

Brother Murphy had shuffled his feet awkwardly when handing her the note with an apologetic smile that revealed his reluctance to address the subject.

Two amber sconces attached to the stone portico cast their glow over a massive brass lion's head knocker. Soju was about to raise the knocker when her eyes went to the words on the doormat at her feet. "Service entrance at the rear." Carefully lowering the knocker, she was about to turn away when a curtain in a bay window alongside the door parted to reveal the plump face of a middle-aged woman. The woman rapped on the glass and held up a restraining hand. The curtain dropped and a moment later the door opened. The woman, her hair tightly crimped in blue-gray curls, her thin lips contorted in a message of irritation, shielded herself behind the door.

"You the maid from Catholic Charities?" she demanded, and without waiting for a reply, added. "You were supposed to be here no later than three." The woman puffed her cheeks petulantly, her eyes making a disdainful head to toe inspection of Soju's stocking cap and travel-weary clothes. "You know it's past four."

"I'm sorry." Soju was about to explain.

"Never mind all that. You are Chinese?"

"No. Japanese."

"Japanese? I was led to believe all the girls from Catholic Charities were Chinese Catholics."

Soju smiled apologetically.

"We never considered taking a Japanese into our home. What are you? Buddhist?" the woman added skeptically. "No matter. Shake that snow off yourself and come inside before we both freeze. I'm Mrs. John Callahan. I assume someone from the agency brought you out?"

"I came on the streetcar."

"That's nonsense. The car line is blocks away from here." She paused, expecting an explanation.

"It was snowing and…"

"Never mind that," the woman interrupted, having convinced herself she wasn't about to hear the truth. "You might as well stay.

I see you came ready to move in." Her disparaging glance went to Soju's bag. "Leave the bag right here for now. I'll show you what I want you to do with what's left of the day. I assume you expect to be paid for today as well." She turned and started off at a near trot across the dimly lit hall and up a banister staircase, laying out house rules as she went, casting an occasional backward glance to be certain Soju remained in tow.

"Our family is Catholic. But don't worry about that. We won't be imposing the church on you. A person is either Catholic or is not. Never have understood how anyone not born a Catholic could just decide to become one. I'm like the Jews that way. A little skeptical. But that's neither here nor there. Prove yourself satisfactory and you will have Saturdays to yourself and Sundays until our late afternoon tea. Ella, our day cook, does the evening meal so you won't have to worry about cooking. I will want you to serve weekdays and Sunday evenings. You can forget that today. We are eating out," she added with a look that made Soju feel she had cheated the woman. "You are to have no visitors in the house without my prior permission, especially gentlemen friends. You will prepare your own meals in the kitchen." Mrs. Callahan continued scurrying from room to room, throwing open doors, adjusting a chair here and a curtain there.

"The judge. Mister Callahan, my husband, is the senior counsel for Armstrong Insurance. He has served on the bench, and in this house prefers to be referred to as the judge. Our friends call him John the Just. You will simply refer to him as Judge. He is usually home for dinner by six. He and I will both be late this evening." The woman cast an exasperated glance at her watch. "It's nearly four o'clock. And I have been standing around here all afternoon. They told me you would be here at three. I have wasted the entire day waiting for you."

They returned to the entrance hall where Mrs. Callahan began working her arms into a fur coat. "You can learn the rest as you go along. I must be going, though I don't know how I'm going to drive anywhere in this terrible weather."

Soju found herself alone with her suitcase at the foot of the grand staircase, her head filled with a confusion of beds to be made, rugs to be vacuumed, sheets and towels to be washed. The woman's parting words, punctuated with sharply pointed emphasis, left an indelible impression. "In the future, always use the servants' entrance."

It took Soju twenty minutes to find the maid's room next to the washtubs in the basement, a stark four walls with a crucifix above the bed and two small windows facing ground-level air wells. Both windows were insulated against the cold by heavy, red velvet curtains, the lace trimming suggesting finer days when the curtains had served as a ball gown.

Chapter 40 Angler

The rocky soils of Northern Ontario offered no teasing signs of an approaching spring. There were no sprouting daffodils, no tender crocus blooms. The seasons arrived in Angler Detention Camp with a jolt, taking little more time passing from winter to summer than it took for the changing of the uniformed guards. One day the frozen ground broke, brittle cold crumbling beneath the weight of a shoe, the next a scorching sun abruptly and impersonally baked a summer crust even over the shaded corners of the yard. Isao Wakabayashi could only dream of a British Columbia spring where the soft rain from the ocean encouraged the tender spring to sprout and blush with blossoms. He could only dream of the fragrance of new-mown grass and the feel of the soft, damp soil surrendering easily to his hands.

His first winter in Angler he had watched and waited through the days of March and April for signs of spring while the weather remained bleak. Each day the passing clouds from the barrack window set him to doubting whether winter would ever release its hold. Then during a single night in early May summer arrived, summoned by sheets of lightning ripping across the night sky followed by torrential rain. By dawn, spring had come and gone.

Isao chose a patch of the gravel-encrusted exercise yard near the barbed-wire fence. Using a twisted, two-tine dinner fork and a stick, he scratched out a bed and planted the tomato seeds rescued from the pocket of his jacket. When the wind threatened the shoots, he cut the tops and bottoms from empty cans and set them over the plants to shelter them from the malevolent sun lingering in a cloudless sky. In a matter of days hot winds had scattered the cans and the remains of his withered plants over the yard and beyond the barbed-wire fence.

***

The day of Isao's arrival, the camp commandant, a slim man whose mustache and prominent cheekbones appeared to have been sculpted from a Rudyard Kipling fable, stood at the camp gate.

Colonel Wheatly Brown, believing he had an eye for co-operative detainees, chose Isao from among the new consignment.

"Wakabayashi?" He spoke the name as if he were welcoming an old school chum. "A word with you inside." Isao followed the briskly stepping commandant to his office, out of sight of the others.

"Cigarette?" The colonel was satisfied that he had his man, yet he experienced a moment of uncertainty when Isao accepted the cigarette and slipped it into his jacket pocket. "Wakabayashi, we are aware one or two in this new contingent are capable of making trouble for the rest. You don't need me to tell you who they are. We both know who they are. You have heard their nonsense about Japan winning the war and all that rubbish. Now, you can make things a lot easier for us and for yourself with your co-operation, Wakabayashi." Isao realized this was the colonel's way of informing him they had heard of his predicting a Japanese victory. "You are a married man with children, Wakabayashi. Some day you may be out of here, back with your family. If you are sensible, you and I can prevent trouble, eh?" Isao merely nodded.

"It would benefit you as well as the others if you were to help us keep all that talk about Japan winning the war out of the barracks, eh? The others would be more inclined to cooperate if there was less of that kind of nonsense." When it became apparent Isao was not about to speak, the commandant sniffed, twitching his mustache. "I understand, old chap. Nobody wants to be a snitch. But should you cooperate, Wakabayashi, we might be able to make some adjustments in your time here. I'd think that over if I were you."

Returning to the barracks, Isao gave the commandant's cigarette to the aging barber and said nothing of his conversation with the colonel. A year passed and he had given up his proclaiming a quick end to the war following the devastating news of a series of sea battles with the American Navy. Still, he assumed his latest summons to the commandant's office was to hear of an additional need for cooperation from the detainees.

A camp guard escorted him to the administration building, indicated a bench in the hallway outside the colonel's office, and then left him unattended. Isao waited through the morning while others came and went in and out of the office door. Shortly before noon the same guard reappeared and was puzzled to find Isao still waiting.

"You still here?" The guard frowned. "It's Wakabayashi, right? Didn't I tell you Colonel Brown was waiting for you and to go on in the minute someone came out? You should have gone on in."

The commandant rose from his desk the moment Isao entered the office. "Aah, Wakabayashi." He pushed forward a straight-back oak office chair. "Take a seat, old man. You have been working in the kitchen. Right? Food holding up?" Isao nodded. "Passable, anyway, eh?" The commandant laughed. "We all share the same grub here." They both knew he lied. The colonel came around the desk, hovering over Isao, his oversized mustache concealing his upper lip so that Isao couldn't tell if he was still smiling. "I'm told you stay pretty much to yourself, Wakabayashi, what with your kitchen duty and all, eh?"

"I am a gardener," Isao replied. "There is no garden here."

The commandant forced a polite chuckle. "True. True." He locked his hands behind his back, pacing to the window. "January can get bloody cold in these parts. I imagine a man who works at growing things could get bloody tired of all this, eh? Well, you will be pleased to hear that I may have some good news for you, Wakabayashi. You see, the government is prepared to let you leave here and go where you can make a decent living for yourself and be with your family." Without waiting for a response, he added enthusiastically. "I am assuming you would like to join your family?"

"I do not talk about the war anymore and I do not know any troublemakers," Isao replied.

"Of course." The commandant brushed the suggestion aside. "Nevertheless, there are conditions to be imposed if you are to be released, you understand? Wartime conditions and all." The colonel brought himself to attention as if suddenly remembering there was a war on. "You are to be included in the government's Japanese relocation plan, Wakabayashi. To participate, you must agree to make no attempt to return to the West Coast of Canada. You are, however, to be given the opportunity to work in Ontario agriculture. How does that sound, old chap?"

"My home is in Vancouver."

From the downward cant of the man's mustache Isao was certain the commandant was no longer smiling. "You can damn well forget British Columbia, Wakabayashi. You no longer have a home there. An Order in Council was issued January of this year, 1943, ordering the custodian of British Columbia Alien Property to put all Japanese properties up for disposal." The commandant turned his back and looked out across the yard as he waited for the news to sink in. "So you see, that's the end of that idea, old boy. There's nothing out West for any of you people anymore. Best you get that through your head."

Isao sat quietly, weighing what he had heard. "Are we all to be released?"

"As of today? No. Yours is a special case, a test, I assume." The commandant went to his desk and shuffled through a file. "The government is closing some of the British Columbia internment camps, including the camp where your family has been interred. The plan is to bring some of those families together so they can help ease the labor shortage. Your train to Toronto passes through here at 4:45 this afternoon. Should you agree to the conditions I have outlined, that doesn't leave us much time. You will be in Toronto tomorrow morning. Now don't start asking too many questions, Wakabayashi. People beyond my jurisdiction have been working on this. Start asking questions and you could find yourself a guest here for another winter."

***

Back in the barracks, Isao wrapped his safety razor into the folds of his zipper jacket with the precise care he tended his garden tools, folded the single blanket on his bunk, then sat on the edge of his mattress, watching the hands on the wall clock. The Powell Street barber, observing these things from the adjacent bunk and seeing that Isao had finished, came and sat with him.

"The others know you are leaving, Wakabayashi-san."

"I am going to be with my family." Isao spoke quietly, hoping what he was saying would not sound as if he were boasting.

A little man with a scraggly beard stood up and shouted from across the barrack. "They are playing a trick on you, Wakabayashi-san." The man's beard wiggled savagely each time he opened his mouth to shout. "You must refuse to go. You know Japan is winning the war."

The barber stood up, facing the man. "We all know Japan is losing the war," he said in a reasoning tone. "What has been done to us was wrong. Time will make others see that." The old man's eyes went to the ember of his hand-rolled cigarette and he spoke as if he were seeing something of the future in the rising wisp of smoke. "In time of war, fear twists the mind so that there is no thought for tomorrow. But what has been done to us will be undone one day."

"Loyalty to the Emperor will be remembered," the little man muttered defiantly from across the room.

"Pay no attention, Wakabayashi-san," the old barber said. "Our lives are running out in this place. Those among us who have been made blind by injustice are unable to see this."

"Is the clock telling us the correct time?" Isao asked.

"I will ask the others," the old man said.

"Never mind. It is time for me to go."

Isao went to the barrack window. Across the yard the clerk from the commandant's office came out of the administration building, his head bowed to the wind as he ran toward the army bus parked at the gate. Isao was grateful for the cold and the approaching darkness that would keep the others from the yard. He smiled inwardly and took a perforated coffee can from the windowsill boasting several frail, green shoots.

"Tanaka-san. You will honor me if you accept these. One day there will be sunshine here. If you keep these out of the wind and the cold they will grow. Give them some cold tea. The acid helps. Perhaps you will have tomatoes when the summer returns." The barber accepted the can and bowed.

At the door a blast of wind struck Isao, sandy particles swirling around his head in capricious clouds, biting his face with a thousand teeth. He lowered his head, turned a shoulder to the wind and started across the yard, his ear catching the distant cry of the transcontinental train. It was a sound he had listened for each day.

The train's call brought forth the picture of the black coveralls with the large red ball painted between the shoulders that had been issued to the detainee's on arrival. "That is not the rising sun on your back. That is a target for the guards to shoot at when you run," a camp prisoner had informed him. Hurrying toward the bus he remembered, and was grateful he no longer wore the black coveralls with the red ball, yet he slowed his run and began to walk.

Chapte 41 Soju's Unwelcome Summons

Twenty-seven hundred miles east of the Yamhill Valley, Soju Wakabayashi's two years of service in the Callahan home was coming to a close. She had been constantly encouraged to remain inside the Callahan house, especially during daylight hours, warned by the Callahans of the hostility awaiting the Japanese in the outside world. The Judge made a point of openly discussing these dangers during dinner conversations in a voice Soju came to suspect was intended for her ears.

Despite their warnings, there were summer Saturdays when Soju took it upon herself to slip out for solitary walks through the quiet, tree-lined streets of Broadmoore, hoping to avoid the jingoistic fervor that drove her family from the West Coast. She never learned of the Callahans' real concerns until the day she was told to pack and leave.

It was an early August Sunday afternoon when Soju returned from an afternoon walk beneath the great-leaf sycamores lining the Broadmoore streets. She went straight to her room and began changing into the French Maid apron and black-skirted serving uniform the Callahans required when the buzzer sounded a series of frenzied summons to the kitchen. Soju glanced at the bedside clock. It was three o'clock, unusually early for Sunday afternoon tea. She hurried up the stairs, the buzzer still sounding impatiently. Bridged Callahan met her at the top step, her face a picture of purple exasperation.

"Well," she announced bitterly. "I hope you are satisfied now that your little deception has finally finished your stay with us." Mrs. Callahan braced her hands on her hips, her lips distorted in anger. "You have been discovered, Soju."

Soju's first thought went to the bundle of discarded Toronto newspapers beneath her bed. She had been clipping news from British Columbia, collecting memories of home. With the thought came her recollection of Otake-san and her father being imprisoned for spying because of their love of Japanese papers.

"The newspapers?" She stammered. "I saved only the papers that were…" She never got to finish.

"Don't talk foolish to me, girl. The entire community is aware you have been living in this house. I suppose that it never occurred to you that you do not belong here?" Soju was confused by the sarcasm in Mrs. Callahan's words. "You are an Oriental. You have been living among Caucasian people." Mrs. Callahan spoke as if she were addressing a troublesome child. "Your being here is a violation of our owner's covenant. Judith Packer delivered the notice to our door this afternoon while you were out strolling brazenly through the neighborhood. She handed it to me as if she was serving me with a warrant." Bridged Callahan released a sigh of surrender. "How many times have we tried to warn you, Soju?" A sudden sense of defiance stopped Soju from saying anything. If she had been looking, Mrs. Callahan would have seen it in her eyes.

"The judge is waiting for you in his study," Mrs. Callahan said in a sharp voice lacking any trace of conciliation.

A tangle of thoughts was racing through Soju's mind as she approached the study. She was surprised to find she felt a sense of great relief, having never realized how much she wanted to be free of the stone house to see her baby. She knocked almost eagerly on the open study door.

"You asked to see me, Judge Callahan?" She was facing the back of John Desmond Callahan, Q.C.'s, imposing head, the long strands of his yellowish-gray hair combed delicately over the flat, bald crown.

The judge appeared to not have heard her knocking, his chair turning slowly at the sound of her voice. His long, angular jaw pressed between thumb and forefinger gave the impression he was emerging from deep, meditative thought.

"Aah, Soju. Come in. Sit down, dear girl. Sit down. Let's not be so formal with one another." He got up from behind the mahogany desk and offered her a soft-back chair, then began pacing the room with his head down, a practice perfected before countless juries, never taking his eyes off the one he was addressing.

"Soju. Mrs. Callahan has explained the problem your living here has created for Mrs. Callahan and myself. Dare I go so far as to say that you are our problem? Do you follow me? Our Home

Owners Association is aware that you have been living here and the association is demanding the enforcement of our neighborhood covenant. A covenant is an agreement, Soju. When we bought our home here we agreed who may and who may not live in this community." He continued pacing, never losing the reassuring smile which worked so well with confused witnesses. "Simply stated, Soju, Orientals are not permitted. No. Correction. Orientals are not permitted to dwell overnight. Mrs. Callahan and I innocently believed that because of the shortage of domestic service, no one would heed the covenant. It seems we were wrong." Callahan inhaled deeply.

"But I am afraid, Soju, your comings and goings were more than the neighbors were willing to put up with. So now we are forced to tell you that you must leave." The judge, looking for the impact of the news, saw only Soju's steady, expressionless stare. "You brought this on yourself, you understand. Of course we are sorry to lose you. However, as the only Catholics in the homeowners association, we are in no position to contest the issue." Callahan went to his desk and retrieved an envelope. "This is to pay you up through today, Soju. Mrs. Callahan would like you to serve tea tonight. You can leave first thing in the morning. It's not as if one more day is going to land us all in jail." He laughed artificially." I have included a few extra dollars in the envelope to tide you over until you find another position. Accept it as a token of our goodwill."

***

The following morning Soju was about to close her suitcase when she looked up to see the stout body of the lady of the house filling the doorway to the maid's room. Mrs. Callahan's eyes were fixed on the partially packed suitcase.

"Already packed, I see." She lifted a sweater from the case, poking her fingers into the packed clothes. "I have brought you a Baltimore Catechism." She smiled benevolently and laid the small black book on top of Soju's clothes. "Consider it my parting bonus, a gift for the good of your soul, Soju. Should you need a reference," she added casually, "tell the Catholic Charities people to contact Bridged Callahan. You know I will always be fair."

Soju thanked her, closed the suitcase, and slipped her arms into the sleeves of her overcoat so as to not have to offer her hand. Mrs. Callahan sighed and moved out of the doorway, allowing her to pass.

"You do realize we would not be going through this if you had made better use of your free time."

Soju chose not to answer. She had eight hundred and thirty dollars saved from two years of table waiting, laundry, window washing, and serving cocktails to Bridged Callahan's afternoon bridge parties. The purse included the Judge's ten dollar parting bonus. She tucked all but the ten dollars into the toe of a cotton stocking and crammed the stocking into a pocket of her suitcase; she then folded the ten in the palm of her free hand and plunged the hand deep into the security of her coat pocket.

The moment she stepped free of the house she felt the welcoming touch of the morning sun on her face, an affectionate greeting to her new day. She tossed her head like a young colt freed to run and breathed deeply the scent of a freshly cut lawn. Her feelings of freedom were caught up in the distant song of an unseen bird singing in the sycamores. A stranger smiled as they passed in the street and for a moment she was too startled to return the smile. The sun, the stranger's unexpected friendliness, and her light step all marked the moment as if she were emerging from a long, unpleasant dream.

As whenever she was alone, Soju's thoughts went to her baby and to Michael. Toshio's last words before boarding the bus to Niagara nearly two years earlier had assured her Michael would write the minute he received her letter. "Then we will see what kind of guy he turns out to be. You should have written to him long ago," Toshio had scolded. "He is going to be mad as hell you waited so long to tell him about his baby."

Then the month passed and there was no letter. Soju wrote again. Once a month, one letter followed another, only to disappear into the red metal mailbox at the Eglington Street corner. At first, she wrote of how she missed him. Then she wrote asking about his dreams of becoming a policeman like his father. Then she wrote of silly things, the weather or mischievous gossip about the Callahans. Hurrying down the shaded street to the streetcar stop she was composing still another letter with the news of her going to see their baby. She would write to him about the sunlight on her face and how it helped her to remember their days at the beach. She would write of the scent of the grass and the shimmering shade of the sycamores and tell him the world was opening its arms to her. And perhaps she would write of how much she hoped that one day they could be together. So consumed was she with her thoughts she that failed to notice the streetcar conductor holding the trolley car door for her at the corner until he called out.

"Get a move on, little lady." The conductor grinned good-naturedly, holding out a hand for her suitcase. "You look ready to travel."

"I am. I'm going to Niagara Falls," Soju explained excitedly, her joy apparent in her smile. "I'm going to see my baby."

***

Sweating soldiers in woolen khaki, their bulging kit bags hoisted to their shoulders, jostled through the bus depot, making their way among families and fractious children. Soju, stepping around and over scattered baggage amid a cacophony of children crying, chasing, falling and laughing in the oppressive depot heat, made her way to the pay telephone. She had exchanged Callahan's parting ten dollar bill for a ticket to Niagara Falls and checked the depot clock. The waiting line for the phone melted away with the first call for the Niagara bus. Soju stepped into the booth and repeated the number given to her by Brother Murphy. After a moment the operator instructed her to deposit twenty-five cents and a woman's voice came on the line.

"Could I please speak to Isao Wakabayashi," Soju asked.

"Who?" The woman was shouting into the phone, as if by raising her voice she could overcome the humming of the long distance line.

"Wakabayashi? Isao Wakabayashi or Toshio."

The voice repeated the name incredulously. "Wakabayashi? The man working for my husband? What do you want him for?

Wakabayashi doesn't have a telephone. He give you this number?" Soju tried to explain but the woman shouted her down. "He is in the orchard, working," the woman shouted again. Soju hurriedly explained. The call for the Niagara bus sounded a second time.

"What you want me to tell him?" the woman repeated irritably. "I'll try and get a message to him. You say your name is So Jew? And you are coming today? From Toronto? On the bus? If I see him I'll tell him." Soju accepted her uncertain promise and hung up.

The afternoon sun wallowed over the highway like a giant ember drawing waves of translucent heat from the pavement to the sky. The summer-hot wind through the open bus window tossed Soju's hair in tangles over her face. She closed her eyes searching for a comfortable dream to escape the heat and found Michael waiting at the garden gate in the snow. She took his hand and slept.

When she awoke, she shielded her eyes from the slanting sun, aware of a cool breeze on her face. The soldier at her side was sleeping, his head propped against her shoulder, his lips rippling with each heavy breath. Soju eased her shoulder free as the bus turned into a broad promenade, the curb-side streetlamps lining the road resplendent with hanging flower baskets in summer bloom. The sun had dropped to the horizon and cast a glistening reflection over the Niagara River.

"There she is folks, Niagara Falls," the driver announced, giving his passengers a long, close look at the cascading waters. "End of the line for honeymooners and picture takers." The driver's call awakened the soldier, who lurched to his feet. "Comfort stations at the far end of the terminal," the driver suggested with a wink into the large rearview mirror above his head.

The soldier snatched up his duffle bag and rushed to the open bus door. The driver's glance met Soju's eyes as she looked up at his reflection, his stare following her until she was about to step off the bus. He pulled the lever, partially closing the door.

"Hey. I'm out'a here in ten minutes. How about I give you a personal tour?" Soju pretended she had not heard and stepped down. After her brief pause by the luggage bin in the belly of the bus, the driver watched her head into the terminal with a shrug of indifference.

Soju searched the empty depot benches for a sign of her family, afraid her message had not been delivered. Then suddenly Yuki appeared, scurrying between the empty benches. She came bent over from the waist, as if she were dragging a heavy bag. When she cleared the line of benches Soju saw that her mother was reaching down for the hand of a toddler whose straight, copper-tinted hair shone like a halo in the late afternoon sun.

***

August 6th, 1945. The B-29 bomber Enola Gay dropped a single atomic bomb on the city of Hiroshima, Japan. A second bomb was dropped three days later on Nagasaki, causing Japan to agree to surrender terms on August 15th. On September 2, 1945 in Tokyo Bay, Mamoru Shigemitsu, Japanese minister plenipotentiary, led a contingent of Japanese in formal silk top hats and cutaway topcoats to the deck of the Battleship Missouri where the Japanese emissaries signed the unconditional surrender of Japan, ending the war.

Chapter 42 August 15 1945

Following Lauds the morning of the Feast of the Assumption of the Blessed Virgin, the novices were going through the motions of picking prunes in the seminary orchard. Michael took a moment before the call to noon prayer to rest in the shade of a heavily laden prune tree, easing his half-filled harvesting halter from his shoulders. The moment he lay back in the tall grass with an eye on the seminary building atop the hill, he spotted the Father Minister's short, round figure looking down on him from the edge of the orchard. Michael struggled to his feet, but not before the Father Minister had started cautiously working his way toward him through the orchard. Michael hoisted his halter to his shoulder and resumed picking prunes.

The demands of his temporal responsibilities had left the Father Minister's jovial features with a permanent frown. The fifty-five-year old Italian Jesuit used this countenance as his badge of authority, especially when supervising the novices at work. His responsibilities as Father Minister included the staffing and inventory of the seminary kitchen as well as the budget and the harvest, which was intended to help pay for all the others. It was a responsibility that rested uncomfortably on the soft round shoulders of the overweight priest who, Michael could see as he drew near, was in a state of total distress. The former Latin teacher collapsed in a heap at Michael's feet.

"Ah, Michael!" he uttered, drawing a deep breath. "I am disappointed to find you lying down on the job while so much remains undone." The priest smiled with a hint of admonition as he surveyed the prunes remaining in the trees, his cherubic smile never completely erasing his nervous concern.

"Good morning, Father Sirianni." Michael shifted the harvest halter on his hip and reached for the prunes overhead.

"No. No. Sit down, Michael. You were about to rest? There is no need for you to get up on my account. As a matter of fact I have come to have a moment's talk with you, my son. So sit with me. Please." The Father Minister sighed benevolently and Michael went to his haunches. The priest reached into Michael's halter and selected a ripe prune. "When we chose to become Jesuits, Michael, we were aware that we were choosing a life of sacrifice and we were renouncing the material pleasures of the world for the Glory of God. We accepted that ours would be a lonely life." He raised the prune to his mouth and bit down. "Ahh, these prunes are almost too ripe for the picking." He dabbed at his chin with the sleeve of his cassock, swallowed the fruit with a satisfied gasp, and spat out the stone.

The Father Minister patted the grass with the palm of his hand, repeating his invitation. "Come, sit with me a minute, son." Michael had already guessed from the tone of the invitation that the priest's seeking him in the orchard was a prelude to bad news. He became certain of it when the Father Minister began softly reciting the prayer of St. Ignatius of Loyola, emphasizing the last line.

"Lord, teach me to be generous, to serve You as You deserve:
To give and not count the cost,
To fight and not heed the wounds,
To toil and not seek for rest..."

Michael forced a smile and took up the prayer.

"To labor and not ask for reward,
Saving that of knowing I am doing Your will."

"How about another prune, Father?"

The Father Minister nodded approval.

"I don't know about this being such a lonely life, Father." Michael took a second prune from his halter. "But today at least we can say it is a fruitful one. There are enough prunes to keep us picking for a week. I suppose we should be thankful we don't have an apple orchard." His jest was lost on the priest, who removed his biretta to swipe his fingers over the sweat in the lining.

"Your mother is not coming for your perpetual vows, Michael," the Father Minister announced abruptly. "She has written you a letter saying she cannot come. You are aware that in the absence of the Superior, as Father Minister I open and read all the scholastics' mail." He handed the envelope to Michael as if he were offering corroborating evidence. "Your mother writes that she has not been feeling well. The doctor has advised her not to travel. There was also a problem of securing transportation. I imagine it is as difficult in Canada to get gasoline ration coupons as it is here." He studied Michael a moment before he went on.

"Michael, we are aware how much a novice counts on his family for support at the time of taking his vows." Michael slipped the opened letter into his cassock and began chewing on a strand of dried grass to disguise his disappointment. "You were eighteen when you turned to the Jesuits to save your immortal soul, Michael. I remember your first year in the novitiate. It took some time for you to adjust."

Michael nodded, not wanting to revisit those days. He had come to the seminary a zealot, welcoming the Jesuits' disciplinary chains, often binding his waist in penance for his constant doubt over his commitment. The discomfort and pain quieted his feelings of anger and rejection, feelings he never openly acknowledged. He took the flagellate as well, aggressively strapping his naked back and buttocks until the marks lingered for days. That too helped purge his thoughts. When reports of this reached the novice master he was summoned to a conference.

"The flagellate is a manifestation of conscience, Michael," the Novice Master had cautioned. "These things are not meant to be anything else. We must beware of a tendency to overdo. The chains are meant to be a part of self-discipline, a penance. We must not allow these disciplines to become a form of self-indulgence."

Father Sirianni's silence made it apparent to Michael that all this was passing before the priest's mind as well. Michael started to his feet once more. The priest reached out, taking him by the arm.

"Stay with me a minute longer, Michael. You don't mind sitting with a winded old man. Give me a chance to catch my breath before I have to challenge that hill." He folded his legs beneath him in the grass, studying the dispirited face of his prize novice.

Michael was telling himself he had been unrealistic in believing his mother would travel the more than three hundred miles from Vancouver, British Columbia. She was obviously not well. Yet he knew his disappointment was showing despite his efforts to conceal.

"Michael. It would be selfish to expect..." the Father Minister's words were cut short by the sudden clamoring of the seminary bells ringing continually with no purpose or rhythm. A junior who served as Michael's guardian angel during his first year in the novitiate appeared flying down the hill, ducking beneath the branches, shouting as he ran. The wind caught his cassock so that he looked as if he would take to the air with each leap. Michael caught the essence of his shouting, though the words were lost in the boy's excitement and the tolling of the bells.

"The Japanese have surrendered. The war is over," Michael muttered, turning to the Father Minister with a look of incredulity. The young man ran on, slapping the backs of all who passed within reach.

"The war is over," Michael repeated.

Chapter 43 A Place in the Setting Sun

The Proclamation, issued by the Canadian Department of Labor during the final months of the war in Europe:

"Japanese in detention are to be resettled permanently East of the Rocky Mountains or can apply for resettlement in postwar Japan."

***

Shortly after four o'clock on the afternoon of August 14, 1945. Isao Wakabayashi and his sons were moving a rubber-tire flatbed horse cart piled high with empty crates between the rows of peach trees. None of them spoke in their struggle to move the cart through the soft soil. Isao worked between the traces steering with Tatsuo and Toshio pushing. It was near the end of a hot afternoon in the Niagara orchard when Isao stepped out from the traces into the shade where a water barrel stood next to the path. Tatsuo and Toshio dropped to the ground in a sweat. Isao reached into the barrel for the water dipper and stopped, his eye fixed on a wisp of a man beyond the row of trees. It took a moment before he was able to clearly discern the stranger whose summer-green suit so closely camouflaged his presence that he had gone unnoticed among the trees. Isao suspected he had been watching them for some time.

Isao pushed the wooden barrel lid aside and let it fall to the ground, the dry, red earth raising a modest cloud of dust. His sons, assuming he was impatient for them to get back to work, began to get back on their feet. The little man among the trees, aware he had been seen, gingerly began picking his way along the wagon ruts in the soft soil towards them. With each step of his polished brown shoes he seemed to be testing the dirt as if treading through a mine field. His garishly green suit and disdainful steps over the broken soil conveyed to Isao that he was about to meet an unpleasant visitor. A few days earlier, news of the American atomic strikes on Hiroshima and Nagasaki had reawakened his fears and the feeling of helplessness he had felt since the day they first listened to the news of the Japanese bombing of Pearl Harbor.

The little man stopped a discreet distance from the water barrel. He held a manila envelope in one hand and a partially-eaten peach in the other. The man tossed the uneaten fruit into the orchard dust.

"Peaches are a bit hard. But that's the way you have to pick them, huh?" he said, moving the dirt with the toe of his shoe in a delicate attempt to bury the uneaten peach. "Can't ever get them in the store tasting like they do when you pick them ripe off the tree, can you? That's the only time a peach tastes like a peach ought to taste." He wiped his mouth with the back of his hand. "You are the Wakabayashi boys, I take it?"

Sensing the visitor's discomfort, Isao set his shoulders and answered with a note of territorial authority. "I am Isao Wakabayashi." Toshio and Tatsuo rose up defensively at his side.

"Okay then, Isao, you're the one I'm looking for," the man said agreeably. "I am Cyrus Green. Pleased to meet'cha."

He fixed a thumb beneath the lapel of his green suit jacket as if the color could verify the name. All the while he was weighing Isao's demeanor, uncertain whether or not he should refer to him as "Mister."

"Wakabayashi." The man's voice suddenly took on a note of authority. "I represent the Department of Naturalization and Immigration." His receding chin moved sideways as he spoke, the words snapping out as if he were speaking over a wad of chewing gum. He drew a document from his manila envelope. "This is for you, Wakabayashi."

Isao thrust his hands into his coveralls, acknowledging the proffered document with a cautious nod.

"Take the papers," the man urged. "These will provide you and your family with the opportunity of returning to Japan, your own country." Anticipating a show of appreciation and uncertain how the words had registered, he turned to the two boys while Isao continued his non-committal silence. "The Canadian government has no intention of forcing you to go back to Japan, you understand," the man added. "That is, unless you are found to be an illegal immigrant or a review of your stay in detainment should reveal that you have been disloyal to this country. Now should you and your family choose to return to Japan, the Canadian government will provide passage for the lot of you. How does that sound?" he said, beaming.

"Are you telling us the government wants us to take off?" Toshio stepped forward, facing the man at close range.

Isao held up a hand for silence. The man took a quick step back with a hint of fear in his eyes.

"I assume all three of you have been made aware that Ottawa has extended sections of the War Measures Act," Green said officiously. "The Canadian government is maintaining rigid control over all Japanese in Canada. Japanese will not be allowed to return to the West Coast. You do understand that? It is a matter of accepting this offer, or not. You can stay on here in Ontario. You are not compelled to accept."

The man lowered his voice in a note of ominous confidentiality. "However, I can give you no assurance that will always be the case." His lips puckered in warning.

"This much I can tell you. Failure to accept this offer may be regarded at a future date as a lack of cooperation with the Canadian government." He shook the envelope meaningfully. "That's exactly what it says in this document. The whole purpose of Ottawa's extending the War Measures Act is to keep a handle on you Japanese."

The immigration officer sniffed, picking up the heavy trace of sulfur fungicide lingering over the orchard, an aftermath of a spraying. He would go back to his office with stories of the "Oriental odor" he had to put up with while "rounding up the Japs."

Soju had seen the man's car turn into the orchard and, taking the baby by the hand, followed his trail. She was behind Toshio and Tatsuo when Green offered the papers to Isao. Seeing her with the child, Green nodded his head knowingly.

"Are you telling us that if we refuse to go to Japan we may be deported?" Toshio demanded.

Isao attempted to silence him again.

"We are Canadians, for Christ sake." Toshio continued in a loud voice. "My brother and my sister and I were all born here. So was my sister's baby."

The Wakabayashis had given up all pretense of the child belonging to anyone but Soju.

"There will be individual decisions for Canadian citizens of legal age," the man replied, readying himself to leave in a hurry. "Minors, whether they are Japanese or Canadian-born, will be bound by their parents' decision. In your case," he added, carefully judging Toshio's age, "this may not be a decision for your father."

"Is this what I must sign?" Isao asked, his lips barely parting as he drew the document from the envelope.

"Yes. That's your agreement. The statement says that you are willing to return home to Japan," Green replied cautiously.

"Then show me where I am to sign and we will go."

***

The evening of August 31, 1945, the Wakabayashi family — among the first Canadians the Canadian government was shipping to Japan — sailed from Vancouver harbor aboard the S.S. Marine Angel. They were among the 668 Japanese aboard, including 150 who had been interred at Angler. Soju attempted to telephone Michael's home during the brief transfer from the railroad station. When a woman's voice answered, she hung up without speaking. By the end of 1946, the number of Canadian Japanese shipped to a devastated Japan had grown to four thousand, one half of them natural-born Canadian children.

BOOK IV: Love Never Dies

Chapter 44 Solemn Vows

Twelve years of Jesuit excises and disciplines had left their mark on Father Michael Costello. By the day of his final vows, the Jesuit disciplines appeared to have instilled the quiet humility and the spiritual commitment of a disciple of Ignatius. Among those congratulating him, only the Father Minister sensed that the years had failed to erase the secular man. To this experienced teacher, who was also Michael's confessor, Father Michael was seen as having accepted the Jesuit order with an air of resignation, donning the heavy black cassock as an outward profession of an uncomfortable commitment. "I am too much a sinner to become a Jesuit," Michael had once whispered to his confessor.

"Father Michael, your faith is a gift. The gift of faith comes to us in embryonic form, just as those who receive a gift of musical talent, or the gift of the imagination that marks a great writer. Those receiving those gifts must recognize what they have been given and diligently develop them to their fullest. That is how it is that we have an Einstein's theory of relativity, a Rueben's painting or a Pablo Picasso. Get on with what you have set out to do, my son," the Father Minister urged. "There is always this moment of indecision when we doubt our gifts, until we make the final commitment that sets us on the path we are destined to follow."

During his years at Sheridan, Michael became a sullen, solitary figure, dealing with others in a pious manner, especially the fresh faces offering their lives to the will of Ignatius. Following his ordination he was sent to serve a small church in the San Juan Islands for a year where he said Mass at seven each morning and twice on Sundays. He heard confessions Fridays from 4:00 to 5:30 p.m., and Saturdays from 3:00 to 5:00 p.m.; he visited the sick and prayed over and buried the parish dead. Parishioners could complain of nothing specific, yet their number dwindled and the parish council finally wrote to the Jesuit Provincial complaining that their dour priest didn't seem suited to their island community.

Father Costello was then assigned to a boy's school in Tacoma, Washington, where he taught religious studies and found his greatest success coaching the school soccer team. It was an interlude that briefly restored color to his drawn features and for a time restored a lighter step. Following his assignment to a retreat house in Portland, Oregon, he quickly slipped back into his mantle of solemnity, brutally questioning the intentions of those who came expressing an interest in the faith. He led weekend retreats through the silent hours with inquisitional stoicism, and when those who had come on retreat were gone, he would sit in meditation for hours beneath the giant cedars shading the grounds. He became a slouching figure, most often appearing before those on retreat with the cowl drawn wherever he went. Visitors often came across him pacing the grounds with his head thrust forward, his hands locked behind his back as if in search of the scent of his lost purpose.

Eventually the Provincial sent him back to school where he spent quiet years in Los Gatos, California, studying moral theology, cannon law, dogmatic theology and scripture. He completed his doctorate in theology and returned to Sheridan to complete his Tertianship, leading to the solemn vows binding him to the Order of Jesuits for the rest of his life. He was appointed Father Minister, a task he was ill suited to, before being assigned the role of Novice Master, for which he appeared to have been destined.

***

In the early evening of a spring day in 1960, in the hour before Compline, a stillness settled over the seminary, the retreating daylight leaving the sparse hall lights to penetrate the gloom. From beneath the tall wooden doors, escaping blades of light spoke of the young men softly mouthing phrases in preparation for the evening Latin conversation drills. A pungent trace of chapel incense added a sanctifying breath to the still air when the sound of footsteps in the corridor lead to a perceptible pause behind each door. As heads rose from the Latin texts, each novice began calculating the number of steps to determine at which door the steps had ended. A soft knocking and a boyish voice removed any doubts.

"Father Costello?" The chubby faced novice nervously ran his hand through his hair and glanced at the envelope in his hand for reassurance. He was interrupting the novice master at a time when

— as all knew — Father Costello was deep in his evening meditation. A moment passed before he could be heard tapping on the door a second time. "Father Costello?" The boy held his breath at the sound of shuffling in the room. The door opened and Father Michael Costello looked out from the inner shadows of the room.

"What is it, Garvey?"

"Your mother has died, Father," the novice muttered, straining to see the face of the priest in the shadow of the cowl. The boy held out the letter. The novice noticed a sadness pass over the priest's face, then vanish in stoic composure.

"Come in, Garvey." Michael accepted the letter and stepped back from the open door for the boy to pass.

Light from a goose-neck reading lamp over the desk revealed a single cot with a grey blanket folded neatly at the foot of the bed, a straight-back chair, and the narrow desk no larger than a tea tray. Beyond the light from the desk lamp, the novice could see a crucifix on the wall above the bed. In the lone widow, beads of rain slid down the glass like liquid diamonds. Michael made a gesture inviting the novice to the lone chair and seated himself on the edge of the cot. The boy obediently accepted the chair, curiously watching Father Michael, who began by slowly turning the long, white envelope over in his hands. One end of the envelope had been torn off by someone not in possession of a letter opener. It bore Canadian stamps.

Michael looked up at the boy for a moment, searching for something of himself at that age and time. There was nothing. He then tilted the lamp so that the light fell directly on the envelope. The postal cancellation had been stamped seven days earlier. The envelope was addressed to the Father Minister, Sheridan Seminary, Sheridan, Oregon. It bore the imprint of the Vancouver Police Department.

"When did this arrive?" Michael asked.

The question startled the novice. "I don't know, Father. It was held... " his voice trailed off as Michael deliberately tapped the letter out of the open end of the envelope, carefully unfolding the single page. Chief Constable Dougal Mulhern's tight, bureaucratic hand read as if he had been recording a disciplinary hearing.

"It is with regret that I write to inform Father Michael Costello of the death of his mother, Eileen Costello. Mrs. Costello passed away at the age of sixty-eight the evening of March 28, 1960, following an apparent failure of the heart. Arrangements are being made by her surviving family members for Mass of Christian Burial." Michael refolded the letter and slid it back into the envelope.

"How long did you say this letter has been in the rector's office, Garvey." There was no challenge in the question, merely a note of curiosity.

"The Reverend Father is in Portland, Father," the seminarian replied hurriedly. "I believe the letter has been in his office since Monday, Father. It was read by the Father Minister."

Michael studied the young man, pausing to see if the boy had anything more to add. Satisfied there was nothing, he smiled tolerantly and began bringing his thoughts into focus.

"You are aware, Garvey, permission to leave the seminary is granted to us if a relative is dying? From the sound of this letter, my brothers have gone ahead with my mother's funeral Mass. But in this case," he hesitated, realizing he was using the young novice as a sounding board, before deciding to go on. "In this case, I believe my leaving could be approved despite the fact our mother died several days ago. Because of the delay, I could be allowed to go, perhaps to join my brothers in offering a Rosary."

The novice nodded, eagerly endorsing the idea. "The Reverend Father Minister asks that you come to his office after Compline, Father."

"I'm sorry, my thoughts were elsewhere. What did you say, Garvey?"

"The Reverend Father asks that you see him after Compline, Father." Michael did not appear to be listening. "I suppose Father Malloy could handle my Latin and Greek classes. I'm scheduled to return to Los Gatos for a semester in late April. Father Malloy will be taking those classes anyway. I have so much to do here, yet I know my brothers will be expecting me. They will feel that because I am the priest in the family, I should be there for our mother." The Compline bell interrupted.

"What's that, Garvey? Did I interrupt you?" The novice began to repeat the message, thought better of it, and stood up and began backing toward the door. Michael looked up at the crucifix above his pillow, searching for the pain he had expected with the news of his mother's death and was disappointed. There was nothing.

***

Shortly after dawn on a gray morning in the valley, the early light revealing the white plum blossoms clinging to the bare branches of the orchard. Michael studied the ranks of broken clouds racing in from the Pacific, scattering intermittent rain flurries in their wake. He was thinking of the bees and the lesson he learned when responsible for the plum harvest. The spring was too cold for the bees. There would be few plums without warmer weather to bring out the bees to work the blossoms. He shrugged. These were thoughts for the Father Minister. Yet he felt an unexpected sense of relief over his leaving, even for a short time. To the west of the valley the clouds were beginning to break, revealing patches of blue. Perhaps, he thought, the weather will turn before I return.

Father Michael looked down the hill where a sporadic burst of rain danced on the highway pavement. He had spent the morning praying Lauds with the novices before signaling Garvey he was ready to leave. The young seminarian left the chapel and returned a few minutes later carrying Michael's suitcase, refusing to give it up before delivering it to the Valley bus stop. The boy was happy to be walking with the novice master, filled with the pride of a young ball player carrying the bags of a great hitter. Michael sensed the adoration and it made him uneasy, so that he walked quickly, the wind teasing the skirts of their cassocks. The two of them in their windblown robes could have been mistaken for large blackbirds descending through the orchard.

Garvey set the suitcase in the bus shelter at the side of the road and ventured out into the center of the pavement to see beyond the curve. He was in the middle of the road when the morning Greyhound appeared, traveling fast. The boy planted his feet and raised his arms in the pose of a man about to be crucified. There was a burst of blue smoke from the heavy tires as the bus braked sharply, sliding sideways across the wet highway. The driver flung open the door, his face flushed in the anger of fear.

"What the hell? You God damn..." he stopped, suddenly aware of the boy's clerical clothing and the priest standing by the bus shelter.

The novice grinned sheepishly and returned to the side of the road to retrieve Michael's bag. The driver collapsed theatrically against the side of the bus, pushed his hat to the back of his head and popped a cigarette between his lips.

"What'n hell are you people puttin' into the heads of these kids up there?" he demanded of Michael. "Couple more feet and that young man woulda been road kill and with him goes my safe driving record with Greyhound."

Michael had been left momentarily speechless and now turned angrily to the novice. "That was a reckless act, Garvey."

Garvey was slowly recovering his self confidence. "Father, are we not taught to have faith that Christ is watching over us?" He was hoping a theological debate would turn the Novice Master's attention away from the fact that he had nearly been run down.

"I don't follow you, Garvey," Michael replied irritably. He was still shaking from the shock of what he had just witnessed. "There is nothing you have been taught to justify your standing in the middle of the road in the path of an oncoming bus." He took a deep breath, suspecting the boy was talking nonsense to disguise the fact that he too had been badly frightened.

The bus driver inhaled a nervous drag on his cigarette and ground the butt into the pavement with his shoe. "You guys drive me nuts. Look at my bus."

Michael reached for his suitcase.

"Father." Garvey was desperate to put the bus incident behind him. "Do you believe that Christ would really have allowed the bus to run over me?"

Michael shook his head wearily. "Garvey, conversations like this are what led to Lutheranism." His face broke into the faintest hint of a smile, hoping he had not ridiculed the boy. The novice wasn't to be deterred.

"In everything Christ said, there are questions, Father. How can we profess to believe that which we do not understand when we dare not exercise the simple acts of faith he spoke of? Christ told us to have faith."

"Garvey," Michael replied sternly, angry that the conversation was approaching a point of liturgical nonsense. "Christ also called on Peter to step from the boat in a storm. Peter did and began to sink. Are you saying your faith is greater than Saint Peter's?" He smiled, easing the anger from his voice. "I doubt very much it was your faith that stopped that bus from running over you."

"You can be damn sure of that," the driver muttered.

"Besides," Michael added, continuing to talk with a faint forgiving smile. "There were no fifty-miles-an-hour Greyhound buses in Jesus' day." The boy blushed, revealing the humiliation in his eyes. "But thank you, Garvey." Michael's voice softened. "I know you merely wanted to be certain I caught the bus."

The driver looked at the boy from where he had been surveying the wet ground beneath the wheels of the bus. "Why do you suppose we have that bus stop shelter?" he muttered sarcastically. "This bus passes here twice a day. Anyone standing by the side of the road, we stop." With a final despondent shake of his head he climbed back into the bus. Michael saw the driver addressing the passengers, his arms waving in the direction of the priest and the novice. He then took his seat behind the wheel, the engine roared and the bus lurched back off the berm into the middle of the road.

"You asked if I will be all right, Garvey," Michael said, turning to the novice. "The rector has notified our Jesuit house in Vancouver of my coming. They will provide me a bed if I need one." He was moved by a sudden feeling of gratitude for the boy's concern and had to resist an urge to put his arms around him. Instead, he raised a hand in benediction. "May Ignatius protect you and strengthen you in your vows, Garvey." The novice made the sign of the cross as his Novice Master stepped up to the bus. Michael hesitated, suddenly struck with a question that had been bothering him since the boy arrived at his door with the letter from Mulhern.

"Garvey? Was it you that I recall arriving here last year in a large automobile? With a driver? Your mother with you?" The picture was coming back. The vintage limousine. The chunky, fair-haired novice accompanied by a large, solemnly-dressed woman, her tears flooding over her cheeks and leading the boy by the hand. Suddenly he had the whole picture. The woman presenting her son to the rector, so obviously pleased with her sacrifice. It had made him think of the Old Testament scene with Abraham laying his son Isaac out on a rock to be slain as an offering to his God. Fortunately a benevolent God provided a ram entangled in a nearby bush that saved that boy. The submissive look on the young seminarian's face was the same expression Michael had observed on the boy's face that day a year ago. "That was two years ago, Father," Garvey replied. "You are probably recalling when my mother came for my simple vows."

"Yes, that was it," Michael lied. He had not remembered anything of the mother's second visit. "You were fortunate, Garvey. My mother could not be here for mine." During his years of relative silence he had buried that memory, along with others long interred. Michael was suddenly frightened at how easily the boy's innocence had penetrated his reserve. In that moment he had the urge to tell him he was not alone. "Christ's peace be with you," he said tersely and disappeared into the bus.

"And with you, Father," the novice called after him.

***

The aging bus smelled of the diesel oil that had settled in a translucent film over the worn leather seats and clouded the window glass. Michael moved into a seat next to a teenage boy who was wearing a two-tone jacket with large pointed lapels. He was surprised to see the jacket was made from two separate fabrics, the patterns cut so that one side was blue and the other in gray checks.

"It's my brother's. It's a Sinatra jacket," the boy volunteered, catching the priest's interest. "Frank Sinatra, the singer? My brother don't wear it no more. Says it's out of style."

The boy carefully touched his slicked back hair, lifting a long loose strand from over his eye. The hair was parted in the center, the part sealed in place by a coating of glistening oil. Michael settled onto the seat and was instantly enveloped in the scent of strong cologne. The boy studied the priest with a split-tooth smile that reminded Michael of a comic character in an old Our Gang movie, only where the boy in the movies had freckles this boy had teenage pimples.

"You from that place up on the hill?" The boy worked the question out of one side of his mouth around a lump of chewing gum.

"Yes." Michael opened his breviary, hoping to discourage further questioning.

"I seen some of you guys up there pickin' prunes last summer. You one of the prune pickers?"

"Sometimes."

"Don't suppose there's much doing up there, when you aren't pickin' prunes, eh?"

"Plums. We pick plums and then dry them," Michael replied coldly. "Then they become prunes."

The boy remained silent a moment, pondering the difference between prunes and plums. "In Gaston people say you guys get down on your knees prayin' half the night. Is that true?"

"No."

The boy grinned wisely, having debunked the town gossip. "In Gaston you hear all kinds of bullshhh, uh, stories about that place. Like, what kind of things are you guys hiding from up there? People hardly ever see any of you comin' to town. I hear some of you are up there just to get away from women. I mean, it can't be just to be pickin' prunes, huh?"

Reluctantly, Michael was being forced to recognize the questions were questions of inquiry touching on the Jesuit vow to teach the children, to bring the innocent to Christ. It was not up to him to dismiss this boy's curiosity as if it were mere town prattle.

"We are not hiding." He patiently closed the breviary. "At least not in the way you are thinking. The building on the hill is our novitiate. Our place to study and pray. You might think of it as a spiritual boot camp and we are the recruits. That is, the young men who come there are the recruits."

"Recruits?" The word appeared to startle the young man.

"Yes. Young men like yourself who are seeking to become Jesuit priests or brothers."

"You recruit those guys? I thought only the army could do that."

"No. You are confusing recruiting with the conscription. No one is compelled." Michael pondered a moment, reflecting on what he had just said. "Yet there is a similarity. Those who come to us come to read and follow a spiritual routine. Some decide to stay, some leave. We pray and have services and disciplines which we call our spiritual exercises." He smiled at the distasteful expression on the young man's face. "It is true. We are in bed most nights by 9:30." Confident he had said enough to discourage further questions, he opened his breviary once again.

"No girls. No movies, nothin' like that, huh?" the boy insisted.

"No," Michael answered, making a conscious effort to speak tolerantly. Again he closed the breviary. "There was a time — I was your age — when I went to movies a lot." The questions were taking on a new meaning, leading to his reflecting on his own spiritual journey. "Frankly, there came a day when movies left me feeling empty. There came a time when everything I was doing left me feeling I was missing something in my life," he added. "Have you never experienced that feeling? Wondering what you were doing with your life? When the milkshakes, the talks with friends, the movies, all seemed to have lost their meaning?"

"Girl dumped you, I'll bet." The boy's impertinent analysis stunned Michael to the point he was on the verge of ending the conversation. He answered carefully.

"Let's say I was looking for a purpose in my life. I began to think about saving my immortal soul. That is when I decided the best way for me to do that was to become a priest. I take it you are not a Catholic?"

"Uh-uh, not me," the boy protested, backing away from any possibility he might be recruited. "My dad's a logger. I'm probably going to be a logger, too. How long do you put in up there before you get out?" Michael had heard these questions before, posed differently by more promising candidates, but the same questions.

"Two years to our first vows. Our simple vows."

"Vows?"

Michael nodded. "Vows are our solemn promise. In our Perpetual Vows we promise to live a life of poverty, chastity and obedience. We also promise to avoid mortal sin, the sins that threaten to destroy the soul. We also promise to avoid the sins we are faced with each day. We then move to the other side of the seminary for two more years to begin our college life, our Juniorate."

Michael resisted the temptation to laugh at the incredulous look on the boy's face. "It takes us twelve years in all, but we don't spend all those years up there on the hill picking prunes."

The bus stopped at a roadside station where an elderly couple climbed aboard. Michael watched the man help his wife navigate down the aisle between the seats. As they passed, the woman looked at Michael and smiled respectfully. "Good morning, Father."

Michael returned her smile. "Good morning."

When they had passed the boy whispered. "Even old people call you father, huh?"

"Especially old people." Michael found himself beginning to take an interest in the curious soul beside him as the bus began to slow and the driver called out the stop for Newberg. The boy jumped to his feet, stumbling over the priest's lap. For an instant Michael wanted to reach out and hold on to him, to explore whatever it was he detected in the curious questions and searching of this son of a Gaston logger.

"Christ almighty. I almost missed my stop," the boy blurted as he jerked the signal cord. "Been nice talking to you. I'll come up to that place of yours sometime and have a look around. Maybe you will still be up there, huh? My girl lives in Newberg. She's always talking about us getting hitched in a church. Maybe we could come up there and one of you guys could do it for us? When we are old enough, I mean" The boy flung his parting words over his shoulder and lurched between the seats toward the door.

A tall girl, looking chilled in a thin cotton dress, her arms folded over her flat chest, stood waiting on the sidewalk. The rain had let up, the sun breaking through the overcast, raising threads of steam from the wet asphalt. The girl locked arms with the boy, turning him toward the town so that his back was to the bus. At the sound of the bus beginning to move into the highway, the boy twisted free, his eyes following the bus. He waved and Michael tentatively waved back, unsure if the boy had seen him.

***

Chapter 45 Home

The porter was quick to spot the priest on the platform waiting to board the Great Northern Empire Builder out of Seattle. In a move, perfected through years of selecting which bags he would handle, he stepped past the two men in business suits and topcoats waiting with their baggage at their feet and picked up Michael's suitcase. Hoisting the suitcase into the overhead luggage rack he grunted aloud. "Older I gets, the heavier these gets," he chuckled, removing his cap to reveal a head of graying, close-cropped curls.

The porter watched Michael settle into his seat while running his hand over his hair. Michael went into his pocket for a tip. "Bet you heading home to Vancouver. Right? You got that look about you. A man heading home always has that heading-home look."

"I suppose you could say I'm headed home," Michael replied. "It is true, I was born in Vancouver. But I confess I have not been there in nearly twenty years."

"Twenty years!" The porter repeated as if doubting what he heard. "Well, Reverend, I can tell you, you are in for a big surprise. You know what I mean?" The porter set the cap back on his head. "You best get somebody to show you 'round, 'cause there's things in that city that wasn't there when you was there. Things change so fast the place looks different every run. You know what I mean?"

The train began to move and Michael reached up to place a fifty-cent piece in the porter's hand. The porter saw the coin coming and took a step back. "No thank you, Reverend," he said, shaking his head. "It's my pleasure. I lift the bag for you same as I'd do for Father Divine, if that man ever boarded my train. Helping a man of the Lord comes back to me one way or another. Now that would be something, wouldn't it? Father Divine on my train with all his ladies? He was in Seattle awhile back. Never did get to see him." He nodded his head at the wonder of the thought. Michael slipped the fifty cents back into his pocket.

"I hope you don't be too disappointed when you see that home you thinkin' about. Most of it ain't there no more." The porter took a swift glance out at the passing landscape and sat down in the seat facing Michael.

"They had streetcars running up and down the hills twenty, thirty years back, right? Not now. It's all trolley buses running on automobile tires. They tore up the streetcar tracks. I bet you 'member those ferry boats running to the North Shore? That was war business." The porter shook his head ruefully. "No more shipbuilding. Most ferries out'a business. You understand?"

The train was moving swiftly now and the Porter glanced up and down the near-empty car. "Where was it you was livin' when you was in Vancouver?"

Michael explained that the Costello house he was returning to was on York Street, near the Kitsilano swimming pool.

"Uh huh, near the Burrard Bridge, right? Used to be a cafe near there. Tough place for coloreds." He chuckled, remembering. "The old Blue Owl. That's a long time ago. The Armory across the street, that's still there, but the old Blue Owl is long gone. You'll see."

Chapter 46 An Unlikely Mailman

Father Michael Costello peered out the open window of the vestibule between the rail cars as the train slowly rolled into the Vancouver Great Northern Terminal. He was searching the passing faces on the platform, hoping to see one of his brothers. The Empire Builder was running fifteen minutes early. Perhaps they would miss the train's early arrival. The screeching breaks gently nudged the cars against one another; the train come to a shuddering stop. The first face he recognized was Chief Constable Mulhern standing stiffly erect in his parade-ground majesty. The chief stood so close to the track that his chest was close to brushing against the slow moving cars. Dougal Mulhern made an imposing figure in his dress uniform with white gloves and the band of gold braid on his cap. The chief's once robust cheeks had collapsed into a mass of soft flesh forming dewlaps beneath his chin. His entire face had the look of a pink pudding laced with thin red veins.

The moment he spotted Mulhern, Michael saw Seamus farther down the platform, hanging back as if he were hoping to go unnoticed. Then he saw Joseph and was immediately stunned to see how harshly the years had marked his oldest brother.

Seamus — when he stepped up to the train — had the look of a man who had given up on life; his shoulders slouched in a thick-knit Cowichan Indian sweater at least two sizes too large. His heavy beard gave him the haunted look of having missed too many meals. Their glances met and Michael recognized the telltale brown tinge in the whites of the eyes, the discoloring that had marked Eamon Costello's last days.

But it was Joseph the years had treated most harshly. Joseph had come out of the war with a permanent squint so that he looked as if he were in pain or about to break into tears. Seeing him for the first time in nearly twenty years, Michael's thoughts went to the army telegram his mother had forwarded to the Seminary in the spring of 1944. "We regret to inform you that your son, Private Joseph E. Costello, has been wounded in action." Later she sent a newspaper clipping with a half column head-and-shoulders picture of Joseph in his wedge-shaped regimental hat with a terse caption: "Wounded in Italy." A dispatch printed in the Vancouver Sun attributed to a Colonel Hostettler, Canadian First Division, confirmed the story. Joe later claimed he had merely taken a piece of German shrapnel in the leg. Only years later did Michael learn the full story.

"Joe's regiment was pinned down by German 88s holding the Gustav Line south of Monte Casino in the Liri Valley," Seamus wrote. "His outfit lost fifty-two and more than two hundred casualties; a third of Joe's platoon in a single day."

When Michael wrote Joe asking for details, Joe's tersely written reply dismissed the incident as 'a battalion fuck up.' It was only after he pressed his brother again that Joseph grudgingly discussed the engagement in a long telephone conversation.

"There was a stone bridge crossing a pissy little creek in the Liri Valley south of Rome, eh?" Joseph explained, looking back on a scene Michael sensed he wanted to forget. "Six of us were crossing the bridge when it was taken out by a Jerry tank. I just happened to be the one carrying the Piat. That's the army's affectionate name for a Personnel Infantry Attack weapon. An explosive tin can with a propellant mounted on the rear." As he spoke, Joe's story began taking on the aspect of a confessional.

Michael urged him to go on. "I'm your brother, Joe."

"I got behind the tank where the armor was light and took it out with the Piat," Joseph said quietly. He would go no further.

Sometime after that telephone conversation Joseph did write to Michael seeking absolution. Michael held the contents of that letter as sacred as he would were they spoken in a confessional. "I don't want to remember, but it's tough to forget," Joseph wrote. "These days I grow more and more afraid. I can't get it out of my head, sitting for three days with my pants filled with shit in a hole next to the body of a mate with no head and no arms. Ask God about that, Mike. Ask Him what he expects a man to do. On the third day I began to stink so bad I stopped caring if the German guns were on us or not. I thought I could hear the regiment bagpipes and climbed out of the hole and began firing. There was no one in sight. Just me and the goddamn 88s whining through the air. So the captain put me in for the Military Medal."

Every word of that conversation flashed before Michael's eyes the moment he saw the smile cut across Joseph's face like cracked glass. "Hello, Father Costello. Doesn't that God-fearing bunch of Jesuits feed you? You look like shit."

"It is good to see you, Joe." Michael attempted to draw his brother close. Joseph twisted free.

"Look at this kid brother of ours, Seamus. Wouldn't Mom love the sight of him coming home with his neck in the collar, eh?" They were all aware Eileen Costello had prayed that it would be Joseph, her first born, who would one day wear the Roman collar. "Our kid brother has the look of a saint, one of those saints they starved to death." Joseph picked up Michael's bag with a thin laugh.

"He looks the same to me," Seamus mumbled. "Pale around the gills, but pretty much the same. The glasses are new though, eh, Mike?"

Michael had forgotten his reading glasses and in a moment of vanity whipped them off. He reached out to ruffle Seamus' receding hairline with a teasing grin. "The years take their toll on each of us, brother."

"The hair is growing back," Seamus protested. "I've been rubbing it with cascara bark. Mom's old country cure? She swore it removes wrinkles, cures arthritis, and grows hair. See? If you look close, Mike," Seamus bowed his head exposing the thinning crown, "that's hair coming back."

"Mother would be proud," Michael grinned.

"You grow hair on that egg you call your head, and your brother the priest is going to have you canonized," Joseph cracked.

Chief Mulhern took Michael's arm. "Father Costello." He spoke the name as if he were uttering a prayer and kissed Michael on the cheek. "God does indeed work in wondrous ways, Father. And Seamus, never mind the missing hair. We should all be thankful God has brought you boys together again at a moment like this. How long do we have you with us, Father?"

"Just a few days," Michael answered. "And how's your family, Chief?"

"You mean Juanita? She's fine, Father. Married the Glasheen boy. You remember Claude?"

"Yes. Of course. Mother wrote to me that Juanita had married Claude. And they have made you a grandfather as well, haven't they?"

"Twins. Girls, pretty and wild as robins in a berry patch, Father. The image of their mother in every way. Wait 'til you set eyes on those two."

They started toward the cars with Joseph leading the way. "Has everything to do with mother's funeral been taken care of?" Michael meant the question to sound casual, and was surprised at the intense look that passed between his brothers. "Is there anything for me to do?"

"The Funeral Mass was Tuesday last, Father," the chief said. "She's buried at Mt. Calvary. After you get washed up and rested, Seamus and Joseph will be wanting to take you to visit the grave. When you are done out there, Juanita's puttin' on a family dinner in your honor tonight, Father."

***

Little remained in the Costello house that spoke of the eighteen years Michael had spent there before leaving for the seminary. The red and gold portrait of Jesus with His Sacred Heart exposed still looked sorrowfully over the empty front hall. In the upstairs bedroom he had shared with Seamus, the room was empty but for Michael's bed pressed up against the wall with a cardboard carton at the foot of the bed half-filled with memorabilia. There were two thin towels and a used bar of soap in the bathroom and a half roll of toilet paper on the wall roller. Nothing else remained in the house. Joseph was quick to catch the questioning look on Michael's face the moment he stepped into the empty front hall.

"We got rid of everything soon as she died, Mike," he explained hurriedly. "You end up paying a bloody tax on all this stuff if you leave it lying around too long. The sheets, towels, all that stuff, we packed off to St. Vincent De Paul. Mother would have been okay with that. Seamus hung on to one or two of the photo albums." He shrugged and started up the stairs. "We had a couple of dealers in and sold everything else."

"Her personal things?"

"What personal things? There wasn't anything you wanted was there?" Joseph turned on the stairs, his voice defensively angry.

"No, of course not, Joe." Michael attempted to touch his brother once more, reaching out to lay a reassuring hand on his shoulder. Joseph shrugged him off and dropped Michael's suitcase alongside the bed. Michael's glance swept through the empty bedroom. He smiled uneasily. "Same old room."

Seamus hung back by the door. "Takes you back a bit, eh? Mom would want you to be here, you being the last of us to spend a night in the old place. Joe and I are going to leave you for an hour or so. Give you a chance to wash and catch a nap. We'll be back about four o'clock. We can take a run out to the cemetery before heading to Mulhern's for dinner. Okay?"

Michael listened for the sound of the front door closing behind his brothers, then cautiously lowered himself onto the bed, sprung loose his collar and unlaced his shoes. How, he wondered aloud, did I ever, ever manage to sleep in the belly of this mattress? He closed his eyes, inhaled deeply and laid back, searching his memory for visions of his mother.

After a time, she came to him wearing her faded grey coat, her rosary trailing between gloved fingers. In the picture before his mind she knelt alongside his father's grave over a preserving jar filled with purple hydrangeas. He could hear her praying softly in the Irish, and was puzzled by the bitterness in her voice, yet he knew she was petitioning for the preservation of Eamon Costello's soul. It was as if in her praying she was scolding her husband before God. Eileen Costello tended that grave with the stoic commitment of a reluctant martyr. Michael was about to draw nearer to her when he was awakened by an urgent ringing of the hand-cranked doorbell.

He reached for his collar and scrambled down the stairs in his stocking feet. It took a moment for him to identify the face peering through the opaque glass in the front door. Middle age had added considerable weight to Jimmy Henniger's body. The years had darkened his skin and carved deep creases in his face alongside his large, flat nose. There was a look about him that made Michael think of pictures of Babe Ruth with those terminal shadows beneath his eyes that were so prominent in the newspaper pictures of the Babe's last days. All that remained of the Jimmy that Michael remembered were the soft, brown eyes of an adoring disciple. Jimmy spotted Michael peering through the glass and flashed the tentative smile that had once pleaded for friendship on a summer day on Jericho Beach.

Michael flung open the door. "Jimmy." He clasped both hands on Jimmy's shoulders holding him at arm's length. "Let me have a look at you. Lord, it's good to see you. You haven't changed a bit. How did you know I was here?"

"Word gets around. Christ, you even look like a priest, Michael." Jimmy mockingly crossed himself. "Maybe I should genuflect?"

"It's the collar, Jimmy. Put on a Roman collar and even the old ladies get up and offer you their seat." Michael was startled at the sound of his own laughter. "When was the last time, Jimmy?"

"You mean when we saw each other? It was in the Armory, in '43."

"That's right. You got in and I didn't." Michael pulled him inside. "I'll bet you made a great soldier. You got to go overseas, didn't you?"

"Yea. I got to go. You make it sound like I won the Irish Sweeps. Three bloody years with khaki up my ass and my feet bleeding army blood. You don't know what you missed, Michael."

"Tell me about it, Jimmy."

"What's to tell? I was in Sicily for awhile, then Italy. Your brother was there. I caught sight of him for awhile at the Moro River when we came up against the Gustave Line on the drive to Ortona. That was December 6 to the 22nd in forty-four. They called that our little Stalingrad." He paused, waiting to see if Michael had anything to add. "Then I did some time with the Limeys in England. I did the Juno Beach landing with the Third Division under Monty. You never want to see anything like that, Mike. Your brothers ever talk about Operation Goodwood? Joe came in there after that fuck up. Liberated Holland, the lucky bastard. He tell you about it? No? Christ, never mind. I don't blame him. Joe must have had enough to talk about after Italy, from what I hear. When you see him, tell him that I still crap my pants every time I hear a car backfire."

"That day in the Armory? You thought they were not going to take me, didn't you? You and everybody else, including me." Jimmy laughed at the memory. "Then some damn sergeant got the idea the army would make a real man out of me, whatever that's supposed to mean." Jimmy laughed again, a forced, bitter chuckle. "Listen, Mike, should I be calling you Father Costello? I mean, is that what you want?"

"Whatever comes easy, Jimmy. It really doesn't matter that much. I don't even have a place to ask you to sit down. Looks as if my brothers were worried I would get sentimental about the place. Sold everything. Maybe they were afraid I would hang around too long."

"Yea. I know."

"Sit here a minute." Michael offered Jimmy the bottom step to the landing on the stairs.

"I came to see if you had time for a beer, Michael."

"Aah, Jimmy, I'm going have to pass. My brothers are coming around five."

"I didn't come just to bullshit about the war, Mike," Jimmy said. "There's something I need to talk over with you. It won't take long, but I want to go someplace we can relax a little, eh? I don't want to get into it here in your mother's house."

Michael was unsure of the look in Jimmy's eyes. Hurt? Anger? A puzzling shadow had invaded the soft face. What he saw set him to wrestling with his inclination to beg off. "I'd love to Jimmy. But my brothers are taking me up to the cemetery. Jimmy?" Michael's voice took on a tone of condescension often heard by seminary novices. "Do you want me to hear your confession? Is that it?"

Jimmy's lips grew tight in exasperation. "Christ, no, Mike. It's kind of the other way around. I have something of yours I have been keeping for you. Look. What I have to say will take half an hour. I'm only doing this because of old times. But it's your call." He got up and started for the door.

It was Jimmy's manner that made Michael decide. "Wait. Give me a minute to get my shoes. I'll be right down, Jimmy." Michael started up the stairs. "By the way. Who is your priest at the Star of the Sea these days? Your friend Father Lavoie still around?"

"I told you, Mike, I'm not here for you to hear my confession, if that's what you're getting at. If I ever do get around to making another one, you get first crack. Only don't hold your breath. And yeah, the old Frenchman is still in the parish. I hear he's kind of been put on the back burner."

***

Time had changed little about the Georgia Hotel beer parlor except for Barney, whose curly blonde hair was reduced to a tight band of gray curls at the nape of his neck. The dimly lit room retained the damp, cellar shadows of a neglected British pub. Michael was hoping Barney wouldn't recognize him. He was uncomfortable, a priest drinking beer in the middle of the afternoon, a feeling compounded by his being there with Jimmy. They took a table beneath the stairs.

"So, tell me, Jimmy. What have you been doing with yourself since the war?" Michael began casually.

Barney set the beer on the table. The waiter's glance convinced Michael he was remembered or else Barney was jumping to conclusions. Jimmy quickly ordered two more beers. "On me," he said, anticipating Michael's protest.

"What am I doing? I'm in the antique business," Jimmy said. "Remember the funeral parlor up from the corner of Broadway and Granville Street? That's now my showroom. I took over the building. Good place to sell antiques, eh? We dig up old things from estates and find them a new life. Come see the place sometime, Michael. I come across some interesting things now and then. As a matter of fact, that's how I came across some things I have of yours. Did you know your brothers hired Ashton and Tate to liquidate your mother's estate?"

"Ashton and Tate?"

"They are estate liquidators. I steer A&T a little business now and then and sometimes they give me a chance to cherry-pick an estate sale like your mother's. I picked up some of your mother's things, Michael. A couple of Chinese baskets, probably mid-nineteenth century. I figured cumshaw from the Chinks, okay?"

"Cumshaw?" Michael knew what the word meant but was refusing to accept Jimmy's implication

"Chinese pay-offs." Jimmy swallowed a large draught of beer and wiped his lips with his handkerchief. "Your old man apparently did a fair business down around Main Street in his day."

"What's that supposed to mean?"

"Take it easy. All the cops were on the take in those days, Mike. Look away, and make it pay? That was the way they did business. Christ, those days they weren't paying cops much more than car fare."

"Jimmy, you didn't know my dad."

Jimmy shrugged and went back to his beer. "Anyway, you remember your mother's tall, green Chinese vase?" Michael merely responded with a blank stare, unwilling to concede anything. "The vase? You remember?"

"Sure. In the living room. Mother kept it in front of the fireplace. Usually full of dried hydrangeas."

"Now that was a very good piece, Michael. Ming. Worth maybe five- or six-hundred dollars twenty-five years ago. I paid thirty-five hundred for it and I'll come out selling it on the fat side of five grand. Where do you suppose your old man got a five- or six-hundred dollar vase on a policeman's pay?"

"I always had the impression that vase was a wedding gift. I doubt if it cost that much. My mother never even liked it."

"Well, it's no skin off my round and rosy, Mike. But ask your friendly uncle Mulhern about cumshaw if you don't want to believe me. On second thought, you better not ask the chief. Ask your brothers. Why do you think they sold everything in a private lot sale instead of having a public auction in the house? Some of your mother's things were worth real dough. You don't have any idea what your old man bagged, do you?"

"I don't like to listen to you talking like that, Jimmy. Frankly, I don't know why I'm sitting here. You never knew my dad. He gave his life to police work. He was shot and killed in the line of duty. What more do you want from a man? You expect me to sit here listening to stories like that?"

"Okay. So he was entitled. Who cares?" Jimmy began turning his beer glass, making wet circles on the table top.

Michael had been surprised his brothers had cleaned out the house so quickly, but he was not about to give Jimmy the satisfaction of admitting to any doubts. His uneasiness put a defensive bitterness in his voice. "Jimmy. Take my word for it. Chinese vase or no vase, you are wrong."

Jimmy smiled tolerantly. "Yeah, I understand. But I got something for you that I came across in that vase." A sly look passed over his face as he produced a thick package of letters bound with a blue rubber band. "These are all addressed to you. I don't think your mail got through, Mike." He set the package on the table, taking care to cover the letters with the palm of his large hand.

"Letters?" Michael resisted the urge to reach out for the package, fixing his attention on the mocking glint in Jimmy's eyes. "Let me guess. Those are my mother's letters. Letters she wrote to me and never mailed. She never knew where I was going to be next." He realized he was explaining hurriedly, not wanting to consider the thought that had entered his mind. "I can see you are wondering why she would do that. Well, those are likely letters she wrote while I was in the novitiate. That would be typical of her. She wouldn't want her worldly worries intruding on my spiritual progress." He laughed a thin, forced chuckle. "I think Mother was haunted by the fear that I was going to pack it all in one day and come home." He tried for a casual, easy laugh that didn't come off. "How's that?"

"It was your mother who set you up to become a priest, wasn't it?" Jimmy answered.

"I wasn't set up by anyone, Henniger. My mother had nothing to do with my taking my vows. It pleased her, certainly. But the decision was mine. I did what I wanted to do, Jimmy. The Church is where I belong."

"Great. And how about that Jap girlfriend of yours? She didn't have anything to do with you becoming a priest either, I suppose?"

The words struck Michael as if he had been hit in the mouth. He felt the air rush silently between his lips and drew he back involuntarily. "What made you say a thing like that?" he managed weakly. "No. Soju Wakabayashi may have had something to do with the timing of my decision. But I was searching for something

I couldn't find anywhere else. And that's as close to the truth as I know it, Jimmy."

"I wonder if you are going to stick to that story after you read her letters."

"Her letters?" Again, Michael was unable to frame what he was hearing into an acceptable thought. "Her letters?"

"These are old letters, Michael. I suppose I should have burned them, now that you are a priest and all."

"Priests receive letters from women," Michael muttered, aware he was answering blindly, not knowing what he was opening himself up to.

"I thought of burning them. I really did," Jimmy said. "Then I thought maybe they might have something important in them."

"You opened them?"

"When I read them, I decided you should see them." Jimmy continued turning his empty beer glass on the black marble tabletop without looking up. "Hell. Sure I read them. Technically they are my letters anyway. I bought the damn vase. I have the right to do whatever I want with them." He put the empty beer glass to his lips, then dabbed at his mouth with the back of his hand and reached for the full glass that remained untouched in front of Michael. "And so now I'm giving them to you." He pushed the fist-sized bundle of letters across the table and raised his hand as if he were a magician revealing a rabbit with a stroke of magic.

"My guess is you never did hear from her after they shipped all the Japs out of here, did you? Maybe you were hoping she would disappear?" He studied Michael's face a moment. "No. More likely you were pissed off thinking she had dumped you."

Michael was speechless. He picked up the letters, his eyes fixed on the large, schoolgirl handwriting, his thoughts submerged in a whirlwind of memories. "I always thought it was because … because they wouldn't let her write," he said, speaking more to his own thoughts than to Jimmy.

"Sure. And I believe you, Mike."

Michael felt a chill pass through his body as he recalled the cold December afternoon in Sandon Camp. It was all right there in naked detail, awakened from where he had buried the memory deep within his religious commitment. The snow-laden trees beyond the road. The sheer cliffs of frozen rock. The children's caroling voices carrying across the camp on the mountain air. As the picture rose in his mind he could still catch the scent of wood smoke drifting across the camp. The RCMP corporal's words had never left him. "Get smart kid. Forget her. Jap women are not like white girls. It's all jig-a-jig and who's next? There's somebody's little sister waiting for you, you'll see."

"I went to Sandon to find Soju," he said, carefully choosing his words. "She was gone. They told me she had moved to Ontario. She was married. Did you know that, Jimmy? She married a Japanese in the Sandon Camp. When I heard that, I knew it was time for me to put aside my thoughts of her." He smiled weakly, hoping his reasoning had answered Jimmy's skeptical grin.

"You have been misinformed, Father Costello."

For a moment, Michael was silent, before tucking the letters into his pocket, determined to conceal the emotions Jimmy's words had set loose.

Chapter 47 Fallen Hero

It had been raining off and on throughout the afternoon, the heavy grey clouds lingering beyond the row of young conifers lining the cemetery driveway as a buffer to the Gulf winds. Purple rhododendrons, wisps of hair fern, and wilted yellow roses that only a few days past had been freshly-cut tributes to the life of Eileen Costello lay scattered among three over-turned mason jars alongside her grave.

Joseph crouched by the mound of new sod and began gathering the blossoms, his head twitching as if he were attempting to shake the raindrops from his ear. Seamus looked at Michael with a glance that attempted to excuse their brother's nervousness. It was Joseph who rescued the flowers from the church following Eileen Costello's funeral Mass and it was he who had set them in the jars now toppled by the wind. He busied himself with proprietary care, stuffing the stems back into the empty jars, then cast about for a cemetery tap to replace the water.

The scene took Michael's thoughts to a long ago visit to his father's grave. He remembered the look of satisfaction on his mother's face on discovering Eamon Costello's grave strewn with bedraggled and dying flowers. She too had silently gathered the flowers and reset them over her husband's resting place, all the while muttering words she did not intend her son to understand; just as Joseph was gathering them now.

When he had finished, Joseph looked up from his crouch alongside the mound of fresh earth. "What do you want us to do now, Mike? Pray together?" His question caught Michael deep in thought.

"I'm sorry, Joe. What did you say?"

Joseph's voice rose irritably. "I said. What the hell do you want us to do now? You are the priest."

Michael shifted from one foot to the other, freeing the soles of his shoes from the damp sod, leaving foot-size puddles in the depression in the muddy turf. He raised his eyes to look out beyond the cemetery, taking in the winding road over which they had come. Street lights were beginning to appear in the dusk over the city. He felt uncomfortable in the role of God's emissary before his brothers at the grave of his mother.

"Joe." He smiled at his brother squatting among the flower jars. "The priests at Sheridan are offering masses for mother all this week. I think it would please her if each of us remembered her in our own way, unto ourselves. What do you think?"

"Yeah?" Joseph groaned, rising up on stiff legs. Even straight up he was half the height of his youngest brother and obviously uncomfortable in a body which denied him equality with his brothers. "Then suppose you tell us, what the hell's the point in our being here? What's the point of Ma's having a priest for a son in the first place if he's not going to pray over her grave?" He pushed out his foot and toppled a Mason jar onto the grass.

Seamus moved between them and spoke carefully, pronouncing each word as if to be certain his tongue was not about to betray him. "Mike. Joe means that we are here to do whatever you say. We have been waiting for you to kind of lead the way. Is there something bothering you? Are you put out because we got rid of all Mom's stuff? Is that it?"

Even with the breeze in his face, Michael caught the smell of whiskey on his brother's words. Without waiting for an answer, Seamus turned to Joseph. "I told you, Joe. We should have waited for him. We should have explained everything. We both saw how much he was pissed off the minute he walked into the house."

"Okay," Joseph snapped. "You are so anxious to dig up the dead, go ahead. Tell him. Christ. Have you forgotten how we put up with him wandering around the house talking to Dad for months after the old man died? Now you want us to dig up all that meaningless crap and start a screw loose in his head again? Go ahead."

Seamus' face was covered in confusion, but before he could stammer a protest Michael saved him.

"What have I said? What have I done to make you two think that I'm questioning anything?" Michael pleaded. "You are the ones who looked after mother all these years. You are the ones who took care of everything while I was off living a life I chose for myself. Whatever decisions you have made are fine with me.

Forgive me if I have been a little confused, but I have been away a long time."

Seamus and Joseph glared at one another. "There wasn't much in the house you would want, anyway," Joseph grumbled. They had forgotten the grave, the three of them standing in the chill wind now laced with traces of rain. For a brief moment Michael had the feeling they were reaching out to one another – perhaps moved by the nearness of the woman in the grave — trying to recapture something of their boyhood closeness. He didn't want to argue. He wanted to be away from there, to be alone, to re-read the letters stuffed in his coat pocket.

"The Jesuits wouldn't allow you to keep any of that stuff, anyway," Joseph added. "We didn't think they were even going to give you permission to come home."

"We kept your mitt and some of your fishing stuff," Seamus said, hopeful of getting past the tension. "And your Baltimore Catechism from Star of the Sea. It's all in that box by your bed. And that 'Imitation of Christ' Mom got you for your confirmation? It's there in the box. And we didn't let them take down the Sacred Heart icon in the front hall in case you showed up."

Before Seamus could finish, Michael reached out for his brothers, taking one on each arm, and began herding them toward the car. "That's swell, Seamus. Now come on, it's getting too wet out here to keep on about all this. But if you two want to help me get straight in the head, there is one thing I hope you can tell me. It's something I'm curious about, that's all. Do you remember that god-awful green Chinese vase mother kept by the fireplace? Can either of you tell me where that came from in the first place? Dad brought it home, I remember. But where did he get such an expensive doodad?"

Seamus and Joseph exchanged uneasy glances and Joseph pulled free of Michael's arm. "Christ. So, that's what's bugging you? And you making out like you don't give a damn about her things."

"Joe, you don't have to use the Lord's name."

"You may be a priest to your Jesuit pals, Mike. But you're just a kid brother to me. If you want to know what that damn vase sold for, then say so. If it's the money you are worried about, you can quit worrying. We put a third of everything we got in an Imperial Bank account for you, even though you will probably have to give every cent to the Jesuits. It's yours, just the same. What more do you want?"

"Joe. Joe. Please don't talk like that."

"What the hell am I supposed to talk like? You come home sniffing around and giving us the third degree. What do you expect?"

Michael sighed and opened the car door. "It's just that Jimmy Henniger came to see me at the house this afternoon, Joe. He said he purchased that vase, said that it was worth several thousand dollars. The one thing that is troubling me is, where did it come from? Where did dad get it if it really cost so much?"

"I told you," Seamus said.

"Dry up, Seamus, "Joseph barked. "That fruit, Henniger? We didn't sell a thing to him." Joseph's voice began to rise to the point Michael was afraid he was about to lose control of himself. "Whatever Henniger got, he bought through the liquidators." Seamus held up his hand, urging him to ease up. Joseph answered with a derisive burst of bar-room laughter. "Did Henniger have that mutt of his with him, a little fuzzy white-hair bitch? He parades that dog up and down Granville Street on a string. Damn dog walks just like Jimmy, both of them like they are stepping on snakes." Joseph lifted his wrist in an awkward pantomime. "You know what they called Henniger in the Division?"

Michael interrupted before his brother could go on. "Jimmy spoke well of you, Joe," he said softly. Joseph's face fell, leaving him with a blank, sorrowful look as he climbed into the back seat of the car.

"Jimmy took me out for a beer." Michael was finding it difficult to sound matter-of-fact. "What bothered me was that he implied the vase was some kind of a payoff for Dad."

"So what? So was a lot of the stuff he brought home for Mother, the Oriental rug in the living room, the vase." The hostility had returned to Joseph's voice. "Dad got all those things given to him by people he did favors for. People he looked after on the beat."

"You mean he took cumshaw?"

"Cumshaw? Henniger gave you that word, didn't he?"

"Something like that."

"What an asshole. What does it matter what Jimmy Henniger says? Dad is gone. Whatever happened, happened a long time ago."

"Joe, what are you saying?"

"I'm saying Dad earned every dime he ever got. Earned it with his life," Joseph shouted, determined to tarnish Michael's icon of their father.

"Hell, Joe," Seamus muttered, "you don't have to—"

"Tell me this." Michael was trying to defuse a confrontation. "Did either of you ever hear from Jimmy about the letters he found in that vase?" The look on his brothers' faces told him Jimmy had said nothing. "Because Jimmy came across some letters in that vase that were written by Soju Wakabayashi; letters she wrote to me during the war. They apparently began arriving at the house right before I left for the novitiate. One was written when Soju was being held in the Japanese internment camp at Sandon. The last was postmarked from Toronto, Ontario, about the time the war ended. That was the year I was taking my junior vows."

"I'll be damned," Seamus muttered. "The old lady dumped them in the vase. She was always afraid you would go chasing after that gal."

"According to Jimmy, none of the letters had ever been opened," Michael said.

"Henniger took care of that, I'll bet," Joseph muttered.

"Maybe Mom thought seminarians were not supposed to get letters from girls," Seamus suggested.

"She would have been right about that. The rector opens all seminarian incoming mail," Michael admitted.

"So what's got you so worked up?" Joseph demanded, a sudden suspicion in his voice. "A few old sweetheart letters in a Chinese flower pot?"

"What happened to the girl, Mike?" Seamus asked quietly. He was remembering Michael and Soju in a way Joseph could not.

"She had a child," Michael said.

"Cheesus," Seamus muttered.

A long moment of silence passed before Joseph spoke. "So?"

Michael hooked an arm over the front seat of the car and turned, looking his older brother in the eye. "The child is mine, Joe."

"Good Christ," Joseph groaned. "You are a priest." His face softened, his anger slowly giving way at the sight of the pain in his younger brother's eyes. "How could you do that, Mike?" Michael's eyes made him wish he had never asked.

**

Juanita began planning the dinner the minute she heard Michael was coming home. Fussing with the silverware and talking over her shoulder to her father, she was laying out the table settings and spoke without looking up from the table. "I want my babies to sit down to dinner with a priest who isn't their uncle. Father Glasheen comes to this house and frightens the girls with stories of how the devil is waiting for them behind every naughty thought entering their heads. Little girls are entitled a naughty thought now and then. It's good for their lovely souls. Father Costello has a more realistic view of a girl's world than their Uncle Stanley."

"You shouldn't talk that way," the chief said, pacing nervously in and out of the dining room. "Father Glasheen is a diocesan priest. It's his job to set the children on the right path. Father Costello is Jesuit. There's a difference in how they go about their business."

"That's for sure." Juanita laughed a naughty laugh. "Father Michael knows something about life." It was on the tip of her tongue to carry that a bit farther when better judgment and the doorbell intervened.

"That's Michael." Juanita caught her breath. "Oh, daddy. How do I look?" Pausing for a hurried touch at her tight curls in the hall mirror, she threw open the door, brushed past Joseph and Seamus and reached up, throwing her arms around Michael to kiss him hard on the mouth.

"Michael Costello. Just look at you. I swear I am seeing a picture that would make even Saint Ignatius smile. Let me look at you in that Jesus suit and collar," she said, holding him at arms length. "Michael, my very own saint. My God." She pinched his rib cage. "But you are so skinny." Michael smiled uneasily.

Juanita locked her arm in his and marched the brothers into the house.

"You mustn't pay any mind, Father. It's the devil takes her tongue now and then." The chief turned a mock frown on his daughter. "You forget who you're talking to, Juanita. What will the babies think hearing you going on like that to a priest of Holy Mother Church?" He shook his head helplessly, but with a smile of benign pleasure at the picture of his daughter with her arm around the tall priest.

Michael was struck at how the chief appeared to have shrunk now that he was out of uniform. How less imposing he appeared in a cardigan sweater with his shirt open at his wattle-wrinkled neck. Juanita ignored her father with a toss of her curls and quickly introduced her daughters, who had appeared, prim in pink and lace, to stand at their mother's side.

"Angels and sinners they are, and saints to be, both of them," she proclaimed proudly. The girls gave the priest a practiced courtesy.

"Speaking of sinners, Michael," Juanita added, still clinging to his arm. "What's this I hear from Seamus about you being all stirred up over a bundle of long-lost love letters from your forgotten Japanese sweetheart? Is it true?"

"Is what true?" Whatever hope Michael had that his brothers would keep the matter of his letters private had vanished. He threw up a silent prayer there had been nothing said about the baby.

"Seamus phoned," Juanita rattled on. "Told me the hussy wrote you love letters while you were in seminary and that your mother hid them in a flowerpot? Yes. Yes, it's true. She did," Juanita exclaimed. "I can see it on your face. You are blushing. My God. Good for mother Costello. The old girl knew what she was doing, didn't she. What would your Jesuit buddies have said about you having a Japanese girlfriend on the side, hey?" Juanita laughed. "You are going to let me read the letters, Michael," she demanded emphatically.

"There were some letters," Michael admitted. "They served to remind me of how quickly we forgot our friends the moment they needed us."

"Friends? Come on, Michael. It's not just a forgotten friend that's got you blushing like a schoolboy with his pants down," Juanita countered. "It's her letters. I want to read those letters."

"Let's not go digging into the past," Michael said quietly. "Tell me about Father Stanley Glasheen. I confess, I find it difficult to picture him saying the Mass, but then he probably has the same problem with me. I remember you telling me of his vocation before I went to seminary. I didn't believe he would go through with it," he added, instantly wishing he hadn't mentioned the night of that conversation, a memory he was never able to completely set aside. Seamus, glossy-eyed and grinning foolishly, wrapped an arm triumphantly around Michael's shoulder.

"Joe," he called to his brother. "You said Glasheen went into the Church because Juanita turned him down for his brother Claude. That's not the reason, Joe. Stanley became a priest because he couldn't live with Father Mike here standing anywhere between him and God. You always were a bump in Stanley's path to glory, Mike."

"I have an idea," Juanita said, momentarily diverted from the letters. "Tomorrow, Michael and I will drive out to Father Stanley's parish in Ladner. We will just walk in, unannounced. It will knock the socks off him."

"I don't have that much time," Michael said quickly. "But I promise I will write to him, now that I know where he is. Right now tell me about your husband. The chief says Claude is doing well on the police force. Is he going to be with us for dinner?"

"No," the chief answered. "I told Juanita when she was planning this that Claude would be working. The lad is filling in on the desk and there's no way he can skip a shift if he wants to hang on to that job. He's a born policeman, Father. Reminds me a lot of your dad, the way the man makes friends. You'd think he owned the East End. But here, you sit at the head of the table, Father. Will you say the grace for us?"

"Yes, I will, Chief."

Michael waited while they gathered around the table, the candles casting a soft light over the dark-paneled dining room. It grew quiet and he raised both arms evangelically above his head, his eyes open as if he were looking up at the ceiling for God to descend among them.

"In the name of the Father and of the Son and of the Holy Spirit." Joseph, Seamus, then everyone in the room, turned their eyes to the ceiling to see what it was he was expecting.

"Heavenly Father. We gather before Thee filled with Thy Holy Spirit to pray that You open our hearts, that our lives may glorify Thee in all that we have done and have yet to do. Grant us the will to live in truth, that we may be worthy of Thy forgiveness of our failings. For in Thy kingdom, all things shall be known and all truths revealed. Bless us, and bless these Thy gifts we pray, as we welcome you to our hearts and this table, in the name of the Father and of Jesus Christ and of the Holy Spirit." He lowered his arms, all eyes turning to him, his blessing hovering over the table like an unwelcome guest.

"Damn it, Juanita," the chief muttered, fussing with uneasy irritation. "I can't see what I'm eating in this daffy candle light." Juanita turned up the lights, hoping to dispel the somber mood settling over the room.

Throughout the meal Michael toyed with his food, saying nothing of the events of the afternoon. When the maid began to remove the dishes he got up from the table and went out into the hall. Chief Mulhern shot a questioning glance at his brothers. Joseph pretended to be occupied with his own thoughts. Seamus shrugged helplessly. The chief tossed his napkin to the table with a determined grunt, got up from the table and went into the hall, closing the sliding dining room doors behind him. He found Michael in the study examining old police photographs on the wall.

"Father, you have something on your mind?"

Michael answered with a look of cold hostility.

"I sensed you were getting at something with that grace you gave us awhile back" the chief confessed. "I've seen enough men under duress to know when there's something sticking in a man's craw."

"You are right, Chief. There is something in my craw, as you put it."

Mulhern glanced out the open door to the hall, hoping something or someone would divert what he sensed was about to be an unpleasant confrontation. "Well," he muttered reluctantly, "if it's all that urgent, we can forget Juanita's dessert. Close the door, Father."

Michael, struggling to contain the rage that had been consuming him since reading Soju's letters, repressed a caustic 'close it yourself.' How clearly he could now see the Machiavellian hand of the old policeman at work in the deception that sent him home from Sandon. He was certain Chief Mulhern conspired with the Mounties to have them lie to him and escort him out of the old mining camp, sending him home like a runaway child. Likely it was the chief who scripted the story of a wedding. Even the railroad policeman, with his innocent questions, Michael concluded, must have been an agent of this cunning Irishman.

Hearing the news of Michael having recovered Soju's letters had stirred Mulhern's conscience throughout the dinner. He got up from his high-back, leather chair and shut the door himself. Even with the doors closed, voices from the dining room could be heard to rise and fall as the two men fixed their eyes on one another in the silence of the study. Michael fought an urge to shout in the face of the old man. Instead, he spoke in the cold precise tones of a clerk of the court reciting a criminal charge.

"Those letters Juanita was asking about, Chief? They were from Soju Wakabayashi, some written from the internment camp at Sandon. I believe without a doubt that you were responsible for what happened to Soju and the Wakabayashi family. And I now believe that it was you who had the RCMP lie to me."

The color rose in the chief's florid face, but as his indignation began to ebb, he turned gray. "Whatever I may have done, I owe no apology to you or anyone else for that matter. Nor do I intend to attempt to conceal from you what did happen back then, if you are certain that is what you really want to hear, Father. You being a priest, I suppose it would be tantamount to lying in the confessional if I tried to tell you anything but the truth. No. It's time you knew, though I caution you, it's an unpleasant story you are asking me to tell.

"You were just a kid, wet behind the ears with no dad of your own looking out for you. And you were about to make a mistake that would have ruined your life. Your mother and I had to keep you from that. Whatever any of us did was done for your own good, and for the good of your mother, may Jesus rest her soul. Perhaps you can appreciate that, though it would have been better had you never come to this," he grumbled. "That's the way it was intended, with you never knowing."

Michael was on his feet, unable to contain himself. "A mistake! You have the gall to tell me that I was about to make a mistake? What in God's name gave you the right to make a judgment like that about my life?"

"Father. Father. Hear me out." The chief raised his hands to deflect the anger in Michael's eyes. "I'm an old man. There's a lot I have seen and a lot I have done and it's too late for me to change any of it. All I'm asking is that you hear me out as you would hear my confession. It will make what I have to tell you go down easier for the both of us. Just hear me out before you go blaming anyone. I'm going to tell you everything. And before God, I swear I have never uttered a word of what I'm about to say outside of the confessional." The chief's huge body appeared to cringe as he urged Michael back into his chair with a supplicating: "Please." Michael remained rigidly upright and the chief moved his chair closer, his lips close to the priest's ear. He spoke in the whisper of a man exposing his soul.

***

"You know that your dad and I were lads together, born and bred off the Belfast waterfront. I recruited Eamon into the RIC in 1919. We were in RIC uniforms when they sent the Black and Tans over from Glasgow, in the early twenties. A dangerous bunch they were, all of them lads who had made it through the trenches during the Great War. They came looking for the King's shilling and a pint and trouble at every turn in the road and they found all three.

These were men who knew what dying was about and they were none too shy about sharing the experience with any Irishman.

"About the time they started the troubles in Belfast, the IRA began encouraging the likes of your dad and me to quit the constabulary. We finally did that and came to this country. Your dad hadn't the money to bring your mother and your brothers, so they stayed in Ireland for a time. Eamon and I were no more than a couple of pups, leaning on one another every step of the way. Was never a man nor woman came between us, but one. We did not judge one another and I'm not about to be judging him now. But it's a fact, with your mother in the Old Country; your dad had a need for other women. It was a weakness that stayed with him even after Eileen and your brothers came over. There was one woman in particular he couldn't leave alone. That's what made what happened to you so damn hard to swallow."

Michael said nothing, his hostile glare riveted on the grizzled old man.

"Father, the woman your dad was stricken with was Japanese. What happened with you was an unholy coincidence, a terrible twist of fate. In your mother's eyes, the very same devil that possessed your father had reached out to claim his son." The chief crossed himself, seeking to exorcise the thought.

"Eamon was with his Jap woman the night he died," he whispered. "And she was the one whose seed was about to leave her mark on you as well." The chief closed his eyes; his head rolled back as unforgettable pictures began playing before his mind. When he began to speak again, it was as if he were describing a dream unfolding before his closed eyes.

Chapter 48 The Wrong Place To Die

The black and white police Plymouth was traveling too fast to handle the sharp turn into the alley. The tires failed to grip the damp cobblestones and the car slid sideways, slamming up against a row of garbage cans, sending them clattering against the Sun Rise Hotel. Acting Sergeant Dougal Mulhern's massive silhouette came out of the shadows, moving with the speed of a feral cat. He was through the hotel doorway in an instant, charging up the narrow staircase two and three steps at a stride. On reaching the landing, he scanned the corridor, his chest heaving against his tightly-buttoned tunic as he gasped for breath.

"Eamon!" He bellowed down the corridor. "Where in God's name are you, Eamon?" A slight sound in the dimly lit hallway spun him around. A gray-haired Japanese woman in a soiled smock, her face a picture of terror, peered out from a partially-open doorway to a service cupboard.

"The policeman?" Mulhern growled, lunging menacingly toward her. "Where'n hell is the policeman?"

The woman uttered a short, indiscernible cry and attempted to close the door.

"Where is he?" he demanded, flinging back the door. "Quick. Before I kick the bloody hinges off every door in this shit house."

The woman ducked back into the cupboard and a tall Japanese, his hair carefully parted in the center and wearing a floor-length cotton kimono, stepped out into the hallway. The man raised the open palms of his hands in supplication and attempted to bow from the waist.

"No trouble. Please. No trouble." The pain on the man's face made Mulhern think he was about to cry.

"Costello. The policeman," Mulhern gasped between deep breaths, his face flush with anger. "Goddammit. What's been going on here?"

Azumo's eyes shifted to a doorway down the corridor. "Room four," he whispered.

Mulhern started down the hallway, scanning the doors, the layers of aging varnish all but obliterating the numbers. "Four? Dammit. Four? Where in the flaming hell?"

His eye fell on the number directly above his shoulder and in angry reflex he raised his huge fist over the door. Just as swiftly he stopped, his fist checked in mid air. With the stealth of a stalking animal, he glared back at the elderly Japanese with a look that commanded silence, then placing both hands on the door handle, he lifted, easing the weight of the door on its hinges. Silently, the door opened wide enough for a narrow view of the room. Eamon Costello lay naked on the bed, his legs dangling over the side, his head hung over a corner of the mattress. His eyes were fixed on something beyond the room, his tongue protruding grotesquely between slack lips.

"Great mother of mercy, Eamon," the sergeant wailed. "What have they done to you?"

Eamon Costello's uniform trousers lay across a chair at the foot of the bed, his Sam Browne belt was hitched over the back of the chair, his wooden-handled .38 caliber revolver dangling ponderously from the holster. Mulhern's eyes flashed from the revolver to a slight figure crouching beside the bed. He knocked the chair aside and seized the woman by the hair. Yuki Wakabayashi clutched Eamon Costello's tunic to her chest, her face, twisted in fear, was wet with tears.

"What happened? What have you done to him?" Mulhern demanded.

"He sick. Sick," she hissed.

"Sick?" Mulhern released his grip on her hair and knelt beside the bed pressing his finger against the neck of the naked form on the bed, knowing before he felt the grey skin what he would find. The touch of the lifeless flesh raised a groan from deep within his chest. "He's dead. Goddamn you. The man's dead."

Momentarily numbed by a surge of grief, he closed his eyes, struggling to maintain a hold on himself. "Come on Mulhern, think, God damn you. Use your God-given wit, man." He rose up and began mentally logging every detail of the room with investigative precision.

"You." He fixed a cold glare on Yuki cowering possessively alongside the corpse. "Get that goddamn pimp of yours in here." She placed Costello's police tunic on the bed, partially covering the dead man's chest, and, moving quietly as a shadow, slipped along the wall and out into the hall. Azumo appeared in the doorway in an instant.

"Get your worthless ass in here," Mulhern ordered, his voice harsh and tense. "What have you done to the man? Given him dope? Hashish?"

"No hashish in Sun Rise Hotel. He is sick man. His woman wants to call for doctor. But he say no. He say he be all right."

"Don't you lie to me. You lie to me just once and you will never lie again." Mulhern's fist caught the old Japanese by the throat. "Now you and that chippie of yours get the man's uniform on him and get it right. Understand me?"

"No chippie," Azumo wheezed. "Wakabayashi-san no happy girl. She is Japanese. She is his friend. Long, long time, his friend. She is very sad."

Mulhern lifted Costello's service revolver from the holster and tucked it into his tunic. He took another rapid glance around the room, then hurried down the stairs and brought the patrol car out of the alley. He parked the car by the curb in front of the hotel, swiftly taking in every detail on the deserted street. An empty streetcar moving slowly toward Main Street through the corner intersection and a single light bulb left burning in a barbershop window halfway up the block were the only signs of life. The night was warmer now and it had begun to rain. Mulhern left the car door open to the curb and rushed back into the hotel, his face dripping sweat.

Costello's body had been raised into a sitting position on the bed, his head propped against the wall, his tunic buttoned to the neck. His trousers were pulled up over his knees to the middle of his naked thighs. Mulhern gave the pants a powerful tug and cinched the belt around the waist of the corpse. He turned to Yuki, carefully studying her face for the first time. She had put on a housekeeper's smock and tied her hair in a coil at the nape of her neck.

"You are Eamon's Jap," he said quietly. "The one from the boat. That lying son of a sea Turk promised me. Gave me his bloody word he would never again—" Mulhern checked the thought and turned to Azumo.

"You. You are up to your neck in this. You and this...this..."

"No. She is not street woman. She is Japanese," Azumo protested. "She is very sad. She says she wants you kill her too."

"It's not me she needs to be worrying about killing her, goddamn it. Either of you ever breathe a word of this, and I swear I will personally see to it you both hang for murdering a police officer. I don't care how goddamn sad she is, one bloody word out of either of you and I'll hang you myself."

"We not kill him," Azumo protested, shaking his head in the face of Mulhern's fury. "Your friend sick. He comes Sun Rise to see his friend. Want to fuck too much all the time." The back of Mulhern's great hand caught the old man between the neck and shoulder. The blow lifted Azumo off his feet, sending him flying backwards into the hall. Yuki didn't move, frozen beneath the cold ferocity of Mulhern's scowl.

"Get up," Mulhern shouted over the figure sprawled across the hall. "Get up before I kick you down the bloody stairs." He glared at Yuki. "You. Get downstairs to the hotel door. I want to know if there is anyone in the street. Anyone, understand?"

***

The chief slouched back in his chair, drawing his hands over his face with a deep sigh. "The woman was no whore, Father. Not at all," he said quietly. "Your dad was taken with her from the moment she stepped into his life. He came to me the day she came off the boat. There was a light in his eye the likes of which I'd never seen in any man. He told me he had discovered an orchid in the rain. A temptation worth the price of his soul. He could talk that way. Eamon had a way with words."

Michael stared in silent disbelief for a long while, afraid to speak, unsure of the thoughts racing through his head. "But the bullets that killed him? He was shot in the back," he protested weakly.

Nodding wearily, the chief lowered his eyes. "Aye. And those bullets were from Eamon's own service revolver. It was never found."

He pulled open a drawer and removed a wooden-handled .38 revolver and placed it on Michael's lap. Michael lifted the weapon.

It felt heavy and deadly in his hands. Three bullets remained in the chambers.

"That's the weapon. I am the man who pulled the trigger."

A chill ran through Michael's body as he lowered the police revolver onto his lap. "But why?" He posed the question even though the answers were already falling in place.

The chief sighed, disappointed Michael was pressing for details he wanted to put behind him. "I couldn't leave him where I found him. Couldn't dump him in the street like some bum off the bottle. Your dad was a hero to me, boy." The chief was no longer talking to Michael the Jesuit priest. This was the son of Eamon Costello looking him in the eye with open hostility. "I saw to it that your dad died the hero he was. I could never be the man Eamon was. Never had his nerve. He was the thief when he was a boy, stealing food for the table. He was the first into it when there was trouble at the door. I doubt if he ever spoke of the 22nd of August, 1920? But I remember that day like it was yesterday. The IRA's flying squads came to Lisburn and put out the lights of the Royal Irish Constabulary's district inspector. They would have put me away as well, me wearing the RIC uniform. But it was your dad — so quick with his tongue — who saved me. And mind, it was open season on any Irish wearin' that uniform. But Eamon could talk to 'em. He was one of 'em whenever he could get away with it. He won me the time to pack my bags." The memories began clouding the chief's grey eyes, the tears leaking down the old man's cheeks. For a long moment, neither of them spoke.

Finally, Mulhern cleared his throat.

"That night, when my head began to clear, I remembered we had a burglary call to the Campbell Packing Plant. I had no idea what it was I set out to do. I put his body in the car and took it down there. It all came together on its own. Played out like somebody had planned it all. I kicked down the door of the office, messed things up and lay Eamon in the grass. He was going to go out a hero, and I had to shoot him to make that happen. That was the hard part. He lay there facing up at me." The chief's voice began to break and he wiped a hand across his face before going on. "I was going to put the bullets in his chest; make it look like he met his killer head on. I couldn't do it. Not with him staring up at me with that silly, cold smirk on his face." His voice began to break once more. "Forgive me a minute." He fished in his sweater for a large handkerchief and dabbed at his eyes. "I rolled him over and that's the way he was found."

Michael turned away, not wanting to witness the old man's tears.

"I had some help from friends in the coroner's office," the chief added, regaining his voice. "Eamon was found to have died in the line of duty. Your mother received his full pension for the rest of her life and your dad was given a posthumous citation. The case was never solved, though one poor devil, a fisherman, came close to being hanged for it, thanks to some bloody newspaper man who fancied himself a detective. We found a pair of gloves with the fingers cut out near where I lay Eamon in the grass. Somebody made a remark, maybe it was me, how the gill-netters used gloves with the fingers cut out to handle the fish and tie their lines. The next thing I know the detectives were picking up every fishermen within shouting distance. They wanted somebody for the killing of a policeman. In the madness of it all, it was like playing a game. I nearly lost sight of what was real.

"The detectives picked up a Jap on a boat at the plant. It was only by the grace of God that I was able to convince them he was on the river at the time. You might find it hard to believe, but I damn near began to believe the crazy story myself. God forgive me." He crossed himself solemnly, bowing his head.

Michael felt lightheaded and gripped the arm of his chair to keep from toppling over. He felt the sweat beneath his shirt and had to resist an urge to laugh bitterly. It all made sense, a painful, ridiculous sense. His mother's graveside prayers. The Roman collar at his neck holding him to his fraudulent promise. In twenty minutes of quiet talk in a musty library the curtain had fallen on a charade that had shaped his life.

Michael's gaze roamed the room, pausing over the photographs of policemen. Policemen in their shirt sleeves struggling over a tug-o'-war rope. Policemen in a pub, beer glasses raised. There was a picture of the chief, handing a medal to Michael's mother. And there was his father, tall and smiling whimsically, gripped in the embrace of Dougal Mulhern.

"Father," Mulhern continued uncertainly, "your prayer at table. You were asking for this?"

"I wanted to know. I never asked for this."

"There never was a doubt he was dead. His heart was not good. Oh, he could fake it and he did. His having been with the RIC got him on the force here without much question about his health."

"And it was you who arranged for the Wakabayashi family being interned," Michael said in a voice he no longer recognized.

"No. It was the Jap, Azumo; one of their own supplied the information that sent their man to Angler. The rest," the chief threw up his hands in surrender. "You have already worked out the rest for yourself. Your mother knew of Eamon's Japanese woman. She was never told he was with her when he died, though I'll go to my grave believing she knew as much."

"And Jimmy Henniger? He was right about the Chinese vase and the rugs being cumshaw? They were payoffs to my father?"

"A loose lip, that one. I suspected it was him who got you started on this. That vase was the one thing your blessed mother kept before her every day of her life. She once told me she couldn't stand the sight of the thing, but it made her feel better knowing she could smash it if she chose. I think it gave her some feeling of control over Eamon. Maybe because it was Oriental, like the woman she knew was so important to him.

"Your mother had her way of letting on that she knew about Eamon's Japanese woman. There was the day she told me about you bringing home some fish the Jap girl gave you. She tried to make it sound like nothing. You had found a Jap girl, she said. It was just a schoolboy's fancy, she said. But I saw she was frightened. Then you started that talk about getting married. I couldn't stand by watching your mother go through that twice in a lifetime. In fairness, mind, she never did know about your fathering a child."

"She hid Soju's letters in that vase," Michael said as if he were describing a scene opening up before his eyes. "Never opened one of them."

"It's not given to us to understand the ways of a woman," the chief muttered. "But I have a feeling she knew that someday you would discover them."

The murmur of voices beyond the dining room door had grown silent. Michael went back to studying the photographs on the wall, struggling to subdue the urge to shout out his frustration in the old man's face. When he spoke, he made no attempt to look at the chief nor did he conceal the contempt in his voice.

"You have taken a hand in determining my life, Chief. What is it you propose I do now? Now that I know I have a child somewhere in the world that has lived these years without..." He left the rest unspoken.

Mulhern shrunk into his chair and answered in a humbled and broken voice. "A child? Far be it from me to be telling a priest what to do, Father. But that girl and her family have all been packed off to Japan. They chose to go. They were given the chance to change their minds. You have raised a doubt in my mind about what we did. I'll grant you that. Put a mark on my conscience if you will. But what I did I believed was right." There was more question than conviction in what he was saying. Mulhern then drew his heavy chair across the floor to again put his lips close to the priest's ear. "Forgive me, Father, for what I have done. Christ asked God to forgive those who knew not what they did."

The misery in the old man's tear-fogged eyes stirred a feeling of pity in Michael. Training, habit or pity, he was not sure what it was that caused him to raise a hand over the chief's head. "Ego te absolvo. In nomine Patris et Filii et Spiritus Sancti." He closed his own eyes and sighed heavily. "Obviously you are aware that I have fathered a child, left it a bastard in a hostile world. Regardless of anything else we do this day chief, you are going to help me find that child."

"That can't be done," Mulhern protested, visibly shaken at the thought.

"Yes, it can. My brothers are holding my share from the sale of my mother's estate. I have the money."

"Have you not taken the Jesuit vow of poverty?"

"And this will not be my first sin, Chief. Nor will it be yours. And unless you intend to use this revolver to stop me," —the chief cringed — "it will not be my last. I intend to find Soju and I will with your help. It's up to you to get me a passport, quickly. And I expect you to use all your manipulative means to help me find her in Japan. Maybe together we can undo some of the damage we have done."

Chapter 49 In Search of a Memory

It was the first time Michael had flown and he was nervous. From the moment they took off until the DC-8 began descending over Tokyo he felt as if he was flying in the belly of an injured bird struggling to stay in the air. The flight was passing through a turbulent overcast sky when it began its descent into Tokyo. Silently he began offering prayers for all the souls aboard, certain the groaning and creaking of the airframe meant the wings were about to fly off. The wing lights on the swiftly passing clouds told him they were descending rapidly. The 'no smoking' light flashed on and he removed the unlit cigarette clenched between his teeth and crushed it in the arm ashtray. Then the clouds parted, revealing spider webs of tiny lights woven across the darkness as far as he could see.

"Dozo." Startled, he turned in his seat to face the stewardess standing behind him. She had changed from her in-flight hostess kimono into a baby-blue tailored suit. Her carefully coiffed hair was tucked neatly beneath a tiny wedge cap tilted precariously over her brow. She held a tray of tightly rolled hand towels in one hand, silver tongs in the other.

"Dozo," she said again, reassuringly. "Hot towel. It will refresh you." She lifted a towel from the tray with the tongs. When Michael hesitated, her broad, high cheeks rose in a trained smile. "We are soon preparing to land," she added softly. "You try."

The stewardess' voice carried the same melodic hint that had made magic the sounds of Soju's words. Michael accepted the towel.

"You must be tired after such a long flight?" the girl suggested. "You boarded at San Francisco?" She had joined the flight in Hawaii when the DC-8 changed crews.

"No. I started in Vancouver, B.C., and changed planes in San Francisco for Japan." He was glad to be talking to someone and wanted to keep the conversation alive, though he realized the stewardess was not seeking answers so much as she was repeating programmed lines.

"Is this your first visit to Japan?" Without waiting for an answer the girl's smile returned. "I hope you will enjoy your stay and you will come again on Japan Air Lines." Her submissive smile, the lights of Tokyo rising beneath the wing, and the warm towel over his face were beginning to restore his confidence in the airplane.

"Thank you," Michael said. "Could you tell me what time it is in Tokyo now?"

The stewardess extended her arm, offering him a look at the watch on her wrist. "Toky-oo time is now 8:27p.m." Again, the practiced smile. "Do you have someone in Toky-oo to meet you at the airport?" An enquiring smile. It was startling to see how quickly her smile could turn on and off.

"I'm not sure. I think so."

"Oh. I am happy for you." A relieved smile. "It is so confusing in Toky-oo on your first visit." The landing gear rumbled in the belly of the airplane, ending the conversation. The stewardess turned away and began retrieving the damp towels from the other passengers. When she reached the end of the cabin, she bowed and stepped back through the curtains into the first-class compartment.

Michael had never experienced anything resembling the torrential rain lashing the airplane so hard he could feel it vibrating through the cabin. Haneda International's ground crew, in yellow slickers emblazoned with the letters JAL, appeared out of the night battling to bring the steps, up to the DC-8's doorway. Four or five of the yellow jackets grouped around the foot of the steps struggling to hold Japan Airlines umbrellas over the passengers. Michael was drenched before he reached the bottom step and, brushing past the umbrella bearers, he lowered his head into the wind and sprinted toward the terminal, his clothes clinging to his body as if he had been fished from the sea.

Inside the terminal he shrugged to ease his wet clothes from his shoulders and for the first time since leaving Joseph and Seamus at the Vancouver International passenger barrier found himself confronted with the hopelessness of what he was attempting. He put a hand into the damp pocket of his jacket for the telegram that had been waiting for him on his stopover in San Francisco. The message was imprinted in his memory word for word yet he unfolded the paper to read it again. "Tokyo police notified of your arrival. D. Mulhern."

That was it. Michael stuffed the telegram back into his pocket and started toward the immigration barrier, his dripping clothes leaving a trail in his path.

Stopping at the wire partition separating the arriving passengers from those come to meet the plane, he began to search the crowd for a face of a Tokyo policeman. The crowd pressed up against the barrier, some holding hand printed signs written in both English and Japanese bearing the names of the strangers they had come to meet. There was no sign bearing the name Costello. Michael was desperately counting on Chief Mulhern's telegram to have someone from the Tokyo Metropolitan Police be there. Searching the faces in the crowd for a second time, his hopes continued to sink. He was confident that if a policeman had been there he would be able to spot the man, even without a sign. He was wet and shivering when he cleared immigration and began working his way through the waiting area, still searching for a plain-clothes policeman.

Twice he passed in front of Tora Hashimoto — almost brushing up against him — despite the fact the Tokyo detective was standing slightly apart from the crowd. When he did glance at Hashimoto's swept-back, steel-grey hair knotted at the nape of his neck, he dismissed him as a middle-aged nightclub musician. Only when the crowd began to thin did he turn to face the detective a third time, only to again dismiss the Japanese. Michael had spent a lifetime among policemen and in his mind he was certain there was no way this could be an officer of the Tokyo Metropolitan Police Department.

Hashimoto, nursing a damp, unlit cigarette between his lips, silently studied the tall, red-headed priest who was now wandering aimlessly among the scattering of Japanese. The detective had also been caught in the downpour and was content for the moment to stand back, allowing his wet clothes to adjust to the warmth of the building. Finally he stepped into Michael's path and spoke to him in English with bureaucratic precision.

"Costello-san?" He bowed slightly from the waist, dropping his unlit cigarette onto the terminal floor in the one motion. "Tora Hashimoto, detective. Tokyo Metropolitan Police. My office welcomes you to Tokyo. You have had a good flight?"

The abrupt introduction startled Michael. He bent at the waist to return the bow, felt awkward, and changed his mind and offered his hand. "I didn't recognize you. How do you do."

"This is Tokyo rainy season. In spring, everyone gets wet," the detective said with a hint of friendliness and signaled for a porter.

"It was good of you to come to meet me in weather like this. It was a long flight," Michael admitted. "I'm glad it's over. I assume Chief Mulhern contacted you?" Michael spoke the question casually, uncertain of what he could expect from this man.

"Yes. We have had a message from Chief Mulhern of the Vancouver Police. And we have arranged for you to stay at the Tokyo Prince Hotel, if that is acceptable to you. Police stay at the Tokyo Prince. It is a good hotel, not too expensive." He fished through the pockets of his soaked raincoat and fed a fresh cigarette between his lips.

"You speak very good English."

"Aah. Not so good. It has been sixteen years now I try to learn, neh. It is good to speak English in Japan. I learned English from your Canadian soldiers in Hong Kong." The rain glistening on his swept-back hair had formed droplets at the end of his short ponytail. The thought occurred to Michael that the detective looked like a man who had taken a shower with his clothes on.

"During the war? In Hong Kong? Would those have been the Winnipeg Grenadiers?" Michael was remembering the tales of Japanese brutality and the execution of many of the Grenadiers following their defense and surrender of Hong Kong.

"Grenadiers, yes," Hashimoto replied curtly, turning to Michael with a questioning glance. "You know of them? It was a very bad time," he said.

Michael decided to let the subject drop, assuming that if Hashimoto had learned English from the Canadians, he must be one of those who helped the few who survived. The Americans hanged the Japanese responsible. That would explain his having escaped the war crimes trials.

"You wear the Roman Catholic collar?" The detective was leading the way toward a curbside police car. "Others come to Japan to preach. Some wear that collar, but they are not Catholic

384

priests, neh? We have many preachers come to Japan after the war. Some wear your collar but they not priest, like you."

"I understand." Michael was not eager to get into a religious discussion.

"But we have real priests in Tokyo. Jesuits, like you."

"I am not here on behalf of the church," Michael interrupted quickly. "I am wearing these clothes because they are all that I have. Did Chief Mulhern's message explain why I am here?"

Hashimoto shot parallel streams of smoke from his nostrils as he peeled off his raincoat and tossed it in the front seat alongside the driver and climbed in the back. "Our information from Vancouver asked that we be of service to you," he replied. Michael detected a mask of discretion in the detective's answer and was grateful, though he suspected the man knew more than he was revealing.

"My coming to Japan has nothing to do with the Jesuits or the Catholic Church, Detective Hashimoto. I am here on a personal matter. I was hoping the Tokyo Police could help me to locate a friend I have not heard from for a long time."

"At Sophia University we have many Jesuits. They know many Catholics in Japan. Maybe they can help you, yes?" Hashimoto persisted.

"Please understand. I do not plan on contacting the Jesuit Order."

The detective nodded knowingly. "Then you are off duty? So. We will find who it is you are looking for, you and me, neh?" Michael nodded with an apprehensive half smile.

From Haneda, the police car wove through a maze of Tokyo streets, the headlights flashing over wooden fences along the shoulder of the road. Beyond the fences Michael saw the beginning of the resurgence from the war in the unpainted houses, replicas of the shacks that grew up in the thirties at the end of Burrard Bridge.

"You are tired, Costello-san?" Hashimoto asked.

"A little. But I'm not sleepy. My clock is upside down. This is morning for me."

"Then we will leave your bag at the hotel and go have some drink. Priest are allowed to drink, yes?" The detective laughed at his own joke. "The rain has stopped. We can walk. Good for your legs, neh?" Hashimoto stamped his feet on the car floor to illustrate.

* * *

9:15 p.m. Tokyo time. The white, enamel clock that would have looked at home in an American kitchen hung on the wall above the desk of the Tokyo Prince Hotel. Its stark contrast to the hotel's dark, mahogany wall panels and heavy, plush furnishing served as a reminder of the hotel's acceptance of American occupation. Hashimoto caught Michael's questioning glance at the clock.

"Aah. The clock, yes? Clock belonged to United States Occupation Forces. After the war, Tokyo Prince Hotel was billet for American army officers, neh. They left clock." Hashimoto led the way across the worn carpet toward the hotel's improvised front desk. "Japanese did not want to offend Americans. So their gift stays, neh. Now, when Americans come to Tokyo Prince, they see clock and they know we remember them." He laughed, his eyes turning to Michael for a sign of approval. "Keeps good time," he added.

Michael stopped at the desk to glance back over the lobby; an empty, glass-encased cigarette and candy display rack alongside a juke box stood silently unlit in a corner. Two stacks of dusty records in the machine lay in odd piles behind the cracked plastic facing. In an alcove, a large glossy poster of a smiling blonde, her sun-tanned legs sprouting from tight tennis shorts, held up a green package of Lucky Strike Green cigarettes. Scattered about the lobby the upholstered furniture, infused with the smell of years of smoking, testified to the hotel's former elegance. Chandeliers suspended from the high ceiling cast an amber light over the lobby, the light all but lost in the corner shadows.

"Tokyo Prince Hotel was palace for prince of the Japanese Imperial Family," Hashimoto explained with a touch of reverence.

Michael set his bag in front of the desk and Hashimoto issued the clerk instructions in rapid Japanese. The clerk picked up the bag, bowed to the detective and handed Michael a key. Hashimoto nodded approvingly.

"Everything is taken care of. He will take your bag to your room. Now you are ready for walk, neh." Michael was about to protest. His clothes were damp and he was still experiencing chills despite the muggy night air, but Hashimoto was not waiting for a reply and was already leading the way toward the hotel entrance.

Outside, the night was filled with a cacophony of protesting automobile horns and exhaust fumes. Hashimoto set out at the brisk pace of a man focused on a destination, ducking in and out of twisting alleys with Michael breathing hard to keep pace. When they reached the bright neon lights of Nishi Ginza, Michael was about to confess he could go no farther. Before he could protest, the detective raised his hand with a triumphant grin, pointing to a picture-sized neon sign directly over his head. The sign lit up a single pink blossom on a field of pale green.

"Botan." It was the first word Hashimoto had spoken since the hotel. "Botan is Japanese. Means little flower. Button flower in Japanese, neh?" He flipped the lapel on his jacket. "Button flower? So? This is a little flower bar. Good name for a bar for priest to drink, neh? You have saint little flower in your Catholic Church? A priest in Hong Kong said prayers to your little flower saint. Prayers that made him happy before he died. You think little flower saint heard his prayer, neh? You also pray to little flower saint, Costello-san?"

The childhood prayer came to Michael's lips more in reflex than by intention.

"Oh little flower,
Oh priceless Power,
O Gem of priceless worth.
For every hour,
Let fall a shower,
Of roses down to earth."

He looked up at the neon flower, which resembled a carnation bloom more than it did a rose, and thought for a moment to ask why it was that the priest in Hong Kong had known he was about to die. The thought passed, giving way to resentment at the detective having linked the name of St. Therese of Lisieux to a Tokyo bar in a Ginza back alley. Hashimoto studied Michael's face by the light from the neon, reading his thoughts. He shrugged and scurried down a short flight of steps to the bar entrance and beat a rhythmic knock on the door. A panel in the door opened wide enough to reveal the face of a woman, her head crowned with a stunning arrangement of glistening black hair. The panel closed quickly and the door swung open to a chorus of young Japanese women, each apparently caught breathless at the sight of Tora Hashimoto, Tokyo detective.

Hashimoto acknowledged the bowing and smiling in a routine that Michael suspected had been rehearsed many times in the past. The girls parted and the woman whose face had appeared in the door panel emerged from the chorus of excited chatter. She was middle-aged, though her years were well disguised by tastefully applied cosmetics. Her bearing and the way the others parted to make way for her indicated her absolute authority over the giggling girls. She bowed deeply to Hashimoto and spoke to him in Japanese. Hashimoto bowed back and turned to introduce Michael in Japanese. Michael sensed a moment of uncertainty that lasted while the woman openly examined him from the tips of his heavy, black seminary shoes to his disheveled red hair. When she spoke it was as if she were repeating lines of memorized English.

"You are welcome to Botan. We are happy you have come to Japan."

Michael responded with an attempt to imitate Hashimoto's bow.

"Botan is bar for Japanese. There are no hakujin — white persons — come here." The detective explained in English, barely loud enough for Michael to catch. "Momma-san says that you are welcome here tonight. What would you like to drink?"

"Do they serve beer?" Michael's throat was dry and he was feeling as if he might be sick.

"Beeru," the detective repeated to one of the giggling girls. The Momma-san took the detective by the arm and led them to a corner booth where she slipped in between them. One of the girls put a bottle of Suntory whiskey on the table and poured a glass for Hashimoto and one for Momma-san.

"Happiness?" Momma-san tipped her glass to Michael with a look questioning her attempt at English.

"Happiness." Hashimoto repeated thoughtfully. He studied his whiskey a moment and turned to Michael. "Happiness is like my glasses when I put them on to read. I do not see my glasses and go looking for them, even when they are on my nose. We go looking for happiness even when it is right in front of our nose, neh?" He laughed.

"Do you wonder why I laugh at my own foolishness?" he asked, smiling whimsically. "I come to Botan looking for happiness many nights, neh? Yet my happiness may be someplace else where I failed to see happiness, like my glasses on my nose." The detective raised his Suntory to Michael in a one-man toast. "But now you are here with us, and we are going to find your happiness, yes? Kanpai." He raised his whiskey glass to his lips and with a series of gulps followed by a short gasp the glass was empty. He wiped the back of his hand over his lips.

"You are shivering. Are you cold, Costello-san? Some hot drink will make you warm?" He spoke in Japanese to one of the girls. The girl got up from the booth and went to the bar, returning with a small bottle of hot sake.

"Kanpai," Hashimoto said once more, urging Michael to knock back the sake. "Sake will make you warm, Costello-san." Somewhere behind the bar someone had started a recording, a ballad sung in Japanese by a woman with a high-pitch voice.

"Kanpai." Momma-san raised her glass once more.

The detective's eyes were beginning to gloss over and a deep blush colored his cheeks. "Momma-san says you look like John Glenn, Costello-san."

"The astronaut? Tell her I am flattered. I have been mistaken for many things, but never a space pilot." Michael had to raise his voice to be heard over the music.

"An astronaut is a sky pilot, yes?" the detective insisted. "In your army, soldiers say priest is sky pilot, so?" Hashimoto coughed his way through a burst of laughter and began explaining his joke in Japanese to the three bar girls crowding into the small corner booth.

Michael was growing apprehensive over the detective's rapidly changing personality. The music had forced Hashimoto to raise his voice and that seemed to have signaled his aggressiveness as the blush in his face grew more pronounced with each glass of Suntory. The plump bar girl at his side kept refilling his glass.

"Costello-san," Hashimoto said loudly. "Talk to me in English. These women will not understand. Perhaps you will tell me why you are looking to find these Wakabayashi people?"

The question caught Michael off guard. He had not mentioned the name Wakabayashi. The realization that Chief Mulhern had revealed more in his telegram to the Tokyo police than the detective had let on, lent a word of warning. He would proceed with caution. The music ended and the bar grew quiet. Michael looked questioningly around the room, gathering his thoughts.

"It is good for you to speak English. There is no one here who understands," Hashimoto assured him.

Michael's eyes cut to the mirrored wall behind the bar, the reflection revealing Hashimoto looking back at him in the glass with an expression of benign smugness. Michael grew certain he was seeing more of Chief Mulhern's Machiavellian planning behind this man's willingness to help. His glance shifted to the second image in the mirror, a gaunt, almost unrecognizable face. For an instant he believed he was looking into the face of a stranger. The rumpled dark suit and the Roman collar looped loosely around his neck brought him up short. He was shocked to see the toll three sleepless nights had taken on his body. Missing meals, washing in airport bathrooms, and now the damp clothes clinging to his back, had left deep shadows beneath his eyes. A three-day stubble of graying ginger whiskers added to what he saw reflected in the glass. His eyes remained drawn to the bar mirror when a teenaged bar girl, her plump, round body protruding from a satin off-the-shoulder cocktail dress, appeared in the glass. Michael felt the warmth of her body next to his before he realized she was cuddling up against him. The girl dropped her hand boldly into his lap and Michael quickly turned away from the mirror, moving away.

"You must know, Detective Hashimoto, that when countries are at war people are blinded by fear and pain and behave as they would not behave at any other time. Nearly twenty years ago I turned my back on the Wakabayashis when they asked for my help. I have come to Japan to apologize for abandoning them." All but one of the bar girls, weary of the English conversation, had left to attend other customers. The one in the satin dress remained next to Michael, the Momma-san next to Hashimoto.

The detective took a deep drag on his cigarette, inhaling Michael's words judiciously. He held the smoke for a long time, finally releasing it in a repeat of the dragon-like streams through his nose. He appeared to have become calmer, his antagonism no longer visible.

"Costello-san, a moment ago you were looking in that mirror, neh? But what you saw did not exist in the mirror. What you saw was reflection of you and me sitting here drinking with Momma–san and Junko, neh? If I kissed the mirror, I would taste only the lips on the glass. To taste the lips of these women, I must kiss the women who are here beside us, neh?" He patted Momma-san's lap. "She is here, now. Looking into the past is like looking into a mirror, Costello-san. What you see is only what is held in your memory and memory plays tricks on us, neh? We cannot go into our memories any more than I can enter that mirror to claim a kiss from Momma-san. What we see in memory is often only what we want to see."

The Botan's Momma-san signaled the bar for more drinks, followed by a painful silence before Hashimoto spoke again. Michael was aware that while the detective continued to drink, his voice was modulating and the glassy stare the whiskey had created a short while ago was gone from his eyes.

"The Wakabayashi family were your friends, so?"

"More than friends."

"Costello-san, what would you do if I told you the Wakabayashis do not wish to see you?"

"I would want to hear that for myself. Soju Wakabayashi was my friend before I became a priest." Michael hesitated, then decided he must trust this man. "She and I were more than friends," he added meaningfully.

"Aah, but now you are looking into the mirror of your memory. Time changes people. You yourself are no longer the man you see when you look back at the days you knew Wakabayashi-san, neh?"

The girl in the green satin dress sidled closer to Michael and once more slid her hand along his thigh. With the other she lifted his glass with a mischievous smile and began sipping his beer. He was uncomfortable but did not move or acknowledge her.

"My feelings have never changed," Michael replied. "I buried my feelings when I was told she had married another man. But there is more involved than my feelings for Soju. I have learned we have a child."

"Aah so." Hashimoto studied the cigarette in his hand, then crushed it in the ash tray, his half-closed eyes concealing whatever thoughts were passing through his mind. "And is it to renew this friendship that has brought you to Japan? Or have you come to claim your child?"

"I once planned to ask Soju Wakabayashi to marry me," Michael answered quietly.

"During the war? You were going to marry a Japanese girl? You must have been very young, Costello-san."

"I had just to turned eighteen when I went to her. She had been sent away because of the war. People were afraid the Japanese were about to invade. Whatever could be taken from them was taken by the greed that flourishes in time of fear-possessed people." Michael's words came slowly, a deliberate self-indictment. "It became patriotic to steal from the Japanese and to distrust them." He sighed wearily. "I rejected Soju Wakabayashi because I was ashamed of loving her and I was afraid." He stopped, aware he was confessing to this soft-eyed Japanese detective as surely as if he were seated before his Sheridan confessor.

Hashimoto toyed with his glass of Suntory, then nodded in the manner of a man who has reached a conclusion. "Costello-san, I have informed the Wakabayashi family of your coming to Tokyo. They have no wish to see you."

Chapter 50 The Girl with the Auburn Hair

Michael spent the night tangled in sweat-soaked bed sheets, tossing fitfully on the broken hotel mattress, unable to free his mind from Hashimoto's parting words. The two of them had left the Botan bar in a police car driven by the same man who had driven them from the airport, the car and driver conveniently waiting at the corner of the alley. Hashimoto invited Michael to get in the back seat. "We will take you back to the Tokyo Prince. Tomorrow I will see if anything can be done about your wish to see the Wakabayashi family," Hashimoto promised with a look that provided little encouragement. Michael wondered if the man genuinely wanted to help or was merely acting out another of Mulhern's devious detours. At the Tokyo Prince Hotel, the detective stepped out of the car and walked with him into the hotel.

"If we are careful, you shall see them," he promised.

"Careful. What does that mean?"

"In Japan it means one does not go too quickly, or the opportunity may be lost." With that the detective turned and left Michael alone in the deserted hotel lobby.

Hashimoto's parting words continued to haunt Michael come mid-morning when he went to the sink in the corner of his room to splash water on his face. He considered using the bathroom down the hall but having seen the toilet and the wet floors, decided to dress without bathing, eager to escape the closeness of the musty room. His temples were throbbing and the hot water radiator, too hot to touch, made the air difficult to breathe. He tried to open the lone window during the night only to discover it permanently sealed. The struggle left him exhausted.

In the hotel lobby he slumped down in an upholstered chair positioned to give him a full view of the hotel entrance and waited for Hashimoto's return. Throughout that seemingly endless afternoon he would get up to pace the lobby to walk off a chill that seized him one moment, only to be followed by the feeling he was burning up. Late in the afternoon a slow-moving porter approached with a solemnity that suggested the man had been a left-over fixture of the royal staff. The porter bowed and spoke in Japanese, yet when Michael answered in English asking for a bottle of beer, the beer arrived in a brown bottle on a tarnished silver tray. The old man poured half of the beer into the glass and bowed deeply once more. Michael, unsure whether he was waiting for a tip or merely waiting to remove the bottle once he had poured the rest of the beer, picked up the bottle and placed an American half dollar on the tray. The old porter looked down at the coin for a moment, unsure of what was intended, then silently left with the tray and the fifty cents. Michael reached into his jacket for a handful of loose aspirins, swallowed them all and put the beer to his lips to wash them down. He was hoping the aspirins would help clear the dizziness that was making it difficult to maintain his balance. Late in the afternoon the rains returned, turning the road outside the hotel into a shallow river.

Hashimoto appeared on the dot of seven thirty and paused in the hotel entrance to shake himself like a wet dog, scattering rain over the rugs. He then began fishing through his pockets for his cigarettes. Spotting Michael, his face lit up.

"Ah, Costello-san. " Crossing the lobby he popped an unlit cigarette between his lips while continuing to search his pockets. "Do you have a match, Costello-san? No. You don't smoke."

Michael reached into his jacket and produced a box of wooden matches.

"Ahh," the detective murmured, examining the box. "You collected this last night from Botan Bar, neh?" He nodded wisely, lit his cigarette and returned the matches.

Michael rose up out of his chair and felt the floor begin to tilt, the hotel lobby turning slowly beneath his feet like an off-balance Ferris wheel. He reached out, catching the Japanese detective by the arm.

"You are feeling not well, Costello-san? Maybe you should sit down?"

"No. It's too warm in here, that's all." Michael tugged at the seminary turtleneck sweater, loosening its hold on his throat, continuing to grip Hashimoto's arm. "These are the only clothes I have, Hashimoto-san. Will they be all right for where you are taking me?"

"Those are priest clothes, yes? But you do not wear your priest's collar?" Hashimoto's eyebrows rose in questioning wonder, then he shrugged. "What you wear is good." He started for the door, keeping a concerned eye on Michael. "It is better we do not pursue the Wakabayashis too quickly," the detective said as he stepped out into the rain. "We will go for some drink. Drink will help you feel better. Then we decide how to proceed. Yes?" He appeared about to say something more but lapsed into a spasm of coughing, his words muffled in the cup of his fist.

A police patrol car with blue emergency lights and the police insignia on the doors was waiting at the curb. Michael climbed into the back seat and was enveloped in a pall of stale cigarette smoke. He reached for the window crank and discovered he was in the backseat of a car with no cranks and no door handles, the back seat screened off by a wire mesh from the driver and Hashimoto in front. He closed his eyes, leaned back in the seat and began silently trying to recall the prayer to St.Therese that had come to him so easily the night before. Why had it been so easy for the Saint of Lisieux to speak to God? Why had it been so difficult for him? His intent to pray turned his thoughts to the Our Father as practiced by Saint Ignatius, repeating each word of the prayer in cadence with each breath. But his breath was short and labored and he quickly surrendered to watching the passing Tokyo street lights glowing in haloes of rain. The hammer throbbing in his head throughout the afternoon had grown louder, and he pressed his fists to his temples in an attempt to quiet the thunder.

Hashimoto signaled the driver to stop at an intersection of a brightly lit alley and opened the rear door. Taking Michael by the elbow, he bowed his head and shoulders into the driving rain and began leading him through the Ginza. When they stopped the detective gave Michael a look of mischievous triumph.

"You are surprised?" he smiled playfully. They were standing beneath the same neon button flower of the bar they had visited the night before. "We have returned to Botan. Like your General MacArthur, neh?" He laughed, pleased at his play on words.

"MacArthur's return was to the Philippines. We remember Bataan, not as a button flower but a death march," Michael snapped with more than a trace of bitterness.

"Aah so," Hashimoto replied, accepting the history lesson with a slow nod. He skipped down the steps to the Botan and played his knuckles on the door. The hostess who opened the door remembered Michael with a practiced smile and spoke in Japanese. Michael was able to catch the words 'astronaut' and 'American' followed with what sounded like a satisfied sigh.

"Not an astronaut," Hashimoto protested in English. "Sky pilot'o. He is your pilot'o to heaven." The remark produced a look of wonder on the girl's face and a burst of bar-room laughter from Hashimoto.

It took a moment for Michael's eyes to adjust to the interior of the bar. The noise, the throbbing in his head, and Hashimoto's sudden smart attitude had his thoughts going in different directions when his eye caught his first glimpse of the copper-haired Japanese hostess. She stood between two middle-aged Japanese men at the bar, her hair a dark auburn seeming to glow in the subdued light. She was a head taller than the other girls, her appearance so different from the others that Michael was certain that if she had been there the night before he would have seen her.

"Ah. You see her right away, Costello-san," Hashimoto observed. "You should have been a policeman like your friend, Chief Mulhern, neh?" Michael was staring hard at the girl. When he answered, the harsh, frightened sound of his own voice startled him.

"What is her name?"

Hashimoto steered him toward a corner table. "Her name is Midori."

"Midori?"

"Midori means green in Japanese. Miss Green. That is funny, neh? Because her hair is red, not green. She has an English name. It is Mary. In Japanese, Mary sounds like Midori." He shrugged, unable to carry the logic any further and ordered a Suntory and a beer for Michael. "So she has become Midori. Would you like to meet Miss Green?"

The girl had turned her attention from the two men at the bar and was looking their way, aware she herself was being watched. Hashimoto waved to her and she started toward their table. As she crossed the room Michael recalled the words written in Soju's schoolgirl hand. "She is named Mary, after the Queen."

"Hashimoto-san." The girl touched the detective's wet hair playfully and sat down. "You are all wet, neh?" Her voice had a soft texture, her English pronunciation freeing the words only partially from her Japanese accent.

"Yes, and I am also cold. I need something to warm me, Midori-san." Hashimoto laughed and signaled the barman to bring drinks. "We need drink, Midori-san, to make us warm. Will you join us?" The barman brought a bottle of Johnny Walker Black Label scotch whiskey from a shelf above the bar. He sat the bottle on the table and waited while Hashimoto poured the girl a straight shot, then the barman carried the bottle back to the bar. The girl raised her glass to Hashimoto and for a long, deliberate moment her eyes fixed on Michael. "Cheers," she said and knocked back the entire glass. Hashimoto cast a probing glance at the priest, raised his glass of Suntory and swallowed a good part of his whiskey.

"Midori-san, this is my friend from America. I think he believes you are very beautiful."

"S'ank you." The girl laughed modestly. Immediately, the barman returned with the bottle of Johnny Walker and Hashimoto poured her another scotch. The alcohol went down with no effect.

"Do you prefer Midori? Or Miss Green?" Michael asked.

The girl laughed again. "Hi. Midori."

"Your name is also Yuki-san?" A sudden puzzled look crossed the girl's face. She shot a questioning glance at Hashimoto, then poked playfully at the detective.

"So, Hashimoto-san. You bring another detective to the Botan. You too are detective like Hashimoto-san, neh? Hi. You are right. Yuki is my name. So, he has told you everything about me. Shame." She reached across the table to slap playfully at Hashimoto.

"How long have you worked at the Botan, Midori-san?" Michael was aware he was pressing too hard, going too fast and ignoring Hashimoto's rules to go slowly.

"Oh, long, long time. Is that correct, Hashimoto-san?"

"Very long time." The detective answered.

"But you are still young. Seventeen? Eighteen?" Michael knew he was probing.

"Oh, s'ank you. S'ank you very much." She dipped her head in mock gratitude. "Hashimoto-san, why do you never say such nice things to Midori? I think I like your friend better." She laughed an easy, professional laugh and squeezed the detective's hand. The bartender had again removed the Johnny Walker and was signaling that she was wanted back at the bar.

"Excuse me, please? I will come back," she said and left them.

"She drinks tea," Hashimoto explained. "Customer pays for whiskey. Tea in expensive whiskey bottle is good business for the bar and Midori-san stays sober, neh?"

"She is Soju Wakabayashi's daughter," Michael said simply. "She is my daughter."

"Yes." The detective said briskly and downed the last of his whiskey. Michael realized he had moved too quickly. Hashimoto picked up his cigarettes, signaling the visit was over. There was an exchange of Japanese between Hashimoto and the Momma-san, and without so much as a glance from Midori, they were out the door.

The rain had let up, leaving the streets glistening in the Ginza neon. Hashimoto tilted his head to the sky and decided to keep his umbrella at alert.

"How long has she been a bar girl?" Michael was pressing to keep pace with the detective through the crowded street toward the car.

"She has been at the Botan since she was sixteen. She has many good friends there. She is very successful."

"You mean she has many good men friends?" Michael's voice revealed the pain in his question.

Hashimoto seemed puzzled. "Hi. Many good men friends. Even some policemen, neh? Momma-san looks after her. Momma-san sees that only good people are customers of Midori-san at the Botan."

Michael hesitated, unwilling to take the question to a more explicit level.

"Have you told her? Did she know me?"

"I have told her nothing. But yes, I believe she knew you. You ask many questions and Midori-san is very intelligent. There is also the resemblance. Your red hair. Momma-san saw it. But?" He cocked his head whimsically. "Maybe not Midori-san." With that he shrugged, as if it were of no real consequence.

Not another word was spoken until the police car pulled up to the hotel. Hashimoto got out to open the rear door and placed a hand on Michael's shoulder. "Now you have seen her. You must take time to think what is best for you and what is best for Midori-san. Sometimes, when we remove the bandage from old wounds too quickly, it will cause pain and the wound will bleed again, neh?"

"I'll think about that, Hashimoto-san."

"Good. Then I will come tomorrow and you can decide what it is you want to do." Michael remained at the curb watching the police car merge into the traffic before he went into the hotel lobby to look up at the wall clock. It was half past nine. He went to his room, swallowed what was left of the aspirin, removed his sweat-soaked undershirt, and dressed once more. He stopped in the lobby to count his Japanese money, checked to ensure the Botan match box was in his pocket, and went back into the street.

It had begun to rain again, a relentless, warm downpour. Before he had walked a hundred yards the rain was seeping through his seminary jacket, which clung to him like a wet rag. He walked along the curb, waving in futile attempts to hail a passing cab. Finally he gave up and started picking his way through the side streets toward the lights of the Ginza District.

He felt as if he had been walking for miles, prowling one alley after another, losing all sense of direction and time, constantly looking up for the neon button flower. When his shaking legs refused to go farther he leaned against a wall in exhaustion and closed his eyes, letting the rain fall on his face. Opening his eyes he looked up through a sea of defused light at the button flower, glistening above his head. Delusional? He knew he was running a fever. He blinked the rain from his eyes, to disprove the hallucination. The button flower remained, glowing pink and green in the night. He pushed away from the wall, looked about the alley to be certain he was in the right place, and started down the steps to the doorway to the Botan.

At first he tried to imitate Hashimoto's pattern of knocking on the bar door. There was no response. He then began pounding with the flat of his palm, each blow jarring every bone in his body. Still no answer. Defeated, he slumped against the door, gathering the strength to make it back up the steps, when the small panel in the door opened. The round, impersonal face of the bartender who had served up the Johnny Walker appeared in the opening. The man showed no sign of recognition.

"No gaijin. Nihon-jin bar. You go. Closed. All gone home."

The panel slammed shut. Michael slapped desperately at the door once more and waited. The panel opened once more and Momma-san's face appeared. From somewhere beyond her, Michael could hear the strains of classical music.

"Ahh. Sky pilot'o," she said in English, as if she were confirming what the barman had told her. The door opened. "You so wet." The Momma-san stepped back from the open door.

Michael had ceased to be aware of his clothes or that his body was burning up from within. He was concentrating on maintaining his balance standing in the center of the Botan's deserted dance floor, the rain water dripping from his clothes.

Botan bar was built like a cave. There were no windows, only the single entrance door. Tables were set about the room, crowding the tiny wooden dance floor; tucked into the perimeter of the room were a series of booths, each separated by a cushioned plastic divider. Several of the tables were turned upside down on top of one another, indicating the place was ready to be cleaned. In his confusion, Michael tried to concentrate on the music. He could hear it still. He had not been delusional. It was real and not born of the buzzing in his head. Mozart. A violin concerto. It was coming from a record turntable on top of the bar.

Momma-san, muttering in mothering-sounding Japanese, pulled off his coat and his shirt and sat him down in a booth by the wall. She wrapped a dry bar towel around his shoulders, then went to her knees to remove his shoes and socks and stepped back to appraise what she had done.

"Sky pilot'o? You could not forget Momma-san, neh?" She called out to the bartender who came bearing a glass of clear liquid. "Hot sake," she said, handing the glass to Michael. "You drink. Make you warm inside, so?"

Michael lifted the drink to his lips, suddenly aware of Midori-san standing over him.

"Midori-san. Your sky-pilot'o has come back to see Momma-san. He is Momma-san's astro-naut, neh?" She laughed and nudged Michael playfully. She spoke rapidly in Japanese and Midori took the towel from her hands and began drying Michael's hair. He could feel the warm sake beginning to work its way through the tightness in his throat and tried to speak.

"Midori-san." A rasping voice from deep within his chest sounded as if someone else were speaking. Michael recalled voices like that, words heavy with the scent of alcohol that came to him from beyond the confessional screen. "I am a friend of your mother's," he said. "We were friends a long time ago. Before you were born." Midori stopped rubbing his hair and the room began closing in on him, hot and stifling. He leaned back against the booth, cushioning his head which suddenly had become too heavy to remain erect. Midori sat next to him and lifted the sake cup to his lips.

"Drink. You are still cold, Costello-san."

"Excuse me a moment, please," he muttered, the movement of his lips slowed to a pantomime pace. "I can't talk for just a minute." Those were the last words he was able to clearly recall.

***

Vague recollections of that night were to haunt Michael for the rest of his life, scenes he was willing to leave buried in his subconscious. He was able to vaguely recall Momma-san turning off the Botan lights, the red neon tubes over the bar casting a surreal, hellish glow over the room. He could remember stumbling over a chair on his way to the door and being helped to his feet by the barman. He remembered his daughter taking him by the arm up the narrow steps to the alley. Beyond that there was only the rain and voices calling out in Japanese with the Ginza lights glaring all about him. He would recall clinging to Midori-san in the dark alleyway and being unable to breathe, his unlaced shoes on his feet. He had lost his stockings. He retained an indelible picture of sitting on a curb watching the gutter water flowing over the tops of his feet, the loose shoelaces drifting in the water. He tried reaching down to tie the laces but the shoes were beyond his reach.

There were flashes of memory of riding in the front seat of a tiny car with his knees drawn up beneath his chin. Midori-san was driving, speeding recklessly through the dark streets. From that point on his memory presented only a confused sequence of being naked, submerged to his shoulders in a scalding bath. He was relaxed and excited, right up until Hashimoto appeared and the nightmare began.

The detective loomed over the bath as if he had been conjured out of the steam — a surreal figure, no longer mysteriously smiling — talking in angry, urgent Japanese, his face so close Michael was unable to escape the evil smell of his tobacco breath. Others quickly entered his nightmare. Chief Mulhern, his face flushed in anger, shouting in loud, whiskey blurred words: "Why are you naked?" Michael recalled only the shame at exposing the goods of his groin shrunken to a malformed obscenity in the hot water. Suddenly it was no longer Mulhern but his father demanding: "Shame. Have you no decency?" An ancient Japanese, a face from the past lined with deep wrinkles contorted into a distasteful frown, appeared alongside Hashimoto. The old man wore a grey, felt fedora and spoke Japanese, his staccato words landing like bullets in Michael's throbbing head. Beyond that, there was nothing.

Chapter 51 From Out of the Past

The pungent scent of damp cedar summoned Michael to consciousness long before he dared open his eyes, his labored breath enveloped in a warm mist. His mind picked cautiously at the shattered pieces of the insane puzzle scattered through his memory. At one point in his semi-consciousness Soju appeared, her brown eyes filled with anxiety. When their eyes met he reached out to her and the vision vanished, frightened away by the sound of a distant chorus chanting a glorious psalm. He attempted to call to her but when she did not return, the words of an unfamiliar liturgy began echoing through his brain.

"The Lord God formed man. He breathed life-giving breath into his nostrils and man began to live."

In the hours that followed, Michael gradually came to realize his upper body was encased in a mist-filled plastic canopy. Now and again through the mist his vision of Soju returned only to fade from view. His first moment of recognizing he was alive and awake came with a Japanese wearing a nursing uniform. She raised the canopy from over his head and spoke softly in Japanese, as if she were afraid to enter the silence of his nightmare. He realized she was speaking to Soju who was nodding attentively at her side. Soju saw his eyes open and the anxiety left her face.

She smiled. "The nurse says you will get better now."

Michael attempted to answer, but there was only a distant, indecipherable sound emanating from his throat.

"But you don't sound better," Soju added. "You have very bad pneumonia. Don't try to talk." He reached for her hand but the effort to keep his eyes open slipped away and he drifted back into his dreams.

When he woke again the room was awash in daylight and the vapor inside the canopy had condensed, leaving a field of tears on the canopy. Through the tears he saw Soju curled in an armchair alongside the bed, asleep. She wore a plain blue smock and her once severely cut hair was coiled in a silken ball at the nape of her neck. Tiny lines creasing the corners of her eyes were the only claim time had made to the face he had held in his memory through the years. He attempted to lift the canopy. The movement wakened her and she looked over at him uncertainly.

"Good morning, Father Costello." She spoke slowly, phonetically shaping each word with her lips so he could understand through the canopy. She has beautiful lips, he thought, a beautiful mouth. "The doctor says you must be still and rest." He slipped his hand from beneath the canopy to touch her so that she would not vanish. The nurse reappeared and lifted the canopy and spoke to Soju in Japanese.

"The nurse asked me if you are hungry," Soju said. Michael turned his head slowly. He wanted only to remain awake, to feel her hand in his, knowing she was there. His eyes went to her ring finger. He was remembering the ring he had carried to Sandon. There was no ring. This was not a dream. If he were dreaming, she would be wearing his ring. Soju saw him examining her hand and smiled.

"No," she said softly and brushed her fingers through his hair.

"Soju." The sound of his voice, thick and uncertain, startled him.

"Sssh." She placed her fingertips to his lips. "I will bring you some soup, then you must sleep." His eyes followed her to the door. When she returned she carried a cup-size bowl of warm soup.

"How did I get here? How long has it been?" he whispered.

"Hashimoto and my father brought you here two days ago."

"Hashimoto told you I was looking for you?"

"Yes." She placed her fingertips to his lips once more. "Don't talk now. I will help you with some soup and then you must rest. We will have time to talk later." He fought to keep his eyes from closing, afraid of losing sight of her.

"I love you," he said, unable to bring the words past his lips.

***

That evening, in the half light spilling into the ward from the hallway, Soju drew a muslin hospital screen around his bed and bathed him and supported him on trembling legs to the toilet.

"It is the Japanese way for family to wash and feed their sick when they are in hospital," she assured him. "So now, I am your family."

She drew the screen close to the bed, shutting out most of the light, and placed a chair where she could sit and hold his hand. She held it for a long time without speaking, the quiet broken only by the sound of muted footsteps in the hallway and an occasional fit of coughing beyond the screen. Gradually, in halting words, Michael began the story of how he had discovered her letters. As he spoke, the great crystal tears he had never forgotten came trembling to her cheeks.

"Your letters were hidden from me for over seventeen years."

"That was all so long ago. I can hardly remember what I wrote."

"You wrote that the baby's hair was the color of the evening sun. Soju, I have seen her. You were right. God, there is such an emptiness in my life when I think of the years I have never known her. I was meant to be a part of her life and all I am to her is a stranger in a bar."

"But Michael, you are a Jesuit priest."

"I am not sure what I am anymore," he said quietly. "I have been lied to and I have lied to myself. When I went to Sandon, they told me you had married. After they told me I had lost you, I offered what was left of me to the Army. When even the Army didn't want me I gave what was left to the Jesuits, hoping to find meaning to what remained of my life. Yet there has never been a day when you have been out of my thoughts."

"The police told you I had married?" She shook her head incredulously.

"They said you married a Japanese from the road gangs. It was a lie they told because of my father's friend, Chief Mulhern. He is still trying to convince himself there was moral justice in what he did."

Soju remained at Michael's bedside well into the night, her thoughts passing through the days spent in her basement room in the Callahan house writing letters that were never answered. "I waited," she said. "I asked a Jesuit Brother in Toronto about you. He said he heard that you were in a seminary studying to become a priest. That's when I decided Yuki and I would come to Japan with my family. I believed that was what you would want."

"Mea culpa. Mea culpa. Mea maxima culpa," Michael muttered. He could see a look in Soju's eyes, a look he remembered from the day she pleaded with him on Fraser's Wharf.

"When my family came to Japan, we declared Yuki-chan as my mother's child. It has been hard for Yuki-chan. To the Japanese, she is foreign born. Nisei sometimes have a difficult time in Japan. Yuki-chan was born to a Japanese mother in a foreign country fathered by a man who has red hair. Japanese people do not accept mixed race babies very easily." Soju could see the anguish in his eyes and held his hand more tightly. "We have said enough. Those bad times are gone. It is good to speak English with you. Sometimes I am afraid I have forgotten how."

Michael clung to her hand. "What has Yuki-chan been told about us?"

"We have never explained anything to her. When we came here, we went to live with the Nagumos, my mother's family. There was not much to eat. We could have gotten help from the Canadian occupation consul, but that would have meant a loss of face for the Nagumos. Besides, my father was very angry. I worked for an American officer on General MacArthur's headquarters staff. He brought us sugar and cigarettes for my father. He had a wife and a child in Los Angeles. When it was time for him to leave, he went home."

"And you?" Michael attempted to withdraw the question with a wave of his hand. "Forgive me. I have no right."

"Yes, I loved him," she replied simply. "And you? You have been a priest with no woman all this time?"

From deep within his memory the image of Juanita on the sands at Spanish Banks crossed his mind. But he had not been a priest that day and dismissed the thought.

"For me it was different. But there was no other love. There was an old friend, not really a lover, before I entered seminary," he confessed. He was tempted to tell Soju how he had willfully conjured images of her, made love to her, welcoming her to his dreams, rejoicing in confessing his licentious thoughts of her to a priest who would remain forever silent. It was enough to tell her he had loved no other. He was glad she had given him the chance to say that. "You are very beautiful, Soju. I've often wondered if you would remain as beautiful as I remembered."

Again she placed her fingertips to his lips with a coquettishness that made him think of the hostesses at the Botan. "Thank you. Priests do not see many women. But thank you anyway. How old are we now, Michael?"

"I am thirty-five," he replied. "You? You must be going on eighteen? You look much younger."

"You are still hallucinating."

"Have I been hallucinating? Is that why I am afraid to let go of your hand?"

"Last night you sang to me in Latin."

"Redo in unum De um Patrem omini pot-'entem." He attempted to chant the opening lines of the credo he had heard in his delirium. "I heard the angels singing over and over again. I believed I had died and they were singing over my body in the seminary. Did I say that I loved you while I was having those dreams?"

"I don't know. Inside that tent you sounded like a little boy singing in a church choir." Soju's expression grew serious. "The nurse says you will be able to leave the hospital soon. Maybe tomorrow. Then I will take you to stay in the Nagumo house in Yotsoya Station until you are well enough to go home again. Can a Jesuit priest do that? Live with a Japanese woman and her mother and her grandmother?"

"Hashimoto said your family did not want to see me."

"I have told them you are coming. They understand. Even when my letters went unanswered, Toshio wanted to write to you. He has always believed you didn't know. Toshio has gone back to Canada to live. He is in Vancouver. I asked him not to write to you. I wanted to go on believing him when he told me you never knew about our baby and I was afraid he might be wrong."

Chapter 52 Broken Vows

Michael lay back in bed listening to the sounds from the hospital corridor. Relatives of the three patients sharing his ward were preparing the morning meal, the cooking odors from the hall hibachi drifting through the open doorway. Soju raised the window at the foot of his bed to the morning air. She had prepared steamed rice with bean cake and soup and pickles, and brought along a western fork so he could eat without fumbling the food over his bed. When he had eaten, she washed his hands, finger by finger, as she would a child.

Michael's moment of security, his first since leaving the seminary, then ended with the sound of a man speaking his name in the corridor outside the ward. He sat up, certain the voice was that of a priest. Soju also heard the name, though the man was speaking Japanese, and she understood what was said.

"He wants to know where to find Father Michael Costello," she said quietly in answer to Michael's obvious anxiety.

At that moment a nurse entered the ward followed by a short, slight priest wearing a floor-length soutane. The priest's thin, sensuous lips curled up beneath a hawk-like nose in a surprisingly warm smile fixed on Michael. The man's deeply-set dark eyes radiated a spiritual gentleness that softened the hard lines of his face. He approached swiftly, stepping past the nurse, surveying everything in the ward at a quick glance.

"Ah. Father Costello. At last we meet." The man spoke with the enthusiasm of having discovered a Livingstone in the jungle, his voice rich and startlingly deep coming from such a small physical body. He bowed slightly to Soju and came up to the bed with both arms extended as if he were eager to embrace.

"Praise God," he sighed. "We have all been praying that we would find you on the mend. The reports of your passing were obviously premature, as your Mark Twain would have said." The priest grasped Michael's hands. "I joke. Forgive me, Father. But we did hear you were gravely ill."

If the priest detected a wariness in Michael's reception, he wasn't allowing it to temper his enthusiasm.

"I am Pedro Alvaro," he said in a slightly-accented English. "I come from our Jesuit Mission House at Sophia University here in Tokyo. We have been given to understand you are well enough for us to arrange to take you out of here today." The statement met with a pall of silence. The swift change in the priest's enthusiasm revealed he had sensed Michael's resentment. There followed an awkward moment before he turned to Soju and spoke in Japanese. She answered quietly in Japanese, set aside her basket of dishes and started toward the hall.

"Soju. Where are you going?" Michael asked in a plaintive voice.

"Father Alvaro would like to have a moment with you alone."

Michael turned to the priest. "What is it you want?" he demanded, the tremor in his voice suddenly hostile. "This woman is..." He was about to say 'my wife' but checked himself, unsure of Soju's reaction to such a claim.

"Father Costello," the priest replied with deliberate calm. "I come at the request of your provincial at St. Michael's. We have been asked to take care of your hospital needs and to see you safely on your way home. Would you rather I came back later?" Soju started for the door once more.

"Soju, please don't go," Michael realized he was sounding like a child about to be abandoned. "There is nothing to be said here that cannot be said in front of you."

"Perhaps I have interrupted," the priest suggested innocently. "Have I come at the wrong moment? Your provincial thought it best." He smiled uncertainly at Soju. "Obviously, you have been well cared for, but I would suggest you now leave the details of your release up to the order."

"I have had pneumonia," Michael answered. "You are mistaking my illness as my having lost the ability to think for myself."

"Well, yes, Father Costello," the Jesuit replied in a tone of mild reprimand. "You are aware of course that you were required to have your provincial's permission before you left the country. We have been led to understand that you have been under a strain since the death of your mother." The priest folded his topcoat and laid it across the foot of the bed, a move Michael interpreted as the man's assuming authority over the situation. He picked up the coat and handed it back. The Jesuit's tone weakened perceptibly.

"Father Costello, your provincial is concerned with the state of your immortal soul and your vows to the Society of Jesus. You understand you may be endangering those vows. How you conduct yourself now will have a great bearing on the outcome of your disciplinary hearing."

"Thank you, Father Alvaro," Michael replied coolly. "I have been sick and I am still too sick to listen to your homilies on the state of my immortal soul." The priest looked to Soju with an appeal for help, then back at Michael.

"Father Costello, crises such as yours come to many of us. Our seminary years prepared us for that. Before you decide on anything, I suggest you consider spending a few days on the mend with us at our retreat house in Hiroshima. Allow some time to get back on your feet before making irrevocable decisions. Give yourself a few days to pray, to meditate. Whatever has been happening to you has made you vulnerable."

"I am tired," Michael said. "Very tired. I'm so tired I can't bear to listen to this talk right now. What I am tempted to say to you would not be in keeping with your goodwill, Father. So I am asking you to please leave."

Michael's words brought a sadness to the priest's deep, brown eyes. "I understand," he said quietly. "There is the matter concerning this woman that has apparently brought you to Japan." The thought that he had been betrayed by Hashimoto flashed through Michael's mind. "We have seen this situation in others."

Michael started to get up off the bed and Father Alvaro raised his hands in protest.

"My heart aches for each of you," he said quietly.

"It is time for you to leave, Father," Michael said with open hostility. "I am not concerned at the moment with my vows or with your concern for my immortal soul."

Father Alvaro nodded rapidly, eager to ward off any further display of temper. "We will be praying that you think clearly of your commitment to Christ and to the Jesuit Society," he replied. "Yours is a battle to which we are all called in one form or another," Alvaro continued.

Michael rolled his head wearily from side to side on the pillow as the priest started toward the door. Soju stepped aside, allowing his slight figure to pass, the skirt of his soutane billowing mystically down the corridor.

"They want you back," she said, attempting to sound matter-of-fact.

Michael began pulling on his trousers. "And I'm going to be out of here before he returns." As he leaned over for his shoes, the floor began to spin. Soju reached out to steady him.

"You should get back into bed." She went to her knees and slipped his shoes over his feet.

He looked down on her. "Do you remember the first time you did that for me?"

"You had a hole in your sock. But at least you had stockings back then. That's more than I can say for you now. Some things in life don't change much, do they?"

"Some do," Michael replied.

Chapter 53 A Time of Decision

It wasn't until later that afternoon that Michael was able to slump down in the rear seat of the taxi. He had passed the better part of the day staring at his feet – they looked lost in his black seminary shoes without socks—while he waited for Soju to obtain his hospital release. He was relieved to be escaping the hospital without another visit from Father Alvaro and was beginning to recapture a fragile feeling of security in the warm confines of the tiny cab. The taxi worked its way through winding streets guided by Soju's staccato Japanese, finally coming to a stop in the Yotsoya Station alleyway where Isao Wakabayashi first had laid eyes on Yuki Nagumo.

The shaded porch of the sugar house that had once looked out over the alley was gone, replaced by a two-story, concrete brick apartment building. A plate glass window on the street level of the building opened on what resembled an American-style convenience store, the words, "Nagumo Confections" written in gold and black Kanji across the glass. A masonry wall eight feet high ran the full length of the alley, shielding the two- and three-story dwellings that had replaced the open-front shops.

Soju exchanged coins with the taxi driver and led Michael through a narrow side entrance into a starkly-furnished ground-floor room. She moved swiftly to produce a thick bundle of bedding from a wall cupboard, then drew the curtains to filter out the late afternoon sunlight. For the first time since the morning he had walked down the seminary hill, Michael totally surrendered himself to someone else's authority. Soju undressed him in the soft light and bundled his shoulders into a cotton kimono. She left him for a short time before returning with a heated stone wrapped in flannel. She tucked the stone beneath his feet and pulled the covers up to his chin as if she were putting a baby down. All this she performed with the swiftness of a magician's sleight of hand.

"Now. Shut your eyes and I will be back," she whispered and disappeared through a softly sliding door.

Throughout the evening Michael slipped in and out of a restless sleep, awakened once by the rise and fall of muffled voices beyond the door. After what he imagined to be several hours a movement in the darkened room brought him fully awake. By the dim light from beneath the door he saw Soju kneeling beside him. She wore a kimono slung loosely over her shoulders, exposing her breasts. He sat up.

"You have had a good sleep, Father Costello. Now I have your reward." She playfully placed a large strawberry between his lips. "Japanese strawberries. They are full of sunshine. My father says when we eat very ripe strawberries our body receives the strength of the sun. He says special strawberries like this contain magic. They can bring good fortune." Michael bit into the berry, wiping the juice from his chin with the sleeve of his kimono. Soju laughed and with a small damp towel wiped the rest from his whiskers. "You are letting all the good fortune run down your chin."

He lay back, watching as she slipped free of the kimono. The light beyond the door went out. For a moment he heard the rustling of the bedding followed by silence, as if the room had ceased to breathe. In the darkness, Soju's naked body came up against his, curling gently against his back. He attempted to turn to her, but she held him still.

"No," she whispered. "I will keep you warm and you will go back to sleep."

Michael sighed, a surge of well-being flowing over him and he began to silently pray. "Hail Mary, full of Grace, the Lord is with Thee. Blessed art Thou among women and Blessed is this woman you have brought next to me." It was the only way the prayer would come to him and he repeated it, over and over, rejoicing in each word until his breath grew easy and slow in the warmth of her arms.

***

Michael was awakened a second time by voices from beyond the room. He turned and reached out for Soju in the dark, his hand searching the vacant pocket where she had slept. The bedding was cool. For a short time he lay still, straining to catch her voice among the words filtering through the wall. After a time he slept again until a sudden flood of daylight awakened him with a start. Soju was standing by the open curtains holding a small tray.

"How long have I been here?" he mumbled.

"You have been sleeping since yesterday. I didn't want to wake you, but there is someone who has come to see you."

Michael was quick to detect the acrid smell of cigarette smoke. "Hashimoto?"

"Yes. He is talking with my grandmother and my father. He has told them you will be leaving us soon. Hashimoto says you must return to your Jesuits." She handed him a warm, scented towel and a hand mirror. The image he saw shocked him once more.

"Good God, Soju. I wonder why they didn't bury me. I look as if I had died a week ago."

"The doctors said you nearly did die. But now you have come back to life. You are my Lazarus." Soju pulled back the bedding with a note of playful pride. "I wonder if Lazarus was awakened on such a beautiful day as this."

"And beheld anyone so beautiful?"

"Come. You must get up," she replied briskly.

Michael pulled at the skin of his face attempting to erase the deep lines. "How did you recognize me looking like this?"

"Even Yuki-chan recognized you, and she had never seen you before." Soju looked into his eyes, searching for something of the boy who had lived in her memory for so very long. "After you have talked with Hashimoto-san, I will tell you what Midori-san told me happened. Then we will go together and have a bath. Do you feel strong enough for a hot bath?"

"Are you sure you can trust me?"

Soju answered with a puzzled smile.

"I was sick, not dead, Soju. It was hard for me to turn over and go to sleep with you in my bed. I'm not sure about how I would behave bathing together."

"But you are a priest." He could see she was teasing.

"I am a man, if that means anything. And I think of you as a woman. I can't help that, no matter what Hashimoto has to say about things. I once tried to make you my wife, Soju."

She smiled demurely and raised her eyes quizzically. "Tell me again about how you came to marry me."

"When I went looking for you in Sandon I had the ring in my pocket. A diamond ring that cost me sixty dollars. I intended to ask you to marry me right there in the camp by a Salvation Army chaplain or anyone we could find."

Soju pretended to busy herself folding the bedding. "And what happened to my diamond ring?"

"I took it back to the jeweler," he confessed. "He gave me twenty dollars for it."

"Twenty dollars?"

"The jeweler said I had taken all of the romance out of the ring. He told me I should keep it until someone else came along. When he said that, I took the twenty."

"Now I have no ring?"

"No, but..."

She shook her head and laughed. "Enough for now. Hashimoto-san is waiting to see you. First you must shave."

Hashimoto sat on a floor cushion nursing a bottle of Coca Cola. On seeing Michael in the doorway he raised the bottle much like a man would tip his hat to a welcome visitor. "Ah, Father Costello. Soju-san has been making you well, neh?" he said with a suggestive grin. "That is good."

The detective popped a cigarette into the corner of his mouth and got to his feet, offering Michael his hand. A sudden perverse resentment caused Michael to ignore the hand and answer with a ceremonial bow, imitating the Japanese. As he straightened up he looked around the sparsely furnished room. A tiny, grey-haired woman knelt on a large cushion in one corner. A man he recognized as Soju's father sat next to her on a cushion. In an instant, Michael realized that Isao Wakabayashi was the old and wrinkled face from his nightmare. Set in an alcove in the wall was a portrait of a young Japanese wearing an ornate military uniform similar to the picture Michael recalled having seen in the Wakabayashi house off Burrard Street. Yuki came into the room carrying a tray with several bottles of Coca Cola. The old lady got to her feet and bowed stiffly to Michael.

"This is my grandmother, Nagumo-san," Soju said. Michael repeated his abbreviated bow. "You remember my father?" Isao

Wakabayashi rose from his chair with a rapid, perfunctory bow and indicated a place for Michael to sit on the tatami.

"So, Costello-san, how has Soju-san made you healthy so quick? It's magic, neh?" The detective winked and expelled a burst of smoke through a laughing cough.

Michael felt Soju's restraining hand slip quietly onto his lap. He was regarding the detective suspiciously, remembering his tantalizing visits to the Botan, convinced that Father Alvaro's hospital call had been Hashimoto's doing. Hashimoto read his thoughts.

"Your priests have been concerned about you. I am merely an observer. Sometimes messenger, neh?"

"You and Chief Constable Mulhern?" Michael replied sarcastically.

"Yes. Your chief will be happy to hear you have recovered so quickly." An awkward silence hung between them until the detective spoke again. "Perhaps I should leave so that you can share your plans with the Wakabayashis, Costello-san?"

"How can I share my plans when I don't know what you and Chief Mulhern have already planned for me?" Michael's words carried a hostile bite.

The detective hissed appreciatively between his teeth.

The old lady Nagumo spoke in high-pitched sing-song Japanese to Soju.

"My grandmother asks if you and Hashimoto would like to talk in private," Soju explained.

Hashimoto looked to Michael for a response.

"No, Soju," Michael snapped. "Tell your grandmother that you and I have been deceived too long by people talking in private."

Hashimoto nodded approvingly.

Michael turned to Soju and spoke to her as if she were the only person in the room. "I have brought shame on your family. I came to Japan to ask your forgiveness. There is nothing I have to hide from any of you."

Hashimoto cleared his throat. "Costello-san, when I left your hotel you were not well. You were going to bed." He was speaking softly, as if he were coaxing a child. "But you went back to the Botan bar alone. So?"

"I wanted to speak to Midori-san, alone. I have a right to do that without the permission of the Tokyo Metropolitan Police, Hashimoto-san. I suspected Momma-san would call you the moment I showed up." He was guessing, still unsure of the events of that night.

"I see," Hashimoto replied.

"I remember only a few details of what happened. I recall sitting on the sidewalk in the rain in Nishi Ginza. Not much else." He looked to Soju with a helpless gaze. "I have a confusing picture in my mind of Midori-san helping me into a tub of hot water." The rest of that recollection he decided to leave within the confines of his clouded memory, praying that what he was remembering was merely an erotic hallucination, a figment of his fever. His own child, his daughter, had bathed him as if he were a child. "That is all I remember." He turned to Hashimoto, having decided to say no more.

"You were sick with fever," Hashimoto said. "Midori-san thought it would be good to warm you. When you passed out, she telephoned me. Wakabayashi-san and I came and took you to the hospital. You remember that?"

Michael nodded tentatively, the images of Hashimoto wrapping him in a blanket and half-carrying him into the street falling into place. He was also recalling a picture of Yuki-chan, her hair falling in copper waves over her shoulders as she cradled his head in her lap in the back of Hashimoto's police car. He had reached up to touch her face, certain that he was dying.

"And you, Soju?" Michael asked helplessly, searching for answers that would lend some sanity to the night that was being laid out before him in investigative detail.

"I was in Hokkaido with my mother. Hashimoto-san telephoned and told us you were very sick and they had taken you to the hospital."

"Hokkaido?"

"My brother Tatsuo operates the Nagumo shop in Hokkaido. My mother and I went there when Hashimoto-san told us you were in Tokyo looking for me. Hashimoto-san thought it would be good for you to have time to think." She glanced at Hashimoto.

"We did not know what it was that brought you to Japan, Costello-san," the detective explained, exhaling a long plume of cigarette smoke through pursed lips. "You were moving swiftly. When a man moves too fast, deeds are done with little thought." Hashimoto raised his eyebrows and lit another cigarette, placing the butt end of his burning cigarette to the new one in his mouth. "Now that you have had time to think, what is it you wish to do, Costello-san? Both you and Soju-san have already had too much advice, neh?"

"Bachi ga atta," the old woman muttered from the corner of the room.

"My grandmother says we have all been punished by heaven," Soju explained.

"No. Tell your grandmother it is not heaven that punishes us," Michael replied bitterly. "Tell her it is we who punish one another."

Hashimoto struggled to his feet and bowed briskly to Soju's father, then to the old lady, before turning to Michael. "Should you need me, Costello-san, Wakabayashi-san will contact me. I will do what I can when you have decided what it is you wish to do." He was about to leave the room and turned, struck with a thought. "What do you wish me to tell Father Alvaro? When he discovered you were no longer in the hospital, he came to my office asking for you."

Michael merely shook his head. "Tell him whatever you choose."

"Then, I will tell him you will contact him when you are ready."

"Thank you," Michael said, uncertain of his trust in this unflappable Japanese so deeply entwined in the lives of the Wakabayashis.

***

Sunday mid-morning, a day fresh and bright following the overnight rain, Michael Costello's Sabbath obligation was the farthest thought from his mind. Soju dressed him in an ankle-length kimono and led him by the hand through a gate in the wall behind the Nagumo shop into the alleyway leading up the hill to the Yotsoya bath house.

"We are going to a very old Japanese bath," she explained, unable to conceal her schoolgirl excitement at introducing Michael to mixed bathing. "My father proposed to my mother after he saw her in this bath."

Soju steered him past the ancient pile of wooden crates stacked against the bathhouse, the crates partially concealing the entrance. Maneuvering around the puddles left by the rain she pointed him toward a low open doorway partially screened from the alley by three blue banners bearing Japanese Kanji figures, and smiled mischievously at Michael who was pretending to be nervous.

"Maybe that wasn't the way you Catholic Priests would have young couples courting, but it worked for my father. Maybe you will see some girl in there and understand. Maybe you will fall in love."

"I have," he answered. "You know that, though I'm still not completely comfortable with the protocol of this mixed bathing business."

"You mean you are embarrassed to be in a bath with women?"

He faked a frown, aware of her teasing

"No one pays attention to that in a Japanese bath," she said earnestly.

"That may be so. But the idea takes getting used to."

Soju laughed. "You weren't embarrassed when Midori-chan bathed you."

"Maybe that's why I passed out," he said, hoping to dismiss the subject with a weak smile.

"Well, you won't have to worry about sharing a bath with an old woman like me."

"I'd hate to be asked to leave."

"I have it." She was still acting mischievously. "You stand by the edge of the bath and I will announce to all the women that you are a Jesuit priest. Then they will all look the other way."

"Would they do that?"

"You don't think any woman would be interested in anything a priest has to show, do you?"

"Soju? I believe you."

She laughed and handed him one of the two towels from her arm and left him in the morning sun outside the men's entrance. Michael watched her disappear through a separate door while he remained, reluctant to leave the warmth of the sun, feeling the deep chill that had gripped his bones since arriving in Japan loosening its hold.

The bathhouse dressing area was empty except for an elderly attendant and a fat man with breasts like a woman's. The fat man, in the midst of struggling to button his trousers over his belly, looked up, momentarily surprised at seeing a Caucasian stranger. He smiled and spoke Japanese, words that sounded friendly, bowed swiftly and went back to struggling with his buttons.

Michael paid the attendant, squatted to scrub his body in a shower-like stall, rinsed by dousing himself from a pail of standing water and stepped, towel in hand, to the bath. He was mildly surprised to feel so unconcerned over the presence of the naked women in the water. Most were visible only above the shoulders and none seemed to have noticed his arrival, though he instantly realized he was the only man in the bath. He caught sight of Soju, though her back was to him, her shoulders glistening above the surface of the water. He watched a moment before he eased his body into the bath, never taking his eyes from her. Slowly the water allowed him to slip into a restful void, as the words from an all-but-forgotten psalm played through his mind.

"Who is this whose glance awakens my soul like the coming of the dawn? She is beautiful and bright. She is as dazzling as the sun or the moon in the dark of night."

Soju turned to him. Seeing her naked form across the steaming water had summoned the beauty of the Song of Solomon from the recesses of his mind.

She came across the bath next to him, smiling coyly, her hair coiled seductively above her head, her small breasts barely breaking the surface. She brushed against him, excitement in her eyes.

"You okay?" She moved closer, long strands of hair slipping loose and trailing on the water's surface. She appeared like the petal of a water lily floating on the surface. "You looked so far away just now."

"I was." He reached out to touch her, reassuring himself of her nearness.

Afterwards, outside the bathhouse, Michael overturned an empty crate next to the entrance and sat with his face tilted to the sun. He didn't hear Soju when she came up behind him. She stood quietly looking down at him until he sensed her presence and turned, eager to share his thoughts.

"Soju." His voice was firm with resolve. "I will be leaving the priesthood. I no longer intend to pretend I am something I am not. When I read your letters, I knew I would leave, regardless of whether I found you. The priesthood was a gift to my mother but it has also been an escape for me. There has been little in my commitment that would please God. I have always known that. The only prayer I have now is that I be given another chance."

Soju tossed her damp hair in the sun and looked at him without revealing her thoughts. She sat on the box next to him and took his hand. "Michael. We cannot bring back even one of the days we have lost. Watching you in the bath, I realized I have been looking for the boy I once knew. I found myself wondering whether either of us ever really existed in that world, or if any of what we did together ever happened. Does that sound crazy? Can you understand? When I look back it all seems but a dream."

"Before you came," she went on quietly, "I had convinced myself that none of those days were real. You were something out of my dreams. Now you are here and I am afraid of going back, afraid of being hurt. It is less painful to let go of a dream."

He raised her hand to his lips. "Soju, our lives have been played with as if we were toys for others to arrange as they chose. We were meant to be together. We were meant to hold one another, to reach for each other in the night. I have spent nights on my knees before an altar of God when what I longed for was to be beside you, to reach out and touch you. When I reached to touch God, I was still alone."

She released his hand and stood up. "For a long time when we were sent back to Japan, I refused to let go of you. I was the mother of your baby and I wanted you more than anything in the world."

"So now we have a child," he added hurriedly, attempting to get past the memory of her pain. "We have a child that is neither Japanese nor Caucasian. She is the two of us."

"Mary is no longer a child, Michael. You have seen that."

"She is entitled to my name."

"She has her own name. Her name has always been Wakabayashi."

"But now she knows about us."

"That's true. Hashimoto has told her everything about us. He loves her, you know. There is nothing he would keep from her. He is the father she never had. He watches over her at the Botan. There is nothing you and I could give Mary now that she does not already have. She has her car, her apartment. Her grandmother will leave her the store. They are very close and very much alike, Mary and her grandmother."

It was dawning on Michael that Soju had rehearsed what he was hearing. The realization frightened him. She reached out, bringing him to his feet. "Michael, please don't be hurt. But I no longer want to be anything but what I am, a Japanese shop-keeper who is happy in her business."

***

They returned to the Nagumo shop without speaking. At the gate both stopped short, caught up by the sound of animated voices coming through the open door of the living quarters. Soju turned to Michel. "That's Hashimoto."

"And Father Alvaro," Michael muttered, immediately wondering if he had been mistaken in trusting the detective.

The Jesuit priest sat on the tatami in the family room, his back to the wall, his short legs folded beneath him so that his knees formed a miniature tent beneath the skirt of his soutane. Father Alvaro's thinning black hair hung loose over his forehead and fell in lank strands over his ears as he waved his arms in animated discussion. He caught sight of Michael and stopped in mid-sentence.

"Father Costello. I was telling our friend Wakabayashi-san of the work of our missions in Japan." It occurred to Michael the priest had been speaking in English to a man who would have followed him more readily in Japanese, and that whatever the priest had been saying had been intended for his ears. "I have also just learned how Wakabayashi-san came to the church at Star of the Sea, our Jesuit parish in Vancouver. It may come as a surprise to you, Father Costello, but I heard of your Father Lavoie when first I came to Japan."

"Father Lavoie was the one who convinced me to sit for the Jesuit examinations," Michael admitted.

"It is a miracle, the hand of God at work," Alvaro replied. "To think Father Lavoie's work with Wakabayashi-san has brought us together now. Wakabayashi-san informs me he has been baptized but never confirmed. You and I can help him complete his acceptance into the church." The priest's large dark eyes appeared to glow with excitement. "How beautiful are the ways of God with those who love Him." He turned his full smile on Michael. "If we but listen and open our hearts, Father Costello, He speaks to us in miraculous ways."

Michael laughed easily, recognizing he was witnessing a true Jesuit master at his work. "Father Alvaro," he said in a friendly tone. "I have experienced quite a few of these beautiful acts of God, most of them brought about by people who considered themselves His authorized agents."

Father Alvaro ignored the invitation to get back into that. "Your brother Jesuits are praying for you, Father Costello. Ignatius is praying for you. The Society of Jesus needs you. And I believe you need the Church and the love of Jesus Christ." He reached into his soutane for a paper.

"I have a communication from your provincial. He understands the strain you have been under, Father, and has delayed any action on your being ruled fugitivius."

"And I have come to the realization that I was never intended to be a priest, Father. My vows were taken while I was under the delusion I had a vocation."

Father Alvaro, solemnly ignoring what he had just heard, turned a forgiving glance at Soju. "It may be true that you are in violation of your vows in other ways. Yet we have time to straighten things out." He spoke without breaking his tolerant smile. "You recall Ignatius' own struggle with the material things of the world? When he was alone recuperating from his grave illness, he thought only of women and the pleasures of the secular world. He asked for books, hoping to indulge those dreams. The books they brought to him were books of Holy Scripture. The word of God turned his thoughts to the loving Christ, Father Costello. Ignatius' desires for the things of this world left an unsettling void in his heart. Yet when he dreamed of loving Jesus, he was at peace. Is there not in you that same need?"

Michael had heard the same words, almost verbatim, over and over in seminary. He sighed wearily. "Father Alvaro, I have just been told by the woman I have loved during all my years as a priest that our love no longer exists. Now I am being told by someone who cannot understand what passes in my heart that my attempt to reclaim my identity is to deny Christ. I do not deny Him. I love Him as obviously you love Him. Do you not think it possible that He remains present in each of us, regardless of whether or not we wear the Roman collar? Could it not be that in loving Soju as I love her, I am loving Him?"

"Oh, Michael," Soju interrupted, "I meant only that I wanted you to be free to choose."

"Soju. The only thing that matters to me is to know if you will have me. I have nothing. I am nothing but what you have found in me. Put aside what this priest or anyone else has to say. The only answer that matters is yours."

"I love you," she said quietly. "I have never stopped loving you, Michael, even though I am afraid."

Silence fell over the room, broken by Father Alvaro speaking as if he was admonishing a child. "Father Costello. I urge you to come with me into retreat. Give the Holy Spirit a chance to enter your heart and reveal the answers you are seeking."

"I can no longer pray," Michael answered. "There is a great poverty at the center of my spiritual life. Until I found Soju, I prayed in an emptiness and darkness that I did not understand. I can no longer go on repeating those prayers with no meaning. My life as a priest has been a life of deceit, Father Alvaro."

"You know that true prayer is not a petition of words," Alvaro replied. "I ask you to recall that day of uncertainty, the day you first set out for seminary. Each of us constantly reminded ourselves we were saving our immortal souls." Father Alvaro's large, soft eyes were silently pleading. When he spoke again, his words fell one upon the other, in compelling cadence. "To avoid mortal sin. To avoid venial sin. To suffer persecution for Christ. Yet in his love, Christ forgives each of us when we fail. He is saying to you even now, Michael, your sins are forgiven."

"I am not seeking absolution, yours nor His."

A frustrated sigh escaped Father Alvaro's lips and with it went his smile. "You would make a good high school administrator, Father Costello. A good chaplain. A good parish priest. Perhaps someday a provincial. A superior of a province. Accept that. You belong to God." Michael said nothing. "At least consider your options. You can get a leave of absence for a year. The order will probably release you from your vow of poverty so that you can support yourself."

Alvaro went down on his knees. "You say you cannot pray. Then kneel with me, right now, this moment, before I leave you. We will pray together." He closed his eyes and brought his slender hands together at his breast. Isao Wakabayashi, who had been silently struggling to follow the conversation, went to his knees as the priest began. Soju got up and left the room. Michael never moved from his chair.

"Heavenly Father, let your countenance shine upon us that we may be aware of the presence of Christ who has brought us together so to serve you. Help us to overcome the weakness of the flesh and grant to us the resolve and strength in the spirit and tradition of Ignatius. For Thine is the Kingdom the power and the glory, now and forever and ever. Amen."

Michael smiled. "Forever and ever? Father Alvaro, tell me what that means?"

"It means Heaven, everlasting for those who do God's will."

"No. I mean the concept of eternity. How do we comprehend what the words forever-and-ever implies? I confess, in my years in seminary, the logic of those words has always been incomprehensible."

Alvaro remained on his knees and said nothing for a moment, then tottered awkwardly to his feet. "I will write your provincial of our conversation, Father." He raised his hand in benediction over the room and he left. Michael continued to smile as if he had been but a passive observer.

Chapter 54 In Search of a Story

Through the weeks that followed Michael often found himself dreaming, drawing the days of his life before memory's eye, as if his years were unfolding in pictures and time, a ledger revealing his story. Each day the feeling of the sun on his back awakened new memories of boyhood moments with his brothers and the Glasheens. He shivered recalling the wet chill of the water and the warmth of the sun on Jericho Beach, and the hot sand on his belly as he flopped on the beach. And Jimmy Henniger? What it must have meant to him slipping into his sister's underpants. He hoped they were still friends. He rode again the giant Ferris wheel at Exhibition Park and caught his breath squeezed between Mulhern and his father, the two big men holding him to the flying seat. Even then, the old chief had taken it upon himself to assure the safety of Eamon Costello and his sons. These memories came slowly through the lazy afternoons with Soju; each day bringing the forgiveness that comes with understanding. Soju witnessed the visible change taking place in Michael; the gaunt Jesuit, so intently in pursuit of her, was slowly being transformed into the boy she remembered from Fraser's Wharf.

There were long walks as Michael's legs grew stronger and his smiles more frequent. She fed him sushi and miso soup in the alleys of Ginza. They tied their fortunes to the spirit trees at the Shinto shrine and crawled one after the other through the sacred passage in the ancient temple timber, a feat promising long life and love. His emergence from the protective veneer that had followed him to seminary saw the somber smiles give way to laughter, which came easily and often.

"These days will always be ours, Michael," Soju told him, her head resting on his chest. "Even your God would understand. Do you think He will take us from one another again?"

Gently, he raised her head until their eyes met. "I have held you so many times in my heart, Soju. And never have I confessed those dreams as an affront to God."

It was evening and they were returning from the bath when Michael first sensed she was awakening from their dream. He laughed at her telling him it was un-Japanese to walk hand in hand when he reached to take hers. He drew her close to him as they walked.

"When will you leave?" she asked. He was startled. For an instant he considered shrugging off the question. Instead he pretended to be offended that she was even thinking of his leaving her.

"It will be Lent in a few days," he said jokingly. "Maybe I could give you up for Lent, if that's what you want. No, that wouldn't be right. Did you know that the word Lent means springtime? It's an old English word that denotes the season of spring." He pulled her tighter against his body. "And you are my spring, the awakening of my life." They stopped and he took her by the shoulders and kissed her in front of the startled passersby.

"Father Alvaro thinks that without me, you could pray again," she said, making no effort to free herself from his arms.

Michael attempted to make light of the idea. "And I told Father Alvaro he's wrong. I do pray now, I pray every minute I'm with you that I will never lose sight of you again, that I will have you with me forever." She smiled and for the moment, the dream seemed secure.

That night as they lay in the dark, their legs carelessly entwined in the soft confines of the futon, Soju raised the question again and he knew it would not go away.

"Lent is your time of penance," she said, her fingers gently tracing the features of his face.

"I have often heard it questioned why that should be," he replied. "Lent marks the days before the Church celebrates the risen Christ. We don't do penance the days before the birth of Christ. How much more should our joy be at the approach of His spiritual inheritance?" He felt no shame using this talk of Christ to bind her to him.

"But isn't Lent also your time to reflect on the forty days Christ fasted in the wilderness?"

"Yes. And I believe that Christ did not discover who He really was until He went into the desert for those forty days. It was only then that He came to know He was the son of God. It was only then He began to live His story on earth. These days with you have been my retreat, Soju. I had no story to my life without you. These few days I have discovered my own story, not a life of salvation for the world, but a resurrected life for each of us."

"And now?" she asked.

"Where that leads us, I don't know. I could teach."

"Father Alvaro is having trouble accepting us," she answered.

"Yes. And I have the feeling Father Alvaro has begun to search for his own answers as I searched for mine. He is coming here tomorrow. I know he expects me to go with him on retreat to Hiroshima." The news brought a sigh from Soju.

"Will you go?"

"No." He began kissing her lips, her ears, her breasts, as if the kisses would deny the thought.

"If they take you from me now, will they take you forever?" she asked softly.

"It is you who said that which is ours can never be taken from us," he replied.

***

The morning passed without a word being spoken of Father Alvaro. Soju folded and put aside their sleeping futon much as she had each day. Michael sat watching her while they both listened for the priest's taxi in the lane. When it came, Michael went into the alley to head off the Jesuit. He returned to the house to find Soju on her knees packing his small bag. He dropped to his knees beside her, taking her hands in his.

"I don't want to leave, Soju. Don't make me go. If I leave you now, I may be leaving you in the same condition I left you eighteen years ago."

She smiled.

"You would let me know this time, wouldn't you?" He was intending to make light of what she was doing, but the words brought pain to her eyes.

"I tried to let you know."

He drew her to him. "Oh God, Soju. I love you more than I thought I was capable of loving. And now you want to send me off to settle with a God to whom I have broken every promise I ever made. He who made you, made you for me. How could He want me to turn away from his most beautiful creation?"

"Some of His best promised never to deny Him, and yet they did, Michael."

He smiled at her testing him. "Peter was repentant. The only things I feel penitent about are my years without you. Soju, I have so much more I want to say. Let me send Alvaro away. We need more time."

"Father Alvaro asks for thirty days," she said. "When they are finished, he will let you go with peace in your heart. I am merely a woman, Michael. Allow your God to claim you if it is His will. If you do not find Him with your Jesuits, then come back to me, and we will find Him in each other. "

He would have protested, but before he could speak she placed the tips of her fingers over his lips.

"Father Alvaro is waiting."

###

Made in the USA
San Bernardino, CA
20 May 2013